THE FALLEN ONE

A FALCON FALLS SECURITY NOVEL

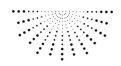

BRITTNEY SAHIN

EMKO MEDIA, LLC

The Fallen One: A Falcon Falls Security Novel

Editor: Michelle Fewer

Proofreaders: Judy Zweifel - Judy's Proofreading; Cindy Shafley

Cover Design: Mayhem Cover Creations

Model / Front Image: Beto Malfacini

Back image: iStock

Ebook ISBN: 9781947717398

Paperback ISBN: 9798882781438

❀ Created with Vellum

To Cindy Shafley and Elizabeth Barnes

Thank you for being there for me while writing this book.
Forever grateful.

MUSIC PLAYLIST

Spotify

Love & War (Yellow Claw G-Funk Remix feat. Yade Lauren) - Yellow Claw

People You Know - Selena Gomez

I'm Not The Only One - Sam Smith

In the Stars - Benson Booone

Dancing With Your Ghost - Sasha Alex Sloan

I Don't Want to Live Forever - ZAYN, Taylor Swift

Born For This - The Score

Monster - Willyecho

Mr. Brightside - The Killers

Dangerously - Charlie Puth

The Fever - Foreign Figures

Lose Control - Teddy Swims

How You Remind Me - Nickelback

Like I Love You (feat. The NGHBRS) - Lost Frequencies

Hanging By A Moment - Lifehouse

Beautiful Things - Benson Boone

Home Sweet Home (feat. ALMA & Digital Farm Animals) - Sam Feldt

Growin' Up and Gettin' Old - Luke Combs

AUTHOR NOTE

Although *The Fallen One* is part of a series, it may be read as a standalone.

The book includes major events in Carter Dominick's life that show how and why he becomes the man he is today. Those scenes start in the year 2011 when his wife was still alive. The present day chapters pick up in the year 2024.

- Enjoy,

Brittney

P.S. - There is a family tree and character crossover information at the end of the book, but it does contain spoilers.

Pinterest Muse Board

PART I

BEFORE...

1

CARTER

ABU DHABI, U.A.E. – NOVEMBER 2011

MAYBE I SHOULD'VE BEEN A PILOT LIKE REBECCA WANTED ME to be. I stared out the window at the F-22 Raptor on the base's runway, noticing two Air Force guys chatting with a few of the U.A.E.'s men. The sophisticated warplane would be heading out tonight, same as last, with a wave of F-16 Fighting Falcons piloted by our allies, the Emiratis.

Not that the Pentagon had officially acknowledged Americans were operating alongside them from the Al-Dhafra base. No, as far as the White House was concerned, we weren't even there.

And for that matter, my team hadn't been in Somalia the last two months, working to dismantle Al Qaeda's foreign fighting trafficking network to Yemen.

"I know what you're thinking." I turned to face Griffin Andrews as we awaited our flight home with the rest of our teammates.

"Doubt it." *Hell, I don't even know what's going on in my head right now.* "But I reckon you're going to tell me."

Fatigue had set in, which had my Texas drawl sliding through. I did my best to abandon my accent whenever I wasn't Stateside. Better not to let the enemies know anything about you. Clearly, I needed to get home. I also needed to fuck my wife. Relieve some tension.

Rebecca and I had been going through a rough patch ever since I went through Selection. She didn't want me becoming a Tier One guy, and that was all I'd wanted since I'd watched *Rambo*, too young to know it was all sound effects and bullshit. So, she'd reluctantly agreed, but her yes had come with a cost—the cold fucking shoulder.

Speaking of inaccurate films . . . I looked across the room where some of our team was gathered around a movie. Instead of Griffin enlightening me with his sudden mind reading skills, the FNG getting hammered by a senior operator captured our attention.

"I'd rather you watch Jerry Springer than this BS. They've got SEALs HALO'ing in at night without NODs. What kind of garbage is this?" Dennison, our assistant team leader, remarked, busting Bradley's balls. "Two things you don't leave home without—night vision and your rifle. If you can watch this and not bat an eyelash at the inaccuracies, I have serious concerns about what you might do if your rifle jams up in a gunfight. Or hell, maybe you'll try and exfil on your dirty side. Or . . ."

He kept going, but I stopped listening. Bradley turned off the TV and tossed the remote, doing a hell of a job sucking it up and taking whatever Dennison served him.

Up until six months ago, Griffin and I were the FNGs, the *fucking new guys,* in the Unit. We'd been happy to relinquish that title, especially given how young we were. Griffin hadn't even punched over to this side of thirty yet, and I was only thirty-two as of June.

Griffin tipped his head, signaling for us to make a clean exit before we got roped into the conversation. And I had a feeling he was about to go Jerry Springer on me himself and wanted to do it privately. Probably attempt to get me to talk through my feelings. Acknowledge the fact that while my wife was pissed I'd joined the Unit, she wasn't angry enough to withhold the few dirty photos she'd gifted me here and there to whack off to—thank fuck for that.

We'd almost made it to the door without drawing Dennison's attention, when he snapped out, "Where are you two headed?"

"Outside for air." *And probably a lecture.*

Dennison locked his arms across his chest. The man was on edge even more than normal, and I didn't like the look in his eyes. The Secretary of State had called in a favor to JSOC —the Joint Special Operations Command—rerouting us here last week for an op instead of home as planned. The man probably needed to get laid, too.

"You've got to be the only billionaire in history risking his neck for the military," Dennison drawled, his Southern slipping through the cracks, too.

Here we go. "I'm not a billionaire." I rotated my neck a bit, knowing I needed to suck it up, pull a "Bradley," and shut my mouth. But, against my better judgment, I was about to get in the man's crosshairs. "My wife inherited the money when her parents died. It's not mine."

Rebecca's parents' private jet crashed three Christmases ago, and now my wife helped run their business empire, which included everything from chain hotels to manufacturing. That was why she lived in Manhattan instead of with me near Ft. Bragg in North Carolina. Not that I was ever home for it to matter where she rested her head at night.

"Marriage means the money is yours, too, buddy,"

Bradley said, deciding to break his silence for me since I still teetered on the border of FNG status. "It's wild you're here when you could buy yourself an island and chill. Billions, man. I can't wrap my head around how much money that is. I mean, what the fuck is wrong with you that you don't just go off-grid, buy your own helos, and maybe an island or two?"

"And miss all the fun with you guys?" I grabbed my Gatorz from my pocket, prepared to exfil out of there before Dennison or Bradley trapped me into opening my mouth.

"Your house in New York is seventy-five million," Bradley went on. "That kind of money is—"

"How do you know how much my wife's house is?" And it would always be my wife's house in my mind. It belonged to her parents before they died, and I was more comfortable on a bed at base than taking a shit on a gold toilet—and fucking hell, there really was a gold-plated toilet in the primary bathroom.

"I was bored. Googled it. Curiosity—"

"Killed the cat," Dennison cut him off, and thank God for that. He cocked his head, giving me the green light to go before Bradley said anything more relating to my wife or her family.

With how wiped out we all were, I might forget we were teammates and working to become friends. I'd take a bullet for the man, but I didn't know him well enough to trust him with my secrets.

Once Griffin and I were outside, I turned to face him. "Spit it out. What're you tiptoeing around?" Sunglasses on, I shoved my hands into my pockets in preparation for what was coming next. Another conversation I didn't want to have.

"I heard you might be leaving us to work for the Company."

Shit. "Who'd you hear that from? I've barely got my feet wet with the team here, why would I leave for the CIA?"

"Because that's what Rebecca wants," he said bluntly. "She's got contacts. Friends at the White House. A lot of them because of her parents. And they're squawking on her behalf. It made it down the pipeline to Dennison, then to Lopez."

"All the way to everyone but me, huh?" The idea our team leader, Master Sergeant Lopez, had heard rumors I might up and leave for the Agency was a gut shot I couldn't stomach right now. I'd need to confront my headstrong wife about the dinners she was throwing with her Washington friends "on my behalf."

"It was going to get back to you at some point, I'd rather you hear it from me."

"Learn that my wife is poking around behind my back trying to get me to leave the Army?" Lifting my hands from my pockets, I tore my fingers through my hair. I loved the woman, but damnit . . . "I'm barely ten years in. I have a list of shit I want to accomplish and another ten, at minimum, to give. I'm not going anywhere."

"You say that, but she's your wife. And maybe you can hide it from the rest of the guys here, but I can see what this is doing to you. The fact she doesn't support you being part of this team is fucking with your head."

He had a point. If I wasn't a hundred percent, distracted by the guilt hovering like a dark cloud, I could get someone hurt. "What would you do?"

"You've known Rebecca for nearly half your life, right?"

"Eleven years." But it felt like I'd known her forever. "Met at Columbia while I was a senior and she was a freshman. Became friends." *She pushed me to join the Air Force, but at the last minute, I joined the Army instead.*

"Didn't start dating seriously until I was a year into my service. Married after she finished grad school." Recounting the bullet points wasn't necessary. Not for Griffin. But apparently my conscience needed the trip down memory lane. The reminders of the life we'd shared and how far we'd come.

He slapped a hand over my shoulder. "It's hard work doing what we do while keeping it together at home. Not that I'd know, being I'm single, but I have eyes and ears. I see and hear what y'all married guys go through."

"You can't seriously be recommending I quit and join the Agency because Rebecca wants me to."

"I'm just saying do what makes you happy. And as long as she's not happy, you're not happy."

I bowed my head, unsure what to think, but leaving the Unit was the last thing I wanted. Well, the last-last thing I wanted was to lose Rebecca. *Fuck.* He removed his hand from my shoulder. Unfortunately, it didn't lessen the weight his words left there. "Do me a favor and come spend Christmas with us next month in New York."

"To help persuade Rebecca you should stay or convince you to quit?"

"To keep me sane when she hosts her fancy dinner parties with her fancy elitist friends in her fancy fucking house."

"You really hate fancy shit, huh?" He laughed. "Won't you have Camila there to keep you from going off the deep end?"

Outside of Rebecca, Camila was the only family I had left. The daughter of my parents' best friends, she'd become like a little sister to me. Always ready to bust my balls and save my ass a time or two.

"No, she won't be there. She's got a work thing." *Spy shit.* "So, do me a solid and come." I cursed at the sight of

Dennison waving us back in before Griffin could respond, and I pocketed my sunglasses.

"Guess we're not making it home for Thanksgiving," Griffin said as we made our way inside.

"We have an emergency situation at the U.S. Embassy here. This is going to be brief, so listen up. We need to head out now." Lopez was in the room now, and the first to speak. "Truck bombing outside the embassy. Marines and DS are under heavy fire. The ambo didn't make it to the safe room. She's being held hostage inside. Same with her daughter who's in town visiting—but they're separated on different floors."

"This is a hostage rescue operation," Dennison chimed in. "We have a five-story building without many windows. The shape is angular, almost pyramidal, and it's not ideal for fast-roping in. So, we'll need to breach another way."

"What about local police? SWAT? Any help until we can get there?" I asked, already on the move for my weapons bag. One that'd been prepped for a flight home, not for an op.

"That's the problem," Dennison answered as I strapped on my plate and vest. "Al-Qaeda members were dressed as local PD, which is how they infil'ed the embassy. And one Marine security guard opened fire on one of the real police officers trying to get in to help after the explosion in the parking lot, creating a fucking mess on top of things."

"Great, so we can't tell the good guys from the bad guys when we do get in." *Fucking perfect.* I holstered my secondary at my side, a Glock 19, then went for my HK416 carbine, a better rifle for close-quarters combat because of the shorter barrel length. "So, don't shoot until we're shot at first."

Lopez nodded. "CIA intel's suggesting this is payback for the Bin Laden kill this year, and they're planning to hit other embassies today, so they're locking every other site down."

"Could've used that intel before they attacked the embassy," Griffin grumbled. He wasn't a fan of the CIA, making my decision to possibly join one day, because of Rebecca's insistence, that much more painful.

"The Marines are reporting the ambo's daughter is on the fifth floor being held hostage by two tangos, possibly in explosive vests. Ambassador Mackenzie is on the second floor with an unknown number of tangos armed with AKs and explosives as well," Dennison shared, eyes on me. "You've got the daughter."

"How old is she? We talking a kid? Five or six?" Fuck, that made my stomach turn. If the guy clacked off his vest, or there was a bomb somewhere inside—screw coming home for Thanksgiving, we wouldn't be coming home at all.

"Name is Diana Mackenzie, and she's not a child. She's twenty, a college student here for Thanksgiving with her mom," Dennison said while kitting up. "She's also the Speaker of the House's daughter. Joshua Mackenzie's not here, but he'll have our heads if his ex-wife or his daughter dies today, so don't let that happen. We clear?"

"I have every intention of saving her regardless of who the fuck her father is," I said, forgetting my place for a moment. "*Sir*," I tacked on.

I met Griffin's eyes and gave him a nod. It was go time.

2

DIANA

On a scale of one to ten, this is . . . unscalable. How do you even rate this kind of nightmare? Had I nodded off while reading? *Ugh.* Why was I hot? And what was that in the air? My entire body did that weird jerk-move from startling when you fall in your sleep, and I—

"Don't move. Not an inch." An unfamiliar voice curled around me as the weight of something heavy banded across my waist.

Who's holding me? Wait . . . not a nightmare. "What— what's happening?" I started coughing, or maybe choking, on what felt like burnt, ashy air as it filled my throat and lungs.

Finally managing to pry open my eyes, the realization of what a bad idea that was had me sealing my lids tight. Was the floor missing inches from where I was lying? Or was this some bizarre fever dream?

Then it hit me. The memories.

I snatched answers from the foggy part of my brain before they could retreat in terror and self-preservation. The hit to my head from the blast had rattled my thoughts and knocked me out.

11

"The floor is unstable. You need to be careful." There was that voice again, coming from behind me. "I need to shift you to the other side of me before you fall."

Fall? I did my best to force the fear to vacate my body so I could get a handle on the situation and reopen my eyes.

"You okay? Injured?" he asked.

"I—I don't think so. I feel fine." That was something. Based on the mystery guy's steady tone, he sounded okay, too.

But there were wires exposed. Crumbled plaster. The building was . . . well, I shouldn't have been able to see into the room next door, but there it was—a wide-open space with no floor between myself and the Deputy Chief of Mission's office.

"This can't be from that guy's vest." I knew a thing or two about chemistry. Enough to know the explosives those two assholes had strapped over their clothes couldn't tear a hole in the room like this.

"There was an explosive device in the office next door. Took out that room and most of this one, including the floor." The deep, slightly muffled voice slid across my skin, hitting the shell of my ear again.

I'd learned the names of every Marine and security officer in the building since I'd arrived. Spoken to each of them multiple times. I would've remembered a raspy tone like this one had I met him before.

"You got to me in time," I said as it came back to me, remembering more of what happened before it'd been lights out.

The man behind me had to be the military-looking guy who'd shown up just before the blast. Rifle in hand, most of his face masked aside from his eyes, he'd taken out the two men who had me hostage. And then . . . boom.

And now I was on the ground about to fall through what was left of the floor. Maybe a twelve-foot drop wouldn't be that bad, but what if I landed on glass or something sharp or jagged, and—

"There's nowhere for us to go," he said, cutting off my panicky thoughts. "We have to wait for an extract. But I need you on the other side of me, okay?"

"What do I do?" At the feel of his hand on my midsection, I tried to turn my head, hoping for a glimpse at the man sent here to save me. Instead, I went still, terror sliding in and taking hold of me as the remaining floor wobbled beneath us. "I don't want to die."

"I'm not letting you die. My people will find us in time."

I attempted to cling to the promising sound of his voice, instinct and hope (maybe even a bit of faith?) telling me we would be okay, but the rational part of my brain clamored for attention. Facts and random information that didn't serve any purpose, except maybe to heighten my anxiety, cut through as I started hacking on the smoke again. Science couldn't get me out of this mess, but maybe the guy with his hand on my stomach could.

"I'm going to slowly pull you on top of me, then around to my other side. The floor is a bit more stable behind me. There's only a foot of space, but you'll be against a wall, and there must be a support beam right below keeping us from going down like the rest of the floor."

I latched on to his strong, calming tone and did as he asked, managing to complete step one: straddle a stranger.

My hands rested on his chest—well, on top of the vest stuffed with ammo—as he held my hips, keeping me safely tethered on his lap. Only his eyes were visible, but it was too dark to make out the color of them. I leaned in closer to him, feeling safer already. Feeling *better*, even. "Oxytocin," I muttered.

"What?" he asked, somehow remaining patient with me.

We both started coughing, and I waved at the tendrils of smoke in the air with one hand, then found his eyes again. "I feel safe like this, and my body must be releasing oxytocin as a result, lowering my cortisol levels. So, basically, I'm less panicky now."

"Ahh, okay. Well," he began, his deep voice continuing to reassure me, "you'll be even safer on the other side of me, and then maybe you'll release a lot more of that oxytocin."

"Okay." Yet, I didn't budge.

"I won't let anything happen to you," he added, sensing my hesitancy about moving again. "What else releases oxytocin? Talk to me while you move."

Jeez, he was good at distracting me. "Aside from physical touch, like hugging, labor can trigger its release. Breastfeeding." I set my hand to the ground on the other side of him, beginning to slide over. "An erection, sex, masturba —" I cut myself off a little too late.

He cleared his throat, doubtfully from the smoke that time. "Lie next to me," he said casually, acting as though he hadn't heard me, and we weren't on the verge of joining the fourth floor.

I carefully finished following orders and shifted to my right side, bending my elbows and forcing my hands to fit between us.

After a few more bouts of coughing racked through both of us—hopefully just enough to joggle his brain and clear away the memory of my rambling—he started talking, but based on what he was saying, he wasn't speaking to me. The only clear word I overheard was, "Break."

"Break," I echoed, not actually expecting him to explain what that meant.

He kept his head tipped back, eyes on the ceiling. No movement aside from his finger resting on something near his throat. It had to be his communication device to his team.

"I have the package. We need immediate exfil." He gave off specific information about our location, but how would anyone get to us? Cut a new hole but through the roof and drop a rope down?

At the visible rise and fall of his chest, I asked, "Everything okay?"

"My teammates are good. And your mom is safe," he shared. "We were the only ones on the fifth floor aside from the bad guys. And the fourth level had already been cleared out."

In the chaos of it all, I couldn't believe I hadn't asked about my mom. "What about the others? There was so much gunfire before you arrived. Is the staff okay?" Thankfully, with Thanksgiving around the corner, there'd only been a handful of people there.

"I'm not sure on other casualties, ma'am."

"Ma'am is my mom. Not that it matters what you call me, I suppose."

"Sorry." He slowly faced me. "Diana."

He gestured for me to lift my sweater up and over my mouth. Not easy to do in the cramped space, but I managed to get my hands to the neckline and cover my lips and nose. Now it was just eyes on eyes.

"Who are you? I overheard Mom on the phone with the Secretary of State this morning. Something about diplomacy didn't work. So, a team of Delta operators were brought in last week for a quick assist even though they were due home already, and now you're here, so—"

"Your mom needs to do a better job at not talking where someone can eavesdrop. Not even for her daughter to hear." Despite the shit lighting, I could make out the visible snap of his brows drawing together. "*Especially* not near her daughter. Knowing things can be dangerous."

"Can't be more dangerous than being taken hostage and having a bomb nearly kill me," I blurted. "Technically, given the floor might disappear beneath us any moment, we can still die." My arms began cramping from being trapped between my body and his. "So, you're Delta, right? Although you all have a few names. CAG. The Unit. Not that you can officially speak on any, right? But at least your people aren't in the media's spotlight, unlike the SEALs who took out Bin Laden earlier this year and are now under a microscope." I needed to stop rambling stat. "Can you give me your name, at least?"

He was quiet for a moment, but then he asked, "Do you *need* a name?" There was a smooth edge to his tone instead of the typical roughness I would expect from a Delta operator.

"I'd like one, but I'd like a lot of things right now. Doubt I'll get any of them."

"Like what?" Ah, he was trying to distract me again.

"Mmm. Room to breathe, for one. Clean air would be nice, too."

"At least we're not on fire," he said, a touch of humor to his voice.

"Well, now that you mention it . . ." I went through a few chemistry notes in my head, trying to determine why the room wasn't a post-bomb inferno.

"You can call me Dom," he said, his words snapping through the chemical equations flying through my mind.

"Like Dom as in dominant, or Dom as in Dominic Toretto from *Fast and Furious*?" *Did I really just ask that?*

"I'd like to laugh right now, but I'm worried the floor can't handle it." He reached for his mask and lowered it to reveal his face, clearly wanting me to see his smile, as if seeing it would somehow help ease my nerves. Because if he was smiling, he couldn't be too worried we'd plummet to our deaths, right?

But also—wow, what a nice face. I bet even better in the light.

"Dom as in Dominick." He re-covered his mouth as he spoke. "The guys on the team call me Dom. And the bad guys call me the devil."

You hardly seem like a devil. But ohhh . . . if he was taking their souls to hell, then I could see that nickname. It made sense.

"I'm going to hold on to you. That okay?" His brows rose in question, and when I nodded yes, he quietly set his hand on my jeaned hip.

"And what does your family call you?"

"How about I ask you a question instead?"

"Distract and deflect. Keep me talking so I don't have a panic attack?"

"That's the idea." I could hear the smirk in his tone; he didn't need to lower his mask to confirm he was smiling again. "Did your mom name you after the princess?"

"How in the world did you know that? Your brief had to have been pretty, well, brief. Those details wouldn't be included."

"You know a lot about the military, don't you?"

"Hard not to when your dad was career military before getting into politics. He was a Teamguy, and I grew up all over the world, surrounded by operators," I admitted. "So,

Mr. Art of the Dodge, how'd you know my parents named me after Princess Diana?"

"A wild guess."

The building rumbled around us, and my heart skipped into my throat. His gloved hand drew me so close we'd soon be sharing a heartbeat.

"Not an answer." I swallowed, my nerves distracting me as the walls continued to groan. "And also, I do *not* want to die like this. I have plans. Big ones. Turning twenty-one in January, to start. After that, saving the world."

"We'll get you to twenty-one, I promise. And all the birthdays between then and your plans to save the world."

"Save me so I can save the world. That *your* plan?"

"Sounds like a perfect fuc—" He paused for a moment as if not wanting to swear in front of me. "Sounds like a perfect plan to me."

Hmm. "Back to my name."

"Back to it." There was that humorous tone again. Not-a-care-or-worry-in-the-world kind of attitude from the sounds of it. I wondered if it was an act for me, or if, like my dad, he used comedy to neutralize tense situations.

"You're a funny guy."

"Not the compliment I usually get."

"Who said it was a compliment?" Was I seriously teasing at a time like this?

"Having a sense of humor is usually a good thing."

"True." I smiled, nearly dropping the fabric covering part of my face. "You are making me forget I could fall to my death. Thank you."

"Anytime." He closed one eye for a second. "On second thought, let's keep it to this one time."

"Good point." Another unexpected smile started to settle on my lips, interrupted by a short coughing fit. My sweater was not keeping the shit air from infiltrating my lungs. I should have kept the talking to a minimum, but the distraction of our conversation was keeping me from imagining all of the less attractive outcomes of our situation. And I had grown a bit attached to hearing his voice. "So. My name."

"Ah, yes." Instead of going on with that thought, he touched the device at his neck and went quiet, focusing as if someone was talking to him. He let whoever was on the line know we were still alive but short on time.

Short on time? Great, there go my nerves again. Flying away.

"Your mom is the ambassador. Your dad is the Speaker of the House. Celebrities and politicians give their kids weird names or iconic ones."

"Not just a door kicker, are you?" I teased, knowing he'd get the joke. "You're perceptive. Clearly, smart."

"All that from a comment about your name, huh?" He chuckled, and the sound went straight to that sweet oxytocin center of my brain. "But I'm gathering you're not *just* a twenty-year-old daughter of politicians, are you?" He threw that "just" right back at me with the perfect amount of sarcasm.

"Almost twenty-*one*-year-old daughter of politicians who named me after a princess as if that'd somehow make me one."

He laughed again.

"I can see the headlines now," I went on, deflecting from the flash of embarrassment cutting through me. At least it sent fear to the backseat. *Fear, always the worst backseat driver,* so my dad liked to say. "Hero fails to save the ambassador's daughter after she triggers his awkward sense of humor with her own, sending them crashing through the floor."

"My sense of humor is perfectly on point." He fake-grunted. "Speak for yourself, kid."

Kid. Ugh, I'd rather be ma'am'ed. "You really are pretty slick at the whole keeping-me-sane and helping-me-forget-the-'I'm on death's doorstep' thing." I went to lower the sweater from my face, but he lightly shook his head, a directive to keep it up. "Or in the hands of the devil. Of course, the devil was an angel before he fell. *But* I get the feeling you're—"

"About to become your second-favorite guy, because my teammate is about to extract us, and he'll be your new hero."

"Wait, really?" My sweater fell, and I choked on some of the disgusting air.

He lowered his mask, revealing his lips. Lips I'd love to kiss as a thank-you.

"The embassy is secure from enemy fire. Our EOD man confirmed there are no more explosives inside. They're thirty seconds out from rescuing us," he said, presumably relaying whatever had been told to him over his earpiece.

"Mm. Well, I suppose you can be my second-favorite, not-just-a-door-kicker-but-humorous, Delta Force–operator hero." *That was a mouthful.*

As the seconds ticked by while we awaited our rescue, he began smiling again, and it did something funny to my insides. Made me warm. Feel like I was bathed in the light of an angel, and definitely not in the hands of the devil.

"What are you thinking?" I couldn't help but ask him.

His smile reached his eyes, and I could actually see his face, light finally shining on us from somewhere and eliminating the shadows that had surrounded him.

"Just happy to have a hand in saving the girl who plans to one day save the world."

3

CARTER

NEW YORK, NEW YORK

THERE WERE TOO MANY PEOPLE AT MY WIFE'S HOLIDAY
party. One short of two dozen to be exact. Unfortunately,
Griffin hadn't been one of the guests, so I had no one there I
wanted to talk to other than my wife. And Rebecca was busy
entertaining people—from dignitaries to dipshits.

One thing was for certain, she was in her element as
Rebecca Barclay of the Barclay billionaires, not Rebecca
Dominick. Not the wife of a guy who made less in a year than
she made in a day. That was probably being generous. She
more than likely topped my yearly salary in an hour.

At the sight of more people crowding in from the private
elevator, I decided to bail for a few minutes to get some air.

It was starting to snow and arctic cold out, so I put on my
coat and took the back steps to the rooftop terrace
overlooking Fifth and Madison. Given the less than
accommodating weather, I'd thought I'd have the terrace to
myself. Apparently, I wasn't the only one willing to brave the
elements for a momentary escape.

The woman had her back to me. Blonde hair pinned up. A long wool coat wrapped around her small form. Eyes either shut or taking in the view of the city.

I didn't remember meeting her downstairs, but maybe she'd come in while I'd been pouring myself a scotch from my private stash hidden in my wife's office.

I contemplated finding somewhere else to have that minute alone I needed since I could only do so much fake smiling and handshaking without losing it. My skin was practically on fire, though, so the snowflakes and cold air were essential.

"Excuse me." Maybe I could get her to go. She turned slowly, lifting her hands from her jacket pockets, then startled back. Damn—*please don't fall over the railing.* And, fuck, was that . . . *Diana?* "Careful." Worried she might fall fifty stories, I quickly joined her at the edge of the rooftop.

"You," she mouthed, the word soft and barely audible. Her eyelashes fluttered in shock. "It is you, isn't it? Your beard is gone, but . . ."

Why couldn't I hide the smile that managed to sneak up on me? The woman was staring at me, starstruck. Like I was some celebrity. It was cute.

After Griffin had rescued us that day at the embassy, I'd barely had a chance to say goodbye to Diana—never even saw the ambassador. My team had been rushed away from the scene, so the media didn't get eyes on us.

"It's me," I finally answered, getting out of my head. "Rebecca invited your mother to the party, I assume?" I hadn't seen her down there, but why in God's name would Rebecca do that? I wasn't allowed to tell my wife classified details about certain operations, and she had no idea I'd been in Abu Dhabi last month. I didn't bother to tell her I'd been part of the rescue team at the embassy, and she hadn't asked.

Hell, why would she? She'd believed I'd been in Africa at the time of the terrorist attack. So Diana and her mother weren't at the party because of me.

"Wait, you know Rebecca Dominick?" She shook her head. "Of course you do, or you wouldn't be here." But then her eyes went wide. "*Dom* . . . inick. You're *Carter* Dominick?"

Her startled step back had me flying closer and snatching her waist, worried she'd go woman-over-building in a second. And fuck, I'd go right after, forgetting I couldn't fly.

When I was confident she wouldn't fall, I let go of her. "Yes, I'm her husband."

"Dom," she said under her breath, still appearing shocked.

I didn't know what else to do other than shrug. "How are you doing? Been okay since . . . well, what happened?"

She stared at me for a solid ten seconds. I counted, using the time to center myself while I figured out how to navigate this situation. I rarely met people I'd rescued after ops, so I didn't know what to do. Okay, that was a lie. I *never* ran into anyone I'd saved. This was my first time, and it needed to be my last.

"No PTSD, if that's what you're asking. I'm good." She clutched the lapels of her coat, tugging them together while visibly shivering. "On break from college. Just visiting Mom's temporary spot in New York while she waits for a new assignment."

Right. The embassy was closed for the time being, so of course the ambassador would be reassigned. "So, where do you go? What's your major?" The art of small talk was actually a skill I'd acquired in the Army's Tier One division. Came in handy more times than I could count.

"I'm at Stanford. Getting my BS in environmental science

with a minor in chemical engineering. And I dabble in nuclear and quantum physics."

"Oh yeah? You know, I happen to dabble in quantum physics in my spare time, too," I joked, grinning like a fucking idiot. *What in God's name is wrong with me?*

When she laughed, it was the first time tonight I found myself enjoying talking to one of my wife's guests. The kid had a good head on her shoulders. And damn was I glad I'd saved that head—and big brain of hers—last month.

"So, your mom knows my wife? Or do you?" I was still trying to put together how Ambassador Mackenzie wound up at our home. Not that I'd checked the guest list. Rubbing elbows, shoulders, or any body part with anyone other than my wife wasn't something I was interested in. I wanted to spend every second on leave with Rebecca. Make up for lost time. Find a way to bridge the gap joining the Unit had placed between us.

She caught a snowflake with her tongue, such an innocent thing to do. "My mom knew her parents, and I guess she stayed friends with your wife after their death. I know Rebecca, too. Kinda-sorta, anyway."

"Oh?" I pushed my hands into my coat pockets, trying to warm them up. I told myself it was because it'd be bad for my trigger finger to get frostbite, but part of me was also worried I might reach out for her again.

"My mom said the Barclays wanted Rebecca to have some real-life experience or something like that, so they had her babysit me a few times when I was younger."

You're still young. I kept that thought to myself and instead went with, "Small world."

"The smallest," she said with a nervous chuckle. When she took a step back, because she apparently enjoyed worrying me, I realized it was because we were no longer alone. "Congressman Paulsen," she said through her teeth, and I turned to the side to put eyes on whoever was there.

"What are you two doing up here alone?" I didn't appreciate the accusation in his tone. He made it sound like I was doing something indecent. On my own fucking rooftop terrace.

"We both had the same idea for fresh air. Well, *cold* air," I said as his loafers tracked through the freshly fallen snow, coming closer to us. At the feel of Diana's hand on my back, I stole a look at her. The tension in her expression told me everything I needed to know—she was using me as a shield. Not a good sign.

I fully faced Paulsen, moving so Diana was sheltered completely behind me. "I think you should go inside. Too cold for your California blood," I added, remembering where he'd said he was from when my wife had introduced him earlier tonight. Apparently, my wife had also donated to his last congressional campaign.

Paulsen angled his focus around me, trying to put eyes on Diana. The guy wasn't much older than me, but he was far too old for her.

"You really should go back to the party." If he hadn't heard the threat in my tone, he'd see it in my motherfucking eyes. I had a feeling this asshole had made Diana uncomfortable before, and if I found out he'd touched her without her consent, he'd be the one slipping and falling fifty stories.

The congressman locked eyes with me before nodding. He didn't want to dance with the devil tonight, which meant he had some sense in him. "I'll be heading home. Good to see you again, Diana. My door is always open to you in San Francisco if you ever need anything."

"Put a lock on your door. Don't let so many people in," I

said, knowing he'd read between the lines to never bother her again. Once he smartly walked away without a word, I turned toward her. "You okay? Did he—"

"I'm good. And thank you for that. So far, he's always taken no for an answer when hitting on me. But he makes me uneasy."

"I'm sorry he was invited, and that he ever made you feel that way." Shit, I needed another drink. I had to deal with bad guys on the regular. I didn't need them at my wife's party. I'd be making sure she removed him from future guest lists, too. No more donations, too. "But if he ever does bother you in the future, you let me know, okay?"

She rubbed her gloved hands up and down the sleeves of her coat, blue eyes flying to my face in surprise.

Wait, what am I offering? It wasn't like I could give this girl my number in case she needed help. That would be awkward, bordering on inappropriate. "Your mom or dad. Tell them, I mean, and they can handle him," I said before she could respond, because who the fuck was I, Batman? "We should probably go inside," I suggested when she only kept staring at me. *Don't want anyone getting the wrong idea, particularly my wife.*

I'd never cheat on her, but Rebecca liked to push my buttons and ask me if I fucked around while deployed. It always made my stomach turn knowing she'd think I'd do that.

"Right." She gave me a sweet smile. "Thank you for saving me in Abu Dhabi. I think I said that then, but in case I didn't because of all the rushing post-rescue—"

"You did, and you're welcome. You were strong. Kept it together when most wouldn't." With the snow starting to fall heavier now, I motioned for her to walk, intending to make sure she got down the stairs safely before I disappeared to a closed and locked room. I needed away from everything.

We only made it three steps toward the door before Rebecca found us up there. "Ahh, good, you two met. I was hoping you would." Rebecca's reaction shocked me, thankfully not giving me her signature *what-the-hell* eyes. "Diana's mom didn't bring her to our wedding, or Mom and Dad's funeral, but we go way back, and I wanted to introduce you two."

"The ambassador was at our wedding?" *The funeral, too?* My memory wasn't that bad, was it? Then again, I'd met hundreds of her acquaintances over the years, and it was hard to keep everyone straight. Our wedding alone had at least four hundred guests.

"Susan wasn't an ambassador then." Rebecca didn't have a coat, so I removed mine and draped it over her shoulders. "But wait, how'd you know her mom's an ambassador? I didn't see you talking to Susan tonight." Her eyes flashed to Diana. "Oh, of course, you told him while up here, right?"

Diana peered at me as if surprised I hadn't told my wife how I really knew her mother, and her, for that matter. "I did."

"Thank God Diana wasn't hurt last month. Did I tell you she was in that bombing? A miracle no one innocent died that day." She pointed to Diana, then gestured for us to head back to the party. "She's a whiz kid. A genius. One of the smartest people I know, and I know a lot of people."

"I'm really not that—"

"Don't be modest," Rebecca cut her off as we descended the steps, the two of them walking ahead of me. Rebecca hooked her arm behind Diana's back in a comforting and guiding gesture. Damn, my wife would make a good mother one day.

If only you wanted kids.

"I'm going to get a drink. Want anything?" I asked the two of them once we were back in the main party area, the room flooded with people. "Shit, you're not twenty-one yet, right?" *Next month?*

"Wow, you two really talked a lot, huh?" Rebecca spun around, handing me back my jacket.

If there was ever a time to tell you . . . "The embassy bombing," I muttered under my breath, letting her connect the dots.

Rebecca's eyes widened, and she peered back and forth between us.

"Is it such a shock?" I tossed my coat on a nearby leather armchair. "You know what I do."

"Will you excuse us?" She gave Diana a polite smile, and I tipped my head to the girl before letting my wife lead me wherever she wanted to go.

"I thought you were in Africa," she huffed in an exasperated tone once we were in her father's old office. Flicking on the light, she made a beeline for the bar and poured us both a drink.

"I was." I closed the door. "We were brought to Abu Dhabi for a quick op. We were about to come home when the call came in about the hostage situation at the embassy."

"You could've died. Diana's mom told me her daughter almost did. Along with the operator who was with her. And that explosion could've—"

"I'm fine." When her worried eyes remained fixed on me, I set a fist to my chest to emphasize the fact my heart was still beating. "I'm here, aren't I?"

"So, you were the operator with her? Susan asked for his name, but she was told it was classified. No wonder Diana

28

had stars in her eyes up there. You're her hero." She shoved the glass in my hand and gulped back her scotch.

Staring at her without taking a sip, I couldn't help but ask, "Are you upset I could've died or that I didn't tell you I almost died?"

"Both?" She arched her brow. "But this is all the more reason you should leave and join the Agency."

My turn to drink. "You know if I join the Agency, I'd be out in the field. No desk job. You get that, right?"

"But no more long deployments, which means we could make love more." She slid her free hand up my chest, and I wrapped my fingers around her wrist, tightening my grip just enough to make sure I had her full attention.

"What is it you really want?" How fucked up was it that part of me hated I loved her so much I really would do whatever she wanted if she pushed hard enough?

I'd convinced her to agree to Selections, but she'd assumed the ninety percent fail rate would've stopped me from joining the Unit. She was wrong. I'd had Griffin at my side ensuring I made it through along with him. So here we were, at a crossroads. Part of me not wanting to give up something I'd worked so hard to achieve, something I was good at. The other part not wanting to lose the life we had together, a life that was increasingly impacted by a job she resented.

"My parents put so much pressure on me while they were alive." She sighed. "I still feel the pressure now that they're gone. Like we need to—"

"No." I shook my head and let go of her. "They wanted us in the White House one day. Senate, then the presidency." I circled my finger like a helo blade spinning. "Is that what these parties are about? Connections to get us there? Because I don't want that." *Please, fucking please, don't try and push*

29

me to say yes to that. "I also don't think you really give a damn about the White House. You just feel the guilt and burden of wanting to make them happy." I went to the desk, abandoned the empty glass, and began working up the sleeves of my white button-down shirt. "Besides, I'm not sure tattoos are the preferred accessory in the Oval Office."

"First time for everything." My wife dragged her palm down her collarbone to her cleavage, distracting my efforts at deflection. She had on a stunning full-length red silk dress. Her blonde hair was pinned to the side with a barrette, and her green eyes were intense and focused on me.

"*You* could be POTUS one day, by the way. Why does it have to be me?"

"As nice of an idea as that sounds, I don't want the job. But I do want to help people. Change the world. And I think between the two of us we could do that. But not if you die. We can't do anything if you're dead."

"I could die in the CIA," I pointed out.

"No, you'd have people protecting you there. I just have a bad feeling is all. If you don't leave the Army, I'm worried I'll lose you forever." She set her glass next to mine, and I pulled her into my arms.

"You're not getting rid of me, I promise."

"No trading me in for some younger girl half my age, either?" She looped her arms over my shoulders and drew herself closer. "Diana's gorgeous. Surely you noticed."

I rolled my eyes. I saw that comment coming a mile away. Surprised it actually took her that long to make it. "I'm not the one with a celebrity hall pass. That's you."

She smirked. "I'll never meet mine. Don't worry."

"I am worried." Well, not really. I knew she'd never use that "hall pass" even if she did meet her crush. I'd also never share her, not with anyone for any reason. "Surprised you didn't invite the actor to your party. He would've said yes for you."

"I did." She shrugged. "He was busy. Another billionaire's event to attend." She stuck her tongue out at me, the little vixen. "Buuut back to what we were talking about . . . what if we put some of this money to better use?"

"Any ideas how?" I leaned in, my lips hovering near hers.

"One or two."

"As long as it doesn't involve giving money to assholes like Congressman Paulsen, I'm open to suggestions."

"Since when is Paulsen an asshole?"

"Has he hit on you before?" I asked her instead, and at her blush, I frowned.

"Forget him and all the men who hit me up for—"

"Better be only for your money and not for anything else." I slid my hand around to her backside.

"Mm. Why does it turn me on when you get possessive?" She chewed on her lip. "Make love to me."

"Here?" I grunted. "It's your dad's office. And someone could walk in." I tightened my hold of her ass, reveling in her quiet moan—a dignified moan if there ever were one. "I don't want anyone seeing my woman. Not for a second."

"It's my office now. And what are locks for if not for keeping people out while you screw your wife?"

4

DIANA

PALO ALTO, CALIFORNIA

"ARE YOU EATING FOR A FAMILY OF FOUR TONIGHT?" My roommate set aside her suitcase and pointed to the mac 'n' cheese box alongside the boiling water in our kitchen. "Was Christmas with your mom that bad? Can't be worse than if it'd been with your dad."

Oh, thank God, you're back. I ran over and hugged Sierra. "It was bad. Like nuclear-level bad."

"Soooo, why didn't you call me?" she asked once I let her go. "Why wait to talk in person?" She reached for the open bottle of Pinot on the counter and poured herself a glass. I may not have been twenty-one for another week, and I was a hardcore rule-follower almost to a fault, but I'd also spent most of my life abroad where you only needed to be eighteen to drink. Some habits died hard.

"I ran into Dom," I admitted.

She spilled the wine mid-pour as she spun her head my way. "You're shitting me? How? Where?"

I turned down the water to a simmer, poured in the

noodles and gave them a little stir as I thought back to bumping into *Carter* Dominick at the Christmas party almost two weeks ago.

"Earth to Diana," she said, waving her hand in front of my face.

"He's married," I blurted. "I've spent a month fantasizing about a married man." My shoulders slumped as I faced her, feeling the creep of a blush work up my neck and into my cheeks. "Not just any married man—he's Rebecca Barclay's husband." I grimaced. "Well, she's Rebecca Dominick now." I probably shouldn't have been revealing his identity since he was a special operator. Fuck, I was a horrible person for that, too.

"The Barclay billionaires? Are you shitting me?"

"You already asked that. But no, I'm very much not shitting you."

"That involves a double-shitting comment for sure. Maybe even a triple."

"At the very least, a double fuck," I said on a sigh.

"They're even more 'old money' rich than my grandparents," she added with a laugh. "But why's a billionaire in the military? That's wild."

I stirred the noodles, then reached for my glass, trying to push aside the very vivid thoughts I'd had about a *married* man. The guy had been the star of every single fantasy of mine after he'd saved my life. He'd unknowingly provided me with heaps and heaps of oxytocin over the last month.

The image of him hadn't been crystal clear in my fantasies because I'd only had a shot of him completely unmasked for all of five seconds, but now I knew exactly what he looked like to a T.

Midnight-black hair. Eyes the color of espresso. A bladed jawline with a strong, defined chin. Golden tan skin despite it being winter. And a rock-hard body he couldn't hide beneath the starched white dress shirt and black slacks he'd worn for the party. He'd towered over me even in heels, so he was at least six foot two or taller.

God, he was hotter in person than how I'd pictured him in my head. And real-life guys were never as good as fantasy ones.

Throw in that hint of a Southern drawl I heard from him a time or two while we'd talked, and . . .

"I'm going to hell. It's as simple as that." I finished my wine and refilled my glass, which wasn't the best idea, but I was on the verge of panicking. Because seriously—I'd used my vibrator to get off to thoughts of Rebecca's husband, and I just . . .

"You didn't know." Sierra slapped her hand over my shoulder, her green eyes laser-focused on mine. "It's not like you've thought about him that way since you found out, right? You're Miss Goody-Goody, and I mean that in the best possible way." She paused, a smirk settling on her lips. "Thinking about him after the fact would be a 'me' thing to do. Your moral compass is straight, mine is wicked fucking crooked," she added, her Bostonian accent cutting through her observation.

"I've tried so hard not to be crooked." My stomach turned. Full-on somersault action. "Every time I close my eyes, I try to have someone else fill his place. I even created a little mantra to remind myself he's off-limits for my fantasies, but his face keeps popping into my head no matter how much I beg my brain not to let it happen and—"

"Girl, calm down. You're only human. I mean, I was beginning to think you weren't, so . . ." She smirked, but when I didn't smile back, she set aside her glass and took mine as well. "The man saved your life. He's like a superhero. And superheroes aren't supposed to exist outside fiction, but in your case, he does." When it was clear to my bestie that she wasn't convincing me of anything yet, she kept at it. "What happened to you is like when hostages fall for their kidnapper and fixate on them. I think there's a name for it."

"Hostage and kidnapper?" This wasn't helping, and I needed my wine back.

"And he's older. Mature. A badass. Plenty of reasons to keep him in your head for 'self-care' when needed. Just pretend he's that rugged hero, Dom, and you don't know who he is in real life."

"He's Rebecca's husband." I emphasized that last word, trying to remind her of how crucially important that key piece of information was. "I would never think about your boyfriend like that. Ugh. That'd be gross."

"First of all, I don't have a boyfriend." She handed my wine back and picked up hers as well. "Secondly, if I had a hot boyfriend, I wouldn't mind if other women eye-fucked him. And third, you barely know Rebecca. She's a family friend, sure. But not *your* friend."

I stirred the macaroni in a daze, sipping my wine.

"But I know you, and you'll feel guilty if you keep thinking about Mr. Billionaire Hero, so we need to find a new guy for you."

"Imagine what my mom would say if she knew I'd been lusting after a married man." The horrible pit in my stomach grew from a seed to an orange in the space of a second. "She'd say I was as bad as Dad."

"Your dad cheated on her while he was married, and he still became Speaker of the House."

Nice recap. Kill me now.

"You didn't cheat or do anything wrong. Did Carter flirt

with you at any point during the rescue or when you met him at the party?"

"No, which makes him that much . . . just more. He's a good guy, and you should've seen the way he looked at his wife. It was sweet. And I'm happy for them both. I just hate myself for wanting him before the party and—"

"For wishing he was single so you could jump his bones?"

I set the glass and spoon down, then slammed my palms on the counter so I could process that horrible truth. "He protected me against that asshole congressman at the party, too. I thought he might throw the guy from the rooftop terrace where we'd been talking if Craig Paulsen so much as tried to reach for me."

"Wait. Hold up." She gripped my forearm, urging me to face her. "You were with this man on a rooftop terrace?"

"In the snow with the Manhattan skyline around us. A flipping fairy-tale setting." I pouted, knowing I was being ridiculous even as I recounted the memory. "And yeah, I wanted to cry when I found out he was Rebecca's husband because part of my fantasies revolved around meeting him again under different circumstances one day, and we'd have some perfect moment and kiss." Ugh, I hated myself. "You're probably right. Hostage-rescuer not hostage-kidnapper infatuation, though."

"That's all it is." She gently squeezed my forearm. "I'll lend you my celebrity crush to fantasize about instead."

"Celebrities do nothing for me, and you know it."

"Fine, fine." She finished her wine and smiled. "Forget the macaroni and the crush. I'm taking you out. You're getting your first tattoo or you're getting laid."

"I don't do one-night stands. Or needles."

"Welllll, if you want to get over Dom . . . you will

tonight." She turned off the stove before I could protest. "You have your whole life and a lot of Doms to still meet."

I laughed. "Doms, huh?"

"Would it be so terrible if the next guy you date is dominant in the bedroom?"

"Yeah, no, thanks. Don't like being tied up. Or having my hair pulled."

Hooking my arm with hers, she led me to my bedroom, a woman on a mission. If I was doing this, I definitely needed to change. Probably into something more flattering than the sweats two sizes too big and the oversized tee that said: **WTF** inside a square, with *The Element of Surprise!* written beneath it. Yeah, I was a dork, but WTF certainly summed up my reaction when I'd bumped into Carter on that rooftop.

"You've never been tied up or had your hair pulled." She stopped walking and unhanded me. "Shit, I'm sorry. The terrorists, did they—"

"No, they didn't," I reassured her quickly so she didn't feel bad. "I just can't imagine myself being with someone who bosses me around, even in the bedroom."

"Not even Carter *Dom*inick?" She playfully lifted her brows a few times.

"Ugh, I hate you."

Maybe he had dominated me in the bedroom in my fantasies a time or two, but I had to forget him and my fantasies. "Okay," I relented. "Tattoo it is."

5

CARTER

"Can you talk to me? You've been distant since you came home."

I glanced at my wife in the passenger seat of her Jag. She'd had a few glasses of wine before we'd left for the restaurant and had insisted on driving. I'd taken the keys from her and slipped behind the wheel despite her protests. We were now on our way to a dinner I sure as hell didn't want to go to.

"Carter." She pouted, and I returned my focus to the road, so I didn't kill us.

"You're the one who's been acting strange since I got back from my trip," I tossed out. A little deflection didn't hurt, but it wasn't a lie either. I'd already reminded her of the fact she'd needed those glasses of red just to force herself to get ready for reservations *she'd* made.

"I love how you call top-secret missions 'trips,'" she said around a hiccup.

"Why don't we just turn around?" I knew exactly how

tonight was going to go—end in a fight after dinner, and we'd sleep in separate rooms. "Cancel dinner with your friends. Spend some time together at home. You can even blame me."

"No. We're already almost there. And they're your friends, too, by the way." She crossed her arms over her chest, eliciting another hiccup, and continued to pout.

I took the water bottle from the cup holder and handed it to her. "*Not* my friends."

"Right, right. You don't have friends who don't wear a uniform."

I frowned but remained quiet.

"That was uncalled for," she mumbled. "I'm sorry."

I relaxed my shoulders, the tension there retreating at the hope there wouldn't be a fight. It was the last thing I wanted after spending the past week chasing down a smuggling ring in Costa Rica. I'd returned home only to have my superiors tell me to back off the new leads we'd developed as a result of that op, ordering me to let the other scum-of-the-earth traffickers just go on their merry-fucking-way. Harper Brooks, the relatively new officer I'd worked alongside, had been even more pissed about it than I was.

But I couldn't tell my wife why my mood was so sour because it was need-to-know and classified. Part of me wanted to break orders and protocol, though, and open up to Rebecca. Maybe, just fucking maybe, she'd understand me a little better.

"Do you hate me?" she asked, catching me off guard.

"Not as much as I love you," I grumbled.

At a red light, she set down the untouched water and leaned over to hold my hand, lacing our fingers together.

"My job is why I'm edgy." *You have to know that.* "And it's why you're stressed out every time I walk out the door. No different than when I was in the Army." I did my best to keep the accusation and "I told you so" out of my voice but couldn't quite keep my foot from pressing a little too hard on the gas pedal when the light turned green.

"You regret leaving Delta for the CIA." She pulled her hand back, like my words shocked her. But this wasn't new information for her. I only said as much every other week. "You blame me for it, too."

If the shoe fucking fits. God, I hated myself for thinking that. Almost as much as I hated myself for resenting her for forcing me into leaving the Unit to join the Company two years ago. The path that decision put me on involved even more red tape and bureaucracy than my previous line of work. I was constantly being told *"no, don't help them"* because the U.S. doesn't benefit from it. It was fucking exhausting, and I wasn't even a full two years in with them.

"You'll never openly admit you resent me. To tell me you're mad I asked you to leave the Army. But maybe you'd feel better if you finally got it off your chest."

Were we really doing this now? Having a come-to-Jesus conversation in the car on the way to dinner with her friends? *I think the fuck not.*

"You're making a real difference in what you're doing now."

Here we go. The speech. The one that always ended with me being a senator and then Commander in Chief one day. The last thing in the world I wanted.

"I mean, you can't tell me much about your work, but I have to believe that what you do matters. And changing the world is what we both want." The sad sigh from her chipped away at the ice walls I'd been working to keep up on the drive. She always managed to knock them down, because like my father, I'd do anything for my wife. Which included never hurting her.

"Remember at Columbia we used to daydream about how we'd change the world one day?"

We'd only been friends then. But what guy was best friends with a woman like Rebecca and not hope she'd see him as more one day? And then after she'd dated all the wrong guys, she finally focused on who was right in front of her, patiently waiting—me.

But *fuck*, what if I wasn't the right guy for her? What if she was meant to be with some fancy dickhead who enjoyed power and the smell of money, and I screwed up her life by admitting I had feelings for her back then? I slowed down at that thought, unsure where it'd come from, and immediately felt like an asshole for thinking it.

"You spend more time with nonprofits and charities than you do with me," I finally spoke up. "You're changing the world like you wanted to. You help people. All I'm doing is putting together target packages that get shot down by people sitting on their high horses with no clue how the real world operates." Maybe I should've been the one to have a few drinks before dinner, especially since her friends we were joining happened to be on those horses—aka, politicians.

"Will you ever forgive me for making you quit?"

"Nothing to forgive." The lie cut through my teeth with too much grit for her to believe. I pulled up to the valet line, waiting for our turn. "I made the choice. Not you." Technically speaking, it was the truth. My hands weren't tied. I could've chosen the Unit over her. But I didn't.

I closed my eyes, remembering her ultimatum, and my reaction to it. "*I choose you. How can I not? You're my wife,*" I'd said, then left the room to nurse my misery alone, knowing my world would soon flip upside down.

At the knuckles thwacking the window, I opened my eyes, finding the valet there. As another man came around and opened the door for Rebecca, I took a few more seconds to rid myself of the foul mood I was in, then exited the Jag, leaving the keys in the car. "Thank you," I said to the guy, then caught up with my wife on the sidewalk, resting a hand on her back.

Her solid gray pencil skirt and blazer perfectly exemplified the powerful businesswoman she was—a woman who had and did it all.

Turning her cheek toward me as we walked, giving me some serious side eye, she said, "I'm miserable because I feel . . . unfulfilled."

That had me stopping in my tracks. I tugged her closer to the nearest building and away from the middle of the sidewalk. "You feel unfulfilled?"

Her tongue skirted along the line of her red lips, the only color on her tonight.

"What if we have kids?" I already knew what her answer would be, but I had to try. I'd never stop trying, just like she never stopped telling me no. "I've been told having kids can be fulfilling." My pulse flew at my neck when she didn't turn me down within five seconds like normal. Was there a chance?

She vanquished my hope the second our eyes met. "Why do you do this to me? You married me knowing I never want children. I was upfront about that."

"I felt that way, too. Then somewhere along the way I changed my mind. Decided the world sucked and needed some little people in it to help make it better. Preferably *our* people. Our children."

"For such a hard-ass, you sound so adorable talking like that," she said around a hiccup. "But my answer won't change no matter how cute you make having your babies sound." She reached between us and smoothed down the collar of my shirt. "Let's just enjoy the process of baby making without actually making one, okay? The plan is for us to be the cool aunt and uncle, remember?"

"Bit of a flawed plan there. I don't have family. Neither do you."

"Camila's basically your sister. Hopefully she has kids one day, and then you can spoil them rotten. Or teach them the ways of the world, or whatever it is you feel like you're missing out on." When I kept quiet, she threw me a bone. "What about we get a dog? I love dogs." She gave me her fake smile, and I hated fake-anything from my wife.

"You're allergic." I gestured for her to start walking again.

"Surely there are pills for that."

"We travel too much to have a pet at home."

"All the more reason to never ask for babies again," she jabbed as we worked our way to the restaurant entrance.

"I could stop traveling if that would—"

"No babies," she cut me off without giving my hope a chance to rekindle.

Not even two seconds inside the restaurant, which was frequented by politicians and other elitists, we ran into a group of people Rebecca knew, but also . . .

"Diana?" I wasn't sure how I even recognized her. It'd been three years and I'd encountered an ocean full of people since, but—

"Diana," Rebecca echoed, confirming I was right. She pulled the girl in for a hug, clearly still feeling the effects of the wine, because she wasn't a hugger.

Diana's eyes met mine over my wife's shoulder, and they narrowed, as if maybe trying to remember my name.

"Ambassador Mackenzie," I greeted, nodding to Diana's mother as Rebecca detached herself from Diana.

"Not an ambassador currently," Susan Mackenzie corrected me. She told the hostess she'd join her dinner party in a minute, and the suits she'd been with walked away to their table, leaving her and Diana there with us.

"Congrats on nearly finishing your grad degree," Rebecca said, saving me from making small talk with Susan Mackenzie. "Any thoughts on where you'll go when you finish? We'd love to have you." She laid on her signature win-anyone-over smile I knew all too well. "Correction. *I* would love to have you at Barclay Energy. We only have a small piece of the environmental saving-the-world pie right now, but with the right people, such as yourself, we could truly make a difference."

Diana peered at me for a moment, and while it was my job as a CIA officer to read people, the blank expression threw me off. "That's very kind of you. I'm not sure what I plan to do next, but I'll—"

"She'll be pleased to consider working with you," Susan cut her off, then tipped her head toward the exit. "May I steal Rebecca away for a moment?" At my nod, she asked, "Watch over my little girl and keep her company while we step out, will you?"

"Mommmm."

I did the math. Diana had to be twenty-four now. But I supposed in the eyes of a parent, she'd always be a little girl. I'd never get to know what that felt like firsthand.

I didn't humor Susan with an answer. There was no point in embarrassing Diana by offering to watch over her like we were in Baghdad at the height of the war instead of inside a crowded restaurant.

When my wife and Susan stepped out, I turned toward Diana and she whispered, "You remember me?"

I nodded, not sure why I didn't verbally answer.

She fingered the collar of her baby-blue silk blouse, then pushed a hand through her blonde hair.

Do I make you nervous? I shouldn't.

"I'm visiting for Easter weekend. Mom dragged me to dinner here with some 'friends' of hers." She wrinkled her nose as if embarrassed by the air quotes she'd used.

To make her feel better, I finally spoke up with air quotes as well. "I'm here for Rebecca's 'friends,' too."

When she smiled at my response, I couldn't help but smile back. It felt good after barely smiling in months.

"Kind of wondering if Mom knew Rebecca had reservations here tonight, though. Feels planned, huh?" She shrugged, and before I could answer, she said, "Mom told me you're no longer in the military." She shook her head. "That came out of nowhere, sorry." When she looked at me again, she clarified, "I may have asked about you once or twice. Just to make sure the man who saved my life was still . . . doing okay."

"Define doing okay." Fuck, where'd that come from? Her blue eyes flew to mine, and I lifted my hand in apology. "I'm not operating, no." *Not exactly.* "But that was nice of you to care about how I'm doing."

"You must do something you hate now. Your eyes . . . they're sad." I lost sight of her blue ones when she hid her face behind her palm and mumbled, "I'm so sorry."

I reached for her wrist and gently removed her hand from her face. "Government work. You're right. I hate it." It felt good to finally admit it out loud and not feel guilty. Maybe the words flowed because she was pretty much a stranger, and it was usually easier to open up to people I doubted I'd see again.

"So, I should turn down the internship the Department of

Energy is trying to recruit me for when I graduate? Work for Rebecca instead?"

I wanted to bark out that she should absolutely say no to both a government gig and working with my wife, but who was I to tell this girl what to do? "Not all work with the government gives you sad eyes."

"Well, I hate yours makes you sad." Her lip caught between her teeth as she stared at me with those innocent baby blues.

Maybe it's not just because of my work.

"I'm overstepping. Sorry, Dom—" She cut herself off, eyes lifting to the ceiling, and I followed her gaze to the chandelier overhead.

"Something interesting up there?" I asked.

Her skin was bronzed, so I had to assume she went to grad school somewhere with better weather than D.C., but her tan couldn't hide the touch of embarrassment fighting its way to her cheeks. "Just searching for what to say. But no teleprompter on the ceiling."

Fuck, I almost laughed. It'd been so long since I'd been around someone as honest and sweet as her, I almost forgot how to communicate myself.

"I'm trying to figure out what to call you now. You once said Dom or the devil, but you're actually Carter." She began talking with her hands. "Or I suppose you're all three."

My smile morphed into a light laugh. "I'm whoever you want me to be." I swallowed the moment I spied her throat do the same thing. *Shit, was that flirty? What the fuck is wrong with me?* "Carter." I began distracting myself by uncuffing my sleeve, prepared to roll it up. *Where are you, Rebecca?* I cast a quick look toward the door, noting her politician friends had joined her out there, too.

"Mister Dominick? Is that perhaps a better name since you're married to my mother's friend, and—"

"I'm old?" Turning to face her, I arched a brow, only to see her eyes focused on the tattoos now exposed on my forearm, the sleeve cuffed at the elbow. I'd nearly forgotten they were there, and in this politician haunt of a restaurant, my wife would probably have my head for exposing them.

"You're not old." She seemed to welcome the blush to her face that time.

Deciding fuck it, I rolled up my second sleeve while shifting closer to Diana.

"And ohhhh, I've got a tattoo now, too."

We were surrounded by other people, but it felt like we were back on that embassy floor years ago. I wasn't sure why the world faded away, but it did. I also didn't want to think about if that was supposed to mean anything, because I *couldn't* think about that.

When she redirected her attention to the ceiling, I couldn't help but murmur, "Are we looking for that writing again?"

She turned her cheek, catching my eyes. We were too close, and it felt . . . well, wrong. Wrong to have my face and body near another woman. And definitely wrong to feel like we'd shared some kind of moment.

I immediately straightened and backed up a step. Because never, not fucking ever, did I have any kind of *moment* with a woman who wasn't my wife. I wasn't about to start now.

Diana probably reminded me of my old life with the Army, being part of a team where I'd truly belonged. Now I just felt alone.

Worried she was still nervous or embarrassed about her tattoo remark, I went ahead and asked, "What's it of?"

The gratitude in her smile was clear as she extended her

arm and pushed her sleeve up to show the inside of her wrist. "It's small and sideways, but—"

"Double helix intertwined with a tree of life," I said, not meaning to interrupt, but it was perfect for her.

"Good eye." She tugged at her sleeve, concealing it again. "My mom hates it."

"Well, I like it." I pushed my hands into my dress pants' pockets, unsure what was taking Rebecca so damn long. I was close to finding my way outside to her when my work cell began buzzing from a message. Shit, that meant one thing —I wouldn't be making it to Easter dinner Sunday. "Excuse me one second." I pulled out the phone and turned my back to check the text. Urgent, as expected. I had to get to Langley as of yesterday.

At the sight of Rebecca finally coming in with a hoard of Washington elitists, I pocketed my phone.

"We're going to see if we can all eat together," Rebecca said before her shoulders fell in disappointment, getting an accurate read on me. "You're leaving?"

"Can we have a word?" I tipped my head toward the door, ignoring the crowd of her friends huddling inside while Susan talked with the hostess about new seating arrangements.

"Don't bother." She brushed past me, and I circled my hand around her wrist, stopping her.

Dropping my mouth over her ear, I begged, "Ask me to stay. To give up *this* job, and I will." *Please, give me that ultimatum before this work kills me from the inside out . . . or this job destroys our marriage.*

"Go," was all she said, and I released her, feeling my walls go right back up at that one word. I tore my hand through my hair as I stood there motionless, unsure what to think or do. "I love you," she forced out, then left.

I turned to see her catching up with some guy in a suit. A

senator, from what I remembered. I'd forgotten his name. She started laughing at something he said, and now I was the one searching the ceiling for writing. For a fucking sign. A clue what to do.

"Find anything there this time? I mean, if we keep looking, just maybe . . ."

I slowly lowered my eyes to see Diana, the area by the door now empty except for us.

"Are you okay?" she asked when I'd yet to breach the silence hanging between us, only filled by distant chatter and music.

"I'm . . ." I gulped, my throat thick with emotion. "Duty calls, so I won't be joining you all for dinner," I shared, going with the more diplomatic answer instead of the truth. *That no, I'm not okay at all. But thank you, a near stranger, for caring.*

"Oh." She gave me a polite little nod. "Off to save the world, then?"

I found myself smiling. Shocking, but it happened. "Now see, the way I remember it—that's supposed to be your job."

6

DIANA

"DO YOU BELIEVE IN SOULMATES?" I ASKED MY BOYFRIEND over the phone while I studied my reflection in the mirror inside the guest bedroom of Mom's Georgetown home—a home bought and paid for by Dad's five-year-old scandal, just like every other purchase made by Mom since then.

"Is this a trick question?" William was in Seattle with his parents this Easter weekend. "You're not expecting a ring when we finish grad school, are you?"

"Where'd that come from?" I placed the call on speaker and set my phone on the dresser while I removed my blouse, leaving me only in a nude bra up top with my gray wool skirt and tights. "We've only been dating six months. Why in the world would I want you to propose? You're going to MIT in the fall for your PhD, and I'm clueless where I'm off to next," I hurriedly spoke up, because the last thing in the world I wanted was a ring.

William started to reply, and I tuned him out.

. . . And the girlfriend of the year goes to?

Not me. Because after seeing Carter tonight, one thing

was sure—I wasn't just a shit girlfriend, I was a horrible human being.

At least last time when I'd lusted after him, I'd thought he was single, and I was younger. Now twenty-four, there was no excuse for allowing a married man to tongue-tie or fluster me. To make my heart beat faster. My skin heat. It'd been a case of goose bumps gone wild at the restaurant.

There had to be a scientific explanation for what was happening to me whenever he was near. I'd do some research later to see what was wrong with me. Maybe there was a cure, and if not, maybe I could invent an antidote to keep myself from wanting someone I couldn't (and shouldn't) have.

I still couldn't believe I'd called Carter "Mister" Dominick. Somehow the word felt naughty when I'd said it to him. It wasn't like I hadn't used that word a hundred times toward my parents' friends over the years. But with him, it hit differently.

"Are you listening to me?" William asked, breaking through my thoughts.

I freed my hair from the ponytail, letting my light blonde locks drape over my breasts, which were too snug in my C-cup strapless bra. "Yeah, I'm listening." *Now I'm a liar, too. I keep getting better and better.*

"Then what'd I say?" Of course he'd call my bluff.

"Break up?" I hastily sputtered what was on my mind, having no idea what he'd actually said.

"Wait, what?"

Shit. Phone back in hand, I went over to the bed. "Um. Do you think maybe we're . . . well, not soulmates?" I tried to muck my way through my verbal vomit screwup.

"Since when is that the criteria for dating?"

I set the phone on the bed and unzipped my skirt. "It

should be. Why waste time with someone not meant to be your forever person?"

"I don't believe in that bullshit. We fit. We work. We should be together. Are you drunk or something?"

One glass of wine at dinner was all Mom ever allowed me. She knew what two glasses did to me—and we were with her hoity-toity friends, so . . . "I'm sorry. Shit."

"Listen, babe, I don't believe in soulmates, but I do believe in us." His raspy, emotional tone sliced and diced me. Screwed with my head. "Can that be enough?"

Could it be? I wasn't sure.

"We'll talk when I see you next week. Okay? I have to go, but just tell me we're good. You're on edge about not knowing what you want to do after grad school, and you're all fucked up in the head about it."

He had me there. But *Mister* Dominick also had me out of sorts. And I wasn't allowed to want another man while being with someone else—*especially* a married man. Ugh, that was a hard no. "Just enjoy the rest of your vacation. I'll see you back at school next week."

"Yeah, okay. Love you." He hung up before I could say it back, and considering how off my head was, that was for the best. I wasn't sure if I could get those words out.

I finished changing into my pajamas so I could get into bed, but at the sound of Mom talking to someone, I went to the door and cracked it open to eavesdrop. That was another thing I wasn't proud of. But Mom had a bad habit of talking too loud, and I'd learned a lot over the years because of it. Like the fact my father had cheated on her, and who he'd cheated with.

I practically choked on my mortification at the realization Rebecca Dominick was downstairs.

"Thanks for having me over so late," Rebecca said, something in her voice pulling me closer.

I crept into the hall and silently moved to the top of the stairs, feeling like that fifteen-year-old kid again while learning Dad cheated. *That* time didn't make any headlines, so Mom quietly forgave him, never knowing I knew about it.

"You barely kept it together at dinner, but you did. You're a Barclay, all right," Mom told her. "And of course I'm here for you. I told your mother I'd always watch over you if anything were to happen."

You did? That was news to me. Great, Rebecca was basically Mom's goddaughter. The guilt was about to hit atomic levels.

"So, what's going on? Is it Carter?"

I plastered my back to the wall and closed my eyes, my pulse thundering up into my ears at the mention of his name.

"He resents me, but he won't say it to my face. Hates me for forcing him to leave the Army." Rebecca's voice was softer that time. Sad. "The problem is, I don't hate myself for it. He made the right choice to leave. And maybe I can't push him to get on a presidential path one day like my parents wanted for us, but . . ."

I had no business hearing any of this, but I couldn't make myself walk away.

"My parents begged me not to date him. They told me to only stay friends, and I didn't listen. They said he'd never be a Barclay, and I was pretty sure that was his appeal back then. He was different. Nothing like the men my parents wanted me to date. But I do love him and don't regret our marriage. You know that, right?" She was borderline slurring. How much did she drink?

I was probably supposed to be loyal to Rebecca since she was a family friend, but her husband saved my life. I didn't know how to reconcile that. He'd also been so sweet and kind to me whenever we'd interacted. Another big *that* in my book.

"I know you love him, you don't need to convince me of that." Mom's voice dropped a bit lower when she spoke, and I couldn't help but edge closer to the top of the stairs despite my conscience telling me to head to my room. "But *you* are a Barclay. Maybe *you're* the one your parents should've been pushing to go to the White House, not whoever you married."

"No, no. I told you earlier, if you ever want a seat at the table, I'll happily write you a check and endorse you for any position, but I'm not running for anything."

Mom? The White House? Okay, maybe eavesdropping was paying off tonight, because she'd never told me this. Dad had ambitions, sure. But Mom? Maybe it made sense. All the parties she'd dragged me to over the years to schmooze and kiss ass with people I knew she didn't actually like.

"I'm . . . I need to get something off my chest to someone before I lose it." Rebecca was near tears from the sounds of it. "I have no one else I trust to talk to."

"What is it?" Mom asked her, and if there was ever a time for me to walk away, it'd be now.

I was twenty-four, not fifteen. And this was definitely not my business. I started to turn, but then Rebecca rasped, "I cheated on him last week, and I can't even look at him. The guilt the second he came home was too much. I've been drinking nonstop."

Holy shit.

"I had dinner with Craig Paulsen—you know, the congressman from California. Although, he's moving back to his home state of New York at the end of his term. And, well, he was searching for financing, and we wound up continuing the conversation in the back of his limo, and we drank too much. And he's such a smooth talker. The kind of man my parents wished I'd married. He's also Patrick Dempsey-handsome, and I just . . ."

Holy fucking shit. I clapped a hand over my mouth. *That slimeball asshole.* Carter had protected me from him years ago, and now the man had hit on his wife.

"We didn't go all the way," Rebecca blurted a moment later. "I stopped it before . . . *that*. But I've never cheated before. I'm not that person. And to make it worse, Carter doesn't like Craig. He asked me not to write him any more checks and made me promise to exclude him from future parties, but I didn't listen."

Shit, he did?

"I love Carter so much. I'm just a mess. But I have to tell him, right?"

"No, don't," Mom rushed out.

What the hell? How could she, of all people, be suggesting that? She'd been the victim of cheating before. She knew the damage it created. The second-guessing. The guilt.

"If you don't want to lose him, don't tell him. Go confess to a priest if that'll help you feel better, but don't tell him."

A priest? Are you for real, Mom? My hand fell to my side, my body trembling now. *Paulsen. Ugh, that man is just . . .*

"You're unhappy, that's all I know," Mom went on when Rebecca didn't speak. "You need to figure out why and do something about it." And then, after one of her patented and perfected dramatic pauses, she added, "Unless being married to him is why you're unhappy—because, then, maybe what you need is a divorce."

7

CARTER

BUDAPEST, HUNGARY – MARCH 2019

DRAWING TOGETHER THE FLOOR-TO-CEILING CURTAINS IN MY small hotel room, I waited for the line to connect with my wife. My third attempt to reach her in the last few days with no luck. My unanswered calls had been met back with quick texts letting me know she was "fine" but it was a bad time to talk. I was growing impatient with her dodging me.

Since she wouldn't pick up, I had to assume she was still angry at me for being abroad on a mission that was one of my choosing.

I'd pushed the Agency to let me follow a lead for an assassin known as The Chechen. He was responsible for the death of an MI6 officer I'd worked with on an op last year, and it drove me crazy he was still out there living his best fucking life.

The deceased officer's fiancée, Zoey, was also MI6, and she hated my guts with a passion—blaming me for Preston's death. I didn't want to give her false hope that I had new intel about The Chechen until I could confirm it myself. So there I was in Budapest, not only apparently wasting my time on a dead lead but pissing off my wife by being away.

But Zoey had lost the love of her life, and our CIA-MI6 joint op wouldn't be considered a success in my book until the assassin was six feet under.

I couldn't forget the day of that op, though. Questioning every decision. Every moment. I'd run through every scenario wondering if the outcome could've been different somehow.

Preston and I had been engaged in hand-to-hand combat with The Chechen, when we learned he'd activated a bomb in the city. I was better with explosives, so I left the primary site to defuse it. I may have stopped the bomb, but Preston died and the animal who killed him got away.

"You left him." That damn phantom ache was back where Zoey had repeatedly beat at my chest after finding her fiancé dead. *"You could've saved him."*

I'd held her wrists so she'd stopped hitting me, but then gave in. Let her do it. Let her *blame* me.

To be honest, if it was her there instead of me, I'm not sure she'd have left Preston's side. She would've chosen to save him over a thousand.

Trying my wife again, I rasped, "Come on, Rebecca. Pick up." Frustrated at my call going to voicemail, I set my phone aside. I had one more possible lead to check and then I'd go home. Maybe take time off and try to reconnect with my wife. Things hadn't been great between us lately.

It didn't help that I could feel her physically pulling away from me in the last six months. She'd gone so far as to sell off almost all of her family's businesses—only keeping one small holding, The Barclay Group—without giving me a heads-up first. Then she began traveling a lot more. Never gave me her schedule or a damn reason why. So yeah, we needed to find some time for each other.

I was a second away from getting my laptop to go back to work when my phone rang.

Rebecca. Fucking finally. "Hey," I answered.

"I'm sorry, I was tied up."

I dropped down on the bed and worked free the top two buttons of my shirt. "With what? Are you even home?"

"I am. I was just working on something."

"You planning to tell me what it was?"

Silence. Typical lately. I'd swear she was the one who worked for the Agency sometimes, not me. She was a better secret keeper. "I want to get away with you. You never sold your parents' place in Sweden, did you? Or was it Switzerland?" I couldn't remember, but it was somewhere near mountains. "Let's go next week."

"You want to take a vacation?"

"I think we need it."

"Not a good idea. Not right now. I'm . . ."

I swallowed. "You're what?" Irritated, I stood and began pacing the small room. "What's going on? Talk to me."

"I can't do this over the phone. But you're right, maybe we should talk."

The blood drained from my face. "Talk?" I waited for her to continue, and when she didn't, I asked, "Are you leaving me?" Was she really doing this over the phone?

She'd brought up divorce once, a few years ago, but the following morning she'd asked to have our entire conversation from the night before redacted—stricken from the record.

"What? God no. How would that look?"

I should've felt relief at her immediate rejection of the idea, but I couldn't feel anything other than anger at her "how would that look" comment. "Then what's going on?" I asked instead of following up on that bullshit remark. I didn't want to get into a fight while I was on the other side of the world.

"There's some things I need to tell you, but not over the phone." Her trembling tone fucked me up right along with her words.

I'd already dealt with a heaping pile of horseshit in the last year, and I couldn't take much more. "You're going to give me a heart attack. Talk to me."

"I can't. When you're home, we'll talk."

"Why would you do this to me? Make me wonder while I'm over here working." I closed my eyes, trying to calm down.

"You brought it up. Asked me what's going on." Her accusation bit into my nerve endings, my fist tightening around the phone as every muscle in my body tensed preparing for the next strike.

It was too late for me to backpedal from this conversation now. "Is it someone else? Another man? Did something happen again with . . ." I couldn't finish that line of thought. Not that she'd ever told me his name—too afraid of what I'd do with that information—but the memory of that faceless fucker transported me back to the moment a year ago when she'd laid the news on me. She'd cheated in 2015, waiting *years* to confess. 2015: the same year she'd tossed the word divorce at me.

I barely heard Rebecca's apology over the phone. I was too far inside my head, back in her office at the penthouse in New York when she'd cut my heart out with her admission.

"I can't live with the guilt anymore. She said not to tell you, but I need you to know," Rebecca had blurted after having too much scotch one night. I'd later learned the "she" advising her had been Susan Mackenzie, but that did nothing

to ease the anger, the pain, the frustration I'd felt toward her confidant. *"I made a mistake a few years ago. Got drunk with a friend, and we kissed. But I stopped it before we . . . I didn't sleep with him."*

My back had been to her. Eyes on the New York skyline. I could still hear the dull thud made by the glass in my hand when it'd fallen to the floor, the crystal so thick it didn't even break. I remembered watching it roll a few feet away, staring at it in a daze.

"Say something." At the feel of her hand on me, I'd slowly shifted toward her, the words stuck in my throat in disbelief.

"Details. I need them," I'd uttered.

"That won't help."

"Explicit. Fucking. Details." My mind and heart had sprinted in a competition toward a finish line in a race I knew I'd lose.

She'd let go of me and backed up. *"Too much to drink. He had his driver bring me home. We were in his limo, and he kissed me. I let him."*

I'd closed my eyes. *"And?"*

"That's it."

"You're lying." I'd swallowed. Waited to be further destroyed.

"He touched me. A little." Her small voice had been just as much of a punch to the gut as her words.

"Where?" My eyes had opened and journeyed down her body, taking in the sight of her in the nearly see-through cream-colored silk blouse tucked into her black skirt. When she'd kept quiet, I'd breached the bit of space between us and undid a few buttons to cup her breast. *"Here?"* Staring into my eyes, she'd nodded. Her trembling lip hadn't stopped me from squeezing her tit. Then I'd let go of her breast to bunch

her skirt up to her waist while backing her against the window. Hand to the glass over her shoulder, I'd moved the barrier created by her panties to the side and thumbed her clit. *"Here?"* I'd gritted out, on the brink of insanity.

She'd squeezed her eyes closed as her answer, a few tears spilling over her cheeks. Each one a dagger to my heart.

"You let him touch you here. Put his tongue in your mouth and . . ." I'd shaken my head in anger at how wet she was. *"Why are you so turned on? Does thinking about him—"*

"No," she'd cried, eyes flashing open. *"It's you. The way you're talking to me. It's turning me on. The darkness in your voice and . . ."* She'd started moving against my hand, searching for relief.

"Who touched you?"

She'd taken hold of my wrist, breathing harder, urging me to keep pushing my fingers inside her. All I could do was stare at her, my eye twitching. *"I can't tell you any more. Please, just forgive me."*

I'd borderline snarled, *"Stop fucking my hand."*

"Want me to beg? On my knees?" She'd pushed my hand away and ducked under my arm, and I'd slowly turned, finding her on the other side of the office, stripping. Taking her time.

Then she'd shocked me by kneeling. One thing my wife wasn't was submissive. Seeing her on her hands and knees, crawling to me, had me forgetting *why* she was doing it. But only for a moment.

She'd made it halfway to me before I lifted my palm, demanding, *"Get up."*

When she'd sat back on her heels, I'd stalked her way, hauled her from the floor, and set her on the desk, my sense of control out the window. My sanity, too.

"This what you want?" Placing my hands behind her

knees, I'd pulled her to the edge of the desk, the momentum flinging her shoulders back, her spine arching, tits in the air, as she braced her palms on each side of her. I'd pushed two fingers deep into her cunt and worked her arousal over her pussy. The memory of the fact some other man had touched my wife had me rasping, *"Is this what he did to you? Did you like it? Did you like some other man fingering you?"*

She didn't answer, her breath hitching as she came all over my hand, crying to God instead of murmuring my name like normal.

"Please be inside me," she'd begged, still riding her orgasm out on the heel of my hand, taking what she wanted because I'd given it to her.

"No." I'd backed up. *"I'm going to a hotel."*

"Please don't leave." She'd crossed her arms over her breasts—a reminder some fucker had touched her there, too.

"You hurt me." My voice had been as raw as my emotions. *"I can't even look at you right now. All these years of putting up with . . ."* Even then, even *fucking* then, I hadn't been able to hurt her in retaliation.

But maybe I should've spewed the ugly shit that'd been on the tip of my tongue? Yell at her for all the times I'd sacrificed my wants and needs for the sake of hers, knowing she didn't give a damn about the consequences of what years of that had done to me.

The control. The manipulation. The gaslighting. All of it.

Fuck, I was burning angry all over thinking about it now.

After she'd recovered her dignity and demanded I stay to work things out, I'd chosen to keep my mouth shut, packed a bag, and left.

The next day, the Agency had called me into work and ordered me to London for a job in coordination with MI6. Then Zoey's fiancé died and seeing her lose the love of her life made me realize I should give my marriage one more chance before I let it die.

I'd come home from that mission feeling defeated and had forgiven Rebecca. Maybe not in my heart, but I'd said the words. It took me months to share a bed with her again, finally convincing myself she'd made a drunken mistake, and it never would've happened otherwise.

"Carter?" Rebecca's timid voice, which wasn't the norm for her, brought me back to the room in Hungary. "Did you hear me? You haven't said anything."

"No, I didn't hear you. What'd you say?"

"I said of course there's no one else." Her pause gave *me* fucking pause. "The things I want to talk about can't be discussed over the phone."

"Then get on a secure line. We're doing this tonight. I'm not waiting," I hissed. When she remained quiet, some dark part of me took over and I whispered, "Sometimes I really fucking hate you."

I could hear her soft breath of surprise float through the line before she mumbled, "Hold on, someone's beeping in."

"Damnit, Rebecca, don't answer that." I was pissed all over again. About her unfaithfulness, her brushing me off now, and preemptively angry for whatever she planned to tell me. "We're in the middle of something. If you care about our marriage, then put me first. Put *us* first."

"Oh-okay." Then the doorbell rang in the background. "Someone's here."

"Don't answer it. Who the hell would come this late?"

"It's probably Susan Mackenzie. She left me a voicemail earlier saying she wanted to meet up. I forgot with our, um, conversation."

"The call just now, was that from her, too?"

"Well, no. It was unknown."

"Something's not right," I said on instinct, a bad feeling in my gut. "Go to the safe room and call the police."

"Don't be ridiculous." She paused for a second. "Just one—"

That bloodcurdling scream from my wife was the last thing I heard before my world stopped as I roared out her name.

8

DIANA

WASHINGTON, D.C.

"WILL YOU MARRY ME, DIANA MACKENZIE?" WILLIAM WAS on one knee.

Is the room spinning? I blinked, chills crisscrossing every inch of my body as I stared at my boyfriend, proposing in the living room of my mother's Georgetown home, knowing damn well she had to have helped him orchestrate the moment. She probably chose the diamond that'd make sinking to the bottom of the ocean happen that much faster. And that was how this moment made me feel right now. Like I was drowning.

"What are you doing?" I tore my eyes away from him and settled them on my mom, standing off to the side of the room, hovering alongside her boyfriend, Jared, the Secretary of Energy. I had yet to grow fond of him, and probably never would. It didn't help that he kept pressing me to work with him at the Department of Energy. He hated the word no as much as Mom did.

"I'm asking you to marry me," William said as if my brain had short-circuited, and I wasn't comprehending him.

Then again, that was what was happening, right? I *wasn't* getting it. Because he shouldn't have been proposing.

Setting my hands to my abdomen, the top of the black dress far too tight, making it hard to breathe, I focused back on him.

My age. Dashingly handsome, so Mom called him, at least. A thick head of blond hair. Blue eyes. Clean-shaven. Smart. First in his class at MIT. Wealthy and connected—Mom's two favorite things. He was perfect on paper and even more "perfect" in person, with those bright, white teeth on display as he smiled at me, assuming I'd say yes. Because who said no to "perfect"?

I had once already, though. I broke up with him years ago after Easter because some other man had made my heart pitter-patter when it shouldn't have.

But then William and I bumped into each other on a plasma energy project in England, chasing the ever-elusive dream of cold fusion, and he convinced me it was fate we were there together. I wound up giving him a second chance, deciding maybe he was right and soulmates weren't a real thing. Two people's energy—*spirits*—weren't truly destined to find one another. That was crazy talk. I was a scientist, and I needed to think like one. Act like one. Live like one. Practical and realistic.

"This is why you wanted to visit the States? To propose *here*?" I pointed to the hardwoods beneath my uncomfortable heels. "Because my mother's house makes 'perfect' sense for this moment?" Shit, I'd meant that last question to remain in my head, and certainly not to throw air quotes at him.

William cleared his throat and swiveled his focus to Mom. He slowly stood, but kept the little blue box open with the not-so-little and far-too-perfect-for-me diamond on display. "Diana." My name was a plea not to embarrass him.

My contacts began irritating my eyes as I stared at him in shock. Or maybe I was going to cry? I'd started wearing glasses two years ago, and I preferred them to contacts, but suddenly Mom's insistence on me wearing them made sense.

Yeah, she was for sure behind William Wallace trying to marry me. Yes, the same name as the Scottish knight, the revolutionary immortalized in *Braveheart*. But he was no hero here to rescue me from the fortress of my mother's expectations.

"Did you make sure we wound up on the project together, too?" I turned and asked her. She was smart enough to put two and two together and understand what I was getting at. I had no doubt she knew exactly what I meant. "You set us up, right?"

"Rebecca Barclay," Mom whispered.

"Rebecca *Dominick*, you mean. She's still married, right?" No divorce from what I knew, despite what Mom had suggested to her years ago. "And are you saying she's why William and I . . ." Mom was no longer staring me down. Instead, she was staring at her phone, mouth open. "What's wrong?"

"Someone turn on the news." She kept staring at her phone, going pale. "Something happened to Rebecca."

Before I could ask her for more information, Jared retrieved the remote and slid open the cabinet to reveal the TV hidden there.

"What's going on?" William asked for me, but we had the answer the second the news started rolling.

"Billionaire heiress Rebecca Dominick of the Barclay family was found dead in her D.C. home last night after her husband called the police to report a break-in," the reporter began. My shock at William's proposal was instantly erased, the bombshell about Rebecca erasing my frustration with him and my mother, sending the room spinning ten times faster than it had seeing William on one knee. "Our source at the FBI is reporting it was most likely a home invasion gone wrong that led to her death." The reporter's "Viewer discretion is advised for what we're about to share next" warning sent shivers throughout my body.

Mom stumbled back and Jared hooked his arm behind her before she collapsed.

". . . Butchered."

"Beaten. Stabbed."

"Blood everywhere . . ."

The words came and went in my head.

The details.

In. And. Out.

"Rebecca's dead." *This can't be real.*

The feed switched to video of Carter Dominick outside an airport, waving away reporters.

"Did you hire someone to do it?" a journalist yelled. "Reports are you'll inherit eleven billion dollars with her dead."

More questions followed Carter as he walked in silence, sunglasses shielding his eyes.

"Are the rumors you work for the CIA true? Do you think her death is your fault?" That question halted his steps, but only for a second, before he began quietly on his way again, the police working to push people back to give him room. The questions continued, a barrage of curious and absurd bombs and barbs following him as he opened the door of an SUV and disappeared inside without answering a single one.

"I can't believe this. This can't be real." Mom lifted her phone, staring at it, her hand shaking. "I—I have to make some calls." She started from the room with Jared following close behind her, leaving me there with William.

I picked up the remote and rewound the news to pause the screen on Carter just before he'd stepped into the SUV.

"You okay?" William asked, joining me.

"No." Unable to rip my eyes from the TV, tears began to fall. "This is going to destroy him. He's a good guy."

"Yeah, well . . . it's usually the husband," he said casually, and I wanted to slap him for that. "You heard the reporter, he has eleven billion reasons to have done it."

And you just made my answer to your proposal easy, you asshole. "Goodbye, William, and take your ring with you."

9
CARTER

NEW YORK CITY, NEW YORK

A SEA OF *THANK YOUS* HAD FALLEN FROM MY MOUTH ALL DAY, and I was drowning in the respects people were paying. I could barely breathe during the funeral, and now at the reception at my wife's New York home, I was suffocating.

I hadn't cried, though. Not once since I heard her scream on that call a week ago. Not even when I saw the police photos from the crime scene. Or when they had me ID her body in person.

Nothing. Not a single fucking tear. I'd been frozen. Numb. In disbelief and shock. Gutted with guilt that my last words to her before she died were of anger. I'd told her I hated her, and I wasn't sure how to live with myself for that.

There had to be something wrong with me. How was I so broken that I couldn't shed a tear despite the fact I was in agony. In hell, being burned alive.

"Thank you," I said to the next person offering me his support. Pierce Quaid had helped Rebecca run The Barclay

Group, and he was saying something about . . . well, fucking something to me.

I swallowed and nodded my acknowledgement to an elderly couple who came up to me next. Apparently, they'd had tea with my wife every third Sunday of every month for the last three years, and I had no clue about it. Just like I didn't know ninety-nine percent of the people who'd offered me their condolences since she'd died.

Not died. Was savagely murdered. Security footage destroyed. No evidence left behind by the "home invaders" who'd tossed my house searching for something. It wasn't for money and jewelry like the Feds believed.

No, she died because of me. Another reason guilt impaled me now. She was murdered because of my job. It had to be why.

The killer was still out there, and I was being told to sit on my hands and let the police and Feds do their jobs. Not fucking happening.

"Hey, come with me." Following the sound of a familiar voice, I spotted Camila at my nine o'clock. She held my wrist as if I wasn't capable of moving on my own and guided me from the crowded room to Rebecca's office.

Keeping my back to the door, the desk caught my eye. The last time I'd stepped foot in this room was when my wife had told me she'd cheated, and I'd snapped. Gotten her off with my hand before walking out. And now . . .

"You looked like you needed a minute." Camila went over to the bar cart and poured two glasses of scotch.

I watched as the only family I had left quietly came back my way, her understated black dress and dark hair pinned into a tight bun muting her personality and helping her blend into the background. Up until recently, she spent most of her life in South America. Her accent was still discernible, and whenever she talked, she always reminded me of my father. I missed his voice. I missed him. Missed my mom, too. And now I missed . . . *I missed my wife.*

"Here." She offered me the glass, and I stared down at the gold-hued liquid, trying to pull myself together. "I didn't know this would happen. I'm so sorry."

"What are you talking about?" The tears falling down her cheeks belonged on my face.

"I . . ." She gulped back her drink. "Never mind. Just ignore me."

I normally would've pressed for more, but I didn't have the energy. "I have to find who did this. The CIA wants me to stand down, but I refuse to believe this was a home invasion." This was the only conversation I could have right now. I needed answers. I needed *vengeance.* "This never should have happened to her. This is my fault. Somehow it has to be."

She lowered her drink to her side and reached for my shoulder. "We'll figure it out. Together, I promise." Meeting my eyes, she added, "Where are your old teammates? I thought they'd be here for you."

"Griffin and the rest of the Unit are in the middle of something *somewhere*, and the Army wouldn't let them leave. This is Griffin's last tour; he's getting out. He's going to come here as soon as he can and help me."

She stared at me with those big, worried eyes of hers. "Help you find the killer?"

"Or *killers*." I swallowed. "If the CIA tries to stop me, then fuck 'em. I'll go off on my own." And I meant that. No one was stopping me. Absolutely no one could prevent me from doing what I had to do to find who was responsible for hurting my wife.

Hurting? My body tensed up, my stomach turning. *Not hurt. Killed.*

"You really think they were after you? You could be in danger, then." Camila squeezed my shoulder a bit harder. "You need to be careful."

"I don't give a fuck about myself, and you know that."

"She wouldn't want anything happening to you."

"Yeah, well, she's dead, so she can't get pissed at me for it," I snapped out, the bitter taste of the words sitting on my tongue. "I need air. To be alone." I removed her hand and gave her the glass.

"Get your jacket. It's snowing," she whispered.

I nodded and left the office, needing to get out of that room, away from its bad memories. I had no plans to find my coat or the suit jacket I'd tossed at some point.

I dodged more condolences on my mission to get to the rooftop terrace, rushing by the woman who'd helped Camila organize everything for today—Susan Mackenzie. She was talking to a former congressman now senator. It took me a second to remember why I hated Paulsen, and then it clicked. He'd been the one who'd approached Susan's daughter the night of Rebecca's party years ago, making Diana uncomfortable.

If I wasn't so messed up, I'd go kick him out. But that would create a scene, and Rebecca would hate me for it. So, I kept on my path for the back stairs.

"Dominick." The grit to that tone and the way my name was said had me stopping near the door leading up top.

I slowly turned to see Constantine Costa, clothed in all black like a shadow—a specter—standing there. My heart pumped the brakes to allow my mind to peel back shrouded layers from years ago, releasing memories involving this particular billionaire my wife had dated in college. Back when Rebecca and I had only been friends. "What are you doing here?"

"Came to pay my respects. And to offer you help in finding who did this," Costa said, slowly approaching me.

My hands locked at my sides, turning into fists. "Why would you think I'd ever want your help? Or to see you again? You broke her heart in college." *And I picked up the pieces.*

"Rebecca's dead. If I can—"

"You're right," I snapped out, my jaw ticcing. "She is. She was none of your concern while she was alive, and she's sure as fuck not now." I somehow managed to keep my voice low so I didn't draw unnecessary attention.

He lifted his palms in surrender. "Fine. But she came to my sister's funeral, and I—"

"She what?"

"She was a good woman. I'm sorry for your loss," was all he said instead, then he quietly turned, and I watched him leave, my world spinning yet again.

How much about my wife's life did I not know about?

It took me a solid minute to move again. To turn and resume my previous path to escape.

Once up top, I shoved open the door, and I could finally breathe. The snow had only recently started, and it was light and melting the second it hit the ground. I walked over to the edge of the terrace, working my sleeves up—welcoming the biting sting of cold on my flesh.

Years of memories with my wife tore through my head. Conversations we'd had. Ones we should've had.

"I thought you might be up here. I was just checking on you, if that's okay." I wasn't sure how long I'd been up there, but those soft words from behind brought me back to my awful reality.

I bowed my head for a moment, then shoved my hands into my pockets and faced the woman I'd recognized from her voice alone.

Diana Mackenzie, wrapped up in an ankle-length black coat, pushed her black-rimmed glasses higher up on her nose as she approached me. She was elegant as ever. Older now, but she'd maintained a youthful appearance. With every step closer, the kindness I'd seen in her eyes years ago seemed to grow stronger. Clearly life hadn't taken a wrecking ball to whatever goodness she had in her the way it'd done to me.

"You may not remember me. I'm Susan Mackenzie's daughter."

"Of course I remember you." How could I ever forget? "But please don't say you're sorry," I added, a bit too harshly for my liking. "Or offer any condolences." There went my voice that time, though, breaking when her eyes met mine. "I, uh, can't handle any more."

She stopped walking and worked her lip between her teeth, clearly unsure what to say after I'd demanded she not follow reception protocol.

I thought back to the day I met her. It felt both like an eternity ago and yesterday. "Distract me instead."

She stared at me in silence, her brows lifting above her glasses as my only confirmation she'd heard me.

"Tell me what you've been up to since we saw each other last." How long ago was that? *Four years?* "Any new tattoos?" She shook her head no, and I wasn't sure what possessed me to do it, but I closed the space between. I reached for her glasses and removed them. "You never took that government job, did you?" I wasn't sure how I managed to remember any details about a girl I barely knew, but it was as if I were drawing them from a hat. They were just there.

Her eyes narrowed. "How can you tell?"

"You don't look sad." I shook my head. "Funeral-sad, yes. Not the other kind."

"Oh." Her eyes moved to the sky, the snow starting to fall heavier, before coming back to my face. "Your eyes are—"

"Not sad. They're dead."

My knee-jerk comment had her studying me, likely trying to find something else to say to break the tension. That, or comfort me.

"You must be cold," was what she settled on as I quietly slipped her glasses back on.

"I can't feel anything." Now I was the one slipping my gaze overhead as if all the answers would be written there— an indication as to how I ended up alone at almost thirty-nine, my other half gone. "I can't even . . ."

"Cry?"

I zeroed back in on her face, thankful she'd said the hard part out loud, because I doubted I'd have been able to. I nodded, the words stuck in my throat.

"Shock. Denial. Anger. That's why. When you saved me, I was in shock that day and . . ." Her voice sounded as fragile as life was.

"I saved you, but I couldn't save her." My hand landed over my heart at the tight squeeze of pressure there. "I listened to her scream a half a world away, and I couldn't do anything. Not a fucking thing."

I told her I hated her just before . . . That line would forever play like a broken record in my head. Haunt me until the day I died.

As Diana wordlessly reached for my other arm, I locked on to the tattoo emerging in view on her wrist as her coat sleeve slid up. Holding my forearm, she offered, "If you're up for it now, maybe it'd be easier to do it with an almost stranger?"

I forced my attention back to her face, and as my eyes grew blurry, I sputtered, "Do what?"

"Cry," she whispered, her voice soft, calming, free of judgment and expectation.

All I could do was stare at her. Unmoving. Everything went quiet as she kept hold of my arm.

Time stopped as we stood there without talking, but the pain started to push forward. I could feel it now. In my chest. Head. It hurt. Fuck, it hurt everywhere for so many reasons. "I should be alone."

"That's the last thing you should be."

Something inside me snapped. Broke.

I dropped to the ground and fell back onto my heels, Diana following me down, never letting go.

Snowflakes hit my face, but there were tears there, too.

Then this near stranger slid around next to me, offering me her shoulder, and I took it. Buried my face in the side of her neck, and I cried for the first time since Rebecca died.

I let go like I'd probably never done in front of anyone else. Rebecca hadn't even witnessed me cry once during our marriage, not even when my father died. Nor my mother's funeral. I'd broke down in private alone.

I snaked my arm up around Diana's back, drawing her closer, searching for some solace in my new hell.

"I got you," she promised, her voice choking me up.

After another minute of losing control, the tears started to slow. Catching my breath again, I turned my head toward her, and my cheek brushed against hers—and God, she was freezing. "You should go inside."

"Not until you're ready to go with me."

I opened my eyes, shocked at the strange comforting feeling taking over my body, and said the first thing that came to my mind, "Oxytocin."

"What?" she whispered.

"Do you remember . . .?" was all I managed out, clinging to her, to the calming feeling her holding me seemed to be providing.

"I would love to say I don't remember my embarrassing comment to you that day, but I do," she confessed, her tone soft. "Surprised you do, though."

"I seem to remember everything when it comes to you," I admitted, unsure why. That little revelation was best left studied at a later date. Or better yet, buried entirely.

"What are you two doing up here?" someone called out.

Diana startled against me, and I realized my arm was wrapped around a woman who wasn't my wife. A woman I shouldn't be seeking comfort in while I mourned another. We untangled ourselves from the hug and I dropped my hand to the concrete, prepared to push upright, but I couldn't get myself to move. Not yet.

"I slipped on the ice, and he accidentally went down with me," Diana said, covering for me. For my tears. Assuming a man like me wouldn't want the world to know he was capable of crying.

Maybe I didn't. Maybe I wanted the world to think I really was the devil. How else would I find Rebecca's killer if I didn't strike fear into the heart of my enemies? Revenge called for other emotions, or none at all.

"Let's get you up, Carter." I finally recognized the voice as belonging to Diana's mother, but I wasn't about to let her help me to my feet.

I stood myself and peered at a woman who, over the years, had become like a second mother to my wife. "Did you know? She thought you were coming to our place the night she . . ."

Susan drew the lapels of her coat together as a breeze knocked snow around us. "Know what?"

"She said she had things to tell me, and she couldn't do it over the phone." My mind was finally working again. "I don't think the home invasion was random. I think we were targeted. I just need to know if they were after me—or her."

Susan glanced at Diana and tipped her head toward the door. "Can you give us a second, sweetheart?"

Diana focused on me, seeking my permission to leave for some reason. Acting on instinct, I nodded my OK, hoping Susan could fill in a few holes when it came to the mystery that was my wife.

Once we were alone, knowing and not even caring that my eyes were bloodshot after her daughter had somehow managed to pull the emotions from me in the form of tears, I ground out, "What is it? What do you know?"

"When she stepped down at work and sold off most of her family's businesses, I asked her why. Rebecca normally told me everything, but she wouldn't answer me when I pressed. I have no clue what was going on in her life before she died. She was being very secretive."

I wasn't so sure I could believe her. "Was there anyone new in her life? Anyone I should check out?" I could normally read people well. It was my job. But I was so out of it I could hardly understand the words coming from my own mouth.

"No," she said, her lips barely opening to deliver the answer.

I cocked my head and dipped in closer, unable to stop myself. "You're sure?" The warning cut through my voice—the "don't lie to me or else" loud and clear.

"Of course. If I knew something that'd help, I would've told the police and FBI when we spoke last week."

"If I find out you're lying to me—"

"You won't."

I stepped back before I yelled at a woman. "Do you blame me for her death like everyone else does?" My voice broke again, the dam open and the emotions no longer held in check. "This had to have happened because of my job." *A smuggler or trafficker that somehow found out my identity.*

"Rebecca wouldn't want you embarrassing her memory or the Barclay legacy by going down the path I fear you plan to go," she said instead.

"And what path might that be?"

"Revenge," she mouthed.

Locking eyes with her, I rasped, "You're wrong. It's everything Rebecca would want." That much I knew about her. That fucking much. "She'd never want me to stop until I killed every last person who did this to her."

10

CARTER

EDINBURGH, SCOTLAND – OCTOBER 2019

GRIFFIN LOWERED HIS SIG AND SHOOK HIS HEAD, EYES FLYING over my attire before he moved his attention back to the dead bodies in the room. "Killing in a kilt. This has to be a new low for us."

"More like a nightmare," I grumbled, not amused by any of this, but especially not the fact we'd had to wear kilts to blend in to infiltrate our target location. A story for another day—or for never. All that mattered was the plan worked, and we thankfully hadn't needed backup since that backup had only just walked in.

"You're a little late to the party," Griffin said as Easton Holloway joined us. "But I know how you Air Force boys are —you hate getting your hands dirty."

"You're a funny fucker, aren't ya?" Easton replied while nearly tripping over one of the dead men. "You two made a hell of a mess in here."

"In our defense, they started it." Griffin shot him a smug smile as I took a knee by one of the dead terrorists—the only

85

way I liked them. "Watch it, man, you're in a skirt. I don't need to see what you're packing underneath."

I ignored Griffin's joke and went for the briefcase cuffed to the man's wrist.

"Wait, I gotta know, how'd you two wind up in kilts?" Easton started laughing despite the grim situation. "When you called me for an assist at the last second, you said nothing about dressing up."

"Don't ask." I wasn't in the mood to talk about Griffin's bright idea to get us inside the building unnoticed, particularly since it'd worked. That admission would only make him more insufferable. Cocky fucker. I could practically feel Griffin's triumphant smirk as I went back to the task of opening the briefcase, using the target's thumbprint on the biometric scanner.

"Is it in there?" Griffin asked, coming up next to me.

I removed the item from the case and held it up, searching for the tracker my inside guy had hidden there. The figurine of King Ur-Nammu from ancient Mesopotamia might have been tiny, but the little object was worth a lot. It'd been minutes away from being sold to some rich dick to help finance an embassy bombing.

My team had been following a trail of stolen artifacts being traded to the highest bidders to finance ISIS terrorist activities. While the smugglers were my targets, there was a happy by-product of chasing down possible leads to find Rebecca's killer—killing men like this and stopping *them* from killing people.

"Got it." I removed the tracker and tossed it to Griffin so there'd be no evidence of how we'd sourced their meetup when the authorities showed up even later to the party.

The artifact tracker was an idea I'd actually borrowed from

a woman nicknamed Red Robin Hood. Becoming something of a legend in the underground world, she stole back artifacts taken by the wealthy and elite and returned them to their original owners. Last I heard, she'd changed gears (and targets) and now sought out other kinds of traffickers. Those smugglers were up next on my list if nothing panned out with my current hunt.

"Who are we giving credit to for this hit?" Easton asked as he removed the duffel bag of cash one of the dead guys had used as a shield before I'd double-tapped him in the head —killing his chance to kill innocent people next week as planned.

I stood and handed the artifact to Griffin, knowing he'd make sure it made its way back to the right people. "Me."

Easton laughed. But I wasn't kidding. This was a decision I'd been coming to terms with for quite some time. "You're serious?"

"When is he ever *not* serious lately?" Griffin reminded him.

Easton dropped the bag of cash, eyeing Griffin as if curious whether he was clued in. He was. So was Camila. They were the only two people aware of stage two of my plan.

I should've had my revenge by now. And the fact the truth was buried beneath so many layers of fuckery told me one thing for certain—her murder had to do with my work at the Agency. I'd predominantly hunted smugglers and traffickers while at the CIA, so I'd created a list of targets from my time there to go after.

Thankfully, I'd been able to recruit veterans from around the world to help, and I compensated them a lot better than their respective governments ever could. But I knew I might lose some of my team for this next phase of the plan. Not everyone wanted to be associated with an enemy of the United States.

"Well?" Easton prompted, waiting for me to continue.

"I need the world to believe I'm a criminal. More than that, actually," I began, hoping I was right in this thought process. "I need people to think I'm the criminal other criminals fear. That means letting people believe I'm also a ruthless killer."

Easton looked around the room at the dead bodies. "The CIA is already pissed you went rogue. You're on their radar. You really want to end up on their hit list, too? The FBI's? Interpol?"

"I have no choice. The only way I'm going to figure out who was behind Rebecca's death is to put the fear of the *devil* in everyone. Good and bad guys. I need to become—"

"A monster?" Easton cut me off.

"Your names don't need to be dragged through the mud with the authorities. Just mine." I handed my rifle over to Griffin. "You're free to go if you don't want to be part of this."

"I'm already in this deep." Easton shrugged. "As long as you don't ask me to cross the line and kill anyone who doesn't have it coming, I'm not going anywhere."

Let's hope the others feel the same. "Thank you." I nodded, then took the bag of cash and tipped my head toward the door. "I'm going to make sure the bank's CCTV cameras across the street put eyes on me leaving. You two go out the back. I'll meet you at the safe house."

A worried expression crossed Griffin's face, but he knew my mind was made up. There was no going back. So, he quietly left, and I did the same.

Once outside, I made sure the bank's security cameras

had a nice clean image of me and there'd be no question I'd killed those seven men, before I started down the street.

A cathedral near a flickering streetlamp caught my attention, stopping my feet and my thoughts. Dropping my focus to the duffel bag of cash in my hand, I took the five steps up to the door, prepared to leave the half a million pounds there. But as I started to lower the bag, the door opened.

I lifted my eyes to see a priest. *Just great.*

He clasped his hands in front of his black robe, his eyes journeying over my body. "You okay?"

I straightened and nudged the bag his way, but he didn't take it. The lighting over the steps was spotty, but he more than likely noticed that in addition to donning a kilt, I was also wearing the blood of the men I'd killed earlier. "Here."

He had to be eighty, and should've been scared of me, already scurrying back behind the safety of his church doors. Instead, he reached out and rested his hand on top of mine and met my cold, dark eyes. "I think you should come inside."

"I think not."

"Confession," he said, a near whisper. "You need it."

"I definitely don't." I hated the whip of chills flying down my body and up the skirt. It was fucking drafty.

"What you say to me will only be heard by myself and God," he said, his Scottish brogue thick. He patted the top of my hand, then turned for the door and waited for me, not taking no for an answer.

"I doubt you or God will want to hear anything I have to say." I steadily stared at him, waiting for him to realize he was inviting evil inside a sacred place. He didn't blink or back away. Against my better judgment, I carried the money inside the holy place and followed him to a confessional.

I dropped the bag and stepped inside the small space.

"When was the last time you confessed?" he asked once he was in the other room, a cutout wall, or window-like thing, between us.

"I don't know. Maybe never?" My parents were Catholic, but only took us to church on holidays. Rebecca had grown up the same way.

"Now is a good time to start, then." He went on, explaining a few details about confession, none of his words registering in my brain. I was too worried I'd burn alive inside that room, losing my chance at revenge, to worry about the procedures and legalities of confessing my crimes to him.

I bowed my head, my heartbeat flying. "Forgive me, Father, for I have sinned." I mumbled the only words that came to me, closing my eyes in the dark, quiet space.

And then I told him everything.

About my wife's murder and my last hateful words to her. That I believed it was my fault and not a home invasion. And how I'd transferred the money Rebecca had left in my name into offshore and untraceable accounts, going off-the-grid on a quest to find her killer.

I shared with him the time I'd spent studying surveillance footage from the night of her death. I'd learned every enemy and friend my wife had made over the years, turning over every rock, stone, and pebble to find possible connections to her murder.

Then I explained that I'd retraced all of her last steps the year before she'd died, finding too many holes and missing pieces to make sense of anything, including the fact she'd been keeping even more secrets from me.

Hell, I even gave him a body count of the lives I'd taken in my hunt for her killer.

"But at least they were bad guys," I casually added.

Once I was done recapping the prior six months of my life in blood-soaked bullet points, I was sweating. And he was still quiet. More than likely shocked and terrified. *But* he was still there. He hadn't bolted and phoned the police.

I needed to bail, though. I left the confessional before he had a chance to tell me how fucked up I was, or what to do in order to get that "forgiveness" I already knew I didn't deserve.

I picked up the bag of money, took a knee, and unzipped it. When the priest stepped out of the confessional, I slid it over to him. "For your discretion," was all I said before taking off.

Hurrying down the steps out front, I quickly took the first side street I saw, but after I rounded the corner, I tripped over something in my path. My heart went into my throat when I saw a small puppy curled up inside a box.

FREE DOGS was written on the outside of the cardboard. Was he the last one left? Why'd he stay inside that box like it was a cage?

The little guy lifted his head, and I was just glad I hadn't stepped on him.

"What about we get a dog? I love dogs." Rebecca's words from years ago haunted me as I knelt and lifted him into my arms.

An Alaskan Malamute or Siberian Husky from the looks of him. White and black fur with two different colored eyes. He couldn't have been more than a few weeks old. Maybe not even that.

"You're all alone," I said to him, drawing him closer to my face, and he licked my cheek. Hopefully he wasn't licking blood, too. I couldn't believe I was going to do this, but . . . "You want to come with me?" He licked my cheek again. "I'll take that as a yes."

I resumed walking, on a mission to find him food. Well, maybe a change of clothes for me first, and then I'd get the both of us a bite to eat. *What do I call you?* Then it quickly came to me. "Dallas." It was the name Dad would've given a pet if Mom had let us have one.

Dallas yelped, confirmation enough he approved of the name.

"Well, Rebecca," I said, studying the dark sky and finding it full of stars, "I finally got us a dog. Just wish you were here with me to take care of him."

11

DIANA

WASHINGTON, D.C. – FEBRUARY 2020

"I'M SORRY I MISSED YOUR BIRTHDAY LAST MONTH." DAD kissed my cheek, then shoved a belated gift in my hand.

"It's fine, and you didn't need to get me anything." I stared at the small present, assuming it was jewelry. I guess my wish for him to understand I wasn't a jewelry person wasn't my gift this year either.

"Maybe it's not for your birthday. We could say it's an early Valentine's Day gift." He reached my shoulder and patted twice. "Come on, open it."

"Valentine's is just commercial BS," I grumbled, attributing my bad mood to both PMS and the fact I was between jobs.

The project I'd been working on at a fusion reactor in France had run out of government funding, which meant I was twenty-nine and living under Mom's roof until I figured out my next steps. And being back at Mom's was the last thing I wanted. Well, I guess it could've been worse. I could've been at Dad's, watching the revolving door of women my age.

"Maybe if you had a Valentine's date, you'd feel different about the day. I heard Mom was trying to set you up with Craig Paulsen." He removed his hand from my shoulder, and I wondered if he felt me cringe at the name. "He's a senator now. Single. My guess is he'll land a pretty powerful role at the White House one of these days."

I rolled my eyes. "At least the guy being single is a criteria for you in picking out my dates." Not that I wanted him choosing my dates. "You do know he's fifteen years older than me and an asshole, right?" I couldn't help but toss out those undeniable facts.

It still made me nauseous my mom tried to set me up with him last month, knowing he'd cheated with Rebecca Dominick.

"He's not that bad of a guy. He has his moments, but don't we all?" Dad shrugged, then swept a lock of silvery-black hair away from his forehead.

"I'd prefer never to hear that man's name again." I set aside the gift, not in the mood to open up a bracelet or earrings and pretend to be dazzled by them like I was one of his girlfriends he won over with sparkly things.

"So." He clapped his hands together, ignoring my comment, and asked, "Your mom back from dinner with Jared yet? I actually need to talk to her."

"Ah, that's why you personally delivered the belated gift instead of having your assistant drop it off."

"You're funny tonight." Dad shoved his hands in his slacks pockets and a goofy grin I hadn't seen in years stole over his face.

Dad wasn't in politics anymore, spending his time playing the stock market on a daily basis instead, but he still had two personal assistants get him everything from his coffee to his dry cleaning. It was like he was unable to do anything for himself anymore. I doubted the twenty- or thirty-year-old him in the Navy would recognize the man he'd become today. It made me sad.

"What do you need to talk to Mom about?" I folded my arms over my T-shirt, pretty much wearing them 24/7 around her. She hated when I dressed "down" and she hated the graphic Ts with silly sayings and puns on them even more. I may have been going on thirty, so it was immature of me to do that, but getting under her skin the way she got under mine was a new favorite pastime.

"Nothing you need to worry about." He patted my head this time instead of my shoulder, and ugh, now I did feel like a kid.

Thanks for that. "She'll never share that money Rebecca Dominick left us, you know that, right?" I cut straight to it.

"Still hard to believe it'll be almost a year since she died," he said, sounding almost somber about it. He hadn't even known the Barclay family that well.

Keeping my arms locked across my chest, I turned toward the windows, focusing on the view of the Potomac River outside the back living room.

"A bit shocking what happened to her husband," he went on when I kept quiet.

I closed my eyes, remembering the last time I'd seen Carter Dominick. He hadn't been at the reading of the will, so our paths last crossed on the rooftop after the funeral.

"Part of me wonders if he hired someone to kill her. Given his reputation now it wouldn't shock me." Dad's accusation had me opening my eyes, glaring at his reflection.

"I've heard the rumors from Mom, and that's all they are. There's no way he's become a criminal, and no flipping way he killed her." I spun around, feeling angry on Carter's behalf. I was beyond sick of people in Mom's fancy circles bringing up his story every chance they got. Whispering between each other at parties or events. The gossip was out of control.

"They're not rumors, sweetie. He's on Homeland's watch list. No-fly list. All the lists." He narrowed his eyes as if worried about my judgment.

Ha. Look at yourself. "There has to be a mistake. He's searching for his wife's killer. He loved her so much, and he's clearly the kind of guy who will do anything for justice."

"I think he did it." Dad's shrug had my stomach turning. The casualness of how he could talk about a man he knew had saved my life all those years ago just pissed me off to no end. Where was the benefit of the doubt? What happened to innocent until proven guilty?

"The police *and* FBI said it was a home invasion, and that there were similar ones in the area months prior to her death. Their house was tossed, too. Things were stolen," I reminded him. "But I think it was a coverup for something. Probably relating to his work with the CIA." Mom had confirmed he did, in fact, work there before he'd gone MIA.

"Yeah, a coverup all right. So no one found out he hired people to kill her." Dad *tsk*ed. "Even if he didn't do it, he's racked up a lot of bodies in this new life of his. Rebecca wouldn't want that."

"Now you sound like Mom."

"Good, glad to know we're still on the same page even if we're not married." He nodded as if delighted at that fact.

"And if someone killed me, would you never stop searching for my killer until you found them?"

Before Dad could answer, Mom walked into the room. "What are you doing here?"

Dad plastered on his fake D.C. smile. "Hey, honey," he greeted.

Mom did something so uncharacteristic for her, and I nearly laughed when she rolled her eyes at his use of the term of endearment. "What do you want?"

"Brought our daughter a present." He pointed to the wrapped box on the table.

"She hates jewelry as much as you hate monogamy," Mom mumbled before quietly leaving the room, and Dad quickly followed after her.

Taking my phone from the coffee table, I went over to the couch and sat, doing my best to ignore their fighting I heard coming from the other room. I'd spent too many years listening to their back-and-forth, and it didn't seem to bug me any less now.

I sent out a quick message to Sierra. She was back from her honeymoon, which meant I could finally text her about random things all day long without being annoying. She'd married Karl Novak. *The* Karl Novak as my mom referred to him. His family ran one of the largest defense companies in the U.S.

> Me: Hey, both my parents are under the same roof as me right now. Send help. And all the wine, please.

Sierra responded right away, sending a photo of herself while holding a bottle of red.

> Sierra: If I could fly to you, I would.

> Sierra: You hear back from any of your applications yet?

> Me: No, but Mom keeps pushing me to work for her boyfriend or for Barclay Energy.

I'd turned down multiple offers Rebecca had made to work for her, too nervous I'd slip and admit I knew about her drunken night with Craig Paulsen. To be honest, I'd been angry with her for cheating on Carter. Even though she was gone, I still couldn't bring myself to work there.

> Sierra: Why are you reallllly texting me? I know it's not just about your parents. Something is on your mind, and it's not work. What's up?

How'd she always know me so well?

Something was on my mind. Well, someone. Dad had brought that elusive someone up.

> Me: You think he's okay? That he'll ever be okay?

> Sierra: You're thinking about him again?

> Me: Just worried, and before you say I barely know him, and I shouldn't worry, I can't help it. I feel connected to him for some reason.

> Sierra: Just because he saved your life doesn't mean you're indebted to him, or need to play defense on his behalf whenever people roast him in public for all the "sins" he's apparently committing.

> Sierra: Also, Karl heard some things. I didn't want to tell you, but maybe I should?

That made me sit a little taller. What could her husband have heard that she was too afraid to tell me?

> Me: Are these things based on facts or hearsay?

> Sierra: Karl saw actual video footage of Carter killing people. Not even with a gun, Di. With a knife. Viciously stabbing them.

I blinked in shock and reread her message.

> Me: If he was seen doing that, then he wanted to be seen for a reason. They had to be bad people.

> Sierra: I don't know. But I think you need to forget him. Let him go. He's not the man you once knew. Rebecca's death clearly changed him. And we still don't know he's not responsible for her dying.

> Sierra: Also, for a scientist, you don't seem to recognize or believe facts and evidence when it comes to this man. I don't get it.

How could I explain the strange pull I felt toward him? I didn't know how to describe it, but deep in my gut, there it was, and time didn't make it disappear. Nor all the facts in the world being tossed my way about him.

I wasn't delusional enough to think the odd "pull" I felt toward him would ever amount to anything, but the world had turned on him. Someone needed to be in his corner while everyone shit-talked him. And that someone would be me.

12

CARTER

REYKJAVIK, ICELAND – APRIL 2021

"Forgive me, Father, for I have sinned. It's been seven days since my last confession."

"Only seven?" the priest piped up, unable to mask his shock.

I hung my head and ran my fingers through my hair.

Swinging by a confessional had become a habit of mine. I didn't even have to be in a city that spoke English, or any of the five languages I spoke. Actually, I preferred it if the priest didn't understand me.

I'd started frequenting confessionals after that night in Scotland whenever the guilt became so thick it was suffocating. I'd unload my soul and leave a bag of cash in exchange for sealed lips.

But the guilt I was now dealing with was pure torture, and it wasn't from killing someone. It was because of sex. Because I slept with a woman who wasn't Rebecca.

It took me two years to have sex again—twenty-four

fucking months since Rebecca had died to be with someone else—and my conscience couldn't handle it.

In addition to the act itself, I was struggling to deal with who it'd been with—a damn target of mine. A criminal. A woman with connections to the most powerful men in the world. I needed her to trust me, so she'd open up to me, tell me if she knew who'd killed my wife. But she didn't want to talk. She wanted to fuck. So, I did.

The problem?

The actual problem?

I'd liked it.

Fuck. What is wrong with me?

"Are you planning to speak?" the priest asked.

"I fucked a woman who wasn't my wife."

"Adultery, ah, the most common sin I hear."

I shook my head. "My wife's dead. She's been gone for two years. But this was the first time since . . ."

"I see." He was quiet for a moment. "You feel wrong for it, as though you cheated?"

Yes, but . . .

"Son?" he prompted.

I'd grown accustomed to that term. It'd bothered me at first, but now it was somehow comforting in the sea of the chaos that was my life—to be someone's son. Someone's something.

"The woman's . . . not good." I wasn't sure why, but I felt the need to hide the reality of my situation from this man. I didn't want him to know I'd taken lives, or that I'd embedded myself in criminal organizations, faking friendships and alliances, all to find my wife's killer. I was starting to feel like I was chasing more than just ghosts, I was hunting a motherfucking unicorn. I came up empty everywhere I turned.

"Is *she* married?"

"No, but she wanted me to . . ." I could talk about violently killing people, but tell a priest the woman asked me to take a belt to her ass and punish her for being bad? That it turned me on? *That* seemed to be a hard limit for me.

Maybe it was harder to confess because my guilt didn't rest on that part of the act. After all, I went back to Alyona Jovanovich the second night for more. Tied her up just like she'd asked.

And that third night, the things Alyona asked me to do to her, pulled me back for a fourth time. Last night. And it'd been the most fucked up of all the nights.

When I'd returned this morning like an addict, needing more, and she'd crawled to me on her hands and knees as I stood there naked and waiting for her, I'd snapped out of whatever twisted spell I'd been under, remembering when Rebecca had done the same after confessing she'd cheated. I'd wound up taking off from Alyona's room with a rock-hard and unsatisfied cock, searching for a confessional.

The guilt stung and burned as I sat across from the priest.

"Two years without sex, and now that I've started, I don't think I can stop."

I also knew *how* I had sex would always need to be that way—a revelation I just came to, but I felt that truth in my bones.

"You will find love again one day, son."

"No, I won't. My heart is dead." *It died even before Rebecca did.* It'd take a miracle for me to ever love *and* trust again. More than that. It'd take an act of God. Even then, it was probably impossible.

"You're in a confessional feeling guilty. Do you think a man with a dead heart would worry about his sins?"

I ignored him, refusing to cling to the idea I could ever

return to being the kind of man my wife married all those years ago. Not with everything I'd done, and maybe I didn't want to be him anyway.

Deciding today's confession was a bad idea, I left before he could offer any more words of wisdom, dropped the bag of cash outside the priest's door, then stumbled into the first bar I came across.

Dropping onto a seat, I stared at a Kentucky bourbon on the second shelf and slapped several hundred-dollar bills on the counter. "The bottle."

The bartender followed my line of sight and set a glass down in front of me alongside the bourbon.

I took the bottle before he filled the glass, turning it around to study the illustration of angel wings on the back. They weren't open and ready to fly, but drawn together as if . . .

I closed my eyes as a conversation from almost a decade ago, with a girl I hadn't seen in ages, filtered up from my memory.

"The devil was an angel before he fell." Diana Mackenzie's words and that beautiful face of hers came to mind.

I clung to the memory of her for another minute, then forced it away, back to the past where it belonged.

Opening my eyes, I capped the bottle and set it back on the bar. "If you'll excuse me." I threw more bills on the counter, deciding what I needed right now wasn't forgiveness. I needed something more permanent. An ingrained, and engraved, reminder of who I was. A tattoo of those angel wings on my back.

Because that's who I am—who I officially am.
I'm the devil.
The fallen one.

13

CARTER

NEW YORK, NEW YORK – NOVEMBER 2021

IT WAS MY FIRST TIME VISITING THE PRIVATE CEMETERY where Rebecca was buried since her funeral two and a half years ago. She had a huge monument alongside her parents' one, just as she'd planned. Rebecca had spelled out exactly how she'd wanted to be buried. Typical Rebecca—needing to be in control, even in her death.

Dallas was at my side, quietly curled up against my leg, waiting for me, giving me the time he knew I needed.

Setting the roses down in front of the marble, I shoved my hands in my jacket pockets. It was early morning and bitterly cold for November, but I had a short window to slip in and out of New York without notice.

I stared at the name on the monument: **Rebecca Barclay.** Not Dominick. That had also been what she wanted. To die as a Barclay. I hadn't thought much of it back then. I hadn't been able to think much of anything other than guilt and revenge. But now? Well now, it hurt. Proved I still had a feeling or two left in me.

Justice had been served, though. After years of creating a network all around the underground world, searching every corner of the earth for her killer—and learning the ugly details surrounding her death—I'd finally found those responsible. I took out every last one who'd had a hand in her murder.

It'd been *her* secrets and lies to me that'd made my quest for justice that much harder and take so damn long. *That* also hurt. The fact she'd kept so much from me. Part of me wondered how much more there was I still didn't know.

"You should've told me. About the blackmail. About everything." I shook my head. "Damn you, Rebecca." A play-by-play of the last few months pushed through my mind like a movie I wished I'd never bought a ticket for. "I could've saved you. Maybe not our marriage, but your life—*that* I could've saved."

I hadn't been crazy, though. Her death wasn't the botched result of a random home invasion. She'd died because of me. Well, because of my job. Not that the world would ever know the messy truth of what happened. I wouldn't let them, because Rebecca would rather keep her secrets buried with her.

I closed my eyes, trying to come to terms with how a celebrity treasure hunter, who was also secretly an overlord for illegal smuggling and trafficking routes, was behind everything.

Andrew Cutter had never been a guest at a party Rebecca had thrown, or on any list connecting her to him in the past. Against my better judgment, I'd reached out to Susan Mackenzie, curious if she knew the name without telling her why I was asking. She'd said no, told me to rot in hell, then hung up on me. So, I still had no clue who brought Andrew into her life or why, and I wasn't sure if I'd ever know.

Rebecca, being Rebecca, must've said yes to Andrew's dinner invite—that she never told me about—given his celebrity and star-like status. According to Andrew's confession, when he couldn't get Rebecca to cheat as planned that night, he'd drugged her and staged photos of the two of them together. Then came the blackmail. The threats to publish the scandal in the news and all over the internet if she didn't do what he wanted.

She died thinking the photos were real. She died not knowing she turned him down, that she'd been faithful to me. She'd thought she had too much to drink, just like the other time, and she did whatever the bastard told her to protect our marriage. She must've not believed I'd forgive her a second time. And I wouldn't have. Especially not with a guy who was her celebrity hall pass's doppelgänger.

The part I also hated was that I knew she'd done everything more so to protect her reputation and family name than to save our relationship.

Regardless of her reasons, Andrew's target had always been me. Once he'd somehow discovered I'd worked for the Agency, he manipulated her, forcing her to break into my files. She'd stolen my private list of twenty-five unclosed cases, and he'd had her funnel them to an unsuspecting target—Red Robin Hood—who also happened to be Andrew's ex-girlfriend.

It was a long and complicated story as to why he used and then killed Rebecca, but ultimately, her connection to Red Robin Hood, who I now knew as Rory McAdams, was how I finally found out how and why she died. I'd wound up partnering with Rory to take him down.

"I worked with Navy SEALs to find your killer," I told Rebecca, as if she were standing in front of me, instead of a cold piece of granite. "You'd have liked that. Probably not so much the way I went about it, or that I broke my promise to Rory and those men when I said I wouldn't kill some of Andrew's men afterward. But they were ordered by Andrew to murder you, so of course they had to die." I let go of a deep breath and opened my eyes, wondering why I still didn't feel better. The case was closed. "I know, I know, I'm still a wanted man, which ruins your name and legacy," I grumbled, hearing her voice in my head, lecturing me about that. "What am I supposed to do now?"

Dallas howled as if answering for her, and he crooned again.

"Don't tell me you think I should do what those SEALs we worked with suggested. Go into private security just because you liked their dog, Bear?" He barked at me, bopping his head yes. "Of course that's what you want." I knelt by him and scratched behind his ears, now eye level with Rebecca's name.

Dallas wailed in delight, and I looked around, confirming we were still alone.

I shouldn't be here, but I had to see you. "You were going to tell me about Andrew, right? It's what you couldn't tell me over the phone? Is that why you changed? Sold off most of your family's businesses?" I stood upright, hands diving back into my pockets again.

Without my focus on revenge, I felt emptier now than ever before. I peeked at Dallas as he stared up at the cloudy sky and howled.

"What do you see up there, boy?" I followed his gaze, half expecting him to answer. "I don't see anything." I swallowed an unexpected lump down my throat, unsure why thoughts of Diana Mackenzie surfaced, but there was a tattoo on my back inspired by her, and she was the only person to ever see me cry in my adult life. The day of Rebecca's funeral, on the rooftop, as we'd both searched for answers in the open sky above us.

I doubted I'd ever see Diana again. Not that it'd be a good idea anyway. She wouldn't recognize the man I was now, so different from who I'd been all those years ago.

No, she needed to stay in the past, just like the rest of my life.

And somehow, someway, I'd have to find a way forward, which required a first step.

I reached into my pocket for my wedding band and stared at it, preparing to leave it behind so I could finally let go. My stomach squeezed, and the breath froze in my lungs. I closed my eyes and curled my fingers inward, securing the ring inside my palm.

I wasn't ready.

Not yet.

But soon.

"Soon, Rebecca—soon, I'll finally walk away from you."

PART II

AFTER...

14

CARTER

"HOW IN GOD'S NAME DID YOU ALLOW THIS TO HAPPEN? A hostile takeover, and you didn't think to call me before shit got so bad you lost the company?" I slapped a hand to the side of my neck, feeling the vein bulging there.

Two and a half years of trying to be a better man, and this news was pushing me awfully close to ripping this guy apart, just like I would've back during my crusade for justice.

I'd trusted Pierce Quaid because Rebecca had trusted him. *My mistake.* He'd fucked up and lost all that I had left of Rebecca.

"You went off-the-grid and left me in charge of The Barclay Group. I did what I had to. And why would I reach out to you? All I know about what you've been up to in the last several years is that . . . well, you probably belong behind bars. If someone finds out you're here, you just might wind up there."

Figured Pierce had the balls to say that to me, like I needed the reminder I was still technically a wanted man by our government, but he couldn't manage to find his voice in time to save the business.

Of course, Pierce had no clue I'd assisted the military on and off over the years. They'd looked the other way, conveniently forgetting my "record" and the fact I was wanted by multiple governments, not just ours, as long as I brought them the results they needed. Hell, I even worked side by side at my security company with the Secretary of Defense's son, Gray Chandler.

And there I was, walking on thin ice, keeping my head low, particularly in cities like New York, waiting for them to officially remove my name from their lists.

How much longer would everyone see me as either the man who had his wife murdered for her money—which many believed—or as the guy who snapped after losing his wife and became a killer?

Part of me wanted to take out a national fucking ad and let everyone know every life taken by my hand had been someone who could've, and possibly would've, easily taken theirs had I not done something. The other part of me, though, was fine with letting people think I was a monster. I wore the suit of asshole well, and I wasn't quite sure if I wanted to lose it.

"Did you even find who killed her? That's what you were doing, right?" Pierce had the nerve to ask me.

"Do you think I'd be here if I didn't?" I cocked my head, continuing to stare him down.

"Fair point." He wrung his hands together, then shook them out at his sides. "And what do you do now? Is it something Rebecca would approve of?"

Did he really think I would tell him what I'd been up to in the last five years? Where would I even start? Maybe with a number? Like how many kids I'd saved from human traffickers in my two-and-a-half-year hunt for Rebecca's killer?

Or there was another number—how many assassins, murderers, and criminals I'd taken out while working with Gray at Falcon Falls Security, as well as before that venture even existed.

Dozens of HVTs had been eliminated, including The Chechen—the man I'd been hunting in Budapest the night Rebecca had been killed. That turned out to be a double-edged sword in itself as Zoey now had her doubts he killed her fiancé after The Chechen had planted the ridiculous idea in her head that someone else had done it, but—

"I guess your silence is my answer." He interrupted my internal ranting, continuing to hang by the door as if on the verge of bolting from his own office, a room that had once been Rebecca's. He'd redecorated and changed it to the point I couldn't even feel her memory clinging to the walls.

"Shut the door." I rounded his desk and dropped down in his chair, intending to come up with a strategy and get The Barclay Group back. Rebecca held on to it despite what she'd been dealing with back then, so she'd want me to save it.

"It's too late. I know you're trying to think of a way out of this problem, but there isn't one. Paperwork was finalized this morning before you startled the shit out of me by busting into my office. I thought you were a ghost—haven't seen you in years," Pierce said after closing the door and facing me.

"And you were never supposed to see me again," I finally said. "But you fucked up and lost all that my wife gave a damn about while she was still alive." I couldn't save her. The least I could do was save her company.

"You haven't reached out in years. For all I knew you were dead, too." Pierce paused to let that bitter truth sink in. I *had* been a ghost to almost everyone I'd known before I'd taken off. "You don't collect a check from The Barclay Group. Your share is automatically redirected to charity. So, tell me why it really matters? The deal may have been hostile, but it was a good one. A lot more money than we deserved."

"It matters because Rebecca cared enough not to want to sell. I had to find out on the news about the takeover, not from you, no less."

He loosened the knot of his red tie, then removed his suit jacket and chucked it on the couch. "Rebecca cared about The Barclay Group because her father did. I swear, sometimes I think I knew her better than you did."

I stared at him, my jaw tightening, as I considered the harsh truth of his words. It seemed everyone knew my wife better than I did. She'd kept so many secrets from me. So fucking many. Every time I found out a new one, it stung. It never seemed to stop hurting, how she felt she couldn't be completely honest with me. I'd tried to keep the past in the past, but it was moments like these that made it impossible to do.

"I'm sorry." He lifted a palm in surrender. "I shouldn't have said that."

"There's nothing left of her now," I said under my breath, the words slipping out before I could stop them.

"You have her money."

"Okay, so maybe you do want to die today." I cracked my neck, then began working my sleeves to the elbows. At his timid gasp, I shook my head. "Kidding."

"You don't joke."

I used to. All the time in the Army. When it happened now, it was because my teammates at Falcon Falls were beginning to rub off on me here and there, even if I didn't want them to.

Pierce headed for the desk as if sensing my walls were

coming down. Not a chance. "I negotiated for most of us to continue working here, despite transfer of ownership. Many were hired by Rebecca herself." He pointed to a folder on the desk in front of me. "So, in a way, her legacy continues. We can keep the research going that she wanted because—"

"Her father wanted it," I finished for him, a bad taste still in my mouth at all of this, hating that maybe this was a sign it was time I finally let go of her.

I snatched the folder and flipped it open, then stopped on one name. *William Wallace?* Now I was thinking about Scotland and that kilt I had to wear, but that day brought Dallas into my life, at least.

I kept reading, and my heart stopped when I saw—"Diana Mackenzie?"

"Rebecca had been trying to recruit her for years. Not just because Diana's mom was close with Rebecca, but Diana's one of the brightest minds out there. It took a lot of convincing, but I brought her on board six months ago. Not an easy sell, that one. It didn't help her ex, William Wallace, already worked here."

Of course he's her ex. I closed the folder as he hiked a thumb over his shoulder.

"Diana's here now. I brought everyone in to meet with the new owners this week. You want a word with her? I, uh, assume you know her since—"

"Bring her here," I said without hesitating, wishing there was a bar in there. I needed something strong. I never thought I'd see Diana again, and now I was seconds away from it happening.

Pierce swung open the door but didn't leave. "I am sorry."

"Are you saying that because you know my reputation

and you're worried I'll kill you for losing her company?" No need to sugarcoat the truth.

"I don't know much about your reputation." He gave me his profile. "Just rumors. Including your kill count being higher now than it was when your enemies in the Army nicknamed you the devil."

"Did Rebecca tell you that's what I was called?"

"Like I said, we were friends."

Yeah, I was once her friend. Should've stayed that way. She'd be alive now, and maybe I wouldn't be so cold. So dead. So fucked up.

"She wouldn't want you hurting me, now would she?"

"Contrary to what you may have heard about me, I only kill dangerous criminals. I'm not actually one myself. So, unless you give me a reason—you're safe."

"Last I checked, murder, unless it's self-defense, is still illegal."

I ignored that last jab, and he left. I'd need to make the meeting with Diana quick. I doubted Pierce would call the Feds to let them know I was there, but I wasn't in the mood to test his loyalty and wind up going head-to-head with law enforcement. That would necessitate calling in a favor to Gray, and I hated playing the phone-a-friend card.

Although my co-team leader and I were getting better at trusting each other, it was still Griffin or Camila I'd prefer turning to for help if needed. Griffin also worked at Falcon Falls, and Camila assisted here and there as well. I never would've survived teaming up with Gray if Griffin hadn't had my six.

It was still hard for me to believe I'd said yes to partnering with Gray in the first place, and it'd happened at a wedding with the President in attendance, no less.

My path first crossed with Gray courtesy of the group of

Navy SEALs I'd worked with to take down Andrew Cutter. Gray's sister—CIA, of-fucking-course—was married to one of the Teamguys who ran off-the-books ops for President Bennett.

Rebecca would've loved me "playing nice" with Gray and his SEAL friends. One of them was President Bennett's son. That was as close to the White House as I'd ever get. Not that I wanted that. Fuck, I'd rather continue being a wanted man than get into politics.

At least I was putting the Barclay family money to good use in funding our security company, which ultimately helped a lot of people.

Steepling my fingers together, I tapped them against my lips as I waited for Diana to show up, unsure what I planned to say to her. Tell her about the tattoo on my back a random comment of hers over a decade ago had inspired? Or about how far I'd truly fallen since that day I'd first met her?

"Dominick?"

My attention swiveled to the door the second she said my name. She was staring at me as if seeing a ghost—appearing even paler than Pierce had when I'd stormed in without warning. "Come in." My hands dropped to my lap. "Close the door."

Instead of doing that, she remained stuck in place, peering at me from behind round gold-framed glasses.

"Are you in shock?" I reclined the chair a bit as I studied her. Her jeans were paired with a black tee that had a beaker on it with the words: *I have many chemistry jokes—I'm just afraid they won't get a good reaction* offered an impression of someone much younger than I pictured when I thought of her. She had to be in her thirties now. Thirty-three? Not a kid anymore. Then again, had she ever really been one when we'd run into each other before?

"I'm not sure what I am," she whispered, finally entering the office. I was relieved Pierce wasn't her shadow, and she was alone. "I didn't expect to see anyone today." She smoothed a hand down her shirt, then flicked at her ponytail as if embarrassed by her appearance.

Me, though? I fucking loved how she looked. Sweet and a little nerdy weren't qualities I'd ever sought out before. Not that I'd ever hit on Diana. She was off-limits for obvious reasons. *But* there seemed to be a strange magnetic pull between us whenever we were close. And, for reasons I didn't quite understand, she'd popped into my head more than a time or two over the years.

"Why are you here?" She wet her lips as I stood, making my way over to her. "I thought you were on the run?"

I stopped a few feet shy of her and shoved my hands into the pockets of my black slacks. "On the run? I guess that's one way of putting it."

She angled her head, her eyes flying down my black dress shirt before moving to my sleeves, maybe searching for the tattoos she remembered being there. "You do some eavesdropping over the years? I assume you've heard some things about me from your mother."

"Maybe."

"I think it's safe to say it's more than a maybe." Unable to help myself, I closed the last bit of space between us, lowering my chin to look her in the eyes.

When she lifted her hand between us, hesitating as she reached for me, I took hold of her wrist but didn't force her hand down.

"I'm just so surprised to see you here, and I'm . . . well, I needed to touch you, make sure you're not a ghost."

Letting go of an uneasy breath, I relented, guiding her hand to my cheek so she could confirm I was real. At the feel of her palm on my heated skin, I dropped my eyes closed but didn't release her wrist.

"Did you find who did it?"

I knew exactly what she was asking. She didn't have to spell it out for me. "Yes."

"That's why you disappeared, right? Why you became, well, who you became."

I nodded and forced open my eyes.

"And now?"

"I'm . . ." I didn't know what to say. Did I let her in on the secret about my team? That I'd lost my way while searching for vengeance, crossed too many lines, and was now doing my part to make up for the wrongs I'd committed along that path? "I didn't know you worked here," I deflected instead, turning the conversation back on her.

"Mom finally got her way and talked me into it. I'm assuming even though you weren't at the reading of the will, you know your wife left my mother twenty-five million dollars. Mom felt like I owed it to . . ." She swallowed, leaving her sentence unfinished between us, as if regretting ever starting it to begin with.

She may have kept other secrets from me, but I knew all the people Rebecca had in her will. If both of us had died, Camila Hart would've received money as well. I'd sent Camila money after Rebecca died anyway because, in a sense, I did die the day Rebecca had.

"Did your mom share the money with you?" The idea of Diana spending Rebecca's money, though . . . I couldn't wrap my head around that thought for some reason.

"No, I didn't want it. Told her to donate whatever she'd planned to give me to charity."

Unexpected relief filled me she not only declined the money but gave it away. Whether she didn't want the money because she didn't need it, or just wanted to help others who needed it more, it soothed a part of my heart. Confirmed there were still good people in the world, who weren't all after Rebecca for her name or her wealth. That thought had me feeling like someone had taken a defibrillator to my heart and shocked it awake.

She slowly pulled her hand back from my face, and I finally let go of her, stepping away so our bodies weren't so damn close. *And* so I wouldn't breathe in whatever sweet perfume she had on. A fragrance tempting my basest self to lick the side of her neck. Taste it. Taste her.

Fucking fuck, I needed to get laid.

Not with Diana.

Never.

"I'm sorry if I came across ungrateful for an opportunity to work here and honor Rebecca's dream for clean energy. I know she wasn't a scientist, but she was passionate about believing fusion could one day be a limitless and viable energy source. That we didn't need to wait decades for it to happen."

Apparently, that was her father's dream.

"But I . . ."

There was a reason the moth went to the flame, and I was just as powerless as I reached out and slipped the back of my hand across her cheek. "You what?"

I couldn't help but notice she wasn't wearing a ring. Was she married to her work like me? Or was she dating that ex again, the one with the name of a Scottish knight, since they worked together?

"It's not important," she said as if in a daze, and I retracted my hand as she shook her head, clearing her mind and breaking our trance. "Are you back-back?"

I smiled. *What in God's name is wrong with me?* "No, I'm

not." Damnit, seeing her was a bad idea. Being around her made me feel lightheaded. Drugged, even. Maybe it was nostalgia from knowing her at a time when I was a different man. I wasn't sure what it was, but it had to stop. I turned and went over to the desk, set my hands on the surface and closed my eyes, bowing my head.

"Why can't you be back?"

"I think you know," I answered, my tone clipped. I was pissed at myself for being attracted to this woman when I had no right to be. Had I found her attractive when Rebecca was alive? Yeah, I had eyes. But there was a difference between finding someone attractive and being attracted to them.

When she remained quiet, I let my thoughts veer off yet again, trying to figure out what was wrong with me, and how to fix it.

I needed to head home and relieve some tension. I was on edge and wound tight about losing the company. A good, hard fuck was what I needed.

There were three women I trusted who were discreet and capable of handling me, mostly because they had their own issues and were as fucked up as I was.

I kept a space separate from Falcon's headquarters in Pennsylvania where I brought those women. It was also where my dog sitter picked up Dallas to take care of him when I traveled for jobs it'd be best not to bring him along. I didn't want my dog sitter, or anyone outside my team, knowing where I actually slept at night.

It was also convenient since one of the three women I'd casually been screwing happened to be Elizabeth, my dog sitter.

Then there was Jasmine, a law professor I'd met at a bar one night.

Lastly was Zoey. Yes, *that* Zoey. We'd started using each

other on and off after working with "Red Robin Hood's" brother, Jesse McAdams—who was now on my team at Falcon Falls—to take down The Chechen. It was an unlikely partnership, but the ultimate end of The Chechen was worth crossing those lines.

Then two months ago, Zoey and I came to the mutual decision to end our arrangement.

Crazy enough, Zoey had been worried *I'd* catch feelings. It was easier to let her go than convince her that wasn't possible. Hell, I hadn't even flinched when Gray walked in on us screwing at a wedding—*I know, I'm an asshole.* That moment proved my heart was as cold and dead as Zoey claimed hers was. Because I'd have lost my mind at another man seeing a woman I actually loved in that situation.

"I suppose I do know why you can't come back, but there has to be something you can do so you can eventually," Diana said, finally breaching the quiet and cutting through my messy thoughts. "If you're still in trouble, though, why would you risk coming here until your name is cleared?"

I lifted my head and slowly turned, finding her too close again. I held myself back from leaning into her, trying to ignore her soft floral scent. Freshly picked, fragrant, and crisp. I'd suck all that sweetness and sunshine right out of her. Then she'd hate me, and I'd hate myself even more. Because she was all that was good and wholesome still left from my past, and I wanted to remember her that way. *Keep* her that way. Which meant staying far away from her.

So, I did the least asshole thing I could think of and started for the door, before I lost what little self-respect I had left and made a move on a woman I shouldn't want and could never have. Because for the life of me, there was something about her that made me crave her, and I needed to get away as quickly as possible. There would be no way to *Father-*

forgive-me my way out of that one. There could be no acting out on the unexpected desire I had for this woman.

Although, was it really unexpected? I'd felt a connection to her before, but I'd refused to acknowledge it. And I needed to do that again now.

"You're leaving already?" Her sad tone had me halting.

I turned, finding her eyes on me, appearing as sad as her voice had been. "Yes." I swallowed. "Because whatever you've heard about me—the truth is much worse."

15

DIANA

"You know, Karl told me this bar is owned by a former Navy SEAL who is also the governor's son." From our table by the window, Sierra shifted on her stool and looked around the nautical-themed bar in Greenwich Village.

"You told him where we were meeting?" I wasn't sure why that bothered me so much. Maybe it was because I wasn't her husband's greatest fan. More like not a fan at all, but I kept my mouth closed because Sierra claimed she was happy.

She focused back on me, picking up her Moscato. "Yeah, he always knows where I'm at. You don't marry a billionaire in the defense industry and get to run around without a fleet of security traveling with you."

Shit, she was right. It'd been a long time since we'd hung out in person. Maybe it was a bad idea to call her to meet with me after all. "So, your security detail is blending in with the crowd here, I assume?"

"Double Oh Seven over there," she said with a light laugh, "is chatting up that pretty girl at the bar, but he hasn't actually taken his eyes off me for a second." She nodded toward a guy hovering by the hallway near the back of the bar. "And Jake is being all Jake-like, acting like someone might sneak in from the back to try and kidnap me."

I focused on Jake and, despite my wild day, cracked a smile. "The fact you refer to him by his name and the other by—"

"Back to why you're here." She batted her lashes with intent, letting me know to drop it.

Okay, then. "Well, I needed someone to talk to." Desperately.

"Luckily, my nanny's back from her vacation to watch the baby, so I could come out. Karl can disassemble a rifle in the dark, but change a diaper? Forget it."

Mmmhmm.

"So, what's the emergency that has you all out of sorts?"

I trusted her. Of course I did, but I didn't trust her husband. If Sierra told Karl that Carter was in town, he'd call in the cavalry and have him arrested. Well, *try* to have him arrested.

Maybe Carter was long gone by now anyway? It'd been six hours since he'd been at the office, and my heart had yet to stop colliding with my rib cage. Even after all that time, and with every dark rumor that'd spread about him since, my body still responded to him.

"Earth to Diana?" Sierra waved her hand in front of my face. "William pushing you to date him again?"

Ugh. My ex from once upon a time ago was a serious pain in my ass. Relentless in pursuing me. There'd be no "third time is a charm" when it came to that man. I'd rather be forever single than give him another shot. "No, there's only one person who makes me feel like *this*." I'd said too much, damnit. Wore my heart not on my sleeve but right smack in my eyes for all to see.

Sierra knocked over her glass and cursed, wiping up the spill with a stack of napkins as she leaned closer and hissed, "Diana, please don't tell me you're thinking about *him* again."

Ever since our text exchange a few years back, I'd stopped mentioning Carter's name to her. Once she'd dropped the news on me that Karl had witnessed video footage of Carter killing people, I knew he was an off-limits topic. Even if she was my best friend.

She shook her head. "You saw him, didn't you?"

"How do you know that?"

"Hence the emergency meeting and the fact you look all flustered. I'd even say like you've been properly fucked."

"I do not look"—I swallowed—"like *that*."

"What happened?" She took my full glass away from me and gulped half of it back. "Tell me."

"You'll tell Karl."

She lowered the glass. "I won't."

"Liar," I called her bluff. "Karl made you hate Carter."

"I've seen things, Di. Things I never want you to see." She finished off my drink. "More than just that one video I told you about."

"And how does your husband have these 'things' for you to see? Why show you them?"

"Defense contracts. Private military stuff. *Bad* guys. It's his world, and he knows all the players in it." She massaged her temples, and this was clearly a bad idea.

But who was I going to go to about today? *Mom? Dad? My boss?*

"Please tell me what happened so I can talk you down from whatever high seeing this man has so clearly given you."

"That's not—"

"You look like you're playing a game of Candy Land right now, but really, you're about to enter an episode of *American Psycho*." She reached across the table and covered my hand with hers. "He's dangerous. I have no idea why you can't get this man you barely know out of your head, but you have to."

"Well, I didn't see him." My lie was so weak it about folded out right from under me.

"The company," she said, putting two and two together. "He came back because of the company, didn't he?"

You know me too well and know too much. I hesitantly nodded.

Looking toward 007, then in the direction of Jake, she chewed on her lip as her fingers flew through her mahogany-colored hair.

"What is it *you're* not telling me?" I asked, chills covering my arms like sleeves.

"Nothing, I promise. I just don't want to see you get hurt. This infatuation you seem to have with him makes me nervous."

"I'm not infatuated." *I don't know what I am other than confused.* I peered out the window and about fell off my chair.

"Is that Senator Paulsen out there?" she asked.

I trembled at the sight of him standing beside a limo, waving me out. I'd seen that man more than I cared to since he'd become friends with my mom, but what was he doing there? How'd he find me? "Shit, I'll be right back."

Sierra held my arm. "You sure you want to go out there?"

"No, but if I don't, I have a feeling he'll come in here and it'll be much worse for everyone."

"If you're not back in ten, I'm sending Jake after you."

"Okay." I left the bar, and once outside, locked eyes

with the man who'd cheated with Rebecca all those years ago. A man who'd made more passes at me than I could count on two hands. "What are you doing here? How'd you find me?"

"Get in the car." Craig opened the door and stepped to the side while stomping out a cigarette.

"Not a chance." I folded my arms, doing my best to stand my ground. A common misconception about me was that because I was brainy and wore glasses, I didn't have a spine. Despite Dad's faults, he'd made sure to raise me to kick ass both physically and verbally if necessary.

"Get the fuck in the car, Diana." He smiled through his teeth that time. "Don't make a scene."

"Why would I—"

"Because you were with Dominick earlier today." He waited for a couple to pass before barking out, "So, get in the goddamn car."

I startled at his words, nearly losing my balance. "I don't know what you're talking about."

He wordlessly gestured me into the limo again.

Tossing a quick look at the bar, I spotted Sierra focused on us. Maybe she'd changed since she'd married Karl, but she'd always have my back. Well, she'd send one of her guards out tonight to have it, at least. I didn't want to make a scene or make things worse, so I did as Craig asked and got inside.

He slipped in next to me, slammed the door and hit a button that slid the glass divider up to block out the driver and locked all the doors. "What'd Dominick want?" He flicked on the overhead lights and turned to face me. "Do you know where he is now?"

"Quaid told you," I said at the realization. "Why would he—"

"Because his loyalty lies with Rebecca not Carter. So, of course, he'd tell me that psychopath made an appearance."

My heartbeat was really packing a punch today. First Carter. Now this. "He's not a psychopath. He went after her killer. He didn't accept what the police said."

"Keep spinning that little fairy tale, sweetheart. It's not the truth. He killed her, and I can prove it," he hissed.

"Bullshit," I shot back, nearly slapping him along with the word.

"He's on the FBI and CIA's 'most wanted' list. Do you think he earned himself a place there by kissing puppies and chasing motherfucking pots of gold at the end of rainbows?"

I pulled on the door handle, beyond ready to leave. I wasn't going to let him talk to me like this, but the door wouldn't open. Great, and now claustrophobia and fear were setting in. "Let me out."

"I'll tell your mother you saw him. She'll assign a security detail to you. Is that what you want?"

My shoulders tensed at his threat. He was right, and having bodyguards breathing down my neck was the last thing I needed. "What do you want? Why do you care about Carter?"

"Because he killed Rebecca." He slammed his fist down on his thigh, likely wishing it was Carter he was hitting instead.

"How'd you even find me here?"

"I'm resourceful."

No, Karl told you where I am, didn't he?

"I need specifics. I need to know exactly what Dominick said to you."

"There's nothing to tell you. I barely know him. He was saying hi. That's it."

He laughed. The bastard. "A man like Carter doesn't say

hi. Quaid said he requested to meet with you and only you."
When I kept quiet, he added, "Did you tell him anything?
Like what you've been working on for Barclay Energy?"

"No. And thanks to Quaid, it's not Barclay Energy
anymore," I snapped back, my intuition telling me Quaid
allowed that takeover to happen. Not that he'd admit that to
anyone. "But no, I didn't talk about work."

"You're sure?" He gripped my leg so hard he'd be leaving
behind a bruise.

I tried to shove him away, but his hand didn't budge.
"What the hell, Craig? You're acting crazy."

He let go of me as if finally realizing what he was doing.
"There's nothing you want to tell me? Because if I find out
later you're keeping something from me, so help me, I'll—"

"You'll what? Not take no for an answer the next time
you bother me?" I bit out, on the verge of tears. Crying
wasn't something I did often, but he was pushing every limit
I had. "You should've stayed away from Rebecca," I added,
still angry on Carter's behalf about not only the accusations
he killed Rebecca, but the fact Craig had taken advantage of
an inebriated woman.

Craig quietly stared at me, then his brows snapped
together. "You know." He looked up at the ceiling, his chest
puffing out from a deep inhalation. "How much do you
know?"

"Don't worry, I'm not in the business of blackmailing
people."

My words had the intended effect, his attention cutting to
my face as if I'd finally gone ahead and hit him. "Rebecca
and I were close friends."

"A friend she didn't tell her husband about?" I defiantly
crossed my arms over my chest. "There's a name for that."

He ignored me and leaned in, his ashy breath hitting my

face. "If you see that man again, do yourself a favor and run. He's dangerous."

"And that man has never made me feel uncomfortable, but you do." I turned and went for the handle again. "Maybe look in the mirror, because it's you who's a threat. Probably to our nation as well." At the feel of his hand on my shoulder, urging me to look back at him, I went still but didn't give in to his request. "Get off your high horse. You don't belong there, and you know it." I swallowed, trying to keep my courage going. "Stop whatever crusade you're on to take him down. Carter's been through enough."

He pressed his chest against my back, fisting my ponytail and jerking my head to the side to drop his mouth over my ear. "You want to fuck him, don't you?" His hot breath at my ear as he tugged my hair had me closing my eyes. I was about to enter fight-or-flight mode, and while I knew how to defend myself, I also doubted I'd survive a matchup with this man. "That's what it is. You have a crush on him. Always have, haven't you?" His free hand slid around to my throat, but he didn't squeeze. "You're not such a good girl, are you?"

"Let me go," I demanded.

"Although, you're a woman now, not a little girl, even if you still dress like one." Another tug of my hair, and I cringed when I felt his teeth graze my earlobe.

"Let me go, or I'll tell Carter about this." *Shit, why'd I say that?*

"Please do. Call him. Go ahead. I'd love nothing more than to see if that man would come running in to save you." He let go of my ponytail, then pressed a button, unlocking the doors. "But you don't have his number, now, do you? Because he doesn't want to fuck you back." He *tsk*ed. "Too bad for you."

"Just stay away from me and my mother." I hated the

break in my voice as I opened the door, not wanting him to know he'd managed to scare me and get under my skin.

Once on the sidewalk, I was about to close the door, but he reached his arm out to hold it open.

His eyes met mine as he murmured, "I'll be seeing you around." Then he pulled the door closed, and I waited for the limo to leave before I faced the bar again.

Sierra came outside, her two guards right behind her but keeping their distance. "You okay? You look pale." She handed me my purse, which I'd left inside, then hooked her arm with mine. "What'd he say to you?"

My head was spinning. "I just want to get out of this town. Go bury myself in my research again." I had to meet the new owners of the company tomorrow, and then I was off to wherever they decided to send me. Hopefully somewhere far away from here.

"Talk to me," she pleaded.

"Your husband told him we were here."

"What?" She let go of me and removed her phone from her Birkin handbag.

"Don't call him. It'll make things worse."

She frowned, then shoved her phone back in her purse. "What'd Paulsen want?"

I tipped my head, studying her. "He wants what everyone wants," I whispered, my skin breaking out with chills again.

"And that is?"

I closed my eyes. "What they can't have."

16
CARTER

VIRGINIA – TWO MONTHS LATER, AUGUST 2024

Hanging back from where everyone was gathered outside, I removed my sunglasses at the sight of Camila holding my teammate's son in her arms. She'd accompanied me to Gray and his wife's party, and they'd just announced Tessa was pregnant.

Aside from Griffin and the love of his life, Savanna, who were back home with Tomas, their newborn, the rest of my teammates were at the party. Not to mention several of the Navy SEALs I'd worked with what felt like forever ago to take down my wife's killer.

Would it really be three years in October since I'd confronted Rebecca's murderer, and was it fucked up I kept track of the time?

A chill rolled down my back at the memory as I refocused on Camila. A strange feeling formed in the pit of my stomach as she held Jesse McAdams's son in her arms, and it took me a minute too long to realize why.

Instead of being parents ourselves, Rebecca had wanted

us to be the "cool aunt and uncle" to Camila's kids one day. I wasn't so sure if I'd ever get that chance to be an uncle to her kids, though, since she didn't seem to have plans to settle down. But I knew one thing for damn sure, Rebecca had been right about the fact I shouldn't be a dad. Not with all the things I'd done in my life.

Not to mention I was getting older. Forty-five as of this past June. And unless I accidentally knocked someone up—God help me, I hoped not—I'd be dying one day as I deserved—alone.

"You okay?" I looked over to find Mason Matthews at my side. He was a former Marine who accompanied Falcon Falls on missions from time to time.

"Better than ever," I said with enough sarcasm to warrant a smile from him.

But in truth, I wasn't half bad. Our last mission had the unexpected outcome of finally removing me from Uncle Sam's lists. Watch lists, wanted lists—all the fucking lists. Not that I planned to live my life much differently, but it'd be nice to walk down the streets without worrying about someone trying to cuff me.

I remained by Mason as he casually drank his beer, despite the fact I was in the mood to be alone. His focus wasn't on me, though. It was solidly trained on Oliver Lucas and Mya Vanzetti, two team members at Falcon. Oliver tossed Mya over his shoulder, and she squealed and slapped his back, begging him to put her down.

I wasn't in the business of knowing my teammates' love lives, but it'd been hard not to hear about the triangle situation that'd been happening between Mason, Oliver, and Mya. From what I *didn't* want to know but did, Mason and Mya once had the same friends-with-benefits thing going on as Zoey and I did—minus the friends part in my case. But now Mason was supposedly moving out of the way for Oliver. Not that Mya or Oliver would admit they liked each other. Their hate game was pretty strong.

But what'd I know? I'd predicted Gray would've wound up with his ex-girlfriend, Sydney Archer, who worked with us. Instead, Sydney married Jesse's brother-in-law, Beckett Hawkins, leaving the path clear for Gray to find his way to Tessa.

Realizing my sunglasses were still in my hand, I put them back on. "I'm getting the feeling you may not be working with us anymore after our last op."

"I think it'd be best for all of us if I didn't," he said, then gave me a light nod—his cue to exfil from the conversation —and he walked over to Gray's brother-in-law, Wyatt Pierson.

I could barely look at Wyatt after what'd happened with his daughter, Gwen Montgomery, on our last mission. Hell, I didn't want to think about it now. Or ever. *I need a drink.*

I started for the makeshift bar set up in the yard, but stopped when I heard chatter from behind me. *Distinct* fucking chatter. As in the name Susan Mackenzie rolling off one of the SEALs' tongues.

"Mackenzie's stepping in as Secretary of State as of Monday," one of them said.

"The current Secretary had a heart attack, and he's not up for the job anymore, so . . ."

The next voice I recognized as Jack London's from our team. "Susan's daughter is apparently some genius, too. She's off saving—"

"The world." I hadn't intended to be heard, but despite the music still blasting, it went quiet behind me.

"You know her?" Jack asked.

I twisted around to face him and the Teamguys standing

there. They stared at me from behind their shades, and I felt the curiosity in their eyes. "I need air, if you'll excuse me."

Jack smirked. "We're outside."

I tipped my head toward the street. "Other air," I said, then started for the gate, accidentally catching Camila's eyes on my way.

Not waiting for her to try and stop me, I started down the road lined with vehicles, searching for my rental.

"Wait up," Camila called out.

Against my better judgment, I did as she asked.

"What's wrong?" she asked, a little breathless from running after me.

"I need a drink," I said through my teeth.

"There are plenty of drinks at the party."

I swallowed. "A drink somewhere else."

"Well then, I'm coming with you." She sidestepped me and reached my rental SUV before I had a chance to order her to stand down.

I didn't have the energy to go head-to-head with the stubborn woman. She really was like a pain-in-the-ass sister, but I loved her. The only woman I'd ever love again, but that was because she was family.

Once I was behind the wheel, she buckled in next to me and wasted no time to press me again. "So, what's going on?"

I started up the Tahoe. "How do you know there's anything going on?"

She jerked her thumb over her shoulder. "Because you left Dallas at the party."

She had me there. "I'll be back for him."

"Speaking of Dallas, have you found someone new to replace Elizabeth yet? You never told me why you let her go."

And you don't need to know why I fired Elizabeth. Oddly

enough, she was loosely connected to my present foul mood. "No, I didn't."

"Would you please talk to me," she pleaded once I pulled away from the curb.

"Susan Mackenzie is the new Secretary of State," I revealed hesitantly.

"The same Susan who was like a godmother to Rebecca and helped me plan the funeral?"

All I could do was nod.

"So, you're thinking about Rebecca right now?"

I nodded again, even though there was a lot more I was thinking about right now than that. Like a truckload of guilt.

I'd considered seeing a priest again, but I was Stateside, and I didn't want to go to confession on U.S. soil, even if I was no longer a wanted man. There were a lot of people unhappy about my name being removed as a traitor and enemy of the State, and one of them was now Secretary of State. Her position of power would be a new problem for me, I was sure of it.

Camila reached for me, and on instinct, I pulled away from her touch. "I don't need you seeing my future."

"I'm sorry, you're right." From the corner of my eye, I noticed her wiggling her fingers. "I wish I could turn this thing off."

That *thing* was her visions. What had started as confusing dreams had turned into her being able to *sometimes* lay a hand on someone and get a glimpse into their future. It was all surreal, and if I hadn't witnessed her help people because of those "predictions," I wouldn't have believed it myself.

"I wish I could have saved her. You know that, right? My abilities weren't what they are now, and I didn't know what would happen to her back then," she said softly.

Her strange words to me in Rebecca's office the day of

the funeral came back to me, finally making sense. They wouldn't have back then since she'd yet to open up to me about her visions.

"Maybe I need to get away for a while. Go somewhere I don't know anyone. Chill on a beach. Touch people again without seeing their fate since it usually only happens if I have a connection with them, or they're tied to a case."

"You just got a place in D.C. I thought you wanted to make a home here?"

"Yeah, I know. But a vacation first might be nice. Six months or so. Go off-the-grid. No technology."

That's a long vacation. But the no-technology part sounded nice.

"But back to you. What else is on your mind? Stop being all broody. Stewing in silence will get you nowhere."

What can I even tell you? That Wyatt's daughter walked into my office while I was getting serviced by my dog sitter.

Gwen was younger than Diana, but they were both blonde with light eyes. Extremely smart and daughters of Teamguys. I was pretty sure Gwen's middle name was also Diana, adding to the damning list of wild coincidences.

Throw in the above with the fact I'd had too much to drink, and I may have been staring at Gwen while she remained stunned in the doorway, but in my head, it was Diana who'd caught me getting my cock deepthroated. Like she was witnessing me cheating on Rebecca.

It'd taken me too damn long to realize it was actually Gwen standing there, not a figment of my imagination. I'd forgotten she had a key to that office and had even given me the heads-up she'd be dropping off files at some point. I supposed she hadn't expected I'd be there so late, and she didn't know my second office doubled as my "hook up" place.

After Gwen had left, I'd not only stopped Elizabeth from getting me off, I'd fired her from watching Dallas. I'd given her a healthy severance check and let her know the casual fucking was done, too.

I hadn't been able to have sex with anyone since that night. I wasn't sure what was wrong with me, but my dick wasn't broken. It still worked just fine when I jerked off. The problem was, Diana Mackenzie kept popping into my head while I stroked my cock.

I'd tried to fight off the image of her sitting on my desk in her glasses and T-shirt, spreading her legs open for me to taste her like a good girl. It was so far removed from my normal desires and how I screwed these days, but somehow, thoughts of her like that was all it took to get me over the finish line.

I justified it by reminding myself I was already nearly there, so, what the fuck did it matter if I thought about a woman I'd never actually set a hand on while it happened?

My conscience seemed to think otherwise. Shockingly, I still had one.

In an even more fucked-up twist, Gwen and I had to partner up in a dating adventure game on our last op—a horrible idea—and we'd wound up having to kiss twice. The first time had been brief, for the sake of the dating show. The second time, though, Gwen had kissed me as part of the cover story. When I'd closed my eyes, I'd let myself imagine it was the one woman I'd never be able to truly have. Diana. What a fucking dick thing to do.

Gwen confessed she had feelings for me on that op, and I'd come up with a not-so-bullshit reason to turn her down. I couldn't exactly tell her why I'd really let her stay in my office that night, staring at her while another woman gave me head. Or tell her who'd been in my mind during that kiss. Not that Gwen wasn't a great girl, but she'd never be *my* girl. *Fuck my life.*

"You need to get laid," Camila said, somehow reading my mind without physically touching me. A new skill? "You're wound up. That's what's wrong."

I smiled at her bluntness, but she was spot on. "How do you always know everything?"

"Don't worry, I'm not offering up myself. That'd be gross. You're like a brother."

This woman would inherit everything if I died, and she was the only woman I'd ever allow myself to love ever again. But have sex with her? God no. "Same page," I said, surprised I managed a laugh despite my mood.

A mood I wasn't likely to shake anytime soon. Especially because not only had I been fantasizing about the new Secretary of State's daughter, I'd also been casually checking in on her in the last two months. And by "casually," I meant I'd secretly had my own cameras installed at the research center in Amsterdam where she currently resided and worked. Keeping tabs on the new company, as well as Pierce Quaid, to ensure no one fucked up Rebecca's legacy (since that was all she'd seemed to care about) with the change of ownership.

The unintended consequence of my efforts to obsessively watch over the new company was to also check in on Diana.

I had no clue why I was so drawn to this woman, but fuck if I couldn't seem to stop myself from caring about her well-being. And after the last few times "checking in" on her, I could tell Diana was getting close to solving something with her research. I could see it in her eyes, and the excited little fist pumps in the air she did while she worked in her lab or behind a desk with her headphones on. I'd gone so far as to zoom in on her phone screen to see what music she listened to while working, pleased by her taste in beats.

Yeah, I was a sick fuck and needed help for a lot of reasons. The sooner I cut myself off from watching the company—*aka, her*—the better.

"So, are you going to tell me what else is going on, or are you going to keep it to yourself like always?" Camila's question pushed through my thoughts.

"Did I keep too much from Rebecca? Is that why she kept so much from me?" I deflected while pulling the SUV to the side of the road and parallel parked in front of a bar. "She died thinking she had sex with another man. Went behind my back to give him my case files just to prevent me from finding out. She'd rather help a criminal than tell me what was going on." Why was I rehashing this? It was history. Nothing would change the past. I was supposed to be letting go. *But what if I missed something? What if there was more she didn't tell me, and—*

"You know what your problem is?"

I unbuckled and turned toward her. "No, but I know you're going to tell me."

"You haven't forgiven her. For anything. For making you quit the Army. For forcing you into a job you hated. For other things you probably haven't told me about. And then, of course, for her keeping all those secrets about Andrew Cutter from you." She started to reach for me, but then went still at the memory of what might happen if she touched me. "So, like I said, forgive her."

I stared at her, probably giving her a blank, confused look. Was she serious? Rebecca was dead. I was the only one who needed forgiving. All the confessions to all the priests around the world would still never get me redemption. Because I didn't deserve it.

"You're mad at her. You won't admit it because she's

gone, but you are. And you're mad at yourself for being mad at her," she said, her accent thickening that time.

And for telling her I hated her before she died. For still hating her even now for all of her secrets. For cheating. For so many things. Yeah, you're right. But I lied like a stubborn kid and said, "No, I'm not."

"You are." She folded her arms, staring me down like only she could. "So, forgive her. Forgive yourself for being mad. Stop carrying her ring with you like a ghost haunting you, too."

How'd you . . .? I shook my head.

Dark eyes focused on me. "And for that matter, while you're at it, no more dressing like you're the head of the mafia, wearing only black all the time. Then, God help us all, go get laid before you snap."

PART III

NOW...

17

DIANA

AMSTERDAM, NETHERLANDS – OCTOBER 2024

THE SCREEN OF MY MACBOOK WASN'T SUPPOSED TO BLINK back at me. Either I was running on overdrive and on the verge of falling asleep at my desk or my computer was having a meltdown.

Checking to see if my laptop was acting up in more ways than one, I hung my Bose headphones around my neck and paused Spotify halfway through "Mr. Brightside" by The Killers.

The loud whoosh of the fan running at max capacity snagged my attention, but only for two seconds, because the cursor on the screen began flying around as if possessed. *Great. Something's up. Not just me at two in the morning.*

I made sure to back up my work just as my co-conspirator in our late-night work session walked into the office we shared. Bahar plopped down in the swivel seat alongside me and reached for the arm of my chair to roll herself next to me.

"Why do we torture ourselves staring at all this data as if it might magically morph into something?" Bahar was from

Turkey, and her accent made the English language sound so much sexier whenever she spoke. I knew Pierce Quaid had taken notice of her, too, but Bahar was only twenty-seven, and, in my humble opinion, he was about three decades too old for her. So far, he'd only flirted and to no avail.

Bahar released my chair to cover her yawn, then ran her fingers through her mass of shiny black hair, shaking her head so the locks shifted to her back.

"Some call this torture, others call it a good time." I was putting in all those long hours with the hopes of finding a clean energy source to help make people's lives easier. And, well, keeping the planet spinning a bit longer would be nice, too. So, it was worth it. "You know you love these late nights, and I feel like we're about to have a breakthrough."

"Or a breakdown." She chuckled. "Kidding, kidding." She pushed away from the desk, sending her chair flying back as she stared into the adjoining room.

Only a glass wall separated us from the lab next door where my ex-boyfriend was currently kissing Bonnie, one of the lab techs. When did they become a thing?

"They know we can see them, right?" Bahar's laughter was genuine that time, unlike her breakdown comment that would've worried me if I didn't know her better.

"Surprised William would be handsy with anyone in public." I would've been happy for the two of them, but I didn't wish a relationship with William even on my enemies. And I actually like Bonnie. "Speaking of weird shit, though" —I pointed to my MacBook—"she's making noise and acting up. I might need to pause my work and bring her to tech."

"I love how you call your laptop a 'she.'" Bahar rolled over and turned the screen to have a look. "Then again, didn't clinical studies recently prove women have more brain cells than men?" Without missing a beat, she angled her head toward the lab where Bonnie appeared to be dry-humping William against a filing cabinet. "Men have even fewer cells when they're thinking with their dicks—example A, Sir William over there. So, it makes sense that a supercomputer would be a girl."

My laugh turned into a long yawn, and I focused back on whatever it was Bahar was doing to my computer, which didn't seem like much of anything. The whirring sound had about as much bite to it as Pierce Quaid's little pooch he'd brought to live with him here. Ironically, Pierce's Chihuahua probably had a better shot at winning over Bahar than he did.

I closed my eyes and tipped my head back against my chair for a minute while she continued to do *something* to my computer. Maybe Bahar was channeling her brother, who was in cybersecurity, and she'd be able to figure out if my laptop was simply as fatigued as I was, or if we had a spy poking around in my hard drive.

At least something would be poking me. It'd been too long since I'd been poked, and after seeing Carter Dominick that day at the office months ago, I'd had no desire to ever be poked again unless he was the one doing the poking. *And. Oh. My. God. What is wrong with me?* I removed my glasses and rubbed my eyes. *Poking? Seriously?* "My brain is more on the fritz than this laptop."

"You've been staring at the same calculations all night to the point your vision, even with your glasses, is probably blurry."

To be fair, she was right. My gut told me I was one number away from turning theory into a reality.

"I think you have a bug," she said without much conviction. "I mean, maybe. Who am I to know?"

I slipped on my glasses and dragged the laptop in front of

me. But hey, the noise had stopped, so maybe Bahar did have the magic touch.

"You know what I've been thinking about, though?" Her tone was almost wispy.

Leaning back in my chair, I turned my focus her way, doing my best to ignore the make-out session still going on next door. There was fusion happening all right, just not the kind we were getting paid to create.

"Time travel," she blurted with as much excitement as someone announcing the winning lottery numbers.

"Time travel, huh?"

"I think it's possible." A red manicured nail stabbed the air. I was jealous she could keep her nails so on point while there. We'd been working almost every hour of every day, full out and nonstop since Barclay Energy was sold and we'd joined forces with eleven other private companies.

I'd thought that sale was a terrible idea, but it turned out to be a blessing in disguise. The new owners provided a massive boost in funding to our research.

"Yeah, you know. With all the research we do in energy, sometimes it has me wondering if maybe what we're doing here could transfer to that, too. I know our work can result in a lot of less desirable things, too. But time travel would be a nice byproduct of all these countless hours we put in, right?"

I highly doubted anything we did could help with time travel, but yeah, the "less desirable" stuff knocked at our doorstep every day. God forbid our research ever fell into the wrong hands. "Maybe it's possible to go into the future, but not to the past." I was too tired to be thinking about this, but since my laptop wanted a break from me, I figured what harm could it do to focus my energy elsewhere. A nap would've been nice, though. "Once the present becomes the past, it's done. Over. Finished forever. Left as memories only." I wasn't a fan of revisiting the past, in my head or otherwise. "So, if anyone's traveled to the future already, well, they're stuck there, because their present became the past the second they joined the future time plane."

"So, the only reason to want to time travel is to escape our present and hope the future is better." She hiked her thumb toward the hall. Three doors down was a room where hundreds of millions of dollars in equipment was being assembled to create a reactor to generate and sustain plasma in hopes our team would pull off a cold fusion miracle. "Or it's probably worse, right? Well, if we don't figure out how to make fusion work outside the sun, it may be." She smirked, picked up her mug and tipped it back and forth and stood. "I'm going to get more. Want any?"

"You read my mind." I offered her my cup that said: **Everything is Energy -Einstein** on it.

Bahar started for the door but halted before the threshold. I'd thought William's tongue in Bonnie's mouth had distracted her, but it was me she swiveled around to look at. "What would you change if you could go back, though? In your own life, I mean? If there'd be no ripple or butterfly effect thing? No consequences?"

I hated my first thought was of Carter Dominick. To thinking about the man I wanted to "poke" me a hundred times over and then some.

The truth softly left my lips as I revealed, "I'd wish my path never crossed with someone." *I wish someone else saved me the day of the embassy bombing.*

She tipped her head, studying me as if expecting me to explain. But how could I tell her about Carter without sounding off my rocker? How would I boil down all the feelings I didn't understand into the sum of a few words?

What if I hadn't met him in the way I had? What if he

hadn't saved my life, and then we hadn't shared a few moments between then and now that had me questioning so many things? Things like the palpable energy that flowed between us when we were within arm's reach of each other. I refused to believe the connection I felt toward him, as if it'd been powered by the sun itself, was all in my head.

So, yeah, I wished we'd never met that day. Because then I wouldn't compare every man I'd met since then to him.

Mom always said to be with a man who gave you security, not butterflies. To which I'd responded, *"Why can't he give me both? Why not be with someone who makes me feel like I can fly, but then know he'll be there to catch me if the wind abandons my sails?"*

And, of course, thinking about my dad, she'd bluntly told me, *"Because he'll be the one to put a hole in your sail."*

After meeting a man who I was sure could make me feel both ways, how could I resort to wanting less, though? Once given a taste of something so strong, so elite at the highest of levels, how do you settle for anyone who doesn't make you feel that way?

"What about you? What would you change?" I finally brought myself back to the present after dipping into that very place I'd wanted to avoid.

"Easy." She sighed. "I'd have become a vet instead."

Ah, now I get why you still like Pierce's dog despite his nonstop barking and his much more annoying owner.

Bahar stepped through the doorway just as I called out, "Wait. I, um. I gave you the wrong answer."

Bahar peeked her head back in. "And it is?"

"Save Rebecca, that's what I should've said." I gulped. "I would save her life."

She had no clue who I was talking about, but she gave me a little nod, then left.

I spun back around toward my desk and bumped into my laptop, accidentally hitting a few buttons. Shoving my glasses higher up on my nose, I leaned in at the realization that—*holy shit.*

I stood in shock, the cord from the headphones snapping free from my phone, and I knocked my chair back. "Oh my God."

I read the slight change to the formula I'd been working on that my bump with the keyboard had caused. Then I read it three more times. *This is bad. Horrible.* The opposite of what I had wanted to create. How'd I . . .?

"William!" I faced the glass wall and began waving my arms, trying to get his attention.

He unglued his lips from Bonnie and looked over at me, a rush of red flying up his face in embarrassment. Brain cells depleted from that kiss, apparently. He smoothed down his white lab coat before rounding the glass divider to enter the office he shared with us. "What is it?"

"I think I accidentally—"

Red lights started flashing, and siren-like wails echoed all around us. William shifted behind me, and it took me a second to lock on to the problem.

Two masked men with rifles were in the lab next door. Bonnie shot her hands up in surrender while lowering to her knees. William, the coward, moved farther behind me, using me as a shield.

Oh my God. "They're on their way to us. We need to get out of here." I whirled around to face him. "Come on." But then I remembered my computer, and what I'd discovered before the sirens, so I committed the formula to memory before deleting it.

"Down. Now. On your hands and knees," a man wearing all black military-looking clothes ordered. Only his eyes were visible, but there was black paint around the circumference of his lids. He had an accent—but at this lab, so did thirty-three people representing eleven other countries aside from the U.S.—and I couldn't recognize where this guy was from.

William lifted his palms. "Please don't kill me."

The man nudged his rifle in the air, a command to walk toward the door.

"What do you want?" I asked as I finally lifted my hands, following William while trying to come up with a plan. We were in the office, not the lab, so I couldn't pull a MacGyver and knock the bastards out with an explosion.

At the sounds of gunshots competing with the sirens for attention, I halted in the doorway and turned to the side. Bonnie was still okay, so it hadn't come from there, but she was being nudged from the room into the hall.

The second the other shooter left the lab, I fixed my attention back to the masked man with us as he traded his rifle for a sidearm. Now was my chance.

I lunged at my target and brought the heel of my hand up beneath his nose while kneeing him in the balls, just as Dad had taught me.

He groaned, then yelled in an unfamiliar language, and I took the chance to strike him again, knocking his Glock to the floor. The rifle was still on a sling around his body, but we were too close for him to get ahold of it and use it, and I had to keep it that way.

From the corner of my eye, I caught a glimpse of William taking off for the hall while I slid beneath the enemy's extended arm as he went to punch me. He had brute strength, but I was smaller and more flexible.

He pulled a knife that'd been strapped at the side of his leg, and I fell back on my ass, preparing to use everything I had in me to kick, but before I had a chance, the sirens stopped and a voice came over the intercom.

"Stop fighting, or your colleagues will die," someone announced in a computer-generated voice. At the threat, I went still, trying to calculate the odds and what to do next.

The masked guy used the distraction to his advantage and secured a strong hand around my ankle, flipping me over. The last thing I remembered was him climbing on top of me before everything went black.

CARTER

OFF-THE-GRID, PENNSYLVANIA

STANDING ONLY IN MY JEANS, THE BELT BUCKLE UNDONE BUT still on, I took a sip of my scotch while opening the door to my second office. The space served two purposes: my own office separate from Falcon's headquarters, and it was where I fucked when I was in town. Tonight's reason for being there was the latter.

The law professor I hadn't seen in six months was outside, and I sure as hell hoped Jasmine could fix me.

"I was shocked to get your message. Been forever." Jasmine stepped around me to get inside and had her coat off by the time I'd closed the door and faced her. Aside from pink lipstick, and black heels, that coat had been all she'd come over in.

I set aside the scotch as she confidently strutted naked across the room. She kneeled by the couch, flicked her black braid around so it rested over one taut nipple, then lifted her wrists, waiting for me to bind them.

I thumbed the tail end of the belt hanging from my pants

and approached her, hating the wrenching pain in my gut, and the heavy weight filling my chest. I shook my head and dropped my hand to my side.

Was it still too soon? I'd been distracted by a case last month. One that'd had me teaming up with an unlikely partner—Rebecca's college boyfriend, Constantine Costa. I wanted to blame working with that man and his family for why I *still* couldn't get hard, even with Jasmine on her knees for me. But in truth, I knew that wasn't why.

Tonight was a waste of time. Because as depraved and screwed up as I'd become over the years, one thing hadn't changed. I was unapologetically loyal. To a motherfucking fault, so it would seem.

I'd never once strayed when married to Rebecca. And now there I was, loyal once again, but it wasn't to Rebecca's ghost. I wished so damn much I could convince myself it was, in fact, Rebecca giving me pause. That it was her memory preventing me from being with another woman.

It sounded better to say I was being loyal to Rebecca's memory all over again, like I had been those two years before I'd met Alyona Jovanovich—a woman I never wound up taking down.

As good as it sounded, it wasn't the truth. No amount of saying it out loud would make it so, because it wasn't loyalty to Rebecca keeping my dick down around other women. I'd become loyal to a fantasy, to Diana. To a woman I couldn't have and hadn't even seen in person but a handful of times.

As of five days ago, I'd stopped checking the cameras I'd planted at the research center in Amsterdam, hoping that'd help this fuckery going on in my head. Help me return to the status quo, which was having meaningless, rough sex.

"You need to go," I ground out, frustrated. "I hoped this would work, but it won't."

160

"*What* would work?"

As she stood and came my way, I lowered my focus to the smooth V between her legs where her hand rested. I didn't feel a damn thing. Not even a subtle dick twitch.

"I'm sorry," was all I said before lifting her coat from the floor to nudge it at her.

"Well, if you change your mind . . ." She pursed her lips in disappointment while putting on the heavy garment.

"I won't." Once she was covered, I opened the door. "Unfortunately." The second she was gone, I shut and locked it, then bowed my forehead against it, my heart hammering out of control.

Far too tense to get behind the wheel of a car, I decided it'd be best to jerk off in the shower here before heading home.

I started for the bathroom, unzipping my jeans, then paused at the sight of my laptop on my desk. Like an addict, I toyed with the idea of pulling up surveillance footage in Amsterdam. Get my dopamine hit from seeing Diana.

Would she be up working yet with the time difference, or still asleep in that little room of hers she'd been living in next door to her lab?

I shook my head in disgust. I couldn't afford to give in to a weakness like this. "Fuck, what is wrong with me?"

I went into the bathroom, turned on the water and stripped down to nothing. Once beneath the hot spray, I lathered up my hand with soap and slammed my other palm to the wall while fisting my cock. I was hard the second I thought about the woman I couldn't have.

My back muscles snapped together as I clamped down on my molars. I dragged my hand along my shaft from root to tip, then across the head and back down, over and over, doing my best not to think about Diana. But like every other time, my obsession with this woman, who I could never be with, pounded through my thoughts anyway.

Visions of her blonde hair falling over her chest filled my mind. Diana, wearing only her glasses, would climb into my bed, a place I never took a woman, and arch her back, her tits rising with each breath as I braced myself above her.

Missionary of all things. Fucking vanilla and *missionary* was how I'd take this woman. It made no sense. But this wasn't real life. It was in my head. And there, I could have her any way I wanted her.

I kept a firm grasp of my cock, my body responding to the image of her spreading her legs for me. I'd take her bare. I'd even kiss the sinful smile on her lips.

My body trembled, already on the verge of orgasming as I thought about filling her tight pussy, knowing the fit would be hard for her to handle at first. But she'd adjust. Take it all. And give back as much as I gave to her, calling out my name on the cusp of coming, and . . . I blew my load like a college kid.

My chest heaving, the endorphins waning, I nearly punched the tiled wall, angry at myself for letting her take over my thoughts again.

At this point, I'd rather suffer the wrath of Gwen's dad, lose all respect from my team at Falcon for having sex with Gwen, than feel this way for Diana Mackenzie.

I was far too close to taking my jet to Amsterdam to beg Diana for just one night. To taste her. Surround myself and lose my mind in her scent of fresh flowers. Then I'd ask her on *my* hands and *my* knees, why I was fantasizing about her, a woman I'd saved a million fucking years ago. Then I'd demand to know why I couldn't stop thinking about her, especially when I barely knew her.

Of course, I really did know her. Like how she took her coffee: steamed milk and a stevia stirred in.

The music she listened to, and her little shoulder dance while at her desk when she really loved a song.

How she'd twirl the few stray strands of hair that always managed to escape from her messy bun or ponytail while she was working.

The way she'd roll her eyes and stick her tongue out at her ex-boyfriend when he annoyed her, but she always waited to do it when he wasn't looking.

Then there was the fact she alternated between plain silk blouses and silly science T-shirts depending on her mood, and I knew her mood depended on the weather.

Worst of all, I knew how damn guilty wanting her made me feel.

After the shower, I dressed and got my stuff together and headed home. There was nothing for me at the office tonight, and packing my laptop away was one more barrier to me giving in and stalking her.

Dallas greeted me at the door. His tail whacked the floor in excitement as I turned off the alarm. He rolled to his back, and I crouched down and scratched his stomach. "I couldn't go through with it," I confessed. He kept flopping his tail around as he yelped back his response. "I know, I know. I've . . . got a problem, don't I?"

When I shook my head and stood, he hopped up to all fours and followed me to the back so I could let him outside. The small house Dallas and I shared had a decent-sized yard for him to run around and was conveniently located five minutes from my "sex" office and ten minutes from Falcon's secret headquarters at Bushkill Falls.

The team had nicknamed our headquarters, a cave behind the waterfalls, Batman's Lair. When we'd first started out, I'd had no choice but to acquire the bunker since I'd still been a wanted man. It was best to remain off-the-grid. I may have been safe from Uncle Sam coming for me, but there were still plenty of people around the world I'd prefer never knew what I did for a living. Or where I slept at night.

I folded my arms, leaning inside the doorframe while I waited for Dallas to wrap up his business.

Not even a minute into him searching for just the right spot to take a piss, my Apple watch buzzed with a gate alert, and I straightened with alarm. Aside from Camila, Griffin, and Gray, no one else knew where I called home.

"Dallas," I ordered. "In." I locked up and went over to my security system and pulled up the camera as the driver of a large, black SUV hit the call button.

My phone began burning a hole in my pocket as it rang. I grabbed it, unsure what to think at the sight of the name on screen. "Secretary Chandler," I answered. "Are these your men outside my house?"

"They're not my guys," he said in a somber tone. "They're the President's Secret Service. POTUS needs you at the White House. Now."

19

CARTER

WASHINGTON, D.C.

THE OVAL OFFICE WAS ONE OF THE LAST PLACES I WANTED to be. Too many memories unfurled in my mind in the space that was smaller than it appeared on the news.

"I can see you sitting behind the Resolute Desk one day, can't you?" Rebecca's words haunted me as I stared at the desk. How many times had she said that to me over the years? Thinking back now, it was like she'd been trying to plant the seed in my head, hoping it'd grow. It never did, no matter how much she watered it.

Standing on the Presidential Seal, I fixed my attention on the yellow-gold curtains behind the desk. They were drawn together, hiding tonight's full moon. "Where'd Secret Service take my dog?" I faced the only other man sharing the room with me.

Secretary Chandler's bloodshot eyes, and the slight wrinkle to his chest-candy-covered uniform, were a strong indicator shit had hit the fan. My involvement was still not clear, and that bothered the fuck out of me. "On a walk. He's fine, don't worry."

"Is Gray being summoned as well?" Considering Gray was a local, why hadn't he beaten me to the White House?

The Secretary took a seat on one of the couches at the center of the room, positioning his ankle over his knee. "My son doesn't know you're here, so no, he's not on his way."

Not what I'd expected to hear. "And who does know I'm here?" I peered at the door Secret Service had snuck me in. Apparently this wasn't a "front-door visit" situation.

"POTUS, of course. Myself."

Fucking obviously. Too tempted to free some of the top buttons of my white dress shirt, which I'd opted for instead of going with all black, I shoved my hands into my pants pockets since this wasn't the time to be casual.

"CIA Director Spenser, Secretary of State Mackenzie, and two others."

Mackenzie's name was a punch to the gut I didn't want or need. "Is Secretary Mackenzie joining us tonight, too?"

He nodded. "But she'll be in a bit later. She's not privy to some things yet."

"Like?" I arched a brow, knowing he wouldn't answer. So, I went ahead and gave one for him. "Something go wrong with your team of covert operatives? The SEALs only a few people know work for you all? The same team I'm not supposed to know about but do."

But if that was the case, that still didn't explain my presence.

"No, they're not in trouble," was all he gave me.

"But someone is?" I lifted my hands from my pockets, hating I didn't have one clue, not a fucking one, why the President would beckon me in the middle of the night to the executive West Wing.

The election was around the corner, but I wasn't exactly on his speed dial for a last-minute campaign donation or a strategy session on how to increase his already record-high poll numbers.

"Something like that." He began massaging his temples, but then jumped to his feet as the door opened.

Finally.

Waving off Secret Service and ordering them to close the door and leave us, the President wasted no time in cutting straight to me. Unlike the Secretary, he'd lost his suit jacket and tie at some point.

President Bennett's handshake wasn't what I'd been expecting, but he offered it to me anyway, and I accepted. "You a scotch man?"

"Sure." I didn't discriminate against whiskey. I liked all types. But the fact he knew I had a slight preference for scotch wasn't shocking. Big Brother was always watching (when I let them, at least).

"Thought so." He motioned to Secretary Chandler, a quiet request to get us drinks as he went over to the front of his desk, leaning against it, palms landing on each side of his body, eyes trained on the floor. The man was a dead ringer for the actor Denzel Washington. One of my favorite movies happened to be *Man on Fire*—not surprising given the plot. Fuck, if only the last five-plus years of my life had been fiction, too.

"Two nights ago, a research lab was hit," the President began as I took my drink from Gray's father. "And by hit, I mean half a billion in equipment was destroyed in an explosion, and multiple people were killed. It wasn't an accident, and it was bullets that took out the people, not the blast." He downed his drink and set aside the empty tumbler. "The thing is, we partnered with eleven other countries in a classified effort to work together on a cold fusion project. And now everyone is pointing fingers—blaming each other and playing the 'who betrayed who' game. We don't know who our friends or our enemies are right now, and tensions between the countries are high."

"Where do I fit in?" I took a moment to sip and savor the drink. Single malt. Probably Macallan from the taste. A good choice for delivering shit news.

"The hostile takeover of The Barclay Group was done by a shell company on behalf of the CIA," Secretary Chandler spoke up, filling in the pieces I should've seen coming, but that news still managed to unearth a motherfucking chill down my spine. "The Agency knew you'd never sell Barclay Energy outright, and their researchers were the closest in the nation to making cold fusion a reality. We coordinated a deal with Pierce Quaid to make it appear like a hostile takeover situation so you wouldn't, well, to be blunt, kill Quaid for losing the company."

For the first time in a long damn time, I felt my heart grow wings, attempting to break free from its darkness. "Tell me it wasn't the lab in Amsterdam."

That one nod from POTUS had everything going dead quiet, and I turned away. The ringing in my ears came next, as if an IED had detonated nearby, screwing up my senses. *This can't be happening.* I tore my hands through my hair. "The Secretary of State's daughter"—I swallowed hard and faced them—"is she dead?" I was on the verge of falling to the floor, knowing a hole would open and take me to hell if they said Diana was gone.

"Diana wasn't one of the ones recovered in the rubble. We believe she was taken, along with Pierce Quaid and several others," Secretary Chandler said, and the phantom ringing in my ears abruptly stopped.

"We don't know who did this, but there are a number of reasons they'd attack that lab. None of which are good." The President closed the space between us. "All surveillance footage was destroyed before the explosion. I sent in my guys on Bravo Team to sweep the area last night and discreetly check the place out, but they came up empty. The lab was highly secure and in a remote area, so there was no other CCTV footage within a five-mile radius."

Surveillance footage. "I need my laptop. Where'd Secret Service take my things? I had cameras installed at the lab. Ones no one would know about. Well-hidden. We may be able to see what happened before the explosion."

"How? Security at that place was tighter than a frog's ass." The Secretary was missing both the plot and the point.

"Not secure enough, considering what happened," I ground out, the irrational side of me taking over, ready to throw down with anyone who may have had a hand in Diana's abduction.

"Forget why or how he did it, just send someone to get his laptop." POTUS lifted his chin in a directive to get a move on.

Once it was only the President and myself in the office, I cut to the chase and asked, "Why am I here? I don't own Barclay anymore, thanks to the CIA. And you have your Teamguys, which includes your own son, to handle the mission and find out what happened and save Diana."

"Save Diana," he said back to me as if he knew those words held deep meaning to me.

And fuck, they did. If only I'd kept checking in on her, I'd have had a two-day head start in finding her.

"We believe this was an inside job, but it has to be an insider from one of the other eleven countries. The CIA director believes there are only a handful of people in this world who might have insight as to who was behind this, and that's where you come in."

"Criminals you can't get to talk, but I can," I said in understanding. "But that was when I was—"

"A wanted man. For the country, and for those missing scientists, we need you to become him again." His calm demeanor as he threw those words at me was a reminder he was a seasoned Commander in Chief and had once been an operator himself. He knew exactly what he was asking of me, and he had no choice.

"That's why Gray wasn't notified. I can't work with Falcon on this." *Not in the field, at least.*

"If anyone ever hurt my son or wife, I'd go scorched earth on the world, too." His hand slipped over his heart. "When this is over, I'll personally clear your name. Set the record straight once and for all."

Before I could summon a response, the door opened. I was disappointed to see the Secretary of State instead of my laptop. Where'd they bring my stuff? Fucking Virginia?

I hadn't come face-to-face with Susan since the day of Rebecca's funeral, and I wasn't sure if I was prepared to do it now.

"Carter," she greeted, tugging at the lapels of her black blazer. "You came."

"I didn't have much of a choice," I snapped, forgetting she was Diana's mother, and not just another thorn in my side.

"You weren't exactly my first pick." Her tone with me wasn't shocking. I'd been on the receiving end of it plenty of times at Rebecca's parties. "We don't know if whoever took her is aware she's my daughter, but once they find out, it'll make things more complicated in trying to get her back."

I began rolling up my sleeves, not giving a damn I was

exposing my tattoos while inside the Oval Office. Fuck protocol. "Finding Diana's my priority. The *whys* and *hows* as to why the lab was hit will be a byproduct of her rescue."

"We already have the best on the planet searching for her and the others." I wasn't sure if the President was directing his comment toward Susan or myself, but I assumed he was referring to his secret SEAL Teams in that statement. "I need you to do what they can't. Your focus has to be on who's behind the lab hit in Amsterdam. Can you do that for me?"

I respected the man enough not to get into a pissing match about how to handle the mission. If I needed to be a monster again, then so be it. I wasn't going to let Diana die. "Fine." He didn't need to know I had every intention of finding Diana first, because fuck rationality and orders. "I need a word with the Secretary alone before we continue."

"You have two minutes. I'll check on your laptop," Bennett said without rebuttal. He knew he needed my help, so he'd give me that time.

"I need to know if I can trust you," I said as soon as I was alone with Susan.

"Feeling is mutual." She kept her chin high, pretending I didn't scare her, but I could smell her fear. Not even her overly-rich-scented perfume could hide it.

"Do you still think I killed Rebecca?" Since that particular mission was classified and didn't pertain to this op, I had to assume POTUS hadn't told her Rebecca's killers were six feet under.

"I don't know who's responsible for her death, but the President assured me it wasn't you, or you wouldn't be standing in front of me right now." Her lip trembled, and it was the first time I'd seen her emotions slip to the surface. "My daughter needs you, and frankly, so does the country. Screw diplomacy in this case. You do whatever you have to do to get her back. I don't care what POTUS wants, I'm counting on you." Now *this* version of Susan I could get along with. But then she had to go and add, "Rebecca wouldn't want her to die, so if that's the motivation you need, think about her. Pretend it's your wife out there, and you have a chance to save her before it's too late."

I angled my head, staring her down. Losing my patience. "I don't need to pretend anything." That was part of the problem. I was already invested in this mission. I cared too much for a girl I barely knew.

Before we could finish our conversation, the President returned, along with Secretary Chandler holding my computer bag.

"What's going on?" Susan asked as I accepted the computer case and sat on one of the couches, quickly getting to work.

"Seems Dominick was spying on the company after the change in ownership," Secretary Chandler drawled, forgetting yet again this was a good thing, that there was hope I might be able to shed some light as to what happened two nights earlier.

Thankfully, I hadn't deleted the surveillance program from my laptop in an attempt to get over my obsession with Diana.

I opened up the hidden app and typed in the code to access the footage auto-saved there. "The last recorded clip before the signal was corrupted was on Monday at twenty-three hundred hours." I began working backward through the clips, relieved they were still there. "That means they didn't discover the cameras."

Susan sat next to me. "That's something."

I searched through the footage, identifying ten different

masked tangos armed to the teeth inside, then paused the moment Diana was on screen.

"Is she . . .?" Susan left off the word *dead* as she cupped her mouth.

I returned my focus to the laptop as one of the men lifted Diana from the ground and began carrying her to an exit. She was limp and lifeless in his arms.

My stomach turned, but I kept my shit together and rewound the footage farther back to see what happened to her before then.

I shouldn't have been surprised she'd put up a fight. She'd always come across as a strong woman to me. Her ex, on the other hand, had done nothing to help her, and it made me want to kill the asshole.

Rage burned through my veins as I took in the scene inside Diana's office. She'd resisted the bastards and fought while her ex hid behind her, then fled. I nearly lost my shit witnessing the masked man strike her in the face when she'd been distracted by something—effectively knocking her out. Another man I planned to identify, then murder with my bare hands.

"What do you see?" Secretary Chandler asked, and I skipped back to the scene and turned the computer to show him and POTUS. I used that time to get a grip so I could think through the problem of how to locate her.

"You have sound, too?" POTUS asked.

"Yeah, give me a second." I turned the screen and made a few adjustments to the program, bringing up the volume.

"What language are they speaking? Anyone recognize it? Eastern European, maybe?" Susan asked as we rewatched the footage unfold, this time starting from Diana being rendered unconscious and removed from the building up until the blast that destroyed the site. "We need a translator."

I listened closely, recognizing the language. "Serbian." The first woman I'd slept with after Rebecca had been Serbian. *Alyona Jovanovich.*

After I'd had the angel wings tattooed on my back, I'd gone back to Alyona's place. Ultimately, she'd helped me connect the dots to the smuggler that brought me to Rory McAdams—Red Robin Hood. I'd been indebted to Alyona for that, so I didn't take her down with the others. I supposed it was my luck I hadn't, because I'd be needing her again.

"We weren't working with Serbia on that project," Secretary Chandler echoed what I'd already assumed. "Must be hired mercenaries for whoever was behind this."

"I think I know how we can find whoever has Diana and the others." I set the laptop aside and stood. "Behind every powerful man is an—"

"An even stronger woman." Susan's words weren't lost on me.

Rebecca. Yeah, yeah, I fucking know. I suppressed my emotions so they didn't bleed into the room. "Are you familiar with Alyona Jovanovich?"

"Of course. She's on the same lists you once were." Secretary Chandler's eyes widened in a light-bulb moment. "You think she's behind this?"

"Not behind the attack, no, but she may know who is. And I can get her to tell me." I checked my watch, needing to be on a plane already. "Last I heard she was in Germany. My guess is Germany's one of the eleven countries you were working with? I'm betting you trust them as much as they trust you right now. So, you can't send a team in to take Alyona in for questioning." *Which is why I'm here.* "But there's only one way I can make this work." I hated what I was about to ask, but I had no choice. "Put me back on the

174

wanted list and give Alyona a justifiable reason as to why I'd come back to her for help after all these years."

"What kind of reason?" Susan asked, fidgeting with her suit jacket.

"Leak a story to the press that there's new evidence I murdered my wife for eleven billion dollars." I waited for the news to sink in before continuing, "Gray and the rest of Falcon can't be on the ground with me for this. I need my old crew."

"And what will you do?" Susan asked, managing to reclaim the same sharpness from minutes ago that her nerves had seemingly whittled away.

"What you all want me to do." *Be the man I once was and take down every son of a bitch responsible for setting a hand on Diana.* I took a pen and notepad from the desk and jotted down names that'd hopefully be the least offensive to Secretary Chandler. "Here." I dropped the pen and handed the list—which didn't include Griffin's name—to Chandler. No one needed to know he'd been part of those dark years with me unless *he* wanted it to be known. "See who you can pull in from this list while I get word out to Alyona I need to meet."

Chandler smoothed his thumb over the shiny stars on his collar. "Why do I feel like you're Bruce Willis giving us a list of his motley crew, and I have to go round them up like we're in some *Armageddon* movie?"

That gave me pause. The fact he'd make a parallel like that at a time like this. "Is this an Armageddon situation, sir?" When everyone remained quiet, my blood pressure spiked. "Does Diana know she wasn't really working on cold fusion?"

CARTER

"SHE WAS WORKING ON COLD FUSION." THE PRESIDENT WAS possibly the only man in the White House and all of D.C. who could stare a man like me dead in the eyes and say those words with a straight face.

Secretary Chandler lifted my list of names, waving the folded piece of paper in the air. He wanted out of this conversation and now.

What had they gotten themselves into? *Really* fucking into?

"Just tell me these names are all Americans with previous top-secret government clearance," Chandler pressed.

"Yes," I gritted out, only willing to drop my concerns about their work in Amsterdam for a greater, more urgent issue—locating Diana.

"Surprised Camila Hart's name isn't on here," Secretary Chandler said under his breath. "You don't think she might be useful to have on this op?"

You know about her visions, don't you? "She's off-the-grid at the moment. If I have to locate her and pull her in, I will. But for now, she stays out of this." I locked my arms over my chest, standing my ground. "This has to be handled my way. No questions. No objections. No need to know how. It won't take long for people to figure out I had a connection to the lab considering I once owned Barclay Energy."

"We figured as much." The President's brown eyes flicked from the list of names and back to me. "We assume you'll have a plan for that?"

I nodded. "Get my people. Leak the story to the press. Add me to the wanted list again," I quickly ordered. "Do that, and I'll get Diana back. And fix this mess you've found yourselves in. Rescuing Diana is my priority, the rest of the plan can go fuck itself in the meantime."

The President arched a brow. "What happened to you agreeing to my other team being search and rescue?"

"That was before I knew all of the details." Before he could deny anything about Diana's research again, I tacked on, "Also, finding Diana will help me figure out who's behind the hit."

The President took less than ten seconds to think about it, then jerked a thumb over his shoulder, focusing on Susan. "Find out who at the State Department speaks Serbian. Wake them up and get them here now."

She started to leave but stopped in place when I asked, "Who else knows I'm being brought in? You said two others aside from the CIA director know I'm here."

"The Secretary of Energy, Jared Felsely. And the chair of the Senate Select Committee on Intelligence." The President slipped his hands in his pockets, but I was more interested in the notable shiver from Susan.

"Which senator?" Eyes on Susan now, I couldn't help but wonder, why she was looking at me like she'd seen a ghost.

"Are you familiar with Craig Paulsen?" Secretary Chandler asked.

Susan's awkward throat clear as she resumed her path to exit the room had me stepping the fuck back. Memories crashed and burned through my mind. She knew something about that asshole. What else had he done to Diana?

I should've handled him years ago, but I'd been more dignified in my approach to pricks back then. Not anymore.

Once Susan left, I finally answered, "Yes, I know him. Why isn't Felsely or Paulsen here?" I assumed the CIA director was busy working with POTUS's SEALs, but the other two should've been present for a meeting like this. Then I could've hit Craig. Screw where I was standing, if he did anything to Diana, I'd stain the presidential rug with his blood.

"Felsely is handling the fallout. As for Paulsen, we thought it'd be best you two didn't have a face-to-face," Chandler shared. "He's not your biggest fan. The only part of this plan he'll like is—"

"Accusing me of killing my wife," I said gruffly, "and placing me back on the wanted list." I pointed to the laptop. "I need a room to work in. I'll make a copy of the footage for your Serbian translator, but the laptop never leaves my hands."

"Set him up," the President directed before Chandler could veto the idea. He motioned for me to follow him to a side door. "My private exit. Come with me."

I reached for the laptop, closed it, then tucked it under my arm, quietly following the President from the Oval Office into a hall and down a back flight of stairs before turning into a small, nearly empty room. My belongings, including my phone, were there waiting for me. They must've been expecting the meeting would go as it did. The only curveball was the footage I happened to have because of my stalker issues.

"You sure you don't want us to accuse you of something a little less *harsh*?"

"It's the only way this will work." I took a seat at the desk and opened the laptop. "I need my team at Falcon to work on the back end of things while I'm abroad. Give them clearance to this mission. Once you've read Gray and the team in, give them a list of the eleven other countries, and every person involved in the project." I lifted my hand, preparing for him to object. "They'll play ball with your SEALs, don't worry. It's not like my team hasn't worked with your people before. We need all the help we can get."

An unexpected smirk cut across his lips. "Your wife wanted you to be the President. At least, that's what Susan told me. You're good at giving orders, so what held you back from seeking Commander in Chief one day?"

I didn't want to think about Rebecca, but in a way, she got what she wanted—I'd made it to the Oval. Just not how she'd planned. "I think you know why. I don't like playing by the rules."

"What part of me pulling you into this op suggests I do?"

Considering he worked with off-the-books SEAL Teams using dark money to bypass Congress to get shit done, I had to believe him.

The President casually winked, then quietly left. Once the door clicked shut, I focused on the laptop, settling in to replay the footage. I went back to the minutes before the alarms started wailing, when Diana had been alone in her office with a colleague.

Turning on the volume, I listened again to what I'd heard Diana say. I'd done my best not to react to her words in front of the others in the Oval Office, but I couldn't hide it now.

"I'd wish my path never crossed with someone," she said, and the look in Diana's eyes had me uneasy again.

Me. It's me, isn't it? You wish you'd never met me. I didn't blame her, but it was the next part that did a motherfucking number on me. The moment she'd changed her mind to wishing Rebecca never died cut me in half. *Of course you'd say that.* It was a good-person thing to say. She was someone I'd never deserve, but she had more than earned my help, and that I could give her.

Like the good psychopath I was, I watched the scene a few more times, including the shocked little O-shape on her mouth after she'd bumped into her computer right before the attack.

What'd you figure out?

I finally went for my phone and made my first call. "Hey, sorry to wake you," I said as soon as Griffin picked up.

"It's okay, I'm sure Tomas was about to get up soon to be fed," Griffin answered, sounding groggy and out of it. "What time is it?"

I checked the time on the laptop, my stomach turning at the image of Diana paused on screen. "It's zero three hundred."

"Who is it?" I overheard his wife, Savanna, ask.

"Carter, sugar," he told her. "Go back to sleep."

Hearing her voice was going to make this next part that much harder. "I'm sitting in an office at the White House right now."

"Yeah, okay. Wasn't expecting that." Now he was awake.

I closed the laptop before I lost my mind staring at the screen. "The President needs a favor from me. And to do it, I need to become the man I was after Rebecca died. You were at my side then, and I hate to ask this of you, but—"

"I'm on my way," was all he said, zero hesitation.

"This is going to be different," I warned. "And you're married with a baby now. If you want to opt out, say the word, and we're good. The White House will know you were with me back then, and—"

"On my way." He hung up before I could offer him a way off the hook again.

Relieved, but still feeling guilty for asking for his help, I did my best to shrug off the emotions I wasn't all that accustomed to and focused on the next call.

I scrolled through my contacts, stopping at the name LIONESS in my phone. I'd never been more grateful I'd opted not to delete Alyona's number.

It'd be morning in Germany, so I wouldn't be waking her. True to form, she didn't make me wait long, picking up on the second ring.

"Carter. Fucking. Dominick." My name came from her mouth slowly and with purposeful intent. It actually pained me to hear her say it. "Who pissed you off this time to have you coming back to me?"

21

DIANA

UNKNOWN LOCATION

I'M ALIVE. THEY NEED ME, I HAD TO REMIND MYSELF, catching my thoughts starting to spin out of control again. Fear was a vise grip, securely holding my throat. So strong it squeezed off the blood flow to my brain, making me even dizzier.

Bahar, William, Bonnie, and I were inside a windowless room, most likely a basement based on the ground and stale air. Our hands and feet were bound, backs to the concrete wall and our asses parked on the cold cement floor.

I had no idea where the others from the lab were, but one of the masked men had wordlessly plucked Pierce, along with his dog, from the room a few hours ago. The fact he'd yet to return didn't do wonders for my current state.

Every night since we'd been taken, we'd been moved together to a new location. Tossed like trash into the back of a truck where we'd spend hours on the road before being dumped into another dark, dank room like we were in now.

We knew our captors spoke in Serbian because Bahar's

grandmother was from Serbia, and although Bahar didn't speak the language, she'd recognized it.

The masked men hadn't spoken another word in our presence since the night of the hit, though, no matter how much we'd begged them to tell us what was going on. And William had done quite a lot of begging—offering everything from our research on a silver platter to every dime in his bank account if they let *him* go.

"It feels like nighttime again," Bahar said, not lifting her head from where it rested on my shoulder just as the door to our prison opened.

"Diana Mackenzie." A man loomed in the shadows of the doorway, then began stalking toward us. William cowered against me on my other side as the masked stranger said, "Secretary of State's daughter, hmm?"

You know I'm more than a scientist. Does that make me your bargaining chip, too? Leverage?

The man quietly took a knee before me. It was too dark in the windowless room, and I'd lost my glasses at the lab, so I couldn't clearly see his eyes through the slit of his mask, but I could feel the dangerous gleam pointed my way. A wicked energy buzzed off him.

I tucked my bent knees closer to my chest as he cocked his head, a smile probably concealed beneath the mask.

"Time to go." He reached into his pocket, and before I knew what was happening, he jabbed a needle into the side of my neck.

"Wait, where are you taking her?" Bahar yelled as my body immediately went limp. Bound hands or not, she tried to reach for me anyway. "Don't take her," she pleaded as he lifted me into his arms, carrying me like a small child.

My arms hung dead at my sides. Eyes rolling back in response to what he'd stuck into my body.

Once in the hall, I sealed my lids tight against the bright overhead lights, unable to handle the sharp contrast.

"Where . . . are you . . ." I slurred, my head lolling to the side.

"One more stop, then off to your next destination."

22
CARTER

JUST OUTSIDE HAMBURG, GERMANY

"Are we sure about this?" Easton asked from the backseat of the rental SUV. We were parked outside Alyona's mansion.

Sometimes I couldn't believe I'd willingly walked into her arms, but she'd been the one to bow to me, not the other way around.

I turned off the engine, catching Easton's eyes in my rearview mirror. "The plan will work."

"PACE," Griffin said, a reminder to Easton who'd been out of both the military and mercenary game for a while now. "We'll be solid. Don't worry."

"Right." Easton sighed dramatically. "The military and their fucking acronyms. You didn't use them back when we, well, you know."

Killed people for a living without government consent? Yeah, I remember. It's why POTUS has me here now.

But there was a reason for PACE planning, and it'd worked with Delta and would now. A primary, alternate, contingency, *and* emergency plan to mitigate risk of operational failure. And I would *not* lose Diana no matter fucking what.

"Just the three of us are really going to walk into this woman's house?" Easton wrapped a hand over my seat, and I unbuckled to swivel around to better face him. To put his concerns to bed before we entered Alyona's home.

"Your nerves are unexpected," Griffin said before I could.

"Too many of us will scare her off," I pointed out. "But me coming alone would alarm her."

From the list of twelve names I'd provided Secretary Chandler, he'd managed to pull together four others aside from Easton (and Griffin). Those four, along with Dallas, were parked ten klicks away from our current location waiting for next steps.

Shockingly, Secretary Chandler hadn't been that surprised when Griffin rolled up at the airport terminal to join me.

"Something told me you worked with him back during his fuck-around-and-find-out days," the Secretary had said to Griffin, and I was pretty sure that comment was Gray's dad trying to get back in my good graces.

"It's been almost seventy-seven hours since Diana was taken," I tossed out, probably more so for myself; a reminder the chances of locating her became slimmer with every passing hour.

Alyona's guards patiently waited outside our SUV, giving us time. Respect. That had to be her doing.

"Yeah, okay," Easton finally relented.

Once we stepped outside, a guard broke forward from the pack of others. "We need to check for weapons." He stepped closer by one of the lampposts so I could get a better look at him.

Franz. Pretty sure that was his name. He'd seen me

coming and going from Alyona's bedroom back in the day, and she more than likely chose him to make me feel more at ease. (Or to fuck with me, which was probably more likely.)

"I have a Glock holstered at my side." I shifted my black jacket out of the way to reveal my piece. "Told that to your guys at the gate. We all do."

Her security guards out front had externally swept the vehicle for explosives and trackers before letting us roll through. Standard procedure, and I would've expected nothing less. Hell, I would've been worried we were driving into an ambush had they not done a sweep.

"We have no plans to hand over our sidearms," I let Franz know. "But go ahead and check for other weapons," I gave him the go-ahead, and he patted me down while two of his other men did the same for Griffin and Easton. "I need to grab the suitcase of cash from the trunk."

"Do it," Franz said, and once I secured the suitcase, I popped it open to let him check. After a satisfied nod from him, I snapped it closed.

We were escorted down a lit-up sidewalk and around to the back of the home, then ushered through a door directly into a living room.

"She'll be right down," Franz shared once we were inside the ornate space, a fireplace roaring. He motioned for his men to leave, and they followed him out, leaving us alone.

Setting aside the briefcase, I approached the fire, resting my hands on the mantel and welcoming the heat.

Alyona didn't make us wait long, which was good, because my patience for everything had evaporated the second I'd learned Diana had been taken.

"Dominick," she said, her distinct and familiar sharp tone easing some of my lingering concerns.

I pushed away from the mantel to face her. Alyona was a

gorgeous woman, I couldn't deny that. In her forties. Smart and sophisticated. Not that I'd felt anything more than a below-the-belt reaction to her in the past, but today, I felt nothing other than the need to hurry through this.

"Been too long," she said, the edge to her voice softening slightly. Her English was as flawless as the five other languages she spoke, and she somehow always managed to hide her accent.

Time didn't appear to change her, or her wardrobe. Black dress pants covered her long legs. Her nude-colored heels clicked across the hardwoods as her dark green eyes remained steady on me as if it were only us in the room.

Her iPad was all that truly caught my attention as she maneuvered my way.

No formal handshake or a hug from her, which I appreciated. With her free hand, she shifted her hip-length long black hair to her back, and I took that as my cue to open up the conversation.

"Did you find who took her?" I lifted my chin in the direction of the suitcase. "Three million like you requested."

Intense emerald eyes narrowed on me. There was going to be a catch, wasn't there? "If I tell you what you want to know, you have to let me know something first."

I casually peered at Griffin and Easton hovering near the door, giving us space. I didn't need space. Just answers. Just . . . *Diana.*

I pushed my hands into my pockets. "You want to know why I'm after her."

"May we play a little guessing game first?"

"You have my permission to guess," I said, biting down on my back teeth, drawing my face a bit closer to hers. Staring her down. Playing her game for the sake of Diana. Giving her what she craved. Her submission. *My* dominance.

"I saw the news." Her eyes could captivate a man into surrender. *Most* men. Not me. Not anymore, at least, but I had to let her think she was managing to seduce me.

I parted my lips a fraction. Allowed my jaw to visibly strain. Let her witness a slight twitch in my hand at my side. Gave her the impression I was seconds away from slapping her ass. Or giving her the hand necklace I knew she craved.

Flames from the fire cast a glow across her face. "There's a warrant for your arrest. You're being accused of murdering your wife," she stated almost matter-of-factly. "But we both know that's not true. You came to *me* to help you find a connection to her killer years ago."

I waited for her to continue, to let her go on with her guess since I'd given her permission to do so.

"I know you haven't been hiding somewhere these last few years. I heard about what happened at The Sapphire. Tell me, did you really kill that assassin with a fork?"

I dipped down so we were eye level. "What do you think?" I murmured darkly, continuing to play the role, knowing damn well she'd have learned about what happened at that hotel long before today. Because she knew everything. That was why I was there in the first place.

Now, if she also discovered I'd been at that hotel working alongside Gray Chandler for a job with Falcon, and not for other reasons, that could be an issue.

"I think there's more than meets the eye when it comes to you. Always has been. But your gaze is a bit softer now. You're not as coldhearted, are you?"

Not what I wanted to hear from her. I needed to take the control back before we'd be forced to move to our alternate plan. "You've yet to guess your theory as to why I want Diana," I reminded her. "You have three seconds." My tone dropped lower that time, letting her know what I'd do if she defied me.

I hated her for making me play this game with Diana's life on the line. Fuck this cat-and-mouse shit.

"Unfortunately, we don't have time for me to disobey so you can punish me." Her expression softened. "Or I should say, this girl you're after doesn't have time."

I did my best to hide my knee-jerk reaction to that warning, knowing if she saw how much I cared about Diana, we'd wind up moving straight to the final backup plan of PACE. *Emergency.*

Alyona lifted the iPad between us, eyes still locked on mine, but she didn't yet offer it. "Your company, all that you had left of your late wife, was lost earlier this summer. If you truly wanted it, you would've fought for it. I know that much." She continued with her guess of my situation, and added, "Diana Mackenzie worked there and stayed on with the new owners. She's the Secretary of State's daughter. And based upon what I discovered, her mother ran in the same social circles as your late wife. Inherited twenty-five million when Rebecca died and used it to help climb the political ladder to where she is now." Tipping up an eyebrow, she finished with, "And now you're once again being accused of killing Rebecca the week her daughter goes missing." She finally handed over the iPad. "How'd I do?"

I accepted the iPad and cocked my head. "You've yet to tell me why I want Diana for myself."

She smiled. "Mmm. That's easy. You believe Susan Mackenzie is setting you up, but you don't know why. All of this can't be a coincidence, that much you know. So, you're after her daughter while you figure out what's happening. Letting people know that if you fuck around, you find out. I always found that wildly sexy about you."

Her eyes skated down my body to my belt. A flick of her tongue between her lips before she added, "Among other things."

Once we made eye contact again, I tipped my head, congratulating her on being right. She'd drawn the conclusion I'd *hoped* she would. And it was also one I hadn't shared with Susan or the others, for obvious reasons. "You were always too good at solving mysteries. Takes the fun out of it," I said casually, lowering the tablet to my side. "Do you know where I can find Diana? Who's behind the lab hit?" I'd only given her a handful of details on our call yesterday, just enough to help her help me.

"Of course," she mused, and relief filled my chest. "You have less than five hours before your chances of finding her become nearly impossible." She pointed toward the iPad. "Once she's smuggled onto the cargo ship, I won't be able to help you anymore."

Cargo ship? I gripped the iPad tighter, doing my best to hide my reaction. "What do you know?"

From the corner of my eye, I spied Griffin and Easton moving in closer at the news we had intel to go on.

Alyona turned to the side, staring at the fire while folding her arms. "You'll be indebted to me after this. For more than three million. Are we clear?"

"Crystal," I hissed.

"And I'll want to finish what we started here as well."

There wasn't a chance we'd ever have sex again, but I forced a nod.

She peeked at her wristwatch without uncrossing her arms. "A few hours ago, the Serbians who took her from the lab separated Diana from some of the other hostages. Those men run a lucrative smuggling operation out of Riga, Latvia. Based on the recon work I had my people do, they'll be placing her on that ship just before nine a.m. Destination unknown."

Human traffickers. I hung my head, chills racking over my skin, heating my body.

Trying to keep it together, I focused on what I knew and could control. Latvia was less than a two-hour flight away. We could get there in time.

"Since when do you associate with traffickers who smuggle people?" I'd never have fucked her had she been that particular brand of evil.

"I don't," she shot out, wrinkling her nose in offense. "Luckily for you, people I know do."

I wasn't sure if I believed her, but as long as the intel was good, that was all that mattered.

"The details on where we think she's being held, along with the number of possible enemy combatants, are on that iPad."

"You know anything else?" I asked.

"Nothing aside from the men who took her are elite. The best of the best." She unfolded her arms to grip my bicep. "Be careful."

"When have I ever not been?" I let go of a deep breath, still uneasy. What was she holding back? It was the same bad gut feeling I'd had when the President refused to talk about the project Diana had really been working on. "If you learn anything else . . ."

She squeezed my arm, then let go of me. "Be seeing you around."

I nodded my goodbye, then signaled to Griffin and Easton to move.

The second we were outside and far away from her guards, Easton dove right in to giving me shit. "Punish her? Really? You two used to hook up? I mean, I get it. She's smoking hot, but she's a criminal. Isn't that a bit below the belt, even for you."

"Redact that part of the conversation from your memory," was all I could manage out, because I hated how right he was.

"Going after traffickers again, though," Easton said, thankfully dropping the other conversation, "it's like old times."

My chest constricted at the thought. Something told me this wasn't like anything we'd ever dealt with before. But we'd soon find out what we were truly up against, and smugglers would most likely be the least of our problems.

CARTER

RIGA, LATVIA

THE SUN DIDN'T RISE UNTIL 0800 IN LATVIA THIS TIME OF the year, which meant daylight was around the corner, making it minutes until the sun was fully fucking aroused, showering light down over us.

The port near our target location was already too crowded for us to blend in and enter that way. I'd had no time to locate a helo for us to make a fast-rope entrance, not that it would've been the best option anyway. No chance we could make a HAHO insertion happen, let alone find a suitable plane to jump from. That left us with a risky on-foot ground approach.

Griffin was on overwatch on the building across the street as our lead sniper. Easton was our radio comms guy. Teddy, a former EOD once attached to SEAL Team Three, was our lead breacher. The rest of us, along with Dallas, were two seconds away from hitting the closed-down and abandoned clothing factory one kilometer from Riga Port Terminal.

We were suited and masked up in black. Nothing

identifiable other than the color of our eyes. NODs—night vision—weren't needed with daylight on our asses, and there was only one entrance for us to breach.

"This is Alpha Two," Griffin came over comms. "You're all clear from my vantage point. Over."

"This is Alpha One, roger. Out." I motioned for my team to move into positions, then took a knee, readying my M4. "Breacher up."

Teddy began wrapping small pieces of det cord around the doorframe of the entrance while we kept eyes on the parking lot and neighboring empty buildings for movement.

Fuse lit. A small bang. And Teddy had us in so we could move on target.

Entering first, I looked around, finding no immediate threats. I patted Dallas's head, giving him the go-ahead to move ahead of me. The camera attached to his brain bucket—aka, helmet—was sending a real-time signal of video footage to the screen strapped to my wrist.

Dallas stayed ahead of me, and every time he cleared a room, the team flowed in behind and checked again, doing a secondary sweep.

No working security cameras visible in the hall or rooms from what I could tell. And aside from mannequins and trash on the floors, there were no signs of life.

The silence on level one had me on edge, worried Alyona had played us and we were walking into a trap—or even worse. That we were too late and Diana was already inside one of the hundreds of containers on one of the dozens of ships docked at the port.

I lifted my fist to hold position the second Dallas signaled to me he heard something. He stopped at the bottom of a metal staircase, ears up and tail moving. I directed the team to stack up and move into formation.

As we crept up the steps, I spotted the door up top open like an invitation. They were more than likely waiting for us after hearing the breaching charge go off.

Once up top, I opted not to send Dallas in ahead. Too risky. Instead, I ordered him to hold his position, then brought my back near the doorway in preparation to round the hall.

Clearing a tight corner with a rifle meant needing to remove the buttstock from my shoulder pocket. I punched it up over my shoulder to reduce the length by a foot, and the second I moved around the bend, I re-engaged to the normal position and fired at the first tango in sight.

My team followed me into the dark hall. Using my scope to paint the targets with a red laser, and the suppressor to conceal the flash and reduce noise, I took out the next target that appeared in the hall.

We peeled off every tango one by one as they emerged into view on that level, taking them out before they had a chance to return fire.

A moment later, my gun jammed, so I let the combat sling around my body catch it and went for my secondary, the pistol holstered at my side. I double-tapped the guy coming at me from the nearby room, then went inside, and my heart fucking stopped at the sight.

There were at least thirty terrified people huddled together on the floor.

Human trafficking pieces of garbage and their buyers were behind this, and all the other rooms over all the years, and the anger burned in my stomach right up into my throat.

But Diana— "She's not here," I said as I dialed in on that horrible reality.

"The other rooms are clear," Teddy said on approach.

"Alpha Two," I began over comms, "package is not here. No jackpot."

"This is Alpha Two, that's a good copy. Preparing for plan two," Griffin announced, which meant we were heading for the port.

I went back into the hall in search of one of the masked tangos, hoping someone was still alive. Locating a moaning asshole holding his side from a gunshot wound, I lifted him toward my face by his vest, snarling, "Where. The. Fuck. Is. She?"

24

DIANA

My vision was blurry, more so from the drugs than the loss of my glasses, but . . . where were we going now?

Up until a few minutes ago, I'd been in a room full of other people, none of whom spoke English. The stench of our sweat and fear had soaked the walls and bled right into my pores.

Our captors had suddenly started hollering at each other in Serbian, and one of them had taken me by the arm, pulling me from the crowded space.

I'd dug my heels in, trying to resist him. My hands were bound, but at some point after they'd taken me away from Bahar and the others, they'd removed the rope from around my ankles. Of course, trying to walk in my drugged condition was a joke. The times they'd permitted me a bathroom break, I probably looked like a drunken sailor on leave after a bar brawl, wobbly and ambling every which way. So, where would I have gone?

My effort to remain in that room had been fruitless. The guy had plucked me from the ground and tossed me over his shoulder, then ran me down a flight of stairs before chucking me into the open bed of a pickup truck, which was where I was now.

Focusing back on my current state, I blinked several times, trying to get a handle on the change from the dark setting I'd grown accustomed to, to the slow rise of the sun kissing the world good morning.

We were still on the move, and from the looks of it, heading toward water. The light was too much for my eyes to be sure, though. The very thing I could rely on to shed light on my current location and situation was completely overwhelming me, so I forced my eyes closed.

I hadn't eaten in days. Only sips of water were provided to keep me alive and semi-lucid. Drugs may have still been knocking around my system, but so was the will to fight and protect myself. With my feet still free to move, I knew this would be my only chance to escape.

A blaring horn sounded from somewhere. Opening my eyes, I looked around, remembering I needed a plan to get away. Damn the drugs for making me forget so fast.

Two masked men were in the back of the truck with me, and it appeared only one person was inside the cab.

The guy at my right didn't bother to hold on to me. He'd never expect me to go from rag doll to action figure. *Now to actually do it.*

If somehow I could channel a heavy dose of adrenaline, I could jump over the side. I knew how to properly tuck in my limbs to reduce the chance of breaking bones upon impact, but in my altered state, could I actually do it? I had to try. To save myself. No one was coming for me. Whoever these people were, they wanted me alive, so they wouldn't kill me. I continued to pump myself up despite the drugs trying to lure me back into a foggy haze of comfort. Telling myself over and over again, *I'll escape. I will. Then I'll find someone to help those people back there.*

A bump in the road sent me colliding with the enemy next to me, and he shoved me away. We were on a backroad, not a highway. Going fast but not fast enough to kill me when I jumped.

With the person across from me looking away, sights set elsewhere, a hand to his ear as if trying to listen to someone or something, that was my cue to exfil, as Dad would say.

No time for another pep talk or countdown, I used the force of everything I had in me and pushed upright to standing, then threw myself over the side. Curling my body up, bound wrists lifted to cover my face, I braced for impact.

The grass alongside the small road didn't do much to cushion my fall.

The sounds of screeching brakes echoed all around me as I rolled, tumbling down a hill. Doing my best to ignore the aches in my body, only focusing on the need to survive, I kept my elbows pinned inward and hands over my face as I fell.

When I finally came to a stop, I made it to my knees, doing my best to get my bearings. I needed to see where to go and pinpoint the threats. Thankfully, my vision wasn't too bad, and I was only slightly farsighted; I could clearly make out objects and people at a distance as well.

By some miracle, I made it to my feet. Adrenaline compelled me forward while I peeked over my shoulder to see three masked and armed men coming for me.

Shouting, not shooting. Gaining ground, though.

I picked up my pace, unsure where I was going but not caring as long as it was away from them.

I spied ships off in the distance, so I began hauling ass toward them, praying my legs would keep going and not give out.

"Stop," someone yelled behind me, opting for English as if that'd make me come to my senses and listen. "Stop, or I'll shoot."

I ignored the warning until a noise whistled by my head and punctured the metal triangular-shaped sign alongside me. I froze in place, unable to raise my hands in surrender because of my bound wrists.

Without my momentum to launch me forward and keep me going, my body gave out, and I fell to my knees.

The next shot fired wasn't at me. I didn't think so, at least.

Breathing hard, I sat on my heels and chanced another look back to see what was happening.

There were more men jumping out of a vehicle now. Same all-black clothes. Also armed.

Unable to tell everyone apart, and not sure if these new people were the good guys or just a different brand of enemy, I knew I had to run again and get to the ships for help.

Get up, Diana. Get up. Finally on my feet, tears flying down my face, I started to speed walk while yelling, "Help!"

A man wearing a bright orange safety vest and construction helmet was on approach.

But . . . *shit. He has a gun.* The man charged my direction, and I was so fatigued and disoriented, I wasn't sure what to do.

I froze and my shoulders startled back at the whistling sound flying by me again. I was a bit slow to react, but nothing hit me. Maybe whoever was shooting hadn't missed. Maybe the bullet wasn't meant for me. It connected solidly with the guy in the orange vest instead.

A second shot nailed him just as an arm snaked around my midsection and someone lifted me from the ground.

I gasped and did my best to resist. To break free from

whoever was holding me, trying to steal away the freedom I'd been close to tasting.

"Stop fighting, Diana." That husky voice rasped against the shell of my ear as he squeezed me tighter against him. "It's me."

No, no it's not . . . you. It can't be. It was a hallucination. The drugs.

More shots exploded around us, and he let go of me, only to sling me around like I was paper-light, using himself as a shield, protecting me from incoming fire.

He aimed his pistol, shooting someone dressed nearly identical to him, but minus the combat helmet.

Too worried my mind was playing tricks on me, and that this wasn't a rescue, I took the opportunity to run again.

Not even two seconds into my escape, I tripped on something and dropped back down to my knees, scraping exposed skin as I twisted to avoid landing on my face. The rope around my wrists was finally loose enough to wiggle my hands free and I desperately pulled at it, finally getting my hands under me and pushing up to all fours.

"Diana." There was that rough voice again at the back of my neck. Desperation in the tone as he neared me.

Shaking and unable to get to my feet, I started to crawl, but I didn't make it far.

An arm looped around my body, but I quickly rolled to my back and lashed out. Kicking. Punching. Moving every part of me, as I struggled to force this guy away.

Because no, it's not you. My delusional brain is out of whack.

The masked man straddled my hips, using the strength of his thighs to keep me pinned there, and gathered my wrists in one of his gloved hands, effectively stopping me from striking again.

"Time to move," I heard someone yell out. "We have incoming."

The man on top of me holstered his sidearm and pushed the rifle hanging around his chest to the side to reach for his —*belt???*

My eyes went wide as his big hand deftly flew over the buckle of his black belt. He had it undone in a second. Then one more second, followed by a snap, and the belt was free from his hips.

He was too close for me to make out his eyes, but there was something familiar about him I wanted to cling to.

"Not you. It's not you," my protest of denial punctured the air, and I tried to break free from his hold again.

"It is me," was all the man said before he stood, peeling my upper body from the ground and . . .

Ohhh shit, you're going to tie me up with that.

"Sorry about this," he grunted, then secured the belt around me, restraining my arms by buckling them down at my sides. Next thing I knew, he had me in the air and over his shoulder.

A fresh wave of gunfire pounded the air, and I caught sight of a dog wearing a helmet running our direction along with two other masked armed men.

"Who—who are you? For real?" I cried as I continued bouncing against his body as he ran with me.

"I told you," he gritted out while abruptly taking a knee. He had his sidearm in his hand in one swift movement, shooting someone that seemingly came from nowhere.

"Carter?" I whispered, doing my best to believe it really was him.

"Yes," he hissed. "It's me."

My heart fluttered. It grew wings of hope that this was real, and I finally slipped free from fight-or-flight mode. The drugs remaining in my system took over, numbing my mind and saving me from the aches and pain in my body as the adrenaline retreated.

And this time, I let the drugs win, slowly succumbing to the darkness. Because if I was with Carter, I knew I was safe.

25

CARTER

Money buys a lot of things. Today, I needed it to buy us temporary lodging. I didn't want to be on the road any longer than necessary. I didn't think anyone was searching for the BMW we'd "borrowed" once we'd crossed into Latvia, but I'd feel safer once my team regrouped.

My team and I had split up fifteen minutes ago. I'd left four men behind to tie up loose ends, including getting those thirty-plus people who'd been in that room to safety. Without those men with us, we were more vulnerable than I wanted to be.

"Stop up there," I ordered.

"A church?" Easton passed a puzzled glance to Griffin, who smirked but never took his eyes off the road.

"Not the church. The rectory next door." I couldn't tell if that term or my request was causing him so much confusion, so I clarified, "The priest's home."

"Yeah, uh, I suppose no one will search for us there." Easton's hesitation wasn't lost on me, nor was his shrug and shake of the head.

Our options for a temporary location were fairly limited,

so we didn't have much of a choice, not with Diana riding with us. The belt I'd used to secure her arms to her sides was back around my waist, and she was stretched out on the seat between me and Dallas, her head resting in my lap.

We may have ditched our helmets, masks, and gloves once we'd exfil'ed, and our rifles were now stowed in the trunk, but we didn't exactly give off "you can trust us" vibes. I wasn't sure how this was going to go when we knocked on the priest's door.

Once parked, I waited for Griffin to hop out from behind the wheel and open my door. "Get the bag of cash from the trunk," I directed while shifting Diana's head to the leather so I could slide out.

Dallas jumped out and remained protectively on alert, glued to my side. I leaned in to carefully pull her out, draping her jeaned legs over my one arm to carry her. I lifted my chin to Easton. "See if he's home."

Nodding, Easton walked ahead of us to the small ranch home a few hundred meters away from where the cathedral sat bathed in morning light.

From the corner of my eye, I spotted Griffin coming up alongside us with the bag of cash—something I never left home without.

Griffin shot me a lopsided grin. "Feels like old times."

Only Griffin knew I used to visit the confessional. Not that I'd intentionally shared that with him. After he'd witnessed me walking into a church with money and leaving without it a few years back, I spilled the truth to him over a bottle of scotch.

Diana began stirring in my arms, moaning a little. I considered shielding her from the sun in case that was bothering her, but maybe some vitamin D wouldn't be such a terrible thing.

When the priest opened up, appearing on his doorstep in his robes, Easton cut to it, asking, "Will you help us?"

The priest was probably in his late fifties or early sixties. Black hair with gray at his temples. Glasses covered his eyes, and those eyes were fixed on Diana, lying limp in my arms.

Hopefully, he didn't see us as mercenaries, a danger to him and anyone else inside, and slam the door in our faces. The last thing I wanted was to force his hand in helping us, but I knew this was likely our path of least resistance.

I stepped closer, drawing my eyes to Diana to help emphasize why we were on his doorstep. "She's injured. We need a place to check and clean her wounds." Emotion pinched up into my throat. What if something serious was wrong with her? "We need to borrow your home for a few hours."

Tipping my head, I gave Griffin a quiet signal to step forward. He unzipped the duffel bag to show the cash to the priest, and the man's eyes widened in surprise.

"Do you have a medic kit? Anything we can use to help her?" I carried on, beginning to worry he didn't speak English. I'd been in such a hurry to get her to safety, I'd forgotten the entire world didn't speak one language.

"Do you know any English?" Griffin asked, reading my thoughts.

"I do," the priest finally spoke up, eyes on me now.

"We rescued her from human traffickers." I decided to go with a dose of honesty. Lying to a priest wouldn't get me anywhere, and the truth was miserable enough. Hopefully, we could garner his sympathy so he'd assist us. "There could be more men out there looking for her. We just need a safe space for an hour or two."

"She doesn't look good," the priest said somberly, zeroing in on the dried blood on her forearm. He probably didn't miss the bruises on her body as well. Contusions from the fight she put up that first night along with that wild but bold move she'd pulled when jumping from a moving vehicle.

"Possibly drugged, too," I shared. "Considering how long she's been missing for, most likely nothing to eat in days."

"I'll help." The priest moved from the doorway and relief swelled inside me as he waved us in.

I repositioned Diana in my arms and took the lead. Griffin, Easton, and Dallas trailed in behind us.

"In here." The priest opened a bedroom and pointed inside. "Set her on my bed."

"It's best if you don't stay here with us," I told him as I laid her down.

Diana's head rolled to the side. Her dry skin and lips were starved of adequate hydration, and I had to swallow the rage bubbling up inside me at the sight of her arms sliding lifeless to the bed. I'd already killed almost everyone who'd gone near her today, but I was itching to remove their limbs one by one.

"If you can point us to your medical supplies, then head over to your church and close up for the day, that'd be helpful," Griffin said, speaking for me as I finally took in the full extent of Diana's situation.

She was so pale, and even in sleep I could see her exhaustion. The hollowness under her eyes, her shallow breathing, the lack of resistance in her limbs gutted me. What if there were other injuries not visible to the eye? *What if they . . .?* I shut down that thought immediately before the priest dipped into my mind and discovered me visualizing murdering a half a dozen people. Could he see my thoughts? Or was that just God?

Dallas jumped onto the bed and curled up next to Diana, setting his head on her abdomen.

I subtly cleared my throat, pushing thoughts of vengeance to the back of my mind, and faced the others in the room as the priest shared, "There's a box of clothes in the office from the clothing drive we had last week. There might be something she can wear."

"Thank you." It was a kind gesture, and soothed some of the suspicion and worry that he was about to toss us out or turn us in. We wouldn't need clothes from him, though. Diana's mother had provided some of her things before we'd flown out. But that bag was in the SUV with Teddy and the others. So, maybe . . .

The priest stepped before me, and I went still as he removed a large silver crucifix from around his neck. "Something tells me you need this more than I do." He gestured for me to bow my head. Unsure what I was doing, I did as he asked, allowing him to place the necklace on me.

Going from a rifle across my body earlier to now a cross —not how I'd expected my morning to go. I closed my palm around the crucifix. "I don't need this."

"You do, my son." He patted my chest and gave me a nod, the warning not to argue coming across loud and clear. "The church can use the money, though. It'll help a lot of people." He accepted the bag from Griffin, then motioned for him to follow him out. "I'll take you to where I keep my medical supplies."

With Easton hovering by the doorway, I instructed, "Take the car and check in with the others. See where they're at with intel gathering and helping those people get free."

"You sure you don't want backup here just in case?" Easton asked, studying me closely.

Realizing I was still gripping the crucifix inside my fist, I let it go. For whatever reason, the necklace both weighed me down and grounded me at the same time. "We'll be fine. I'll work on getting us a new location to go to next. I still have a friend or two in this part of the world." Well, friend was a loose term for assholes who thought I was also an asshole, but they loved the smell of money more than anything, and I reeked of that. "Go," I insisted. "Call me the second you have news. I'll reach out to POTUS to inform him the package is secure."

That "package" softly whimpered, and I turned toward her as she stirred. Dallas lifted his head and licked her cheek before returning his head to her stomach.

"Be in touch," Easton said on his way out. I nodded, unable to rip my eyes away from the sight of my best friend curled up next to the woman I'd been fantasizing about for months.

She's safe. I had to keep reminding myself of that. *The plan worked. Alyona came through, and now—*

"He had a banana bag. Shocking but good news," Griffin said on the move, joining us again. He set a few things on the nightstand by the bed, then busied himself with setting up the portable IV for her.

Dallas appeared to have no plans to go anywhere. *You're trying to claim her as yours, huh, boy?* The little mind reader lifted his head and gave me a light howl before snuggling up next to her again.

"You should get these wounds cleaned, too. Check her for other injuries," he said once he had the IV started. "It's a bit wild we're rescuing her again, don't you think?"

"There's something I should probably tell you." Unholstering my sidearm and setting it by the other medical supplies, I sat at the edge of the narrow bed. There wasn't much room for me with Dallas hogging the rest of the space, but I needed to be as close to her as possible. "Diana didn't just work for Rebecca's old company. She knew Rebecca.

Came to the house for a Christmas party. And to the funeral. Rebecca even babysat her when she was a kid. Crazy, right?" I did my best to play off my words as no big deal.

He cocked a brow. "You're just telling me this?"

"Wasn't relevant before."

A smirk came and went. "But it is now?"

Ignoring him, I ordered, "Just go call Gray." Resting my hand on her denim-clad leg, I noticed a rip over the knee. "Have him tell POTUS we have her and we'll be in touch soon. I'm sure her mom wants to see her alive on screen with her own eyes."

"Let me do a quick perimeter check first, then I'll make the calls."

Good idea. I should've thought of that. I waited for Griffin to leave, and at the sound of the door clicking closed, I scooted a bit closer to check her wounds.

I used the small, wet hand towel Griffin had left behind to pat at the blood on her right elbow, then moved on to the blood at the back of her left hand. Checking the tear in her jeans next, I found a bad cut there. I ripped the material back to give me better access to her knee and sanitized that wound.

Dallas lifted his head and began yelping, which was more like his version of cry-singing.

"She can't be ours. I know what you're thinking, but she can't be." It was ridiculous how much my heart hurt saying that. Dallas clearly felt the same, because he groaned in disapproval. "Lift your head, I need to check her stomach and back."

He didn't budge. So stubborn.

"I'm getting worried at how quickly you've become attached to her." Maybe he saw her a time or two while I'd watched her on the security cameras and recognized her, but I knew him. He was like me. Didn't cozy up to people easily.

Something about this woman drew him to her. *I get it, boy, I do. But we . . . can't.*

I gestured for him to move again, and he only tipped his head left, then right, ears pointed up, eyes on me.

"Yeah, yeah." A smile nearly cut across my lips at how protective he was of her. "I won't lift her blouse all the way up. Promise, buddy."

Diana had on the same bright yellow blouse she'd been wearing when taken days ago. The shirt was missing three buttons and covered in grass stains and dirt. I leaned over and removed a little twig from her matted and tangled hair.

You jumped from a moving truck. What were you thinking? Probably not that I was about to get to her. I admired her guts and self-preservation. Checking her stomach, all I found was a faded scar over her belly button. *Ah, you little rebel. You had a piercing when you were younger, hmm?* I skated the pad of my thumb over the little mark there before doing my best to turn her onto her side without disturbing her.

Thankfully, the IV was helping bring some of her color back. With any luck, she'd wake soon so we could get some food and water into her.

There were a few scratches on her back, nothing too serious. Satisfied with what I found, I gently rolled her around so she was faceup. At seeing her lashes fluttering as if she might come to, relief struck me and I quickly told Dallas, "Down, boy." She didn't need to wake up to a wolf in her face.

I stood and discarded the hand towel and antibiotic cream on the nightstand, unsure what to expect when she opened her eyes. Fear again? Would she lash out and attack me like she'd done by the port when she'd thought I'd been yet another threat?

Dallas circled the bed and parked his ass alongside me, both of us waiting quietly, eager to see Diana come to life.

Her subtle stirring transitioned to full-blown shaking and chills, coupled with yelps of pain. Worried the IV would rip free, making things worse, I removed it as gently as possible, doing my best to hold her down without too much force as she trembled on the bed, eyes still closed. With my teeth, I ripped a piece of medical tape from the roll, securing a small gauze pad over the spot where the needle had punctured her skin.

Dallas set his paws on the bed by her, and all I could think to do next was hold her. Sitting on the bed, I gathered her in my arms and hauled her upright so we were chest to chest.

Her teeth clicked together, shock—and possibly the drugs in her system—causing the intense reaction.

Keeping her tight against me, I surveyed the room and spotted another door beyond the bed. "Dallas, check." He followed my line of sight and went over to the door, set a paw to the handle, and pushed it open, disappearing inside. He quickly came back, indicating the room was clear, and, from the looks of it, a bathroom like I'd hoped.

"Good boy." I carefully repositioned Diana on the bed so I could stand, then scooped her into my arms and walked us into the bathroom.

She was still shaking, eyes closed, and I used my elbow to turn on the light. I carried Diana over to the tub-and-shower combo, tilting my head toward it while saying, "Dallas, open."

He trotted in and pulled back the blue shower curtain with his teeth.

"On," I commanded, and he used his nose to shift the handle up to start the bath water. "That's a good boy."

I waited a few more seconds, hoping the water had

warmed up, then carefully stepped into the small tub. It was a tight fit for the two of us. I was nearly a head taller than the shower curtain rod.

Using my elbow again, I reached the second nozzle on the wall and switched it over to shower mode. Her legs dangled over my arm and hung outside the tub as I held her beneath the warm spray, the light water pressure softly pelting her face and chest.

"Wh-wh-what's happ-happ-happening?"

Relief rushed through me at hearing her voice and seeing her wet lashes parting. I shifted so the water stopped hitting her in the face. "I got you," I promised, unsure why my voice broke when her eyes met mine.

"Car-Car-Carter," she stuttered, but her trembling was slowing a bit. "It's you, right?"

I wasn't sure how clearly she could see me without her glasses, but hopefully she'd be able to remember my voice. "Yeah, it's me," I said as she kept her eyes on mine, her teeth clicking together less. "Does it hurt anywhere? Anything feel broken or sprained? Fractured?"

She took her time, and I watched her for signs of pain as she processed everything. Shock was a heavy drug on its own. Throw in what happened to her, plus real drugs, and she must've been reeling. "I—I don't think so. A-achy. Hun-hungry, maybe."

That's manageable. Good.

"You—you can put me—me . . . duh-down."

"No, I'm not letting you go." I'd almost lost her earlier. If she'd made it onto one of those ships, I couldn't imagine what would have happened after that.

"I think I can stand." Her words came out smoother that time, and although I could easily hold her all day if she needed me to, I did as she asked. I gently shifted her around so her sneakers could find the floor of the tub, then I circled my arms around her waist to ensure she didn't fall.

Her knees buckled, and she flung her arms up over my shoulders to hang on to me. Despite the fact she seemed to be shivering with less intensity, her frazzled, terrified look remained.

Staring into her frantic and apprehensive eyes, I did the first thing that came to mind. I hugged her. Threading one hand through her wild blonde hair, I cupped the back of her head, bringing her cheek to my chest. It was something I never did, but with her it was purposeful and natural. Comforting even me.

Too late to do anything about it, I hoped the crucifix didn't dig into her skin, disturbing the solace she needed.

"Oxy-oxytocin. You remember."

I remember everything when it comes to you. "Yes," I admitted. "Is it helping? Me holding you?"

"Yes." I kept her tight against me, only slowly peeling free from her embrace when she whispered, "Skin to skin would make it better, though."

Dallas remained on post, watching us as I hesitantly reached for her hand to shift it to the wall at our side.

Relieved to see she didn't fall without me holding her upright, I quickly removed my long-sleeved black shirt and tossed it. Her eyes roamed over my body, her gaze cutting down my chest and abs, momentarily distracting me from what I was supposed to be doing. I cleared my throat before I gripped her waist and directed, "Your turn."

She lifted a trembling hand between us, fumbling with the first of her buttons. The longer she took on the second one, the more she started to tremble. If she truly needed skin to skin to calm her, then fuck it, I needed to help.

"Let me." At Diana's nod of permission, I turned her so

her back was to the wall. Bracing her rib cage with my elbows, I ripped the shirt open.

A little gasp fell from her lips and I gritted my teeth as I held myself back, using every ounce of self-control not to lean in and taste that sweet sound.

The fact she was standing there and not screaming in pain confirmed nothing was broken or fractured. She was lucky. But when she attempted to move away from the wall and free herself of the shirt, she winced. That fall from the truck had to be catching up with her. No, not fall—she'd hurled herself over the side. And I'd about jumped from my SUV I was in at the sight.

I helped her peel the wet and ruined blouse from her body, doing my best to ignore the lacy bra. *And* avoid gaping at the swell of flesh heaving behind it as she continued to shiver between deep breaths. Dragging her back into my arms, her breasts smashed against my wet skin. I closed my eyes at the feel of her hands on my bare back. My heart slowed for the first time since POTUS dropped the bomb on me she'd been taken. "Better?"

"Better," she repeated, still shuddering.

The longer we remained quietly standing there beneath the warm water, the more she softened and relaxed against me.

"It's really you, right? This isn't a hallucination? Or a dream?"

I held the back of her head and dropped my mouth over her ear. "It's me."

"You saved me again," she murmured.

Opening my eyes, my heart in my throat, I rasped, "I'll always save you."

26

CARTER

"Your boots are wet," Diana whispered.

Keeping my arms locked around her, I pulled back to find her eyes. "What?"

"Operators hate getting their boots wet. And you're doing that for me." For the briefest of seconds, the innocence of her words made me forget she'd just survived hell. Had shaken uncontrollably in my arms mere moments earlier.

What could I say to her, though? That wet boots were the least of my problems? That it seemed I'd do anything for her? "We're both getting a lot more than our shoes wet." I kept my tone light, grateful she was far more relaxed.

"I think I needed this shower." Shivering again, the opposite of what I wanted, she frowned and stared up at me. "I want to wash their filth off me. Erase everything from these last few days."

Their filth? "Did they hurt you? Touch you?" The questions snapped out before I could stop them. Anger radiated through me as my body tensed. My mind drenched in blood-soaked thoughts of what I'd do to anyone who'd hurt her. If I'd already killed them, that wouldn't be enough for me.

Peering up at me with her big blue eyes, she shook her head. "No, not like that."

I did my best to dial down my heartbeat and command my derailed thoughts back on track.

She lowered her arms from my shoulders and bent them between us, drawing her hands beneath her chin. "Something about being clean makes me feel in control again. I haven't been in control since . . ."

Tightening my hold of her, I smoothed my hand up and down her back, attempting to soothe her before her shivering turned into shaking.

"Does that make me weird? Wanting to be clean even though I could've died?"

With her lips pressed against my chest, her words vibrated into the walls of my body. There was pain in her tone. A little misplaced guilt, too. I'd take it all from her if I could. Absorb whatever she was feeling and carry it instead.

"When I was growing up, and my parents used to fight, I always felt the need to do something that helped me reclaim control of the situation. Clean my room. Organize my closet. Balance chemical equations." Her teeth were clicking together again. Nerves trying to get the best of her.

I had to get her focused before I lost her to the chaos the trauma and the drugs were creating in her mind. "Not strange at all." I continued rubbing small circles on her back with my palm. "I did the same when my parents argued. Well, not science stuff, but I had to distract myself, so their fighting didn't eat away at me. Usually hid in the woods out back and worked on building a fort. Never did finish one. Not much of an architect."

My stomach squeezed at not only the memories, but the

fact I'd shared them. That was something not even Rebecca had known.

Her cheek was no longer glued to my chest, and I dipped my chin to find her blues pointed up at me. She was probably as shocked as I was at my confession. "I'm sure you were great at a lot of other things, then," she said so softly, so fucking earnestly, that a bit of the tension in my body managed to loosen up.

"Maybe." I forced a smile, then rolled my lips inward to suppress that emotion, unsure how we'd gotten there.

She turned her cheek back to my chest again, maybe searching for her own strength in the strong and steady beat of my heart.

After a few quiet moments passed, she suddenly rasped, "Oh God. There were other people with me back there. We— we have to save them."

At least I could give her some good news on that front. "My guys are on top of it. They're freeing them now." I reached between us, searching for her face, worried she was still concerned about something. "What is it?"

"My colleagues are out there somewhere, still in danger. I'm safe, and they're not. I don't know how to handle that."

She hid her eyes from me, but I didn't need to see them to know how she was feeling. The sting of her guilt punctured into me as she spoke, and it burned up into my throat as I remembered the times in the Army I'd survived while others hadn't. It was a bitter pill I'd never learned to swallow.

"You have to believe they'll be okay," was the best I could give. Close enough to the truth without being overly optimistic or completely giving up hope. "No feeling bad. What's important right now is that you're safe, and my team will find the others. Got it?"

"I'll try to think like that."

I recognized that sentiment. And she was about as convincing as I'd been the first time I'd felt it. Took me right back to my first year in the Army, when I'd lost my first teammate. My CO had ordered, *"You put one foot in front of the other, and you keep moving forward. Now get your ass up and do your job."*

What was it about this woman that had me reliving moments I'd kept locked away for so long?

"Do you know where you were before today? When was the last time you saw your colleagues? Anything you can share may help my guys locate them." I hadn't planned to break out those questions yet, but if it'd help her feel better to know we had every intention of rescuing the others, and that she had a hand in helping, we could do this now.

"Last I saw anyone else from the lab was yesterday. Well, last night. There were only a few of us that'd been kept together. They moved us from place to place every night since the lab was hit. I—I don't know more than that." Her shoulders collapsed from obvious guilt.

"I assume they drove you a few hours each time they moved you to keep your whereabouts unknown until you hit your final destination." But why they suddenly separated Diana from her colleagues last night . . . *that* I didn't understand.

"Remember Pierce Quaid?" More chills rocked through her body beneath my palms. "They took him away first. I was the second taken from our group."

"We'll find them all," I reassured her. *Even your coward ex if he was one of the ones with you.*

"You think you're ready to get out now? We need to get you somewhere safe."

"You just said I was safe," she reminded me, and shit, she caught me.

Fuck. "*Safer.*"

Her lips pursed in hesitation. "Can I rinse off the rest of my body first?"

Their filth. Your need to feel in control. Right. "I can't leave you in here alone." I wasn't sure if staying was smart either. I'd need to become clinical, detach myself from this moment to survive the primal compulsion inside me to claim her as mine. To offer to protect and comfort her forever.

She'd already been through an ordeal and felt out of control.

Calm, comfort, control—that had to remain both my mantra and my mission.

"Okay, then can you help me get out of these clothes?" She shifted beneath the water, catching a drop on her lips that I had the ridiculous urge to suck free. "I'm sorry." Eyes open and on me, she added, "That'd probably make you uncomfortable. I'll stay like this."

Uncomfortably hard, yes. Help her undress and rinse off? *Really? That gave new meaning to control.*

I glanced over at Dallas. "Out. Door," I ordered, and he jumped to all fours. He took a few steps back and clamped down on the handle with his teeth, pulling the door closed to leave us alone.

"Talented dog."

"He's a little cocky. Don't let him hear you say that."

Beneath my palm, her cheek lifted into a smile. It was an entirely too intimate and completely unnecessary position, so I let her go, narrowing in on my next problem—how to remove her clothes without getting a hard-on. It wasn't like I'd just spent months jerking off in the shower to thoughts of this woman.

Calm. Comfort. Control. "We need to make this quick. Then I want to get you some food while we call your mom."

"My mom . . ."

"She's one of the reasons I'm here. The President, too." I did my best to hide any emotion from my voice, particularly the worry, because I wasn't sure if she knew exactly how much trouble she may *still* be in. "You're important to quite a lot of people." *Apparently, to me, too.*

"My mom," she said again as if in disbelief. "She asked *you* for help?"

"Her love for you trumped her hate for me." I stepped back in the tight space, trying to determine how to get her naked without my cock tenting my fatigues.

"Thank you for saving me," she whispered, pulling my attention to her face. "Did I say that yet?"

My pleasure didn't feel like the appropriate response, so I nodded. "How good is your vision without glasses?"

Not sure why that concerned me. It was my 20/20 eyesight that'd be problematic. Keeping myself in check while I stripped her down wasn't exactly the challenge I'd signed up for. How would I navigate a situation that felt a little too close to fantasy becoming reality?

"Farsighted," she answered, "but not bad enough that I can't make out the color of your eyes. Or how you're looking at me right now."

"And how am I looking at you?" My voice was far too gravelly, a solid indication my constraint was slipping. We were bordering on having some kind of moment, and there were still too many reasons moments of any kind couldn't happen between us.

"Like I'm a victim you feel sorry for, and you're not comfortable taking care of me, but you're doing it anyway."

That was the furthest thing from the truth, but I was grateful she couldn't see the real reason I was struggling. That I was also fighting for that control she claimed to need.

"You're strong." I swallowed. "You jumped from that truck to save yourself. That takes guts. You're a survivor." *You're also the only woman I seem to want.*

At her nod, even if it was a hesitant one, I forced myself to tackle the task at hand.

Calm. Comfort. Control. "Want your hair washed, too?"

"If it's not too much trouble. I don't have a lot of energy, but I can try and do this myself."

"No, I got you." I located the shampoo—well, what I hoped was shampoo since I didn't speak Latvian—and squirted it into my palms. "Turn around. Hands on the wall for support." Fuck. Those orders came out rougher than intended, and my dick twitched when she obeyed them so easily.

Back to me, hands on the wall, she angled her head so her face wasn't right beneath the small barrel-shaped spout, and I began massaging her scalp. I'd never washed a woman's hair before, and I had no clue what I was doing, but the little moans of pleasure suggested I must have been doing something right. At least making her feel better.

And making my cock harder. *Fucking fuck.*

The soapy water ran down her spine and over the curve of her ass. Her jeans, that I'd need to help her remove without going fucking feral, molded tighter to her under the water, accentuating her figure.

"Better?" I asked her when I felt *my* control waning. Gritting down on my teeth, I turned her into my arms.

Her pupils were still a bit dilated from the drugs, and I wanted to kill those men at the factory all over again.

"Much better." Her blue eyes dipped to her breasts, and she drew the side of her lip between her teeth. "How do we do this?"

Hell if I know. "One second." I stepped one boot outside

the tub, leaned over to get a facecloth from the counter, then stepped back in. This time I had the good sense to pull the curtain closed in case Griffin got worried and checked on us. I didn't want Diana to be even more embarrassed by him seeing her half-naked. And I wasn't exactly sure I would be able to keep my shit together if that happened either.

As I lathered soap on the small cloth, she went for her bra clasp, and completely stole my ability to regulate my breathing.

"Turn around," I suggested, much rougher than I'd intended. Her eyes went wide and her mouth rounded in a little O, realizing what she'd nearly done in front of me.

Once she was in position with her hands on the wall and her bra removed, I lathered her back, then under her arms, before carefully cleansing any visible wounds. I couldn't bring myself to move around to the front of her body. Soap up her nipples and not snap? That was a chance I wasn't willing to take.

I set my chest to her back, the cross between us a metaphor I didn't want to examine, and covered one of her hands on the wall with mine. When our fingers locked together, I stared at our united hands, oddly mesmerized by the sight.

What the hell am I doing? I pulled my hand away and nudged the cloth at her with the other, a silent request to wash her own breasts.

Understanding my request, she silently accepted it and kept her other palm positioned on the wall for support while she cleaned herself up.

It didn't take me long to determine even that simple task was too much for her. The arch of her back became more pronounced as her spine curved forward, and her hand slid down the wall.

"Diana?" I reached around, my hand resting momentarily at the base of her throat before cupping her chin to prevent her from knocking her face into the shower handle. My forearm was now cushioned between her soft breasts, and I grated out a quick, "You okay?"

"Heart is going fast. A little dizzy."

Mine, too. I banded my other arm around her midsection and gently nudged her to face me in the cramped space.

I used every ounce of my restraint not to lower my eyes to her tits. I didn't need to know the color of her nipples, have that image forever burned into my retinas where I'd then download it to memory for permanent safekeeping.

I really needed to get her out of there before she collapsed, *or* before I lost my mind.

"I hate asking this, but at least, can I"—her head bumped into me when she lowered her focus to her jeans—"wash myself there quick?"

There, huh? I did my best to swallow the *fuck no* trying to break free, looking everywhere but where she'd mentioned. I spotted the facecloth by our shoes, and I'd been too distracted to notice she'd let it go.

"If you can lower my jeans a bit, that should be good. I'll be fast. I'm sure you want to get out of your clothes, too."

She had no idea. I inhaled a deep breath and steeled myself for what I needed to do next. "I have to kneel to get the facecloth and lower your jeans, and it's a tight space." I guided her hands to my shoulders. "Hang on to me, okay?"

She nodded, and when I was satisfied she wouldn't lose consciousness, I moved back as much as the little area afforded my big body, took a knee, and grabbed the cloth by her sneaker.

As efficiently as possible, I worked through the necessary steps to complete the task. I held the facecloth with the edge of my teeth to free up my hands, unbuttoned her jeans, dragged the zipper down, then hooked my thumbs in the waistband in preparation to take them down to her knees. "Still good?" I managed to ask without losing hold of the cloth.

"I'm . . . fine." Her tone was as shaky as my damn hands.

Remembering we needed to hurry, I shoved down the wet fabric, successfully leaving her pink panties in place. Another deep breath. Pulling on all my resources to keep my mind out of the gutter. My rifle jamming up under heavy fire was a far easier situation to handle than this.

Her wet panties molded to her clit, every bit of her revealed behind the thin fabric, and I mentally scheduled a visit to the confessional. I'd need to drop another bag of cash into a priest's lap as I asked forgiveness for the erection I was sporting.

I was such an asshole to get a hard-on at a time like this. I repeated my new mantra—*calm, comfort, control*—hoping it was enough to carry me through.

Diana's hands were firmly anchored on my shoulders, and as I started to stand, her palms walked along my pecs. I took the facecloth from between my teeth and squeezed my eyes closed as I returned upright.

Securing a hand around her hip while going for the soap, I rasped, "We need to move fast." *For my sake.* I offered her the cloth, tensing as my blood continued its downward path, away from my brain and directly to my cock.

As she began washing herself, I lifted my chin toward the ceiling, searching for answers there, unlocking another memory of those lost years behind us. Another connection better left in the past, particularly since it involved my late wife.

I kept my hand at her hip in case she lost her balance and

waited for her to finish rubbing her pussy two inches from my dick.

"Done. Thank you." Her soft voice a siren song, and a reminder of how fucked I was.

I didn't waste time killing the water, sliding open the shower curtain in one sweeping motion, and stepping out. Putting a safe distance between us, I picked up a towel to use as a protective divider, but then I realized my error. Her jeans were at her knees and her shoes were on. She'd never be able to climb out without face-planting over the side.

"Don't move," I hissed while setting aside the towel. I closed my eyes, reached out, and lifted her up and over to me. So much for that safe distance. "Still okay?"

"I think I can hobble to the bedroom from here."

"Doubtful," I said gruffly, hoping she didn't mistake my frustration for annoyance when I was only angry at my body's response to her. "Wrap yourself up in the towel." I gave her a few seconds to follow the command, then called out, "Dallas, open," before lifting her without warning.

She looped her arms over my shoulders, making it easy for me to toss her legs over my other arm to carry her.

I finally parted my lids, thankful to see her covered as I'd asked, and I stepped away from the door as it opened inward.

Holding Diana like this unleashed a painful memory, dredging up images I thought I'd buried for good. Rebecca's rejection of my attempt to carry her over the threshold the night of our wedding was a stark reminder of what I'd lost, and the connection still tethering all of us together. *Not the time to think about that, damnit.* "Good boy," I told Dallas, leaving a trail of water as I walked us into the bedroom.

I set Diana in a seated position on the bed and dropped to my knees, quickly finishing the process of stripping her before she could witness my arousal.

"Thank you," she said as I reached for her ankles and swung her legs onto the bed, encouraging her to lie down.

"Of course." I stood. "Don't try to get up. I'm going to find you something to wear for now, some food, and a phone to call your mom, okay?"

She nodded and set her head on the pillow, her wet hair spilling around her face, the towel fisted over her breasts.

Dallas hopped up onto the bed. "Watch her," I told him, not that he had plans to leave. "I'll be a minute." I took my piece from the nightstand and holstered it in place at the side of my wet pants as I left the room. Once in the hallway, I closed the door and rested my back against it, taking a few calming breaths.

Griffin spotted me from the office across the way as he ended a call. His gaze flew over my naked chest and wet clothes.

"Don't ask," I grumbled, pushing away from the door to join him. "She doesn't like being dirty." *And I'm the definition of that.* Another reason I could never be with her. I'd stain and destroy her sweet innocence.

"And what? You tripped and fell into the shower with her. Hell, you left your boots on."

"It was a time-sensitive operation." I went over to a box marked **clothes** and rummaged through it. "Do we have a status update from the guys? You talk to Gray? POTUS?" I pressed on, not wanting to talk more about my shower with Diana.

"Yes to all three."

I removed an oversized black long-sleeved shirt and pair of sweats from the box. They were three sizes too big for her, and she'd more than likely remain bare underneath until we had the bag her mom packed, but it was better than a towel.

"And?" I went over to the couch and began unlacing my boots.

It took Griffin two seconds too long to wipe the smug smile from his face before he shared, "Our guys have two men alive but unconscious in the trunk of the SUV so we can question them later. Teddy's hanging back on overwatch at the neighboring building by the factory in case any more asshole smugglers make an appearance. With the police swarming the place, thanks to the anonymous tip about the thirty people we found there, I doubt we'll get lucky enough to grab any more of them, though."

"I need to get us to a new location. May be better to drive instead of fly." There were a few options I had in mind for next steps. "As soon as Diana talks to her mom, and I have a word with POTUS, we'll move out." Boots off now, I stood, cracking my back. "There's still a possibility that—"

"Yeah, I know," he said, saving me the effort of delivering a warning. Daylight would buy us some time to move out, but not much.

"Gray all set?" I asked him while picking up the clothes I'd set by the chair, and he nodded. "POTUS?" I was anxious to get food and water for Diana and get back to her, so I was keeping this status update as brief as possible.

"They're relieved we have her, and POTUS has Bravo Team working on an extraction plan so they can get her Stateside. We'll most likely be meeting them at an old CIA black site."

I wasn't a fan of passing Diana off to someone else so I could continue playing dress-up as a bad guy. Considering the circles I'd soon be running in to get answers, she was safer with Bravo than me. Not to mention how even being close to her made me act and feel. Her safety and well-being needed guarding in more than one way.

"They're expecting a call from her. They have a secure line waiting." He offered me the phone, and I tucked the clothes under my arm and took it. When his eyes narrowed on the cross still around my neck, he asked in a more somber tone, "You okay?"

I bowed my head as I admitted, "Not even a little bit."

27
DIANA

"He called you Dallas, right?" I scratched him behind the ears, and he lifted his head and licked my cheek. "I'll take that as a yes." Petting him managed to soothe my nerves almost as much as hugging Carter in the shower had.

No, that was a lie. Carter had calmed me down while also making me a hot mess. My legs had gone from shaking from shock to quaking like I'd been standing on an active fault line when he'd soaped up my hair and body. He'd been great at distracting me thirteen years ago when saving me the first time, but him taking care of me today was a whole other level of holy-shit-distracting.

Days of being held hostage, deprived of food, and drugged, but all it took to wash away the pain was that man *actually* washing me. Not to mention the holding part. The rush of oxytocin was real.

Him gently taking care of me in the way he had, as well as being respectful and not ogling my naked body, was evidence of what I'd known all along. He wasn't the man my mom, Sierra, or anyone claimed him to be. No way could he be so kind and sweet to me while also being some psychopath. I still couldn't believe my mother had a hand in choosing Carter to rescue me, but I was relieved she had, or who knew where I'd be now.

I wasn't in too much pain after jumping from the truck, which was probably thanks to the drugs in my system. I'd never anticipated I'd have to use the escape strategies Dad forced me to learn after the embassy bombing, but his over-the-top lessons had saved me worse injuries today.

Dallas must've heard the rumbling in my stomach, a reminder I was famished, because he bopped his nose against my face as if worried.

"I'll be okay," I reassured him. "Thanks to you and your dad. Well, I think he's your dad." He nudged his nose my way again. "He is, right?" I smooshed his face between my hands and leaned toward him, nuzzling the tip of his nose, grateful for the soothing effect his furry presence provided.

My hand went still behind his ears at the memory I wasn't totally rid of *everything* from my hellish week. Testing my strength while keeping the towel drawn together, I attempted to sit. Nothing worse than wearing old underwear.

Dallas shifted his head off my lap to give me space, and I forced my legs over the side and set my bare feet on the floor. I had to hang on to the small wins right now. Like the fact I didn't flop back over. The IV bag by the bed was probably one reason for that.

Next step, get my panties off. I parted the towel to assess the situation as to how to remove my panties without collapsing onto the floor.

Letting the towel fall, I hooked my thumb at the waistband of the wet panties and shimmied my ass on the bed to help move them farther down. Once they were to my knees, I wiggled them down my legs and kicked the panties free from my ankles.

At the sight of them on the floor and exposed to anyone who may walk in, I knew what I had to do next. I could spread my legs open for the doctor at the OBGYN's office, but I had to hide my panties from being seen by the man who held me up in the shower.

I hadn't been saved from human traffickers only to die of embarrassment when Carter walked in and saw my underwear there.

Here goes. Re-wrapping the towel around my body, I lowered myself to the floor and reached for them. Snatching the pink undies, I shifted over to hide them inside my wet and discarded jeans, lost my balance—of-freaking-course—and had to let go of the towel to save myself from a lovely face-plant disaster.

Dallas jumped down next to me, barking to alert his dad.

"Shhh, Dallas," I pleaded once I'd corralled my thoughts, but it was probably a little too late. "Don't rat me out. I wasn't supposed to move, remember?"

The door flung open like a storm had blown it inward, and I peeked over my shoulder to see that storm staring at me, his muscular body filling the doorway.

"Diana." Carter dropped what he was holding and flew to my side, taking a knee. "You okay? What happened?"

"I'm good." I tried to hold the towel together but that required balancing myself on the hand still awkwardly holding my panties. Little drops of water from my heavy, wet hair rolled down my scalp to my cheeks and splattered onto the hardwood, and I stared at the droplets in embarrassment until Carter picked me up.

On his feet, my ass now cradled between his arms, I managed to pin the towel over my breasts. Hopefully, I'd been fast enough to hide the nakedness he'd worked so hard not to see when I'd practically served it up on a shaking, exhausted, terrified, grungy platter in the shower.

Carter stared at my face, and despite the fact I didn't have on my glasses, I could easily make out the definition of his bladed jawline tensing beneath his black stubble. His nostrils were flared, and his eyes skated to my hand next. You know . . . the one still fisting the panties.

"Sorry," I said when he continued to quietly study me. "My panties," I blurted, my nerves splintering into fragments of chaos. "I was trying to hide them."

He angled his head, his *"why on earth would you do that?"* expression loud and clear there.

Instead of making me spell it out for him, he lowered me to the bed, placing me in a seated position, and stepped back. Dallas immediately joined me, curling up at my side.

Searching for something to say that would make me sound like the grown-ass woman I was now rather than that young college kid he'd saved forever ago, I found myself following his strong tattooed forearm as his palm went to his head. I became jealous of his hand as it raked through his wet hair, mussing it in a way a girl could only dream of doing.

My traitorous eyes flew next to the hard planes of his bronzed chest, and when he turned, I couldn't hide my gasp at the sight before me. I'd somehow missed the angel wings that took up his entire back when he'd first left the room. The tattoo was utter perfection.

Still robbed of speech, I gaped at him while he bent over to pick up what he'd dropped to get to me. It took a few seconds for my brain to resume functioning at normal levels, and I quickly slid the panties under my ass.

Facing me, clothes and a water bottle in hand, he came over. There was a large crucifix around his neck I only just noticed.

So, that's what was digging into my skin in the shower.

He quietly set down the pile of clothes, then removed the cap from the water bottle. His eyes were on my bare thighs as he offered it to me, and I caught a light shake of his head while accepting the drink. The water was heavenly for my parched throat, and I sucked down the entire thing.

"I have broth heating up in the kitchen. You need to slowly ease into food or you'll get sick." He took the empty bottle from me and crushed it between his palms before tossing it onto the bed.

"You haven't changed yet." My gaze snapped to his belt, triggering a memory from earlier.

He followed my line of sight. "Sorry about that," he remarked. "We were being shot at, and you were resisting."

"I've never been belted before," I whispered, feeling my body instantly blush.

The side of his lip hitched. "I'd hope not." He closed the space between us and leaned in, our cheeks nearly touching, and my heart thwacked with ridiculous disappointment that it was only to show me something.

Ah, a phone. It'd been bundled up inside the clothes.

"Do you want to talk to your mom?"

"Maybe not in a towel?"

"Probably not the best idea." He grimaced. "POTUS might be on the FaceTime call, too."

"The President. Right. How? Why? I mean, what happened? To the lab? To me? Why are you here? How'd you find me?" I was rambling, the reality of my situation hijacking my thoughts.

Carter backed up, his hand resting atop the gun strapped to his side. Then those tight, strong abdominal muscles flexed before my eyes.

Thank God my vision isn't that bad . . . because damn.

"We don't know why your lab was hit yet." His words pulled me free of my misplaced stupor and back to the matter at hand. "But the President thought I could help, so he brought me in."

"Aren't you . . .?" How could I finish that and not sound like an asshole? Just the past summer, Craig Paulsen said he was on all the bad-guy lists. Had something changed? *Please say it has.*

"I'm not who you think I am, Diana." He shook his head. "Or maybe I am." I lost sight of those dark eyes as they cut to the hardwoods.

"But you're here. You came for me." Now I was the one tightening my stomach muscles. I could feel the familiar dull ache of fear trying to claim control.

"Of course I came for you." There was a touch of insult in his tone, as if shocked I'd ever expect him not to.

"So, um, how'd you find me?"

His dark eyes flew to my face, and he observed me for a few intense seconds before revealing, "There were cameras at the lab, ones the Serbians didn't know about. I heard and saw what happened just before, though. It's highly doubtful the traffickers who took you were the ones actually after you. We kept a few alive to question them and see what they know."

Heard and saw me? Why was a fresh wave of *oh-shit* flooding my system? Despite the drugs, it didn't take me long to put the pieces together in my mind and understand why I was becoming even uneasier at that news, at the fact Carter had . . .

"You heard me," I whispered. "My time travel comment." He was smart enough to put two and two together and know I'd been referring to him. When he peered around the room instead of keeping his eyes on me, I couldn't help but dip into a past memory and ask, "Looking for a teleprompter?"

That had his attention squarely hot on me, and his tone an octave lower as he said, "You wouldn't have been able to save her." He paused for a beat, and my heart skipped three. "So, your first answer was probably the better one." He turned away as if his words hadn't anchored me to the same sad and dark place where he seemed to dwell. "Get dressed so you can talk to your mom. Do it from the bed."

His husky voice wasn't lost on me, but I also didn't know how to interpret it after what he admitted. How could I explain to him why I'd given Bahar that answer without feeling like a horrible person since he'd been married when we first met? Did I drop the news on him now of all times that I'd had a crush on him when I was younger? That I *still* so obviously had feelings of some kind for him.

I let the towel fall, deciding to postpone that talk for another time. Shivering again, I did as he asked and pulled the black oversized shirt over my head. Then I shifted to my back so I could slide on the black sweats without tipping over. No undergarments, but I was good with that. I wasn't exactly keen on the idea of wearing someone else's underwear.

"You doing okay?" His arms were still locked at his sides.

His broad back muscles pinched, drawing the angel wings together as I let him know, "You can look now." When he faced me, I was mid-struggle to get back upright, so he quickly came over for an assist.

His hand went to my forearm as mine went to his, and our eyes remained fixed on one another. I'd swear there was a change in energy between us. I felt it shift, the same way I'd felt guys I'd been dating in the past pull back before they ghosted me. A woman always knew what was coming.

I squeezed down the lump in my throat, reminding myself

I had to focus on what was important, which was finding Bahar and the others.

He released me and stepped away. "Griffin," he hollered out a moment later, startling Dallas.

The door opened, and a man dressed similar to Carter, but with a shirt on, joined us. He was about Carter's height, with the same dark hair, golden skin, and overall hard-ass look as Carter.

Why was he so familiar? "Do I know you?"

"The embassy," Carter said, turning to the side so he could look between the two of us. "He was the one who saved us from joining floor four."

It took me a second to connect the dots. I'd seen both of them without their masks that day but for only a few seconds. "That means you were Delta, but now you're operating together again." I set my palms at my sides for support. "I'm confused."

Griffin folded his arms, hanging back by the door. "I was Delta, yes. And we do work together now."

"We're in private security." Carter frowned as if that was bad news.

But, if he was doing that kind of work, that had to mean his name was cleared. "That's why my mom and the President came to you?"

"It's part of the reason we were asked to help," Carter shared, his tone as low as my mood on a non-sunshiny day.

"So, you're no longer a wanted man? You're off the list?" I asked, feeling a surge of relief on his behalf.

"I *was* off the list. It's complicated." Carter's words sent a fresh wave of chills over my skin. "Can you get the broth from the kitchen before I burn the priest's home down?"

Priest?

"Sure." Griffin unfolded his arms. "Easton will be here in

five minutes with her things."

"My things? What things?" I asked him after Griffin left us alone.

"I didn't look inside the bag your mom gave us, but I assume clothes and spare glasses."

I doubted my mom planned to share more about what was going on than these two would. *Why in the world were we taken?*

When a new memory from the night of the attack surfaced, I shut my eyes to latch on to the details that I must've suppressed during the chaos of being held captive.

"I think someone was poking around my computer." *It wasn't a tech issue. It was a cybersecurity one.* "A hacker, maybe." I opened my eyes. "Why do that if they could just take my computer, though?" I shared my concerns out loud, hoping Carter would have an answer. "And, oh, God, if they were monitoring my keystrokes, then they'll have seen the equation I stumbled upon before the sirens went off." I went to stand, shock propelling me up, but I fell backward.

Carter immediately snatched my wrist as if worried I'd go down three flights instead of having a bed cushion both my fall and embarrassment. Once releasing me, he drew his brows together and prompted, "What equation?"

"Not the answer to making cold fusion a reality." *I'm going to be sick.* "The equation is still theoretical until tested, but I'd always feared my work could be altered to create a weapon." I did my best not to slip back into a state of panic. After everything Carter had done to calm me down, I didn't want to regress.

"Diana." My name was a rough plea from his lips that time, worry cutting through.

My eyes fell closed again as I revealed, "I think I accidentally solved how to devise an EMP weapon."

28

CARTER

This genius woman was staring at me with big, blue eyes, and I wasn't sure how to tell her the project she'd been working on was *exactly* what she feared. The good guys had set her on that path without her knowing. And now the enemies might be in possession of it. The lines were murky as fuck.

Diana was Einstein smart—possibly with an even higher IQ than him—but not even the smartest people could always see what was right in front of them. I'd been guilty of the same. I hadn't seen all the signs and clues about my wife's secrets over the years. People tended to overlook things and make excuses when they trusted someone.

"You don't look shocked," she said, breaching the quiet first. I'd left her revelation marinating in the air between us for too long, lost to my thoughts.

I slid my hands into my pockets, fighting the wet fabric, which also reminded me I was still shirtless. That wouldn't be ideal for a call with her mother and the President. "I'm not. Not exactly," I reluctantly tossed out. "I'd thought you were going to say you could perfect a neutron bomb, not create an EMP weapon, though. I guess it makes sense since you're working in energy."

She wiggled her fingers as if trying to rid herself of tension before working that plump bottom lip of hers between her teeth.

"The use of an electromagnetic pulse weapon has been a concern of the government for over two decades now." I opted to remain standing, even though part of me wanted to sit beside her and pull her close to me. I had to stop treating her like anything other than part of my mission. I couldn't lose sight of the op because my head was off. Her life and national security depended on me remaining focused. "There are trade-offs with everything," I went on. "Even with the seemingly good inventions. The greener we get in energy, the more vulnerable we become to these new-age types of attacks."

"Voltage surges in our electric systems could be catastrophic," she said softly. "End-of-days kind of bad. An attack could take the power grid down for years." She was trembling again, and my hands strained in my pockets as I resisted the impulse to offer to hug her and provide a hit of oxytocin for the both of us. "I knew the risks of working with fusion, but I was trying to help make a difference." She opened her palms and looked down at them as if she were the Lady Macbeth of clean energy.

I couldn't handle that sight, so against my better judgment, I sat alongside her. "You *are* making a difference." I took her hand, so much smaller than mine, and our palms slipped into what felt like the most comfortable position in the world, lacing together and resting on my thigh. I forced myself to ignore why things were so effortless with her, needing to get to the reveal of what I knew instead.

"What is it you're afraid to tell me?"

Ripping off the Band-Aid, I shared, "I found out this week that a shell company for the CIA was responsible for the takeover of The Barclay Group. They were only after Barclay Energy, but couldn't raise red flags by making it look that way." My pulse quickened when she pointed her beautiful blues at me with nervous anticipation. "Those eleven other companies you were partnered with represent eleven foreign governments. The President said it was a classified cold fusion project, but given how terrified they are about the lab hit, and the fact they brought me in, would suggest you were working on more than cold fusion. They kept the truth from you and everyone else there."

It wasn't a move I'd have expected from President Bennett. It made me wonder if his predecessor had orchestrated the plans long before he took over, and Bennett had only assumed the mantle when things were ripe to unfold.

Diana applied a little pressure to our clasped palms and whispered, "The Manhattan Project."

I waited for her to continue, familiar with America's nuclear program during World War II, but unsure where she was going with that comment.

"Compartmentalization," she murmured as if expecting me to understand. "If you're right, then Amsterdam wasn't their only lab. Like the nuclear arms program back in the day, the government would have at least one, maybe two additional clandestine sites in operation."

I bowed my head in understanding. "That's what they did with the Manhattan Project." Pretty sure there was a movie about that recently, not that I'd seen it. I took a few military history courses at Columbia, though, so I was knowledgeable enough on the subject matter. "In case of an insider or a spy, as well as not completely trusting their own physicists, they divided up the work into different locations."

"The sum of all parts equals the whole. If one site falls into enemy hands, the project is still safe from being stolen," she whispered. "I don't think I was supposed to stumble upon a way to make that weapon feasible on my own, though."

Doubtful. But you're you . . . I'm not shocked. If anyone knew what Diana had discovered, she'd be more valuable than all the fucking parts. She was all they'd need.

"The President didn't mention other locations, right?" Her eyes were open and on me again, so I shook my head no.

"If they exist, you think they were hit, too?"

"Only one way to find out. The President's not going to tell us anything over the call today, though. He'll want us at a secure location first. A CIA safe house." She only gave me a hesitant nod to that. "You think it'd be a nuclear or non-nuclear?"

"Non-nuclear, but just as effective at the end goal." She wet her lips. "I panicked when the sirens went off and erased the equation from the laptop so no one could get it. But the more I remember, the more I think someone may have been monitoring my computer. They could already have what they need even though I deleted it."

"They'll want you regardless. You said it's still a theory until applied. They'll need the brainchild behind the numbers to ensure it's successful." Not what I wanted to tell her, but it was the truth. She was invaluable, including to the President and CIA.

"If you saw me on the other security cameras, then the people after me must've seen me, too. They may have zoomed in on my screen and—"

"The main cameras were corrupted and destroyed before they infil'ed the lab." That was now a blessing in disguise.

They wouldn't have seen Diana's shocked expression while staring at her screen moments before the siren had sounded.

"Wait, then how'd you see me?"

About that. My free hand raced along my jawline as I considered how to share that information without letting her know I'd developed an unhealthy obsession with her. "There were other cameras there they didn't know about." I waited to see if she'd accept that pathetic explanation without question, to not see what was in front of her again since this time the answer was me.

She pulled her hand free from mine. I was worried she'd accurately read the particular brand of psychopath in my eyes and knew I'd been stalking her. Instead, she went a different direction and said, "My mom pushed me to work for Barclay, and her boyfriend is the Secretary of Energy."

I was curious to see what puzzle pieces her brilliant mind clicked together.

She leaned forward, setting her elbows on her knees in a position that would likely make her lightheaded. So, I hooked my arm with hers, urging her back upright so she didn't faint.

Despite everything she'd endured this week, she was somehow still capable of carrying a deep and important conversation.

"My mother had to have knowingly set me up for this project. How could she do that to me? How could she not tell me what I'd really been working on and who I'd been working for?"

"It's possible she didn't know until now." I honestly didn't know what to believe, but I'd play devil's advocate if it'd help keep her from breaking to pieces. She'd already been through too much to also feel betrayed and misled by her own flesh and blood.

"No, she had to have known." A few tears fell, but it was

the way her brows suddenly snapped together that had me growing even more uneasy. "Craig Paulsen is part of this, isn't he? He's friends with Mom and with . . ."

Her wide-eyed, panicky look had me holding my fucking breath. That name. That man. The bad gut feeling I'd had at Susan's reaction to him in the Oval . . .

What are you afraid to tell me? I stood and faced her, feeling a weird rush of *something* roll through my body and land in the pit of my stomach. Was this anxiety?

"Craig, um, found out you and I spoke the day of the takeover in New York. He forced me into his limo to talk. He wanted to know what you said to me and if I told you about my work. I—I hadn't understood why he'd been so riled up then, but he clearly didn't want you knowing anything," she rushed out.

I took a knee before her and held her hands between my own as I rasped, "Did he hurt you? Touch you?"

Her silence was a disaster to my state of mind. *Does he need to die? Say the word, and I'll make it rain with his blood.* "What is it, Diana? Because so help me, I'm on the verge of losing it." So much for calm, comfort, and control. I was on the edge of becoming irrational, but I couldn't prevent my reactions any more than using the power of my mind to stop a speeding train.

"He warned me you were dangerous, and he mentioned he was friends with Rebecca before she died."

I blinked. Replayed her words. My body going cold. "But did he hurt *you*?" That was all I could think about right now. *Her.*

A flash of surprise crossed her face, but I couldn't figure out why. "Not really, no. Just scared me."

"Define 'not really.'" Counting back from three, I waited for her answer.

"Just, um, squeezed my leg and yanked my hair. Said a few things that made me uncomfortable. Nothing I couldn't handle," she sputtered.

So, he needs to die, is what you're saying. His name jumped to the top of my hit list.

"I assume my boss, Pierce Quaid, told him you were at the office that day. Pierce was taken with me, though, so I don't think he's in on the lab hit, but he probably did know the CIA was behind the transfer in ownership."

At some point during our conversation, my hand had moved to my sidearm. To say my trigger finger was itchy was an understatement. I kept it there as I pieced more of the puzzle together. "I trusted Pierce because Rebecca did." I remembered what I'd been told in the Oval Office about the hostile takeover. "Pierce did know, and Paulsen is aware I'm here now."

"Mom knows both Pierce and Craig." She cringed. "I'm pretty sure that confirms she knew I was working on more than clean energy."

"Not necessarily. She only became Secretary of State this summer, and it was originally supposed to be interim. This plan had to be in motion long before she got the job. Not to mention her job is diplomacy, not defense. But it doesn't mean her strings weren't being pulled by her boyfriend since he's Secretary of Energy. Or by Craig without her knowledge to get you in the door of the company."

Her shoulders dropped. "I hope you're right. I don't want to totally hate my mother."

I tried to consider what else to say to ease her concerns, but the image of Craig inside that limo with her came back into my mind, sending me over the edge again. "What'd you tell Craig when he cornered you that day?"

"I didn't tell him anything other than he was wrong about you, and that you're not a bad guy." She lifted one shoulder.

So freaking innocent, and I'd swallow you fucking whole. I have to stay away, damnit.

"I also told him to leave you alone."

Her words created a tight band of pressure inside my chest, and I drew my hand over my heart. Here I'd been thinking that organ of mine, caged protectively within my rib cage, only functioned to pump blood. Yet, her words practically stopped it from doing even that.

"You okay?" She successfully stood without help, only to shoot her hands out in front of her for balance.

"Diana," I warned, worried she'd fall, but my terse tone didn't stop her efforts to get to me.

She placed one hand on my shoulder, then reached for my new accessory and closed her other hand around the crucifix. Sad blue eyes lifted to my face as she repeated, "Are you okay?"

"You shouldn't be asking me that. *I* should be asking you."

"I brought up Rebecca, and I know that may not be easy for you."

All that she'd been through, and there she was worried about my feelings. Not only did she not fear me like she should've, she seemed to care about me. For both our sakes, I had to make it stop. It wasn't safe for her to even know me, let alone defend me to assholes like Craig.

"Rebecca's not who I'm thinking about right now, trust me," I revealed, the opposite of what I should've shared.

"Who are you thinking about, then?" She appeared to be holding the cross so tightly it'd likely leave an imprint against her palm, which had to be symbolic of something I didn't care to consider right now.

I reached for her wrist and slanted my face so our lips were closer as I confessed in a damn near hoarse voice, "I think you know."

"Hey, it's us. Can we come in?" Easton asked from the other side of the bedroom door.

Good timing. He'd saved me from nearly kissing this woman. What had I been thinking?

Diana released the cross and peeked back over her shoulder at the bed.

Right . . . your panties.

Her face flushed, and she went over and hid them. No falter in her step that time, which hopefully meant the effects of the drugs were wearing off.

"Come in," I said to Easton once she seemed comfortable to have visitors in the room.

The door slowly opened, and Easton walked in, followed closely by Griffin, who had a mug in his hand.

Griffin glanced at me funny, and I realized why.

"Can someone get me a shirt?" I tore a hand through my semi-damp hair, swiping away the beads of water lingering there from my impromptu shower. "Maybe pants, too. And dry fucking shoes."

A lopsided grin from Griffin caught my eye before he handed over the broth to Diana.

Easton angled his head as if waiting for me to ask him for something else, too. When I glared at him like an impatient CO, he asked, "Want an update first?"

I closed my eyes for a second, frustrated with myself. "Yeah, of course. Anything new?"

Easton ping-ponged his focus between myself and where Diana now sat next to Dallas. She was busy waving away the steam while bringing the mug to her mouth.

"The driver of the truck had a thumb drive on him," Easton reported. "Aside from a few phones, that's all we pulled."

"We'll get the two men you have tied up to talk at our next location." I folded my arms. "Anything on the phones or thumb drive?"

Easton grimaced, apparently not happy with the shit news he was about to give me. "No one on the team has the necessary skills needed to decrypt the USB, so we can't see what's on it. We used the dead men's thumbprints to check their phones, but so far, nothing of value there."

I nodded and turned to Griffin. "Get the laptop. Make two copies of the thumb drive. Email one to POTUS and the other to our people. Sydney and Mya should be able to figure out what's on the USB."

"You sure you don't want to pull Gwen into this? Her hacking skills are unmatched," Griffin said, and I took a few seconds to consider that option.

"She's not working with us, remember?" Both Gwen and I had made that decision only a week ago. Even though she swore she no longer harbored any feelings toward me, she'd decided it was too awkward to be on the team after she'd confessed them. I didn't blame her for wanting to part ways.

Hard to have a professional relationship with someone who'd seen another woman gagging on my cock. And it really sucked at times like this, when her tech skills would be a huge benefit to the team.

"I know, but she's the best, which is what we need," Griffin insisted.

But he had no clue what went down this summer with Gwen. If he did, he'd understand my hesitation to reach out. Unfortunately, this wasn't the place to reveal that particular set of circumstances. So, I had to hope he'd just leave it be and trust Mya and Sydney to take the reins on this one.

"Who's Gwen?" Diana asked softly, and I rolled back my shoulders, uncomfortable all over again.

Thanks, Griff. Where would I even begin? *She's a twenty-four-year-old I convinced myself was you one night while Dallas's dog sitter sucked me off, and from that moment on, my dick has only ever gotten hard with thoughts of you.*

"She's a cyber genius," Griffin offered, since my mouth remained shut. "Boss man here co-runs our security company with her uncle. Her father's a SEAL, like yours. Probably a bit overprotective. He'd have planted a damn tracker on her ass and found her by now, but—"

"Griffin," I cut him off with a warning glare. What the fuck was he thinking?

"Right, sorry." Griffin shook his head in apology. "I'm a few months behind on sleep. Newborn."

"Sleep deprivation didn't seem to prevent you from helping save me, though. Thank you." The sincerity in her voice was something I'd never grow tired of hearing. "Congrats on the baby, too."

"Thank you." Griffin smiled, and I could tell he was two seconds away from powering on his personal phone to show off pictures of his infant son. That'd have nothing to do with his lack of sleep either.

I pointed to the broth, reminding Diana to drink up. I was grateful to see more color returning to her complexion.

"You know," Griffin went on, "I wouldn't be surprised if you and Gwen run in the same circles, seeing as her grandfather is Secretary of Defense and your mom's the new acting Secretary of State."

Yeah, it seemed everything was a family affair with our people. The lines were gray, murky, and always crossing. "He's not her grandfather by blood but by marriage," I reminded him, then moved on to the business at hand, eager to abort the conversation altogether. "Just go ahead and upload the contents of the thumb drive for Mya and Sydney to deal with for now." My tone had more bite than before, and Griffin glared at me, unamused. "They'll decrypt it and see if there's anything helpful there."

Griffin hesitantly lifted his palms, patting the air. "Fine."

"After the call with POTUS," I began, "I'll find us a new location once we're mobile. I'd like to put some distance between us and the port before we head to the President's exfil spot."

"Which direction are we heading?" Easton asked. "And plane, train, or automobile?" His smile stretched. These guys loved to push my fucking buttons.

Like old times, I supposed. "We'll cross the border into Lithuania and get a place there." I gave Griffin my attention and added, "Let Falcon know our destination, too."

Griffin nodded, an uneasy look remaining in his eyes. He started for the door but stopped when Diana asked, "So, the people who were with me in that room are definitely safe?"

"Yeah, the authorities have them now," Easton answered.

"But I assume you were split up from the other scientists somewhere earlier in the week?"

She lowered the mug to her lap and nodded. "Compartmentalization," she whispered, and were more pieces of the puzzle clicking together for her?

I understood where her head was at with that thought, but I'd forgotten Griffin and Easton hadn't been part of our conversation about the EMP weapon. "We'll fill you in soon." I tipped my head toward the door. "Clothes first so we can make the call. See if the priest has coffee, too. I could use some."

Easton winked, damn him. "Roger that."

Once they were both gone, I went over and checked the mug, making sure she was making progress on drinking it. "Keep at it."

She met my eyes but didn't do as I asked.

"What's on your mind?" I reached out and petted Dallas's head, waiting for her to share her thoughts.

"Compartmentalization," she said again. "What if we were all taken in different directions, not just myself and Pierce Quaid? And the goal was to reunite us somewhere and work for them there?"

"You're thinking they split you up to throw us off their tracks leading to the final destination," I said, translating her words. "A backup plan, too. If one of you is rescued, at least it's not *all* of you." These fuckers had their own PACE plan.

"They want us alive, then, right? So, my friends should be okay. We have time to find them." Her hand was shaking a little. Not enough to worry me that she was slipping back into shock, but enough that I was worried she'd spill the hot broth and burn herself.

I stopped petting Dallas and took the mug, setting it on the nightstand. "I'll find them, don't worry."

"And if there are more labs that were hit? More people missing? We have no idea how big this whole thing is."

"I'll handle it, I promise."

She stood but stumbled, so I secured my hand around her forearm to steady her.

"Easy there. You haven't eaten in days. You've been running on shock and adrenaline, but without those drugs in full effect, the pain and hunger are probably kicking in."

"I'm feeling better and also worse at the same time. Is that normal?" Her eyes fell to my hold of her arm. I had no plans to let go until she was back on her ass and safe from collapsing.

"I think that's normal," I reassured her, then nudged the air with my chin, a request to sit. "Once we finish the call with your mom and the President, we'll get on the road, okay? You can sleep in the car. We're going to need to leave a trail of breadcrumbs to our next location, though." I hated this part, but we had no choice.

"I'm bait, right?" she asked, reading between the lines.

"In a perfect world, I'd never allow you to be bait."

"But things are far from perfect," she mused. "If someone gets their hands on an effective EMP weapon, all hell will be unleashed. It's not just the loss of conveniences like Wi-Fi and electricity that'll wreak havoc, it's the loss of the things that depend on those systems. Banking. Infrastructure. Communication. It'll send communities into chaos. Then fear will take over. People will turn on one another."

Yeah, it'll probably be even worse than we can possibly imagine. "I know, but I won't let anything happen to you. By this time tomorrow, you'll be placed in very capable hands, and they'll protect you." I meant that. Word for fucking word. I hated losing sight of her, but I trusted Bravo Team.

"What if I don't want someone else to protect me?" Her

eyes slowly moved up to my face, and I wanted to kiss away the little quiver in her lip.

"I have orders from the President. Rescue you first. Find who's responsible after that." Technically, rescuing Diana hadn't been step one, but I'd made finding her my priority regardless. "I can't do what I need to do with you at my side. It's too dangerous."

"So, who are the breadcrumbs for? Why is it safe to make me bait now and not the day after, or the day after that?"

Dallas howled as if hating the bait idea as much as I did.

I glanced at him, sometimes feeling as though he could read my mind. *I know, but what choice do we have?* "Say the word, and I'll get you to the President's men tonight instead."

"I think you skipped over a few things I just said." She'd called me out, and I pinned her with a hard look, hating the conflict warring inside me at how to truly handle the next steps when it came to this woman.

But no, the farther away from me, the better. Safer for her. Not just for this mission but in general.

"I have concerns that the woman who helped me locate you may be playing both sides. Until I can be certain she's not, I'd rather not pass you over to Bravo Team. If she's fucking me over, she'll ambush the extraction," I finally shared, opting to be honest with her.

"What makes you think she's betraying you?" She started to wiggle free of my grasp, a cue for me to let go of her arm, but I waited until she was seated by Dallas to do so.

"Those traffickers took you from that room this morning five minutes before we arrived. It was too clean. As if someone tipped them off we were coming," I explained, once again securing my hands in my pockets so I wasn't tempted to reach out for her. "She could've alerted them they'd been blown to protect herself from anyone thinking she was the one who provided the location. She cut the window down to five minutes knowing I'd still be able to get to you in time, though." I sure as fuck hoped that was all Alyona had been doing. It'd be a typical chess move of hers to make. The problem was I knew she was capable of making other moves, and I had to be certain she didn't have any other plans, too.

"Who is this woman?" She scratched behind Dallas's ears, and he moaned in pleasure.

Lucky bastard. "She's just someone I used to know."

"Well, if she helped bring you to me, then I'm indebted to her even if she played both sides."

Her words had my spine going ramrod straight. "You don't want to be indebted to that woman, trust me."

"But you are now, aren't you? Because of me?" Her eyes softened as she studied me, her hand stilling on Dallas.

"The last person in the world you need to worry about is me," I said gruffly, emotion tight in my chest and moving into my throat.

I lost her eyes to her lap, but only for a second before those beautiful blues returned to my face. "And if I do anyway?"

30

CARTER

Inside the priest's office, I dug into my bag Easton had dropped off and hurriedly changed.

Unaccustomed to wearing anything around my neck, I was about to remove the chain, but Easton poked his head into the office stopping me.

"You sure you want to do that?" he asked, brows lifting. "A priest gave it to you. You might combust or turn to ashes if you take it off."

"I'm already going to hell, what difference does it make?" My words were as heavy as the cross around my neck, but I let it go, feeling it fall back in place with far too much finality. "You send the files over?"

Griffin joined us and set down a bag at his side—food for the road from the looks of it. Unfortunately, no coffee in sight. "Yeah. Is there anything you want to tell us before you head in for that call with POTUS and get on the road?"

I went ahead and filled them in on the conversation I'd had with Diana about the EMP weapon and a possible attack. When I finished with the bullet points, Griffin continued eyeing me as if I were keeping secrets.

Pinning me with a knowing glare, he grunted out, "Is that all?"

I sighed, not in the mood. I wasn't sure what shit he wanted to get into, but I knew this wasn't the time for one of his lectures. Or for me to spill my guts like only he had a way of getting me to do. I'd need scotch for that anyway. "Any change in Alyona's movements?" I asked instead, because well, priorities.

"Nothing yet, but Germany's a short flight away. Also, Teddy and the others are on their way here. Since we're not interrogating the two guys in the trunk right now," Easton began, gesturing toward the door, "we should probably hit the road so we can get it done at our new spot."

Thanks to my scorched-earth days searching for Rebecca's killers, I'd made contacts and connections in nearly every country known to man, so I wasn't concerned it'd be hard to find a new location for us at the last second. "The call will be fast. POTUS won't admit Diana was working on a classified project for an EMP weapon. Not yet, at least." I'd have to pry that information from him once we were at a more secure spot. Or better yet, have Gray pull it out of his Secretary of Defense father.

"And that's what we're really thinking the President was having them do?" Griffin asked, the touch of doubt unmistakable. Hell, I didn't want to believe it either.

"Only one way to find out." I started for the door, anxious to get back to Diana, telling myself it was because I didn't want her testing out her legs and standing while I was gone.

While she was with us, I had every intention of being the one to provide the help. I was also a greedy asshole and knew our time together was limited and wanted to make the most of it. *Make the most of it? Who the hell was I right now?*

"I'll let the boys know we're prepping to go," Easton said once we were all in the hallway.

"Yeah, thanks." I stopped outside Diana's room, but with Griffin right on my back (and my case), I didn't open up yet.

"You sure you don't need to get anything off your chest?" Griffin and his worrying about me, damnit.

"Is this payback for what I put you through when we were protecting Savanna?" I kept my voice low and faced him. "Are you about to put me through the wringer as well?"

Instead of appeasing me with a *no*, he pushed with more force that time, asking, "Is there something else going on I should know about?"

That *something else* was on the other side of the door. "No, everything's fine."

"Thank God you're not a woman. When Savanna uses that word, I know I'm screwed." He shook his head, and I motioned for him to drop the conversation and assist Easton.

"Fine," he said as a smile passed between us at his ridiculous rebuttal, then he headed outside.

Once alone, I thought back to the last few words Diana and I had exchanged. After she'd declared she'd worry about me no matter what, Easton had walked in with her bag, saving me from being an asshole and demanding she not give a damn about me.

After a resigned sigh that did nothing for my overall state of mind, I opened up.

Diana was sitting upright on the bed and appeared stable even if banged up and exhausted. She perched her light-framed glasses on her nose and smiled at me. "I managed to change on my own, that's progress." She had on dark denim jeans and a Stanford sweater with white Converse. More color back in her face, which was also a good sign.

Unsure what to make of this woman, I wound up studying her like she was a living and breathing museum exhibit.

What was it like to be someone who could smile after everything she'd gone through and not want to lash out at the world? To not be consumed by darkness?

I was a little envious of that, but far more relieved that was the case for her. The last thing I wanted was her hellish week to stain her outlook on life.

"I'm about all set," she said while tidying up her things on the bed as if preparing to leave for a five-star resort. She returned her toothbrush and deodorant to the bag and kept a hairbrush on her lap. Apparently, her mom *had* packed like Diana was going on vacation, and I wasn't sure if that frustrated me or made me grateful.

"You went to the bathroom on your own," was the best I could come up with as I remained leaning into the interior doorframe, some invisible force preventing me from approaching her. She began combing her wet hair. "Not alone. Dallas had my six."

Fuck me. Dallas had my six? Of all the things she could say, those four words were apparently my kryptonite. If I didn't have my shoulder against the doorframe, I would've been the one falling.

I cleared my throat, trying to rid myself of the emotions twisting me up like one of those old wind-up mantel clocks my father used to collect. He always told me the most precious thing we had in life was time. I'd never appreciated those words until lung cancer had taken him far too early, stealing away my time with him.

Now, time was knocking at my door once again. In this case, as to how many more hours I had to share with Diana.

"So, uh, you're doing better." Yeah, I was batting zero right now in terms of communication.

"Much better. I finished the broth, and Easton dropped off some yogurt. Ate that as well. I'm feeling more alert and energized, and I think the drugs are almost gone from my system." She glanced at the phone on the bed, Dallas's tail inching a bit closer to her with each wag. "So, yeah, I'm ready for that call. Just not ready to face my mother."

I finally joined her in the bedroom, and she lifted her eyes, taking me in from my change of boots all the way to my chest covered in a black shirt. The crucifix was now hidden, and I wasn't sure if I was hiding it from her or the world in general.

"We'll make it fast. Proof-of-life kind of thing." I picked up the phone and called the number Griffin had already preprogrammed, then switched it over to FaceTime and handed it to her.

"Diana?" Susan's voice was the first one I heard.

I rounded the bed to stand behind her so I could see the screen and let Susan see me.

"Hey, Mom." Her tone was soft, but she kept steady. Resolute. God, I admired her strength, and if I was being honest, her brilliance, too. "I'm, um, okay. He saved me. *Again.*" Diana tipped her head my way as her mom quietly stared at the both of us.

Susan gave me a terse nod and a quick thank-you before diving into sharing her overwhelming relief that Diana was okay.

"Does Dad know what happened?" Diana asked as the President came into view next to her mother.

"He knows you were taken and are safe, yes," Susan replied before deferring to President Bennett.

"Glad to see you're all right." The President shoved his hands in his slacks pockets, shooting me a wary look. "We're still working on a location for the extraction plan."

"I know the truth." Diana's words stole President Bennett's attention. "And I'm not okay with it."

She was bold, standing up to POTUS like that, and it elicited a strange reaction from me at a time like this—the need to smile. I covered my mouth with my hand to hide it until I could will the emotion away.

"You told her *what* exactly?" The President narrowed his eyes, waiting for me to answer.

That effectively erased the smile from my lips, and I let my hand fall. "Nothing you want to discuss on this call. Just tell us one thing. How many more labs were hit that night?"

He gripped his temples, and on a sigh, he revealed, "One, but it was American-led only. No other countries were aware of the location." He paused to let that sink in. "Each country had their own lab, separate from the collaborative efforts of the project in Amsterdam."

This was even more compartmentalized than we thought. "Were their labs hit, too?"

"They won't tell us. We're trying to find out, but—"

"But no one trusts each other right now," I finished for the President, putting two and two together. "Where was the American-led lab located?" I was agitated all over again at the need-to-know situation. How the hell did they expect me to help if they kept me in the dark?

"Montana." He slowly lifted his head, and I read the anguished look in his eyes. I knew he wouldn't say more, but he didn't need to. I'd heard a rumor or two over the years about what our government had been testing out there.

"End the call," I told Diana.

"Wait." The President abruptly held up his hand. "I still need you to do what I asked. Are you changing your mind?"

"No, sir," I hissed. "You'll hear from me when we're ready for her extraction."

Diana turned on the bed to peer at me as if searching for what to do.

"End the call," I said again, and she did as I asked. "Dallas, time to go."

He immediately jumped off the bed, then spun in a circle before sitting, clearly waiting for Diana to get up, too.

Rounding the bed, I went over to her and offered her my hand. She accepted my invitation of help without question, but I could tell there was something brewing in her brain.

She didn't keep me waiting long. As soon as she was fully steady on her feet, she pulled her hand back and rested it on her hip. "What is it you know? What's in Montana other than the second lab?"

"A bunker," I revealed. "As in *the* bunker."

This wasn't just an EMP device our government decided to develop. No, the two labs existed because someone more than likely had already created a catastrophic EMP weapon, and America was on the chopping block to be their target.

That was why POTUS supported this project, even if he may not have liked going behind people's backs to do it. He knew if the U.S. didn't have something to threaten the enemy with—whoever they were—they'd deploy the weapon and end our country as we knew it. It was Cold War shit all over again. Peace through the threat of mutual annihilation.

Now our labs were destroyed, leaving a potentially new enemy with the ability to gain access to the weapon before America could. It was a nightmare, to say the least.

"What are you thinking but not saying?" she asked, reading me damn well.

"If America collapses, the politicians and the rich have an underground bunker to live out their days while they plan a way to make a comeback. I'm guessing our government has a reasonable belief we're on the verge of that happening."

"That's real? Not Hollywood stuff?" I could see her drifting within the conversation even as her brain was still cycling over the details. "I mean, people have been saying cold fusion is mythical, but I didn't let that stop me from believing. So, I guess a doomsday bunker is possible, too."

"It's real, and I know this because Rebecca was approached years ago. She was offered the opportunity to buy us a spot there for a just-in-case day." They hadn't told us the location or details since we'd turned down the offer, but the second POTUS said Montana, I knew that had to be where it was at.

"Ohhh."

"I asked Rebecca to turn them down. Save myself while others die? Not happening." The fact Rebecca could ever believe for a minute I'd do that was . . . well, she apparently hadn't known me well, just like I hadn't known her.

"That sounds like a you thing to say."

"How do you know what I'd say?" I hadn't meant to snap out those words, but I was on edge, tense, and for one of the first times in a long time—nervous.

"I just . . ." She swallowed, red traveling up her throat and into her cheeks. "Because energy doesn't lie."

Energy? Was that what *this* was?

"Does, um, this news mean things are worse than we thought?"

I stared at the floor, unable to tell her the truth. *It means we might already be fucked.*

DIANA

VILNIUS, LITHUANIA

OVERPROTECTIVE WAS AN UNDERSTATEMENT. CARTER'S behavior toward me was beyond vigilant. I didn't have to hear him outside the bathroom to know he was there. Nor did I need X-ray vision to see through the door to know I'd find him there with arms folded, a shoulder resting against the doorframe, checking his watch every thirty seconds waiting for me to finish my second shower of the day.

The shower was needed after five hours on the road, most of it spent asleep with Dallas's head on my lap.

Earlier that afternoon, we'd arrived at a two-story cottage home outside the capital of Lithuania. The cobblestone street had disappeared into farmland and dirt roads that eventually led us to our current destination.

How Carter happened to score us a romantic-looking getaway outside the city was beyond me. He must've arranged it all while I'd slept. I wasn't even sure how we'd crossed the border without being stopped. The man was a mystery. Always had been, and most likely always would be.

What frustrated me was that we'd been at this cute little place for hours, Carter and his men busying themselves with work, and all they'd let me do was eat, sleep some more, and twiddle my thumbs in between petting Dallas.

The haze of the drugs had lifted, which meant the aches and pains had slipped in. Advil had replaced Sierra as my best friend. But maybe now that my head was clear, I could be useful if they'd let me try and help.

Of course, I'd leave the interrogation of the two Serbian traffickers—thankfully happening in the shed out back and not in the room next door—to the team.

At one point, Carter had returned to the cottage with blood on his forearm and shirt. He'd peered at me, then at his arm, then shook his head and disappeared, returning with a white shirt. Probably not the best choice since he'd returned from another go at the men in the shed with blood on that shirt, too.

After he'd changed *again,* donning a black shirt (*way to make smart choices)*, I'd casually let him know I was going to shower. A more thorough one this time. Pretty sure Carter hadn't rinsed all the soap from my hair earlier. Of course, I wouldn't mind having him massage my scalp again while I was more coherent and not shaking nonstop from drugs and fear.

So, there we were. Shower complete. Teeth brushed. Hair clean and towel-dried. Carter still hovering outside the room, babysitting me when he ought to be working.

Unmistakable frustration pushed through his voice as he asked, "You almost done?"

"I could pass a sobriety test, just so you know," I called back through the door. "Ask me to touch my nose. Walk in a straight line. No problem." But prevent my heart from skipping into my throat every time this man locked eyes with me? Nope, that I couldn't do.

"You could still lose your balance. You've been through a lot."

If he was going to be stubborn, so was I. "I'm fine."

"Griffin reminded me nothing good ever happens when a woman says she's fine."

I could've laughed at that, but I abruptly swung open the door instead, and he nearly fell into me. *You really were leaning right against it, huh?*

He shot his hand out against the door, steadying himself as his gaze flew over my PJs. Of course Mom had packed as if I'd been going for a nice stay at the Ritz. Pink silk pajamas with my initials monogrammed on the front pocket.

Locating my glasses on the vanity, I slipped them back on. Those full lips of his wore a smile beautifully, and somehow he also managed to pull off handsome even when frowning like now.

"You need to change." Carter and his way of grunting words like each delivered a command all on its own.

"Do you find my pajamas that offensive? We are sleeping here, right?" I flicked the front of my shirt. "Nighttime protocol dictates sleepwear." Now that I wasn't drugged or hungry, I was back to myself again. That me would take orders if it meant keeping safe and not compromising the integrity of his mission, especially with so much on the line—but I drew the line at having him dictate what was acceptable clothing.

Still waiting for him to answer me, I set my hip against the counter, trying to pull off casual when I was fairly certain the moon could knock out of orbit and I wouldn't notice, completely captivated by the very way this man stared at me.

"I'm fine with your pajamas, but we're not going to be

here long, and we're about to have visitors. So, you may want to hold off with the nighttime protocol until we're at our next destination."

My eyes cut to his hand on the door, to the visible veins running along the back of it and up across his arm. "What kind of visitors?"

Carter brought two fingers to the side of his face, then tapped at his ear. "My team can hear us, and I can hear them, so I'm muting the comms on my side."

"Ah. Those devices have come a long way since the embassy." I worked a little smile to my lips, and he lowered his hand from the doorway, eyes moving over my shoulder toward the shower. "I assume you have the comm in your ear so your teammates can let you know when the guests arrive?" At his nod, I asked, "What kind of guests are we talking about? Polish-the-good-silverware kind? Or should we be sharpening the knives?"

That subtle lift of only the side of his lip could destroy me. Sink a battleship. Just take me out. I was in trouble. So much trouble. Falling hard. Falling fast. *Who am I kidding? I fell thirteen years ago (figuratively and literally, almost through the floor if not for him).*

"Somewhere in between those two." He turned, heading into the small bedroom, which was only a slight upgrade in size from the priest's room.

I followed him and made a beeline for my bag atop the bed to find something more suitable to wear. Of course Mom didn't include any T-shirts I'd left at her place in D.C. "So, who are these visitors?" Jeans would have to make do. A gold V-neck silk blouse for the top.

"The woman who helped me locate you will be here soon." He pointed to the ceiling. "Helo. Fast-rope approach.

We have eyes on their movement. No surprise attack, don't worry."

Somehow, I wasn't worried. Being in Carter's presence may have made my pulse soar, but it wasn't because I feared for my life. No, I felt safe with him, like there was an impenetrable force field surrounding me.

"So, she's betraying you?" *Sounds like knives are needed, then.*

Still in the black fatigues he'd changed into in Latvia, he hid his hands in his pockets. "I'm assuming she figured out you're more valuable than she originally realized, and she wants you for herself."

"Why didn't she come for me at the warehouse instead? Why let you get to me first?"

"By letting me take you, she doesn't get blamed. She can be the hero. Locate us and turn you over to whoever wants you." He kept a few feet away from me, quietly observing me. Continuing to remain calm.

"Is she a criminal, then?"

"Yes."

"Then why in the world would you go to her for help in the first place?"

"Life isn't always so black and white."

His nonanswer started to betray his confidence that "everything would be just fine," and the muscles in my body tensed up, my back aching all over again. *Come on, Advil. Don't fail me now.* "Are you hoping she'll lead us to who's after me?" *Is that the play?*

"Doubtful she knows who's after you yet, but she's connected enough to get word out she has you. And once the people after you find out, they'll offer her a deal." His eyes fell to the clothes in my hand like a silent request to change. "I had concerns she might double-cross me, but those concerns grew when someone gave the Serbians who had you the heads-up we were coming." While he'd shared that concern before, the next part was new. "Those doubts were confirmed when my people identified eight of her best men on the move to Lithuania tonight."

"So, this peaceful little safe house is about to become a warzone?" I should have been terrified, but my heart was still stuck in traffic, only ebbing along ever so slowly. Beat for beat. Not wild or frantic like it should've been.

"No, it's fine."

I smirked the second he'd tossed that word right back at me, and was he fighting the desire to smile back?

"Sorry, wrong word, huh?" And there it was. The sexy side smile he rocked so well. "We'll be good. Not fine, but perfectly okay."

"Mmmhmm." I really did want to sink my teeth into his answer and believe him. *But* eight of this well-connected woman's men were about to show up, so there was that not-so-little detail to consider.

"She won't fire at my people as long as we don't shoot first, but I need her to think she has the upper hand when she arrives."

"And then what?" I picked up my change of clothes.

"I take back control."

"How?" After the week I'd had, I wasn't a fan of being in the dark.

"The less you know, the better." Not what I wanted to hear, but he quickly pinpointed the reason for my scowl and before I could speak, added, "She'll be able to read you too easily. And we can't give this woman any ammunition, trust me."

"I'm not great at bluffing, but I consider being a shitty liar an admirable trait. Ranks right up there with having a sense of humor."

"Can't argue with you there." That deep tone of his and the harsh look in his eyes made me wonder if he was thinking about a few lies he'd come across in his own past. Did they have to do with Rebecca? "So, if you'd like to remain in those silk pajamas that show your . . ." He cleared his throat, eyes falling to my breasts.

I brought the clothes to my chest when I realized my nipples were poking through the fabric. *Kill me now.* This man provoked such strange reactions from me. Aroused at a time like this? What in the actual hell? "I'll change."

His gaze slowly moved up the column of my throat to my face. "You'll be by my side the whole time when she arrives. There's no safe room here, but they'll never hurt you. Not only because of who I am, but because of who you are."

"Who you are." Who is that exactly? "But?" There had to be one coming.

Lifting his hands from his pockets, he surprised me by reaching out to remove my glasses. Cocking his head, he said in a low voice, "She likes to play games. She'll say and possibly do things that may make you uncomfortable." There was more he was saying without actually verbalizing it, I could feel it. "We have a history, and she may try and use that to her advantage."

Ohh. Cue the upset stomach and the world flipping upside down.

Slipping my glasses back on, he reassured me, "Don't worry. I won't let her take you. Nothing will happen to you."

"Okay," I forced out, quickly heading back to the bathroom. He wouldn't leave me alone, and if he had visitors to prepare for, I needed to hurry.

Once the door was closed, I hurriedly swapped my PJs for

the jeans and blouse, then returned to the room, finding him leaning against the bedroom door, one booted foot propped up, eyes on me.

"Where do you want me?"

His eyes widened ever so slightly as his gaze shot to the bed, jaw going tight, only for his eyes to land back on me as his boot hit the floor with a thud.

I tamped down the heat flaring inside me, waiting for him to speak. When he kept quiet, I restated my question. "What should I do?"

He fixed the chain around his neck and patted his chest as if ensuring the cross was still hidden, then pushed away from the door. "We'll get you a plated vest to put on under your shirt, not that you'll need it, but I'd rather be paranoid than unprepared." He erased the space between us but didn't reach for me. I wanted him to. I wanted to go back to the hugs and hand holding like he'd done earlier when my state had been much more precarious than now. But he was mission-focused now, and as he should be.

I also felt him erect an invisible wall between us, and maybe it wasn't a bad idea to try and build my own before I became so attached to this man my heart became a permanent transplant in my throat. I cleared the knot forming there and asked, "Did your team learn anything from the USB? The interrogations?"

He angled his head, gaze going to the ceiling.

"No teleprompter up there," I blurted, my stomach squeezing from memories of the past. That also reminded me, where was his Southern accent? I hadn't heard it slip through once today. Then again, I wasn't exactly myself earlier.

Carter's piercing eyes fixed on me as his lips drew together in a straight line. That bladed jawline of his alone could be what sharpened those knives. "My people decrypted the content on the USB."

I wished he trusted me enough to treat me like part of the team. Like I had a right to know the full scope of the situation without having to ask.

His team had coddled me, acting like I was their patient today, not the reason why we were in this mess. Then again, I couldn't blame myself for this situation. I'd never meant to stumble upon a theory that could be actualized into a weapon. I'd unknowingly been part of a project that could have catastrophic results.

Maybe I should've known? Did Bahar? Did William? Was I the only one so focused on my research I hadn't seen the bigger picture? Were there red flags I'd missed? Ignored? Shit, I was slipping back into guilt mode when I knew damn well that didn't do any good.

He palmed his jawline, and I took notice of the distinguished touch of silver here and there in his facial hair. A little at his temples, too. Why was that so damn sexy?

"I lost you." His brows slanted.

"How could you possibly know that?"

He leaned in, dropping his mouth over my ear, sending shivers and chills down my spine and through my limbs. All the delicious side effects of this man's presence that I shouldn't experience or feel right now. "Because energy doesn't lie," he murmured, and well, there it was. The scintillating Southern cut through those four words and right into me.

We had bad guys to stop. A world to save. And I was paying attention to his voice and the sexy way he'd just thrown my own words back at me. I needed to stop wondering why I felt so energetically connected to this man. "The, um, USB." *Focus. Don't feel the pulse of electricity strumming between you right now. The bad guys are coming and danger is around the corner.*

Carter straightened, his chest lifting from a deep inhalation as if realizing he'd also been distracted. "The traffickers were taking you to Oslo. Once there, they'd be provided new instructions for the next location, along with payment."

I took a moment to digest the news. "Anything else?"

"The intel on the USB matched what the men we've been questioning tonight said. They don't know who hired them. My people are working to chase down their previous movements and track the emails, but they're not optimistic. That concerns me, because my people are good."

"But the best is this Gwen person, right? Maybe she can help?"

"My team already reached out to Gwen a few hours ago. She'd prefer not to work with me, but since she doesn't need to join us over here, I guess it's fine."

"Why doesn't Gwen—" I cut myself off, leaving the question hanging. *Not my business.* I didn't need to know about his history with another woman. "I trust you'll do what's best for the country."

"And for you." His Adam's apple rolled. "I'll do what's best for you."

"I believe you." I nodded, trying to suppress the flutter of emotions and bitter sting of jealousy.

"Because energy doesn't lie?" He did that sexy side-smile thing again, holding far too much power over me with that look alone.

"Right," I said, a bit breathlessly. "But I'm pretty sure our story was written thirteen years ago." The Fates may have been playing a cruel game, dropping this man in and out of my life over the years, but it was clear now what their endgame was. "You're the guy who's meant to save the girl, so she can—"

"Save the world," he rasped, brows snapping together as the memory of that day must've rekindled in his mind, too.

"We're connected for a reason," I whispered, hating the sadness finding its way in my voice, "just maybe not for the reason I'd originally thought."

"JUST PUT THESE ON AND TRY TO RELAX." I HANDED DIANA the Bose headphones and MP3 player I'd had Teddy buy at the airport in Hamburg before we'd flown to Latvia the other day. I couldn't walk around shopping with my face all over the news, so he'd had to do it for me.

Diana accepted the headphones and MP3 player, staring at them with parted lips. "These are just like the ones I had at the lab, only blue."

I strapped my preferred blade to the side of my leg, then checked my sidearm, making sure it was fully loaded before returning it to the holster, leaving it unstrapped for easy access. "Yeah, they were out of pink at the airport."

The little gasp and her cheeks flushing had me realizing my error. "I noticed them on the security cameras before the lab was hit. Thought it'd be nice if you have something familiar to help." Hopefully I dodged a bullet.

I shrugged, uncertain why she kept looking at me like I'd done something special. "What?"

"Nothing." She shook her head as if she could physically remove a thought with that little movement. "Well, thank you, but I'm not a child who needs to block out the sound of arguing. You do know that, right?"

She'd finally gifted me with her sweet (albeit sassy) voice, and the fact my first thought was to spank that ass of hers for the attitude was *not* good.

"Give us a second," I told Easton and Griffin, the only two in the room with us.

Griffin checked his watch. "ETA is five minutes."

Fortunately, shooting him my, *I know, I know,* look was enough, and he tapped Easton on the shoulder to get a move on and follow orders.

Teddy and the others were already in position waiting for Alyona's people to drop in from the sky. Once the two of us were alone (aside from Dallas), she went over to the armchair by the unlit fireplace and sat. She looped the headphones around her neck and plugged the cord into the MP3 player.

Dallas curled up by her bare feet and gave me a little yelp, apparently angry at me for some reason.

Yeah, yeah, join the club.

Diana reached down and petted him, and her blouse was loose enough to reveal a hint of the chest plate beneath it.

"Do people still use these?" She tilted the MP3, continuing to stroke Dallas's head.

"I guess so, or they wouldn't sell them, right?" I winked. *What the fuck was that about?* Add it to the ever-growing list of strange shit I did around her.

The fact this woman was peering at me with a sultry expression, though, really did have me wanting to take her over my knee. I didn't even need a reason why other than she shouldn't have been turning me on at all, never mind minutes away from go-time.

But she was, damnit. The image of swatting her ass, then smoothing my hand in small, soothing circles over the red mark of my handprint there, before plunging my cock in her pussy had me . . . *Fuck.* I wouldn't survive twelve more hours near her at this rate. I needed to get her to Bravo Team as soon as possible.

"To answer your smart-ass comment-slash-question about why I'm giving you that," I finally cut back to it as she pulled her hand away from Dallas's head, much to his displeasure, "I can't have you looking like you're sitting here waiting for war when they show up."

She granted me one of her innocent smiles. *Yes, keep reminding me you're sweet so I stay away.* Keep my darkness —my immorality and filth—from contaminating you.

"That makes sense, and um, sorry for the smart-assery."

What could I tell her? That her sass aroused me? That was messed up for too many reasons to process right now.

I fixed my attention on her slender fingers holding the MP3 player as she began to scroll through the songs I'd downloaded on the flight from Hamburg to Riga. She rewarded me with another smile I didn't deserve, but it was one that met her eyes, making the time I'd taken to download the songs worth every second.

"You and I have the same eclectic taste. I like everything except for the songs I don't."

Somehow that made perfect sense to me.

"You did this for me or . . .?" That hopeful, appreciative look in her eyes as she waited for me to answer sent me back a step.

I had to stop these moments that kept happening between us. Put the brakes on it again, the same way I'd done that Easter weekend inside the restaurant a decade ago.

Only, every time I tried to kill the connection between us, I wound up allowing myself one more moment. I told myself it was okay to let myself experience some of her hope, optimism, and sunshine. Let it soak into me so I felt alive.

Just. One. More. Time. I was out of time, though. No more "just one" to be had. This thing between us had to end tonight before she was hurt because of it. Because of me.

What'd you ask me again? Shit, the music, right. "Teddy uploaded the music. I have no idea what's in there. You must have the same taste as him." Thankfully, my poker face was far better than hers. Hell, it had to be to keep me alive over the years.

"Oh." The disappointment that one syllable managed to pack sent me rocking back on the heels of my boots, and biting down on my back teeth to keep from confessing the truth.

I stalked you. Learned we love the same beats. We also hate the same ones, too.

Easton and Griffin returned, saving me from another "just one more time" moment with her. Easton quickly alerted, "Sixty seconds to arrival."

I tapped my left ear, unmuting my comm so the others could hear me again.

I dug into my pocket and discreetly positioned a second comm in my right ear. An operator always had a backup plan, and then two more.

"Headphones on," I directed Diana, not missing the sudden stiffness in her shoulders and hands, her nerves probably taking back over. At the feel of my phone vibrating in my pocket, I retrieved it. The name LIONESS was on the screen. "She's calling."

"Wait, why would she do that?" Diana asked instead of following my orders to listen to her music. "Is she changing her mind? *Not* coming?"

"No, she's giving us a heads-up she's about to drop in," Easton told her before I could.

I waved my hand, reminding her to put on the headphones.

"Why?" Diana's curiosity could get her killed one day. What if I couldn't be there to save her next time?

While I froze for the briefest second, reflecting how I could never let that happen, Easton informed her, "Because she knows not to fuck with Carter unless she wants this to turn into a slaughter fest."

I waited for the phone to ring once more as Diana finally did as I instructed, then I placed the call on speaker. "Alyona. Are you checking that the mission was a success this morning? I'd have assumed you would've already heard we acquired the package."

Diana must not have hit play, because she shivered the moment she heard the reference to herself. Had I really expected her to jam out to Nickelback's, "How You Remind Me," the first song on the playlist, instead?

"I did hear it was mission success." Alyona's tone was a few decibels above necessary.

"Then what's going on? Sounds like you're on a helo. Going somewhere?" I asked, playing a part I wasn't in the mood to play. Not when the *package* was involved and staring at me, wide-eyed behind her glasses.

"We need to talk. I'm dropping in now." Alyona was never one to waste time, I'd give her that. Plus, the familiar *whomp! whomp!* of the blades chopping the air filtered through the cottage, leaving her zero room to fuck around with her so-called pleasantries and stall.

"Order your men on the perimeter to stand down," she issued the command.

"You know I'd never shoot first when it comes to you, but

if you walk in here with your weapons pointed, I may change my mind," I warned. "The lack of heads-up about your visit is testing my patience, Alyona."

"We won't draw our weapons if you don't," she responded, the line going dead before I could reply.

I pocketed my phone and glanced at Diana before turning to Griffin. "Stand down," I ordered my guys over the comm in my left ear, then tipped my chin toward Diana, a silent order for Griffin to be on guard alongside her chair.

With her safely positioned between my two best friends, I swiveled my focus to the doorway, waiting alongside Easton for Alyona's arrival.

"They're on the property now. Four tangos plus the Lioness," Teddy said in my ear. We didn't use our usual call signs. No need. This wasn't a mission. It was a trap.

I counted back from ten, knowing it'd take her no longer than that to make her way through the small cottage to get to us.

Two men entered first. All black military clothes, same as us. Rifles slung across their chests, but not in hand. Alyona walked into the room behind them in her standard operational clothes. Jeans, boots, and a fitted leather jacket.

"Carter." Alyona may have been addressing me as she waved her two men off to the sides of the room into readied positions, but her eyes were pointed intensely at Diana.

Dallas wasn't amused. He sat up and snarled, showing his teeth.

"Down, boy," I ordered. He gave me a hesitant look before stilling his snarl, but maintained his guarded posture. *I know, damnit. I know.* I pivoted to the side so I could face Alyona while keeping Diana in my peripheral view. "Why the unexpected visit? You have your three million, and you clearly gave the Serbians the heads-up we were coming. I assume you wanted to wash your hands free of any involvement in our op." No point in sugarcoating.

Alyona stopped before me, setting her hand on my chest, and her brows slanted in surprise, discovering the crucifix there. My shirt was the only barrier preventing it from branding her skin.

I gripped her wrist and removed her hand, surprised she didn't shoot me a coy look or one of her standard playful smiles.

"What are you doing here?" I asked again, more bite to my tone that time. I wasn't in the mood to play games.

"New information surfaced, and I'm here to make a deal." There was a slight quiver in Alyona's voice, the only curveball of the evening so far.

"What kind of deal?" *Stop looking at Diana, damnit.* "And eyes on me," I barked out a bit aggressively even for me.

"You rocked the boat by taking her," she said while peering at me, "and because I helped you, so did I."

I tensed, waiting for her to get to her point.

"Someone discovered I helped you," she continued. "Despite my efforts to put space between us, they found out."

"Me, specifically? Or helped the *masked* men at the port they still can't identify?"

"They didn't mention you by name, no," she clarified. "I have forty-eight hours to hand over the package, or I'm finished."

From the corner of my eye, I noticed the *package* stir in her seat.

Alyona glanced over at one of her armed men and gave him a little nod. When he reached into his pocket and strode over, offering her a phone, Dallas growled and resumed his defensive stance.

Diana reached out and rested her hand on his head, perhaps realizing he was on edge. Or maybe she needed him, not the other way around.

"You ditched the iPad back in Riga. Made it harder for me to locate you," Alyona noted as she scrolled through the phone, and her guy kept his eyes trained on Dallas as if worried he'd bite.

Maybe you should. "You think I didn't know you were tracking me with that thing?" I arched my brow. "Besides, I know you enjoy your games. I couldn't make it too easy for you to hunt me down." She'd clearly found the breadcrumbs we'd strategically left for her between Riga and here. "After you tipped off the Serbians their location was compromised, it was a coin toss if you'd track me down," I answered honestly. "In your attempt to remain blameless in Diana's rescue, you inadvertently put a target on your head."

"I was ill-advised, and that person has been handled." She nudged the phone my way.

I swiped through the screenshots, reading over the messages. Checking out the photos there. "They're blackmailing you."

"That's a lot more than blackmail." It was quite possibly the first time I'd ever seen this woman rattled.

Alyona also had no idea blackmail was what ultimately led to Rebecca's demise, and now wasn't the time to be weighted down by the past. I needed to stow away that memory for another time. If Alyona was truly being screwed over because I'd come to her for an assist, then I owed it to her to help before she died because of me.

Proof, yet again, Diana wasn't safe around me. I had to remember that. Never fucking forget it. It also . . . crushed me.

"They have me by the balls, Dominick." She focused on

Diana. "They know every one of my offshore accounts. The location of my properties. They have my parents' and sister's addresses."

"This has intelligence written all over it." *POTUS is right. The lab hit was an inside job.* "Not the CIA or NSA." Anyone with that level of intel on her in our government already knew Diana was secure, and they wouldn't need Alyona's assistance. "Someone has been stockpiling shit against you, and they were waiting for the time to use it."

"Regardless," Alyona began, closing her hand into a fist and placing it over her heart, "I need the package more than you do."

"No." The word came out before I could stop it, ricocheting around the otherwise quiet room. I heard Dallas begin to growl, and it only firmed up my resolve Diana wouldn't be going anywhere with anyone other than me. "I'm not letting you take her."

"The package has a name," Diana spoke up at the same time Dallas's growl intensified.

Alyona whipped her green eyes her way, but only for a second before pinning me with a hard, determined look. "Don't make me fight you, because I will. I won't let these assholes hurt my family."

"Then fight back. You're not one to give up like this." I'd never known her weaknesses before, but her family . . . apparently they were her kryptonite. "Our interests are aligned. Whoever is blackmailing you is my target, too. I'm sorry I involved you, but we'll take this group down. There's a lot more at stake than you realize."

"I'm not taking chances. Let me have Diana, and you can track her to the drop-off point. You can find out who's after her that way, but I need to do my part and hand her over."

I wanted to help her, but I wasn't going to sacrifice

Diana to do that. "Blood will spill between us before I so much as consider that plan," I seethed, hating she was putting me in this position, even if I first put us here by reaching out. "We'll find another way. We'll let him or her *think* you have Diana in your possession. Buy us time in figuring out who's behind this." I angled my head toward her two men on guard in the room. "Tell your guys at the house, and the men you have as a backup five mikes out, to stand down."

"What makes you think I have more men in the wings?" she challenged.

"It'd have been unwise for you not to, and you're anything but that." I tensed at the possibility that . . . "Are you currently transmitting your location?" Was this a Trojan horse play from her, or another error in judgment? "Were you tailed?"

"You think I'd let someone follow me here and lose any leverage I have to keep myself and my family safe?" The woman wasn't an eye roller, but at my doubting expression, she honored me with one. I just had no desire to punish her for it like I would've in the past. No, whatever I'd felt for her, even though it'd been sexual only, was gone. Left in the past where it belonged. Where it'd die.

"I knew you were coming," I shared. "We spotted your men crossing the German border. It's possible someone else knows, too."

"We know each other well, Dominick. You saw me because I let you. Because I wanted you to. This phone is also untraceable. So no, I wasn't spotted by anyone other than your people." She stepped back and opened her arms. "Go ahead, have your people check us for trackers."

I wouldn't be refusing that offer. Considering she was stressed about the blackmail, I also wouldn't make the assumption she was playing with a full deck. I had to assume the worst, that our location was potentially compromised.

"Check them," I told Easton, then I covered my other ear where my secondary team awaited orders. "Did you hear that?" I asked Gray over comms.

"I did. We've got eyes in the sky and are checking for any additional movement. It's pretty quiet out here. Her backup crew is still holding position, and no radio transmissions from them yet."

I relaxed the smallest bit after Gray shared what I wanted to hear. "Roger. Keep me posted. Out."

I hadn't planned to bring Falcon there, but the moment I'd had concerns Alyona might be a problem for me, I'd pulled them into action. I'd had the team (minus Gwen) board my second jet and fly to Europe, arriving in time for the showdown with Alyona. They were currently my alternate, contingency, *and* emergency plans all rolled into one.

"Another team in your ear?" Alyona asked while lowering her arms. "Always prepared."

"They're clear, boss," Easton said, returning next to me.

We still needed to move to a new location, and soon, in case Alyona had been careless and followed.

"What do you really want with Diana?" Was Alyona attempting to lure me into agreeing with her? That wouldn't be happening. "This isn't just about her mother setting you up for Rebecca's murder, is it?"

"Wait, what?" Diana's words, and her small gasp, pulled my attention to her just as her headphones fell around her neck.

"You didn't tell her?" Alyona's soft tone didn't last long, and the sting of bitterness at her situation cut through her teeth. "He believes your mother is responsible for the international headlines blaming him for murdering his wife."

This was an obvious crushing blow to Diana's already fragile state. She could only take so much, and we didn't have time to dive into this now.

"Your mother is why he's not only a wanted man, but his face is being broadcast all over the world," Alyona said, cutting into Diana even deeper that time.

Diana dropped the MP3 player and it tumbled alongside Dallas's paws. He howled and sat taller, bopping his nose into her leg as she stood.

I patted the air, needing to calm the waters before things escalated and I needed to do something rash to settle her down. *Physical contact. Oxytocin. Skin on skin.* The fact those thoughts had pushed through my mind at a time like this . . . I needed to get my own shit together, never mind Diana losing hers. "It's okay, I promise." My acting skills were subpar, but at least Diana surrendered a small nod. No evidence of trembling, which was another good sign.

"I've never seen you patient like this with anyone before." Alyona tossed the burner phone back to her armed guard. "You clearly lied to me about why you wanted her." She made a clucking sound with her tongue before calling me out, "You *wanted* to save her."

Doing my best to mask my irritation at how this situation was unfolding, realizing hand-to-hand combat with Alyona's men would've been preferable to this conversation, I jutted my chin and hissed the truth, "If Diana winds up in the wrong hands, your parents and sister are in danger regardless."

"How so?" Alyona didn't cower back when I towered over her, boldly locking eyes with me while waiting for answers.

"I can't tell you more, but your parents live in Germany and your sister is in the U.S." According to what I'd seen on the blackmail screenshots, at least. "Both are potential targets for an attack. Not just a city. The whole fucking country."

Germany was one of the countries partnered on the project, which meant Germans were potentially at risk from an attack, too. But I didn't need to reveal more details to Alyona than I already had.

"You know me. I'm not lying." I set a hand to my chest, feeling the crucifix under my shirt beneath my palm. "So, what's it going to be? Are you helping us take down the bastard who's threatening you, or are you going to fight me instead?"

"You have twelve hours to convince me working alongside you is better than going up against you. After that, I skip to my next plan." Alyona shook her head, then brought her wrist to her mouth and ordered, "Stand down. Do not engage."

I covered my left ear to listen to Gray as he announced, "They're packing up into their two SUVs and holding position."

"Roger that," I told Gray. "We need to exfil within thirty in case they had a tail."

"Agree. Prepping the team now," Gray answered.

"Be in touch soon," I said, then muted my comm and redirected my attention to Alyona. "I assume you've already tried to track the blackmailer down through the emails they sent, and you came up empty?"

"My people hit a wall of encryption they couldn't crack. We had a short window, so we moved to the alternate plan in tracking you down," she responded.

"Looks like we're in contingency territory now," Easton spoke up.

"We have people who can get past the layers of encryption." If not Sydney, then Gwen.

"So, what do we do now?" Diana asked, drawing my focus. She was still standing, stroking Dallas's head as she visibly held her ground.

"First step is to not kill each other in the next twelve hours." Alyona approached Diana, and Griffin took a protective step forward right along with Dallas. "You're the person endangering my business and family. I'll work with you, but I don't like you."

"Yeah, well, I don't like you either." Diana frowned, then chucked the headphones onto the chair and sidestepped Alyona. "If you'll excuse me . . ."

"Where are you going?" Unable to stop myself, I gently took hold of Diana's arm, worried about her being alone with Alyona's armed men there.

"I need a minute to think." At Diana's words, I shook my head no.

"You can have that minute, but it won't be alone." Still keeping hold of her, I told Griffin, "We roll out soon. Keep an eye on them for me."

"Roger that," Griffin said, and I unhanded Diana as I muted my second comm.

Alyona grabbed hold of my arm and pushed up in her combat boots to reach my ear. "She's *your* weakness, isn't she?" I looked over my shoulder and met her eyes. "Just don't let her be your downfall."

33

DIANA

"I HAVE SO MANY QUESTIONS." I BEGAN PANIC-PACING. NOT proud of it, but it happened nevertheless.

"How about we start with one and go from there?" With the heel of his hand, Carter gently closed the door. Lock engaged, he faced me.

The vest beneath my shirt was like a corset, making it hard to breathe. I began fumbling with my blouse buttons. "Okay, to start, can I take off the chest plate?"

He grimaced, but I was pretty sure that broody look was about the situation and not me. He held up a hand, and my fingers went still on the buttons. "We could have incoming. We're in the clear now, and my people will give us a head start to exfil before anyone can get to us, but I'd feel better if you kept it on."

Could have incoming? Great, more reason to pace. "Fine." I bent forward instead, palms on my thighs, nails digging into my flesh, as I searched for the deep breath my lungs didn't seem to be interested in providing.

After the day I'd had—no, the *week* I'd survived—the

good, the bad, and the ugly kept stacking up. I'd never felt so out of control in my life.

It wasn't like the fate of the world potentially rested on our shoulders and whether we stopped someone from creating a device to devastate multiple countries . . .

At the sight of his boots stopping in front of me, I forced myself to stand. Despite our current situation, this amazingly strong but closed-off man kept offering me his patience and his protection.

I thought back to that woman's words a few minutes ago. *"I've never seen you patient like this with anyone before."* The man had been the definition of understanding at nearly every one of our encounters over the years. I'd assumed that was the norm for him, despite his gritty persona.

"What happened out there wasn't what you expected, but it's good for us, right?" I asked one of the more pressing questions. "Bad for her, but a possible lead to help locate who's after me."

He quietly nodded.

Now for the question I wasn't sure how to ask, but I had to know. It was too painful for me to leave problems unsolved. An equation incomplete. A lack of closure always triggered a sense of anxiousness, and ever since the day I'd met this man, it'd felt as though our story was incomplete. I blamed my issues for feeling that way, but there was one way I could start to feel some closure.

"You want to know about your mom and the news story," he interrupted my chaotic thoughts.

My turn for a nod.

He curled his hands into fists before pushing them into his pockets. It was as if he was resisting the urge to do something. *Reach for me? Please do.*

"In order to find you, to find out what happened at the

lab, the President asked me to become the man I once was. To do that, I needed him to add me back to the wanted list. Being pinned for my wife's death was the most plausible way to do that. It was the only thing I could think of on such short notice." His tanned throat moved from a hard swallow as he quickly cut through the layers of his plight. "I needed to win over Alyona's trust, and since she was the one who pointed me in the right direction of Rebecca's killers before, I knew this cover story would work best." He kept his eyes steady on me, divulging more than I'd actually expected, and he'd done it so matter-of-factly.

Did it not hurt him to share that? To have to do all of that for me? He'd been through too much already.

"So, you'd been removed from the list before this week?" I thought back to my exchange with Carter at the New York office, then time jumped in my head to that night when Craig Paulsen had cornered me. Something had changed between then and now, and Mom must've known but never bothered to share the good news. Carter's name had been cleared, and she kept it from me. Damn her.

"My work in private security helped get me off the list, but there were conditions."

"Such as?"

A flicker of a smile came and went. "Being a good boy."

The gravity of our conversation didn't stop me from matching his quick smirk with one of my own. Carter was every bit a man, but his comment was proof that the humor I'd witnessed in earlier years was still there.

"But you intentionally damaged your reputation to save me."

"I don't care about my reputation. Regardless, I'd do what was necessary for the mission and for . . ." He left his words lying heavily between us as the energy around us thickened.

For who? For what? Me? My eyes flew to his hands, straining in his pockets with even more visible force than before. "I'm so sorry you had to do that."

"Not your fault," he replied, voice void of emotion again.

I couldn't help but whisper the first thought that came to mind. "Why does everything somehow feel like it keeps leading back to your wife?"

Carter lifted his hands from his pockets and took a step toward me, only to lock his arms tight at his sides and refrain from what I was pretty sure he almost did. What he wanted to do. What I wanted him to do.

Hold me.

His brow furrowed as he said in a somber tone, "Rebecca *was* my wife."

That past tense clarification seemed to be a thousand words all rolled into one. And yet, I still couldn't translate it, or the look in his eyes.

"So, um." I backed up a few steps, finding myself flush up against the wall. "My mom doesn't really blame you for her death?" Not important in the grand scheme of things, but it mattered to me.

"I'm pretty sure she'll always blame me one way or another. Maybe I do, too." That heartbreaking tone, God help me, it hurt to hear him talk like that.

"No." He carried such a huge burden, and his shoulders may have been broad and strong, but it was still too much for only one person. "I don't know how she died, but I know it wasn't your fault. You love her."

"*Loved.*" There was the past tense again, opening like a black hole about to suck me straight through.

Energy really didn't lie, but it wasn't being straightforward right now either. I was confused at how he felt toward me, and what he was saying without saying it.

"Do you get your life back when this is over? Your name cleared?"

"What life?" he asked, almost a hint of sarcasm there. But I didn't take him for a sarcastic guy, so maybe his knee-jerk response was to mask his true feelings. As if realizing I was reading him a little too well, he tacked on, "Don't worry about me, please. Let's focus on what we can control."

"So much easier said than done when I'm in the process of spinning out."

"You're a survivor, Diana." He'd said the same in the shower, hadn't he? If only I could remember those moments a bit more clearly. "What you went through today, and yet you're still looking at me like . . ." He turned his cheek, breaking our eye contact. Almost as if he was uncomfortable, or maybe searching for how to continue.

"How am I looking at you?" Did I just echo back something he'd said to me that morning, too. Were we in déjà vu territory? Past lives? Hell, I wasn't sure what I believed in anymore, but I knew I had a connection to this man beyond this mission and our other encounters.

Facing me again with slanted brows, he removed my glasses and held them between us. "Do these things have magical powers?"

"What do you mean?" I murmured, my heart finding a comfortable home in my throat. We were close, so close, the air between us practically hummed with that energy.

"They seem to shield you from the darkness of the world." His eyes boxed me into that moment, and I was helpless to move or think. "They protect you from seeing me for who I really am."

I shook my head, and did my best to formulate coherent thoughts and voice them. "No. If anything, they help me see clearly." Unable to stop myself, I took his face between my palms. The scruff on his face, a week or so old given the look of it, was softer than I expected. Despite the tight clench of his jaw beneath my touch, I didn't let him go. "I can see the real you, Carter."

He rotated his neck, and I followed the path of his movement, refusing to lose hold of him as he warned in a low voice, "I'm just a wolf in sheep's clothing fooling you into believing I'm a good guy."

"What if it's the wolf I want?" Heat flew through my body and between my thighs. Glasses or not, I recognized that look in his eyes. Dark and haunted, capable of penetrating every wall I'd ever put up over the years. Every single layer of protection peeled back.

My glasses fell from his hand, and before I knew it, he had my wrists secure in his grasp, my arms above my head up against the wall, pinning me in place.

"You're too sweet for me," he gritted out, breathing deeply. "I need to hear you acknowledge that. I will *not* corrupt you." In contrast to the harsh tone, he gently rested his forehead against mine. "Do. Not. Let. Me." Each word banged through the walls of my chest, and I felt them echo inside me and vibrate around my heart.

He was trying to stitch the warning into the very fabric of my being when all I wanted to do was beg him for the opposite. Plead with him to give me the thing I'd guiltily craved since the moment it'd felt like time stood still between us years ago.

"What if it's to calm me, though? What if I need something from you only you've ever been able to give me?" I didn't fight or resist his possessive hold. I embraced it. Gave in to the feeling of being dominated by this man, an experience I'd only lived out in my fantasies.

"You're going to need to spell this out for me." He lifted

his head and brought his body closer to mine, and I shuddered at the feel of his hard length straining against me.

You feel the same. You desire me, too. Emboldened by that realization, I pleaded, "Kiss me."

"No." He shook his head. "I can't do that." Yet, he wasn't budging from our locked position. He rotated his hips, allowing me to feel his arousal, making me lightheaded. "You were a hostage this week. Could've died. You're . . . *you.* I refuse to be the one to destroy all that's good inside you."

"You want someone else to destroy me, then?" I challenged, not prepared to back down when the taste of his lips was so close. "You just implied there'd be a someone who will do it."

His mouth tightened, and while caging me with both his eyes and body, he released his hold of my wrists only to slide his palms up to my hands, lacing our fingers together. Arms still up, hands held, he brought his mouth to my ear, sending chills throughout my body. Goose bumps traversed every inch of my skin.

Eyes closed, I murmured, "A kiss won't corrupt me, but if your lips don't touch mine . . . you just might kill me."

He went so still, so quiet, if not for the feel of his body heat and his hands locked with mine, I'd have believed he'd left me. Then came the order, "Look at me, Diana," that had me arching into him. "Are you sure you want my mouth on yours?"

Lids parted now, I watched as he searched my face for a sign of doubt, one he'd never find. Not even after today's events.

"I need to know if what I'm feeling is real, or if I'm imagining it. Please. Help me understand," I begged, my voice saturated with thirteen years of guilt and longing for this man.

"Of course it's real." The tight strain of his jaw became more prominent. "It's so real I'm going to do something I haven't done in a very long time."

"What's that?" I asked, breathless.

He angled his head while tightening his hold of my hands, and the words came out slow, firm, and deliberate: "Lose my control."

34

CARTER

My mouth crashed over hers. I took it. Claimed it. Fucking owned it.

Swallowing her moan, our tongues met, and she let me lead but gave back as much as I gave her.

I kept my hold of her, keeping her pinned between my body and the wall, not prepared to let go. She was mine. Fuck was she ever. This kiss confirmed it, lighting up every one of my senses.

Tasting her. Smelling her. *Feeling* her. I'd never been lightheaded from a woman's mouth before, not even . . .

I nearly growled out my anger, furious with my mind for taking a detour from an experience with heaven. Or as close to it as my dark soul would ever get.

"Carter," she cried into my mouth.

I captured her bottom lip and sucked it. Then trailed my mouth to her jawline and over to her ear. "What do you want?"

"To touch you," she begged. "Please."

I'd already lost control. Snapped. Why not let the train of my denial keep running a bit longer?

Breathing hard, my dick straining against the heavy weight of the cargo pants as she shimmied against me, I released her hands, uncertain what she planned to do but curious to find out.

I wasn't accustomed to letting someone touch me while I . . .

But wait, we weren't . . . Shit, I had to end this.

She tore a hand through my hair and grabbed hold of my back with the other while rubbing up against me, and I—

Just one more minute. I'd give myself just one more.

I held her hip with one hand and hooked my other under her knee, drawing her thigh to my side so she could better feel my cock.

I stole my name falling from her lips with a kiss, not wanting anyone to hear her. Not any of her moans, either, which were meant for me and no one else.

Using the wall for support, I kept her back to it so I could work my calloused palms to her ass, hating the denim getting in my way of feeling her flesh. I couldn't mark her skin with my hand, this woman was too precious and sweet for that, but it didn't stop me from thinking about doing it.

A tight band of pressure journeyed from my abdomen into my chest as I swallowed another one of her breathy sighs.

When she began kissing my jawline, still fisting my hair and burying her fingers into my back, I about unzipped my pants and plunged my cock into her.

"Diana . . ." *Fuuuuck.* "You need to stop grinding against me."

This was only supposed to be a kiss. Just the one-and-done kind. What was happening between us now was utter chaos, and I didn't know what to do with that. I didn't have a damn clue how to handle this woman.

"I'm sorry," she panted. "I've just never felt . . ." Her

tongue skimmed along the seam of her lips, and I leaned in and caught it. Sucked it.

I had no control when it came to her. Absolutely none.

If the chest plate wasn't inconveniently blocking her tits from me, I'd be taking a nipple between my teeth.

Months of watching over her. Stroking my cock to thoughts of her. Now she was shoved against a wall, writhing in my arms and calling out my name, and I was acting like a man possessed.

"Damnit," I ground out, angry at myself, and I forced myself to let her go.

She startled, her foot quickly falling back to the floor, and she lifted her palms between us. A plea to a frightened animal not to react.

Three steps back, drawing my hands to my hips, I studied her. Those swollen lips were slightly parted, and I wanted them to open up. See if she could fit my cock between them.

Determining if that sweet mouth could take all of me would need to be tackled *second*, though. First, I'd put my mouth on her cunt and make her come.

The list of what I wanted to do with her—to her—grew as I stared at her, trying to remember where we were and what the hell was going on.

"You felt that, too, didn't you?" she whispered, drawing two fingers across her lips in a ridiculously sensual way. I doubted the little motion had been purposeful, meant to turn me on, but it did.

"No." I hated how that lie felt on my tongue.

"You're a shitty bluffer, too. Right now, at least."

She'd called me out. And rather than pushing me away, it made me want to punish her. Lay her out on the bed, wedge my shoulders between her thighs and lash her clit with my tongue. Make her writhe and tremble, only to pull away a moment before she came, not letting her get off until I gave her the command to do so.

I turned, dragging my hands through my already-messed-up hair.

"I don't understand what's happening between us any more than you do," she said in a shaky voice. "I only know that when I'm around you, I feel a certain way. I always have."

My arms dropped to my sides as I gave in and faced her, which turned out to be a bad idea. She was touching her mouth again.

. . . And I caved.

I barreled back to her before I could allow the rational part of my brain to take over. Took both her cheeks between my palms and kissed her.

At the feel of her mouth on mine, the harsh, anxiousness inside me retreated and a sense of calm washed over me. *Through* me. My mouth relaxed and our kiss became soft. To my surprise, I let *her* dictate the kiss, and she planted light, tempting little brushes of her lips over mine.

I released her face and pressed her against the wall again. Palms over her shoulders. My attempt to reclaim control failed, because I was too entranced by how she was kissing me, imbuing her sweet innocence in me.

Was this what peace felt like?

Groaning, relishing in her touch, I sank into the feeling for a bit longer.

That sense of peace didn't last long, because peace was never forever. The internal war inside me won out. The memory she was off-limits, that I was dangerous for her, infiltrated my thoughts, and I broke our kiss and pushed away from the wall.

"This can never happen again," I gritted out, hoping she

wouldn't resist and fight me on that. I needed her to listen. To understand and believe how truly bad I was for her. She needed to see me clearly for who I really was, and I had to stop giving her hope I was anything other than a monster.

She covered her mouth, remaining against the wall as her sad eyes cut to the floor.

"A kiss could get you killed," I said under my breath, my hand slipping to the butt of my sidearm strapped at my side. "I forgot where we were and what's at stake."

"I understand." The hurt bled through her tone. But Alyona was right, this woman was my weakness. And I wouldn't let Diana die because of that.

I knelt for her glasses and offered them to her. "The sooner I turn you over to the President's men, the better." She flinched at my dismissal, but wordlessly accepted her glasses, gripping them in her hand rather than putting them on. "We need to get on the road to the next location." I had to get back to business and remain mission-focused. Forget my body's response to her. Forget the fact she'd awakened something inside me that was supposed to have remained dead.

"Okay." No argument from her. Good. *Also,* surprising. "Where to?" She put on her glasses and combed her fingers through her hair. It'd gone rogue from our heated exchange, and I couldn't deny how much that affected me too.

"There's an old CIA black site on the border of Poland. We need to get there before zero three hundred. From there, you'll go with the President's men." I'd done my best to keep my voice professional and clinical, which wasn't easy to do with her. No matter how much I wished away the discomfort gathering in my chest, nothing helped. Now that I'd experienced how she felt and tasted, my obsession for her would morph into something dangerous. "With Alyona in the mix, we can't bring her to the safe house with us. We'll need to split up once in Poland."

She pointed to my other ear. "You have a second team to watch her?"

"Yes, but they'll be with us until we hand you over to Bravo Team. The guys here, aside from Griffin, can keep an eye on Alyona and her men." I couldn't let Alyona put eyes on the rest of Falcon.

"Bravo Team," she echoed, no longer fixing her hair. She'd moved on to tidying up her overall appearance, and it was distracting. Reminded me of what happened between us. "You trust them, I assume, or you wouldn't turn me over."

"Five of the best operators on the planet, yes."

"Okay." Again with no resistance, which was what I wanted.

So why in God's name did part of me wish she'd fight me on this? Beg me to protect her instead? It felt like tearing out a piece of my beating heart knowing I'd be parting ways with her again. And why did that fucking organ, one I'd thought died years ago, only come alive when she was around?

Shaking out my arms, trying to rid myself of the tension there, I tapped my ear. I'd been so distracted, I hadn't realized I'd double-muted the comms, unable to hear anything from either team. Not just the other way around.

Of course, Griffin would've knocked and interrupted if something was wrong. Unfortunately, no one had banged on the door to stop the madness of my tongue entering Diana's mouth.

"We ready to roll out?" I directed the question to the team on-site.

"Yeah," Griffin answered. "Do we have a secondary location to escort Alyona and her people to?"

"I'll work on that once we leave." We'd be driving again

instead of flying, so I'd need both my pilots to head over to Poland in the meantime.

"What are we doing about the two in the shed?" Easton piped up over the line. Shit, I'd nearly forgotten about them.

Diana was now sitting on the bed, quietly packing her bag, staring off in a daze.

I let go of a heavy, anguished breath and said, "Kill them."

That had her attention. "Kill who?"

I muted the comm to tell her, "The pieces of shit we were questioning. We can't take them with us."

On her feet, eyes wide, she came over to me. "You can't just kill people like that."

"Why not? They sell people for a living. You want them in jail playing an Xbox instead?" *Screw that.*

"You can't just go Hammurabi's Code on people." Arms folded in challenge, she stared me down.

That boldness had my dick *and* hand twitching, not that my cock had yet to settle down. No, it was still ready to go. Ready to claim her. "I can, and I will." I dipped my chin to better meet her eyes so she'd clearly see the wolf she was facing down.

"I don't know the kind of man you were after she . . ."
Died.

Her lashes fluttered. "But that's not who you were before then. You were a good guy. Delta Force. You wouldn't kill an unarmed man."

But she was wrong. So wrong. I would've, if someone ever hurt her. Rules of engagement or not, even on Delta. "You didn't know me then, and you don't know me now." I needed to do a better job to fortify my walls, erect some solid emotional barbed wire, to keep this woman from getting to me again.

"I know what you're doing. It doesn't take a genius to figure it out." She shook her head, eyes narrowing. "Go ahead, be a dick to me if you think that'll help you get over what just happened between us." She lifted her chin, standing her ground. "Let me know how that works out for you."

Oh this woman.

Our little staring contest ended, but only because *she* clearly decided it was over, going to her bag and zipping it up.

Unsure what the hell to do, I tapped my comm and hissed, "Don't kill them." She spun around, but I squashed that hopeful look by adding, "Because I'm going to do it myself."

3 5

CARTER

KOLONIA, POLAND

THE FORMER CIA BLACK SITE WASN'T ON ANY MAPS, BUT IT was still owned by the American government. And while it hadn't been operational in over a year, its age and the elements catching up to it, it'd make do for the meeting with Bravo Team to hand over Diana.

Standing by my co-team leader's Suburban, I asked Gray, "You're certain only your father and POTUS know we're here?"

"Aside from Bravo, of course, yeah," Gray confirmed, eyes on the rest of Falcon as they unloaded equipment from the other two vehicles.

Sydney was already inside the building powering on the lights, and when the overhead ones outside blasted on, I had to squint with how damn bright they were in the dark of night.

"Don't trust her mother?" Gray asked, drawing my attention.

To be fair, I didn't trust anyone outside my team. "More

so the people Susan Mackenzie associates with. Not sure who's really on our side or not."

"We're not on the same one?" Gray locked his arms over his chest. I'd once thought of him as a schoolboy West Point grad who'd never cross the lines. Now I knew better. Gray was like me, and he'd do whatever necessary to protect those he cared about.

"I'm not so certain." I wouldn't count anyone out as a threat until this case was locked up and closed.

I caught sight of Griffin offering Diana his hand to help her out of the SUV. She'd either fake slept en route there with her headphones on, or she'd truly passed out.

I'd been parked in the front passenger seat, quietly looking back at her every other minute the whole ride. It was possible I was on edge because of her, and misplaced my concerns on the President's "trusted" people because of it. Better to be on guard than regret something later, though.

Diana peeked around Griffin while he escorted her toward the building, and I could easily make out the frown marring her lips. She'd given me the cold shoulder the last few hours. Well-deserved and then some.

Griffin nodded, letting me know he'd continue watching over her while I was outside. I'd opted to bring Griffin back with us, right where he belonged, with Falcon. Easton and the others could handle Alyona and her men at the temporary location I'd secured for them twenty klicks away from our current spot.

"She going to be a problem for you?" Gray asked, and I stole my focus from that problem back his way.

"Yeah." No use in lying now. "She knew my wife, and it's complicated."

"I'm aware. My father read me in on the situation."

"Based on the fact you can barely look me in the eyes

right now, I'm guessing he told you a little more than that."
Something I won't want to hear.

"I'll fill you in with everyone inside."

Fucking perfect. At the sound of the door thudding shut, and with Diana safely inside, my hand went to my chest as the pressure there returned. "Once she's tucked away somewhere with Bravo, I'll feel better." *Now I'm lying.* Turning her over was what needed to happen, but it was the last thing I wanted to do. "I assume your sister has been pulled into this?"

"Yeah, Natasha's doing what she can legally at the Agency to find the source of that email to Alyona. Check its credibility, too. Make sure she's not playing us. And Gwen's working on things from . . . other angles."

Illegal hacking, and I was good with that. Whatever it took to complete the mission was fine by me.

"They'll reach out when they have something."

We started for the main building; aside from Mason Matthews, who was doing a perimeter check, everyone had already gone inside. I owed Mason a favor for joining us at the last second, considering only that summer he'd decided it'd be best to part ways with Falcon. First him, then Gwen. We were losing people. At least it wasn't only because of me. "Where are Mya and Sydney at on running through the lists of names connected to the project in Amsterdam and the American-based one in Montana?"

Gray stopped outside the door and faced me. "They still have a lot of intel to weed through, but they had to put a pin in that research for the time being when you requested us here to assist you."

Right. "I didn't want to pull you in on the ground. Sorry about that."

"You should've from the start. We may not have been part

of your old life, but we're part of your new one." That was almost too sentimental for Gray. "Our covers won't get blown. Mya's an expert at giving us new identities. We'll be fine."

Fine? Fuck that word, because Diana was anything but fine, and I was now part of that reason.

"Things worked out when we had to go with you to The Sapphire, and that was your old stomping ground. Our covers were solid there, and they'll be here, too," he reminded me.

About that. "Alyona knows what happened at the hotel." *Another reason she's twenty klicks away right now.* "I'd rather her never cross paths with the team in case she ever saw any images of y'all, too." That hotel, a sanctuary for criminals, was connected to an op that brought Gray to the love of his life.

It felt like yesterday they'd announced they were having a baby—the same day I'd learned Diana's mom was the new Secretary of State.

Gray set a hand on my shoulder, and I focused on his palm resting there, confused at the gesture. That was a Griffin thing to do. "You going soft on me now that you're going to be a dad?"

He smiled and pulled back his hand. "My sister calls it the 'Tessa effect.' She says my wife's cheerful personality has dulled some of my grumpiness." He tossed a hand through his hair as if uncomfortable he'd even admitted that. Or maybe shocked. Made two of us. "Griffin told me you left those two men alive back in Lithuania despite wanting to kill them. Diana having some type of effect on you, too?"

When I'd gone to pull the trigger in that shed, Diana's sad blue eyes came into my head, and I'd been unable to take their lives. "Maybe a wild animal will take them out." *Circle of life and all.* "If not, I'll send in a tip to the local police tomorrow." I was the one going soft, damnit.

He angled his head toward the door. "Does she know you didn't kill them?"

"She doesn't need to know." I had to place some space between myself and Diana before I put my mouth on hers again. The next time, I wouldn't be able to stop at that.

"If you say so," he said reluctantly, fortunately letting go of whatever was on his mind. I needed the hard-ass operator back, not a man in touch with his feelings.

"Let's just go inside." I pulled the door open with more force than necessary and waited for him to walk ahead.

We went down the hall, following the chatter to find everyone inside an old office. Rows of desks and nothing else there aside from our equipment.

"I think we've been at a few parties together before." Sydney was in the process of shaking Diana's hand. "I'm Sydney Archer."

Diana's eyes narrowed on her as if trying to place her from her past. "Ohhh, of the Archer billionaires?" She let go of Sydney's hand. "Sorry, I usually spent my parents' parties with my headphones on or my nose in a book. Or both." An embarrassed little blush worked up her throat into her cheeks. "Not much of a social butterfly."

I hung back near the door of the room, too mesmerized by this woman to budge. It was for her own good, and everyone else's in that room, that I didn't move another muscle. The irrational part of my brain wanted to go to her. Take her from the room. Take her away from there altogether and hide her away myself. But this wasn't about us, and I needed to get my shit together and my emotions needed to stay the fuck out of the plan.

"It's such a small world, though," Diana noted with a

little shrug as Sydney tipped her head to Gray. "Were you ever Sydney Maverick? I feel like . . ." Diana let her words trail off, and Sydney nodded.

"By marriage, yes." Sydney picked up a laptop, and started for a desk but then stopped. "Wait, that's right. My ex is friends with your father, and my dad's close with your old man as well."

"Really is a small world," Oliver piped up, stepping forward to offer his hand. "So small these two even once dated," he added while pointing to Sydney and Gray. Sydney subtly flipped him the bird. "That's a Mya thing to do, not you," he joked, then offered his name.

"Sydney's now married to my brother-in-law, Beckett, though," Jesse said, then introduced himself next.

"So, this is really a family, not just a team?" Diana knelt alongside Dallas as he wagged his tail, waiting for attention from his new favorite person.

I'd definitely been replaced. Couldn't even blame him. She was far more easy on the eyes than my rugged-ass self, not to mention much sweeter.

"Family," Mya said under her breath. "Yeah, you could say that." She gave her a bright smile while teasingly elbowing Oliver to the side to get to Diana. "Oliver already gave you my name with his little jab, but I'll follow up with the formal intros. I'm Mya."

Diana smiled, remaining crouched while stretching out her arm to shake Mya's hand. When her sleeve shifted, I glimpsed Diana's tattoo, triggering a memory or two from my past. Like that Easter weekend.

"So, let's see." Mya looked around the crowded room of operators shuffling about, prepping equipment. "You know everyone now but Mason and Jack. Mason's outside, but where'd Jack go? He's our other comedian on the team. If you couldn't tell, Oliver likes to think he's one, too."

Oliver rolled his eyes, and Mya smacked the air in his direction.

"Jack went to call his wife," Griffin shared on his way over to me. "Here," he quietly said. "A burner for when you're ready."

I wasn't remotely close to being ready for that part of the plan, but I'd be damned if I'd let anyone else do what had to be done. I pocketed the phone and pushed away from where I'd been leaning into the doorframe. My slight change in position sent Dallas scrambling to all fours in preparation for orders. I had none to give him right now, other than to keep doing what he was doing, which was relaxing Diana, so I gave him a signal to stand down, and he relaxed back alongside her.

"Jesse and Griffin, why don't you join Mason outside to keep guard," Gray said as I checked the time. Two more hours until Bravo extracted Diana.

"I'll take overwatch. Be on the roof." Griffin picked up the case that held his preferred long gun, gave me a nod, then left the room with Jesse.

Diana stood tall, removing the headphones from around her neck, and set them and the MP3 player on a nearby desk.

I tracked her every movement like a man obsessed, watching as her deft fingers twisted her hair into a side braid. Mya wordlessly removed a rubber band she had on her wrist, her gaze flicking my way for a brief moment, before offering it to Diana.

The tempting goddess ignored the old desk chairs strewn about, opting to head back to Dallas, kneeling next to him. Dallas lowered his head to her lap, and she casually stroked his fur. Images of my head in her lap morphed into visions of her stroking my cock, the visuals clearly and frustratingly following the words in my thoughts. I shook my head to clear it, moving my eyes from her hand, following the graceful line of her arm up to her shoulder and across her chest.

She didn't have the vest or chest plate on anymore, and her bra was clearly too thin. I could make out her nipples poking through the silk. I rotated my neck, desperately in need of tension relief, and knowing the only way I'd achieve it was by plunging my cock into Diana.

Jack joined us just before I became completely unhinged, saving me from tossing Diana over my shoulder and carrying her away.

After a quick introduction, I sent Jack to the roof with Griffin. Despite being at a CIA safe house, the last thing I felt right now was safe, not with Diana there.

I looked at Gray as he sat on the desk next to where Sydney worked. "You said you have news to share? Maybe we recap everything we know first."

Gray gave Sydney the cue to take the lead on the summary of our shit situation, and she hurried through the details. "Monday night both labs were simultaneously hit. Equipment was destroyed. The lead scientists were taken as hostages, and what we know because of Diana, were then split up and in the process of being moved to new locations. No demands have been made, and we've picked up no chatter about who's behind this. All we know is that a group of highly trained Serbian human traffickers were in possession of Diana, preparing to place her on a ship for Oslo. Final destination unknown."

"Now it's Friday and . . ." Mya checked her watch. "Well, I guess it's technically Saturday, and Alyona allegedly needs to turn Diana over to an unknown blackmailer before the end of the weekend."

Based on the tight lock of Gray's jaw, he was about to add more to the equation. "What I'm about to share with everyone is classified and doesn't leave this room," he began. "The United States, along with eleven other countries, was part of a classified and top-secret joint project to do two things."

That much we know.

"Was the Netherlands part of the project?" Diana asked him. "Now that I think about it, though, no one I worked with was Dutch."

"No, they weren't. The Dutch were uninvolved and unaware, which was why it was chosen as neutral territory to host the project," Gray answered. "There were concerns that if one of the twelve countries housed the central project, it might increase the risk of betrayal. The leaders of the countries involved were already paranoid about having their own labs operating separately from the main project as well, so it makes sense they chose a place like Amsterdam."

"Looks like someone screwed everyone over anyway," Oliver said, taking a knee by one of the weapons bags off to the side of the room.

"POTUS won't confirm your bunker theory in Montana, but given the second lab was there, I can see them choosing a location for the project in proximity to an underground site like that," Gray shared.

Diana stopped petting Dallas for a moment. "And our project wasn't focused on cold fusion, right?"

"Yes and no." Gray's nonanswer had Diana frowning.

Sydney picked up the train of thought. "Scientists have been pushing politicians for years, issuing warnings about a massive solar storm coming in the next decade. One that could effectively knock out more than just Wi-Fi, but destroy the entire power grid. A storm like that could set us back years. And we all know what will happen if people lose electricity and Wi-Fi."

"Talk about chaos." Oliver stood, holstering a Glock 19 at his side.

"What are you trying to say?" Diana asked.

A direct hit from Gray was coming, I could feel it.

"Your wife's company, Barclay Energy . . . well, your father-in-law pressured the government to do something long before anyone else."

Not what I'd been expecting Gray to say, and my pulse quickened at the news.

"After your in-laws died, the work at Barclay Energy shifted direction, and the concerns about a solar storm went quiet for a while," Gray continued. "Then in 2018, your wife started asking questions. Speaking up about it again. I'm not sure why, but she was pushing the government to get on board with creating countermeasures for a possible solar storm, as well as how to deal with an EMP weapon. She believed a breakthrough in cold fusion was the answer."

I felt Diana's gaze on me and I peered her way, remembering her words to me earlier. She was right. Everything did keep circling back to Rebecca. "What are you saying?" I asked Gray, my eyes still glued to Diana as her hand hovered over Dallas's head.

"Susan Mackenzie confirmed that's the real reason your wife told her she sold off almost all of her business holdings except The Barclay Group," Gray revealed. "She wanted to focus on her father's clean energy ambitions, and she was also worried about an impending attack, either from Mother Nature or from an enemy."

I turned from the room, unable to look at Diana, Gray, or anyone in there for that matter. I needed a moment to think. To process the bomb he'd dropped on me.

You didn't sell everything off because of Andrew Cutter and the blackmail? Why the hell didn't you tell me about this? I shook my head, realizing I was acting as though Rebecca could hear me and might miraculously provide an answer. *Susan lied to me. I asked her point-fucking-blank at the funeral reception if she knew what had been going on with Rebecca.* What else was that woman keeping from me? Hell, the both of them.

"I didn't know." My shoulders collapsed at the soft tone of remorse in Diana's voice.

I slowly turned to face her, recalling the rooftop on the day of Rebecca's funeral. Somehow, staring at Diana managed to dull the sharp edge of pain inside me. All it took was her eyes on me to get my heartbeat to work at a more normal rhythm. How was that possible? "I'm guessing my ex-wife . . ." *Did I just accidentally call Rebecca that?* I'd never made that mistake before. I pushed aside that thought and recalibrated, doing my best to keep my tone void of emotion. "I assume Rebecca went behind my back and invested in the government's top-secret Montana bunker—the one they don't want to admit to yet—before she died, too."

After an uncomfortable amount of silence passed, Diana peered at Gray and asked, "You said the project was twofold. Does that mean we were working on both an EMP weapon as well as a countermeasure to safeguard from a weapon or storm? Is that why your yes or no response to me about cold fusion?"

Once Gray nodded, I followed up with a question of my own. "If the government didn't seem pressed to do anything in the past, why the sudden change in heart? Rebecca's been gone for years." *I suppose Pierce Quaid took the helm of Rebecca's "passion project" along with Susan, but still.*

"Six months ago, it was confirmed the Chinese

government was on the verge of a breakthrough with an EMP weapon that could take down not just a city, but an entire country. Even one as big as ours," Gray shared. "That's why they began the joint project among twelve nations, hoping to beat them to the punch. Pull together resources and the brightest minds in the world."

One of those bright minds was on the floor with sad eyes petting my dog.

"Like with the nuclear arms race," Diana said softly, "we're now in a race to make an EMP weapon in hopes that if we have one, the enemy won't use one against us to avoid a counterattack."

"If it was the Chinese government, they wouldn't care about keeping Diana and the other physicists on the project alive, right? They'd want to kill them along with the research." Sydney closed her laptop and added, "Well, unless they haven't had success yet. By stealing the world's best scientists, they not only set back the rest of the countries in the race for a weapon, they get help to finish first."

"They'd still need someone to help sabotage the project from within," I pointed out. "Possibly someone working in Amsterdam, and maybe even at the lab in Montana." *At least a few traitors.*

"And we still don't know if the other eleven countries had their private labs hit, too," Gray said. "If they hit all twelve independent labs, that'd make this one of the most well-coordinated attacks I've ever heard of before."

"More than likely narrowing our suspect list to an enemy state," I said in agreement.

"A wealthy, oil-based country with billions to lose if cold fusion's successful could also be behind this, and it may have nothing to do with the EMP weapon aspect," Diana tossed out her own theory. "An oil-rich nation would have the means and motive."

"We can't rule out anything." *You're brilliant, and that option is horrible as well.* "We should consider all motives and everyone a suspect until we know more."

"Our best lead right now is Alyona's blackmailer," Mya said. "I'll touch base with Natasha and Gwen to see where we're at on that."

I reached into my pocket, wrapping my hand around Alyona's phone while focusing on Diana. One more part of the plan still needed to be put into place. Record a video of Diana for the blackmailer . . . and I'd need to tie her up to do it. *Fucking hell.*

36

DIANA

THE LEGS OF THE CHAIR SCREECHED, CREATING TRACKS through the dusty floor as Carter dragged it across the room. He positioned it against a windowless concrete wall and dropped a black duffel bag by his booted feet.

"Are you okay?" It was my first time being alone with him since he'd marched from the room back in Latvia, intending to kill those two men.

His back went stiff at my question, but he didn't face me. "Not really. I have to strap you to this chair and take a video of you for Alyona's blackmailer. I'm sure you're as eager to do this as I am after being held hostage and tied up all week."

"That's not what I meant." I approached him and reached for his shoulder. He whirled around, capturing my wrist midair as if I'd been about to hurt him.

His nostrils flared as he zeroed in on my wrist, then his eyes went wide as he let me go.

The definition of "not okay" was written into every line of his face and body. His quick, almost angry reaction had to be based on more than the burden of tying me to a chair to make a fake hostage video.

I didn't even think it had to do with our kiss—a kiss I'd replayed on repeat the entire drive there, pretending to sleep so my face didn't give me away.

"Rebecca," I whispered, once he calmed down a bit. "What you heard couldn't have been easy."

He turned his focus to the little blue chair, as if acquiring a new target, and gruffly replied, "The woman lied to me more than she was honest with me. I've long ago learned to accept that. I'm more concerned with why Rebecca suddenly gave a damn about solar storms, EMP bombs, and cold fusion at the time she did."

There was so much *more* sitting between us I doubted he'd share. The fact he'd even spoken to me about her at all was shocking.

"Let's just get this over with," he said, pivoting quickly while kneeling alongside his bag, producing a—

Rope. I had to ground myself in the moment so I didn't start panicking.

I waited for the anxiety to eclipse logic and reason. For that rope to remind me of the true savages who'd taken me that week. Only . . . it didn't seem to be coming. Instead, seeing this man's strong hand holding the rope sent my stomach somersaulting in an entirely different way.

Am I turned on? I did a quick check to make sure the door was closed. The idea of someone seeing me bound didn't exactly send a happy thrill up my spine. And yet, this man tying me up did. *What in God's name is wrong with me?*

Standing now, he allowed the rope to unwind at his side before effortlessly making several loops like he was an expert in restraining people. "Why'd you ask me if I'm good?" he asked casually, catching me off guard with both his tone and question. "Aren't you mad at me?"

My shoulders fell at the memory of our last exchange

back in Lithuania. Or was it Latvia? I was losing track of where I'd been at this point. "No," I admitted. "I'm not mad at you."

He glared at me as if displeased by my answer, momentarily stopping twining the rope when catching me in a lie.

I didn't want to be dishonest, so I revealed, "Okay, maybe you weren't my favorite person when you decided to become all gloomy-killer-guy back at the other house. I was kind of angry."

He didn't cock his brow in question, and instead, a touch of a lopsided smile came and went. I'd take that adorable partial grin from this man. Then secretly hoped I'd successfully elicit a full-blown toothy smile from him one day. "Gloomy, huh?"

"*That's* the part of what I said you're latching on to?"

He returned to his work with the rope, going quiet on me.

I wound up doing the opposite. Opening my mouth. "Is it bad I was more upset that you decided to throw our kiss out the window as if it didn't happen?"

No response. Not even a reaction.

The quiet began to eat at me as he took longer than I assumed necessary with handling the rope.

A little frustrated *hmph* noise fell from my lips. "You don't plan to speak, do you?"

He lifted his chin, a silent request to sit. "Remove your glasses. Mess up your hair a bit. Unbutton the bottom and top buttons. You can't look too perfect." His orders were delivered with precision, in a no-nonsense way like he'd rather be anywhere but there.

Worked hard to do that, huh? "Commands don't count as speaking."

"Pretty sure they do," he grumbled, his personality cutting back through again.

I was ninety percent certain he was pushing me away because he was scared of what he felt when our mouths touched earlier, and maybe even before then. It had to be true, because I was equally terrified. I wasn't sure if I could *science* my way out of what was going on between us, not in a rational sense, at least. But he seemed content to try and brood his way out.

"Fine. I'll do what you say." I set my glasses on top of the bag, then removed the rubber band Mya had given me and freed my hair. Slipping the band onto my wrist, I did a headbanger movement trying to make my hair a little wild. Whipping back up straight, I tore my fingers through it, locating Carter's harsh stare pointed at me as if I was doing the whole "messy look" wrong.

"What? Not *disheveled* enough for you?"

His nostrils flared again, but he just continued to stare at me and brood away.

I untucked part of my shirt from my jeans, then undid two buttons and positioned my rear end on the plastic chair. "Satisfied, *sir*?" I asked with a bit more sass that time, growing frustrated at him all over again when I should've been focused on what the Secretary of Defense's son had shared with us ten minutes earlier.

"Don't call me that." His gravelly voice sent my back flush to the plastic behind me. "Not a good idea." He dropped to his knees before me, swallowing hard, a move I didn't miss now that we were nearly eye level. "This is harder on me than you."

"Doubtful."

He set his hand on my knee. "Trust me." Those two

words managed to stamp out my frustration with him. "It's hard for me to tie you up."

"Aren't you good at torturing people?" *Okay, that was a low blow.* Also, maybe I was still upset he'd killed two people when it hadn't been self-defense. And I'd asked him not to. More than anything, though, I was upset he was going to just turn me over to other people rather than bring me home himself. Pass me along the chain and possibly never look back. Never see me again.

Seemingly unfazed by my insult, he ran with it in an unexpected direction, murmuring, "You have no idea just how good I am at tying people up." Lifting his hand from my knee, he inched back a bit, focusing on my sneakers. "I just don't want to tie *you* up."

That *you* barreled through my mind, leaving so many questions in its wake. And I hated knowing he wouldn't answer me if I bothered to ask him to clarify.

When he began working the rope around my ankles, and the pad of his thumb brushed up over my skin, I shuddered. How could such a small sweep of his touch across my skin have me melting into a puddle of aroused goo?

When his hand went still—strong and tight, like a cuff above my ankle beneath the denim—I realized his eyes were shut, and he was dragging in an intensely deep breath.

Oh shit. "That's why." It finally dawned on me. "You don't want to tie me up because you *do* want to tie me up?"

He was quiet for one of the longest minutes of my life before peering at me. "I've got issues." His anguished tone made it obvious it'd pained him to admit that. "If you haven't noticed."

"Don't we all?" At the tight draw of his brows, I couldn't help but blurt, "I have anxious attachment issues." I wasn't sure why I was doing this now, but something inside me wanted him to know he wasn't alone in the issues department. "Years of therapy helped me figure out why when a man ignores or ghosts me, it makes me feel not so great." He kept quietly staring at me, lips parted. So I kept going. "It's because when I was growing up, my father used to give me the silent treatment whenever he fought with my mom. I'd begged him to talk, at least to me. To not go quiet and ignore me because of her. But he'd just look at me and remain quiet. It could go on for days." Aside from my mother, only Sierra and my therapist knew this. Of all the times and places for me to unzip my lips and share this.

But my parents fighting didn't feel like sharing new information with him. Had I shared that in the shower that morning, too? The drugs had laid a blanket of haze over most of that experience, so I wasn't totally certain what I'd said or done.

Still quietly staring at me, his hands unmoving . . . it was like he'd seen a ghost. Not the best thing considering I was already haunted enough by Rebecca's memories. I should've felt guilty for kissing her husband tonight, but I kept reminding myself he was single now, and . . .

"So, yeah, when people ignore me, it triggers my anxiety. Not so great for dating and the whole ghosting thing that happens so often in the modern world," I sputtered since he'd yet to say anything. Or tell me to shut up. "You know what's frustrating, though, is that I know the problem and still can't seem to stop my reactions when it happens. My walls are never tall or thick enough to prevent the pain. And you being quiet on me right now has my stomach hurting, and pulse flying and—"

"I'm sorry." He released both my ankle and the rope and leaned into me, startling me by cupping my cheek. "I didn't

332

mean to hurt you." Genuine. Raw. Real. Everything about his words and this moment was that.

I blinked back tears, hoping like hell they wouldn't fall. He didn't need my tears. He needed my compliance. I shouldn't have opened my mouth and info-dumped on him, not even in an attempt to soothe his soul by letting him in on the secret that we were both imperfect.

"You don't need to apologize, I was just explaining why I got bratty when you went quiet on me, and to let you know we're not that different. We both have issues." Could I really compare my anxiety triggers with his apparent enjoyment of tying people up? Not exactly apples to apples, but still.

"We're *very* different," he said in a somber voice, letting go of my cheek.

I didn't need to hear more warnings about him being bad for me. He'd always be the nice guy who'd kept me sane and safe on the edge of what was left of that floor over thirteen years ago. I'd never forget the man who'd patiently dealt with my social awkwardness each time we'd spoken over the years. Or the grief-stricken man who'd cried into my shoulder at Rebecca's funeral reception.

Carter unexpectedly sat back on his heels, secured the rope in his hand, and quietly returned to the work of tying my ankles to the chair.

"I don't want someone else protecting me. The safest place is with you." The few tears sliding down my cheek would be great for the hostage video, but I still didn't want them there. Tears would put up another wall between us. Justify him seeing me as someone he'd "corrupt." The world as we knew it could quite possibly be on the verge of ending, but there I was wanting to beg him to keep me. To *corrupt* me.

"I have to turn you over to Bravo." His words came

across sad that time, like maybe he didn't want to turn me over after all.

"Aren't you a man who gives orders, not takes them?" I tried to fight back future tears from falling. They needed to stay in the past.

The slight hint of a smile from him threw me off yet again. "You love to provoke me, don't you?"

The fluttery feeling in my stomach shot between my legs and pulsed there. "Only when you can't see what's right in front of you."

That semi-smile quickly transitioned into a grimace, and he gestured for me to place my hands behind the back of the chair. I did as he asked, and he leaned in so close our mouths nearly touched as he bound my wrists. "The problem is," he said steadily, eyes locking with mine as his hands deftly worked with the rope, "I *do* see you. More than you realize. And that's problematic for many reasons."

The EMP weapon. Bad guys. End-of-days scenario. I know, I know. But what else was he trying to say there? What was the "more" part of that statement?

Tying off my bindings, he set one hand to the wall over my shoulder and dropped his mouth over my ear. "I already told you why you need to stay away from me, and you're not listening." His deep, intense tone had me pinning my thighs together.

"Make me behave, then." I wasn't sure where the huskiness in my voice came from, but I craved more of that boldness from my tongue. I scooched around on the seat, a reminder my hands and ankles were tied to the chair, and I was at his mercy.

"You have no idea how badly I want to make you behave," he said into my ear, his low rumbly voice cutting through me.

"If we had time, would you?" I squeezed my eyes closed, waiting for his rejection.

"Yes," he rasped, shocking me, then his teeth grazed my earlobe.

"What would you do to me?" Had I ever been this aroused in all of my life?

At the feel of his hand circling my throat, I opened my eyes. He was gently holding me there while staring at my face. His grasp tightened a touch as his palm shifted higher and higher until his thumb hooked the side of my chin, urging me to slant my head a touch. "You're dangerous."

Me? I'm the dangerous one? I swallowed, knowing he'd feel the movement, his hand still attached to my throat like he owned my breath, words, and my very being.

I'd be lying if I said I wouldn't happily hand over all three for one night with this man, and I wasn't a one-night kind of girl.

"I'm dangerous because I scare you." The truth always managed to escape me so easily around him. "You like to be in control, and you hate that you lose it around me." If true, then well, ditto, because my heart always took over for my head in this man's presence. I became numb to logic. Ignorant to reason. Possessed by need. Swept away by desire.

Still holding me, his other hand braced against the wall, he was the one angling his head now, drawing his mouth near mine. "You're wrong."

I shook my head, closing my eyes, trying to maintain my confidence and not let my inner awkwardness come out like normal. "No, I'm not. Remember, energy doesn't lie."

"You're wrong," he repeated, grinding out his words that time. "I don't hate that you make me feel out of control." His lips brushed against mine, but he didn't kiss me. "I think I love it, and that's why I need to stay away from you." He released my throat, and at the loss of his touch, I opened my eyes to find him pushing away from the wall to stand.

But no matter how much physical distance he put between us, the moment would never be gone.

He could put an ocean of reasons between us as to why we should never kiss again, and maybe they'd all make sense given the hurdles we were facing, but—

I let go of my runaway thoughts when his hand abruptly went to his sidearm and he turned his head, listening to something.

Then I heard that something, too.

Gunfire from outside.

We were under attack.

37

DIANA

THE DOOR FLEW OPEN, AND ONE OF HIS TEAMMATES —*Oliver?*—warned, "We're outnumbered and surrounded. No idea where they came from, but they're seconds from breaching." He removed a rifle slung across his body and offered it to Carter.

I jerked against the chair, trying to free my hands, shocked at how I'd gone from having an intimate moment with Carter to placing him in danger, distracting him.

"Is there a safe room here?" Carter asked him, somehow keeping calm as he swapped his Glock for the rifle.

"No," Oliver said, and I flinched at the explosive pops of sound coming from just beyond the exterior walls.

"Anyone hurt yet?" Carter asked, continuing to remain calm, cool, and collected. Just how he needed to be, I supposed.

In my head, though, that "yet" was floundering around, terrifying me. Someone could get hurt, and it'd be because they were protecting me.

"No, they're on comms with Gray. You don't have your

earpiece in, though." Oliver dug into his pocket for something as Carter slung the rifle across his body.

Placing the object Oliver gave him in his ear, he ordered, "Go, help the others. I've got her."

Oliver nodded, then took off, closing the door.

Carter locked it and hurried back toward me. "I'm sorry," he said while tapping his ear, then he dropped to his knees at my side and began untying my wrists. "How many tangos do we have?" Carter asked, presumably to someone over his earpiece as he quickly freed my hands. "That's too many. How far out is Bravo? Can we hold them off until they arrive?" He started freeing my ankles, war continuing to blast all around the building, sending my pulse thundering into my ears.

How in the world had I allowed myself to be wrapped up in such a false sense of security up until now? I'd thought everything would be fine, because the good guys were always supposed to win. I let myself get carried away with emotions when the dangerous facts had been staring me in the face. "I'm sorry," I whispered.

Carter shook his head as if telling me not to apologize, then finished freeing my legs as he told someone over his comm, "We have no choice, then. Get Teddy and the others here. Yeah, Alyona and her people, too." A pause before he went on, "If she wants to save her ass from the blackmailer, she'll help."

"Alyona? Are you sure we can trust her?" My timid voice managed to break through what sounded like a machine gun outside.

"There are at least twenty heavily armed men. Jesse, Griffin, and Mason can't hold them off much longer. They're going to get inside, and we need to survive until Easton and the others can get here." He helped me to my feet, unholstered his sidearm and positioned it in my palm. "Tell me your father taught you how to shoot."

"You're letting me help?" I asked in surprise.

"I'd prefer you not kill people, but better them die than you, don't you think?" Locking eyes with me, he tapped his ear for a moment, which I was now confident meant he'd muted his teammates. "Yes or no, can you accurately shoot?"

"Yes. And not just stationary targets. Dad taught me to shoot moving ones too," I confirmed. "My glasses would be helpful, though."

Without missing a beat, he picked them up, cleaned them with his shirt, then slipped them onto my face.

"The safety," he reminded me.

I fumbled with the weapon, nearly dropping it, my nerves besting me at a time when I had to pull off calm and steady.

Taking hold of my face between his big hands, he reassured me, "Hey, you got this."

Ignoring the terrifying noises swarming all around us, I managed to nod and meet his eyes.

"I won't let anything happen to you. Tell me you hear me. Tell me you understand."

"I—I do."

He leaned closer, still holding me. "Say it like you mean it. Say you're going to be okay. *Believe* it."

"I'm safe with you, that's all I know," I confessed.

He brought his lips to my forehead and kissed me there. Freeing his hold of me, he dropped his focus to my hands and shifted them a touch. "Don't teacup it. More like butterfly wings."

Right, Dad taught me something similar.

"If you need to use this, there's an optic mounted. Your target won't see the red light, but you'll be able to. Got it?"

"Yeah, got it." N*ot really.*

He readied his rifle next. "No windows in here. Concrete walls. You're going to stay put with the door locked and light off, okay? I've got to go out there and help them. I'll block the door, but if someone makes it inside, you shoot first, ask questions later." He brought his hand to his ear. "Unless it's me, of course. Don't shoot me." He surprised me with a wink, then took off toward the door.

Doing my best not to shake so I could better butterfly-hold the pistol, I brought my back to the wall by the chair.

"Inside still clear?" Carter asked someone over comms. "Send Dallas down here, then." He unlocked and opened the door, and a handful of seconds later, Dallas, wearing his helmet, came flying into the room. "Guard," he commanded, and Dallas obediently rushed to my side.

Carter sent me one last look, then reminded me, "Lock up after. Lights off."

"Oh-okay." I wanted to run to him, but I stayed in place, the bullets pelting the exterior of the building fading into the background. "Be safe. Please."

The lights died a moment later, and Dallas howled in alarm. "They breached," he let me know. "I'll be back for you, I promise."

The moment I heard the door latch shut, I pulled myself together, hurried over and locked it. No need to kill the lights, they were already out for the building. "Dallas, where are you?" I searched around in the dark.

He came up next to me and guided me over to a wall. I set my back flat to it, weapon in one hand, resting my other hand on the top of his helmet.

The walls had to be thick—thick enough Carter must've felt I was safe from a stray bullet, or he'd never have left me —but I could still hear the distinct sounds of fighting and gunfire.

Dallas let go of a little distressed moan, worried for his dad.

Yeah, I'm worried about your dad, too.

I counted the seconds that passed. Then tried to keep track of the minutes. He'd said it'd take time for backup to arrive, and that was assuming that woman and her men would offer assistance.

My nerves stretched thinner and thinner as I listened for Carter outside the room. No one had broken in, which meant he had to still be okay. That was what I had to keep telling myself, at least.

How'd anyone find us if not because of Alyona, though?

The *whys* and *hows* right now didn't matter as long as Carter and his teammates survived the ambush.

At the door handle rattling, my shoulders jerked back in anticipation of what was to come. My vision had adjusted to the dark, but just barely without any form of light filtering in.

Dallas shifted positions when the door stopped shaking, only for an abrupt blast to blow the door off its hinges.

On instinct, I dropped to the ground, pulling Dallas against me to protect him and shield our faces.

Working through what happened, I realized we were okay. *But if someone made it in here, is Carter hurt?*

Coughing on smoke, and fanning my face, I looked up to see two shadows looming in the doorframe, a spear of light coming from somewhere, maybe a fallen flashlight out in the hall, just behind the men.

Not even a full two seconds later, a third shadow appeared, tackling both men.

Carter. Dallas left my side, joining his dad.

Brute force took the place of gunfire as Carter railed on the men. Grunts and exchanges of blows I could barely make out echoed in the room.

Even with my vision adjusted to the dark and that little stream of light, there wasn't enough for me to see and not accidentally shoot Carter or Dallas. I sat there, feeling helpless.

Dallas was growling, chewing on one of the assailants' ankles, shaking his head rapidly as the man yelled in pain or anger.

Carter appeared to have one of the men trapped between his legs, and he was twisting his arm back, forcing him to drop his pistol. A low, guttural sound left the other guy's mouth, and there was a distinct snap. Arm broken?

I turned my attention to see the man Dallas was biting, reaching for something at his side. Assuming he had a gun he planned to use against Dallas, I shifted the weight of my body over to change my angle to my target. This way, when I shot, if the bullet went clean through, it wouldn't hit a second target, like Carter or Dallas.

Doing my best in the heat of the moment, and using the optic, I pointed the red dot on the target and pulled the trigger.

Impact. Well, I think. Before I had a chance to take a second shot, because the target was somehow still upright, Carter beat me to it. A flash of movement and struggling from the bad guy, and Carter took him down permanently. *A knife?*

Dallas howled, signaling to something or someone, and Carter dislodged what I assumed was the knife he'd just used to kill the guy I'd shot. All in the space of seconds, he was back on his feet. The moment a third man entered the doorway, Carter took him out as well.

The darkness spared me from the gory sight of what would most likely be a pool of blood as the third man crumpled to the ground and fell forward.

Carter stood by the missing door and checked the

hallway. "It's clear." He came back my way, stepping over the bodies. "You okay?"

"I'm fine." With him that close, I finally noticed there was something obstructing his face. *Night vision?* So that's how he was so precise in killing those men in the dark.

He reached for my hand, helping me to my feet. "Stay behind me and grab hold of me so you don't fall," he said, only mildly breathless, then took the gun from me.

Use you as a shield? Not my favorite plan.

"Our secondary team is outside the building now, but we're not out of the woods yet."

Dallas went ahead of us into the hall, and I locked on to Carter as instructed, hands gripping his torso as if my life depended on it.

"You did good back there," he said in a low voice as we traversed the gauntlet of what appeared to be downed bodies.

Did you do all this? Holy shit.

"I'm sorry they got in there. I got pinned down and pulled away for a moment."

"Based on all the bodies we're walking around in the hall," I murmured, "you were outnumbered. And yet somehow . . ." *Kept me safe.*

"Thank you for saving Dallas back there."

Before I could reply, he abruptly stopped and hooked his arm around me, practically squashing my chest to his back.

"It's me. Don't shoot. Lost you on comms," someone spoke up. A female someone. Mya or Sydney, I assumed. Couldn't be Alyona, right?

I felt Carter's body physically relax against me. "My earpiece fell out at some point."

"The inside is clear," the woman said as the power returned.

I stumbled back at the harsh lights in my eyes while

Carter turned toward me, knocking his night vision up to his head. I tripped over one of the dead masked men on the floor, but Carter didn't let me fall. He banded a hand around my hip to keep me upright, then pulled me against him, lifting me in the air and over the dead body to find my feet again.

My personal hero. "Thanks," I said as he set me down, my voice too small for my own body.

"How many more tangos outside?" Carter asked the woman, and I focused on her as well, finally matching the voice to a face.

Sydney had a bow in her hand, casually holding it at her side, and I noticed two of the bodies in the hall had arrows in their backs. *Sydney Archer. Fitting name.*

"Two more snipers out in the woods playing peekaboo," Sydney shared, tipping her head toward a corner, motioning for us to continue. "Easton and Griffin have them covered. But we need to exfil in case more people show up."

"Any casualties on our side?" Carter asked while offering me his hand, and Dallas hopped over one body to get to me.

"Oliver took one in the shoulder. He'll be fine." Sydney peered at me, giving me a little nod, as if telling me, *No worries, all good.*

I kept quiet as we walked the hall, wishing I could close my eyes from the sight, but I didn't want to step on a dead person. Or slip and fall in their blood. As we rounded another corner, I heard distinct chatter back and forth between two people.

"Would you quit being a baby and flipping hold still?" That had to be Mya, right?

We entered the office we'd all originally gathered in, and I was grateful there were no dead bodies in there. Only Mya and Oliver at the moment.

"I'm just pissed that fucker shot this shoulder. My tattoo

is going to be a bear to fix." Oliver was sitting on a desk as Mya wrapped a bandage around his shoulder and arm. "Lost you on comms. You good?" he asked Carter.

"We're fine," Carter said, motioning for me to go farther inside the office. "Glad you're not dead."

"You, too," Oliver returned with a light, almost humorous tone that should've shocked me, but somehow didn't.

"Where's Gray and the others?" Carter released my hand, holstered the weapon at his side, then removed his helmet and night vision, setting it on a desk.

Mya finished the job of bandaging Oliver as she shared, "Jack just restored our power and is doing a third sweep of the building with Gray now. Checking some bodies for insight into who's behind this. The others are outside, but—"

"Alyona and her men ditched us," Sydney interrupted as if wanting to cut to the bad news herself. "Your backup team couldn't help us and keep an eye on Alyona. She took that as an opportunity to take off."

Carter's hands went to his hips in obvious disappointment, or maybe irritation. "She'll be back. She needs Diana."

"Unless she's the one who brought these assholes here in the first place." Oliver stood, putting on his shirt. When he struggled with the buttons, Mya shoved his hand away and helped him. "Thank you, ma'am." He was smirking at her. At a time like this, even after that little revelation about Alyona, and on top of being shot . . .

Who were these people? Hell, in this case, who was I? Only the girl getting aroused by being tied to a chair moments before war broke out. I blamed the stress of the situation.

"We checked Alyona and her people for transmitters. She didn't know we were here either," Carter shot down the idea, the authority in his voice bringing my brain back to the here and now. "She may have pulled her men out of the fight, but I don't think she's connected to who's behind this hit."

"She did give Easton everything she had from the blackmailer before bailing, so maybe you're right," Sydney noted.

"How would anyone find us here, though? Only the President and Gray's father know we brought Diana here," Oliver said, holding his bad shoulder.

"Did you check *us* for trackers?" Sydney asked. "More specifically, *her.* What if whoever had her at the port dosed her with one of those new-age tracker drugs?"

I could see that being a possibility, even if it sounded more like science fiction. I did the mental calculations, and shook my head. "I don't think it'd still be in my bloodstream. It wouldn't last long enough to track us here," I shared as Gray entered the office.

Everyone turned to look in his direction and I noticed how eerily quiet it had gotten. Did those two snipers get handled? *Are we safe for now?*

"We didn't have time to check every dead guy," Gray said as Jack joined the room next, "but I grabbed a phone off one. Removed a few masks to see if I could determine anything identifiable about them."

"And?" Carter asked, beating me to it.

"The five we checked were white, military-aged males," Jack answered. "Could be from anywhere. And we never heard them speak. Not a fucking word, actually."

Gray removed a phone from his pocket and tossed it to Mya. "I used his face to unlock it. It's a burner. Only one text on there. It's some type of mathematical code, or encryption. No words. We'll work on tracing it once we're out of here."

"We need to exfil immediately once our guys outside give us the all-clear. Have POTUS send in a team to do a more thorough check of the bodies. Maybe someone survived out there that can be questioned," Carter instructed to the others, remaining steady and level-headed. "We can't stick around and chance another team being sent in."

"Agreed," Gray said.

"Also, get word to your father we're not turning Diana over to Bravo. We're going dark. From everyone. And she's coming with us," he said.

"Where to?" I asked him.

"Best place for us to be right now is in the air," Carter answered matter-of-factly.

"Just need to survive getting to the airport first," Oliver piped up, drawing a distinctly sharp look from Carter.

"Jack, check Diana and the bag her mom packed for any transmitters," Carter ordered once he was done glaring at Oliver.

"My mom?" He wasn't suggesting she had something to do with tonight, was he?

"POTUS will disagree with not turning her over." Gray met Carter's eyes. "But I think you're right."

So, I'm staying with you? A million other thoughts raced to my mind, but I quickly became distracted by the little device Jack held in front of me.

"The last two snipers are down," Mya announced a moment later. "Griffin just gave word. Do you want Teddy and the others to find Alyona?"

"No, we'll tackle that problem later. I'm sure she's off to get her parents and sister somewhere safe. She'll reach out at some point. She still has the blackmailer's deadline hanging over her head," Carter pointed out just as the small black box in Jack's hand beeped in front of my face. Carter swiveled my way. "Your glasses?"

I quickly removed them, shocked they'd set off the alarm. "Why would my mom put a tracker in my glasses?"

"Not your mom, but your dad would," Carter grumbled, taking the glasses from me and tossing them to Sydney. "He'd be worried we might lose you again, and he'd want a way to find you."

"That's a typical Teamguy thing to do to their daughter," Oliver remarked.

"Either someone knew your father placed a tracker in your glasses and hacked the signal, *or* they were the ones who provided him with the tracker in the first place," Sydney said. "Your father just didn't know their ulterior motives." She quickly began disassembling my glasses, breaking them apart. "That should narrow our suspect list as to who'd send a militia after us."

Dallas came up alongside me and Carter removed his little doggie helmet. I took a knee alongside his faithful companion who was apparently becoming mine as well.

"You find the tracker?" Carter asked when Sydney appeared to have zeroed in on something in my glasses.

"Yeah, and I know who holds the patent on this tech." She looked up at us, eyes thinning. "My father's defense company."

38

CARTER

IN THE AIR – ONE HOUR LATER

"THEY DROPPED A BOMB ON THE BUILDING. WE BARELY MADE it away, and we don't even know who 'they' are, but—"

"Diana . . ." I'd been watching her pacing the plane, stuck in the what-ifs in her mind, for too long. Realizing she was two seconds away from breaking down, I took hold of her arms and pinned her in place before she went flying against a wall during unexpected turbulence. Or maybe I was just looking for any reason to hold her. "It wasn't technically a bomb." Not that I needed to explain the details of the stealth bird that'd flown overhead, silently slipping away after annihilating the old CIA site we'd recently occupied.

"Semantics," she muttered, eyes wide and pinned on me.

"They weren't trying to kill us. They could've blown up the vehicles, but they didn't. They opted not to take the chance since you were in one. You saved us. Bright side."

"Did you just make a joke?"

"Maybe." *Probably not.*

"Someone was ensuring no one survived to be

interrogated by us, that's all. Destroy as much evidence as possible as to *who* was sent after us," I reminded her.

I'd explained it all earlier en route to the airport, but the trauma of what we'd gone through probably blocked it out. She'd clearly been too rattled to fully embrace my explanation. Likely still focusing on how we'd narrowly escaped the intruders only to refocus on our escape from the explosion that had rocked the earth under the vehicle we were in. If not for Jack's excellent driving skills, which his wife had a hand in teaching him, we would've most likely collided with a tree on our way out.

I waited until she was looking up at me before reassuring her. I needed her to see the confidence in my eyes when I told her, "We're all okay. Up in the air and safe." Given the bastards had hacked the tracker in Diana's glasses to find us, but waited to strike until we were at the final location, using the dark of night as cover, I assumed they'd avoid a public spot for another attempt at getting Diana. So, the airport was the best call.

"Safe for the time being, you mean." She was shivering nearly as badly as she had in the shower yesterday. How was that only yesterday? Approximately twenty hours separated us between now and when we'd rescued her from the Serbians. "How long can we fly around in circles, or whatever it is we're doing up here?"

"Long enough. Don't worry." I ran my hands up and down her arms, trying to soothe her the way my mother used to do after my parents fought. I'd always bitten my tongue, never reminding her she'd usually been the cause of that fight in the first place.

The fact Diana and I had *that* in common from our pasts almost did a number on me. Those times she'd told me about her parents fighting felt like another layer of connection, another unfortunate commonality.

"Why are you here with me? I'm sure you're probably itching to be with your team in the cabin figuring out who could've hacked the tracker and ambushed us." She pouted, and it took all my remaining restraint not to kiss it away.

"I trust the team to handle things," I reassured her, and it was true. Sydney and Gray were in communication with both of their parents, as well as Diana's, trying to solve what in the hell went wrong. And who could've known about the tracker. The rest of our crew was busy working on other leads.

Teddy, Easton, and the guys from my former life (aside from Griffin) were on my second jet, charged with running possible scenarios about what Alyona might be up to next, as well as trying to get ahold of her to talk some sense into her.

Everything was covered. Nothing I needed to do right now. Our plans to turn Diana over to Bravo, and for me to slip into the underworld of criminals to uncover who was behind it all, had been derailed because of the ambush. And, to be honest, long before that.

So many unanswered questions, so many unexpected detours, and the only part of the night comforting me was the fact I wasn't passing Diana off to Bravo. I wasn't ready to let her go yet.

After staring at her for a bit longer, waiting to see if she'd say more, I gave in and broke the sound barrier between us. "When my team knows something, we'll both know."

With their uncanny timing, one of them would surely barge in soon and stop me from doing something I shouldn't. Something like sucking her trembling lip between mine and making her forget everything she was nervous about. Distract and deflect by way of my tongue was probably more for my benefit. A sorry excuse to feel her against me after being terrified I could've lost her. It had only been seventy-two minutes since the building exploded shortly after we'd exfil'ed. Seventy-two minutes to reconcile how close we'd come to that unimaginable finality.

"I think I've finally hit my breaking point." Tears filled her eyes, but they didn't escape. She was trying so hard to be brave, determined to stay strong. "You could've died tonight because of me. Oliver was shot. I—I killed a man."

"No, you didn't, I did. You just gave me a head start." I smiled, hoping to stave off those tears a little longer with some dark humor. "Also, the list of people who want me dead exceeds the number of tattoos on my body tenfold. Trust me, you're not endangering me."

"You're not funny."

"Well, shit, I thought you once said I was."

She closed her eyes as she huffed out a small laugh. "Funny and sweet, yes. I did say that, didn't I?"

A drop of liquid rolled down her cheek and she caught it with the tip of her tongue. Resisting the impulse to lean down, capture her pink tongue in my mouth, was threatening to demolish the last of my control.

"You also said having a sense of humor is a good thing, but not a compliment you usually get. That hasn't changed in those thirteen years?"

"You're right, I did say that." How'd she remember that conversation so well? And I shook my head, because, no, things hadn't changed.

"You're distracting me again." She sniffled. "How are you so good at calming me down?"

"Fucking ditto." I shook my head again. Because A, my sleep-deprived brain did me dirty. Had me sharing what was meant to be a thought. And B, I had to cool it with how often I threw the *fucks* around her. She was the sweet one. She didn't deserve my foul mouth. A part of me I'd done a better job at concealing back in the day.

"You're not supposed to distract someone on a mission, and I did back at that house. I'd been pushing you to talk about other stuff while I was in that chair, just before those people showed up. I'm so sorry." She slipped her hand between us and held her stomach.

I was losing her again. She was unraveling, and I wasn't sure if I ought to let it happen. To give her some time to fall apart, then help pull her back together after. Or was I supposed to keep her in one piece and never let her crumble to begin with?

She lifted her hand to her temple. "Pretty sure I'll never look at glasses the same again, always wondering if someone's keeping tabs on me. Feels like I had a stalker, and that's creepy, even if my dad did call in a favor to Sydney's dad for the tracker, and . . ."

Both her father and Sydney's had confirmed the truth behind the device. The jury was still out on who else could've known about the tracker and managed to hijack the system to determine our location.

A stalker. Yeah, you have one. Me. But the checking-in-on-her thing helped save her life, and I had to remind myself of that.

I hadn't questioned the amount of security at her lab, or how hard it'd been to find where the new company had constructed it prior to Diana's move to Amsterdam. I'd assumed the owners wanted to protect their patents and project from theft. In hindsight, I should've questioned everything.

"Glasses or not," she began, and I half expected her to start rambling again, "I can see how tired you are. When was the last time you slept?"

353

I tried to remember and shrugged. "Maybe a few hours on the flight from D.C. to Germany."

"That was a while ago." Turning to the side, I followed her line of sight as she pointed her head toward the bed. "Take a nap now. You can't be running on empty the way you are."

"Giving me orders, huh?" There went my lips again. I'd killed a dozen people tonight, and we had more questions than answers about what in God's name was going on and who was really after this woman, but I was grinning. Maybe I really was losing it from sleep deprivation? A nap wasn't a horrible idea.

I'd taken a sixty-second shower once the plane had leveled out, washed the blood from my body to remove that reminder from Diana's view, but it hadn't been enough to wake me. Doubtful coffee would do the trick right now either.

"I am, in fact, telling you what to do." The twitch of her lips into a slight smile cracked the walls of my chest open. "You're already in comfy clothes. Both of us are."

She lowered her chin, studying my black tee and sweats before moving on to her Stanford sweatshirt she'd changed into post take-off and her kill-me-right-fucking-now gray yoga pants.

"If I tell you that *I* need to rest for a bit, and I don't want to be alone, will that convince you to lie down, too?"

"Playing dirty now." The words eased out a bit huskier than I'd intended, but she had a habit of catching me off guard and making me behave in peculiar ways.

A bit of turbulence hit—*not even complaining about the timing*—sending her stumbling against my chest, and my hands slipped around to her back. I kept my balance, and us both upright, so we didn't wind up falling onto my bed. *Not* the place I needed to be with this woman. She'd find out how much I truly had wanted to tie her up at that house. Of course, I'd have had her naked in that chair so I could eat her out while she squirmed from pleasure and called out my name.

That thought right there alone was exactly why it was Falcon out in the cabin working leads instead of me, because only one head of mine was functioning.

This had to be how Griffin, Gray, Jesse, and the others had felt when our cases had involved the women they were now married to. Thrown off and unfocused. I hadn't been able to comprehend what they'd been going through, because it'd made no sense to me.

Until now.

Until Diana.

The woman making me forget logic and reason.

The woman whose breasts were still plastered to my chest as I continued to hold her against me.

"You've crammed a lot of bad shit into this week." The number of cities I'd been in the space of a day was . . . I'd lost count. Where were we now? Flying over Russian airspace, for all I fucking knew. "So, if you want to take a nap, I'll do it for you," I agreed. Because, in truth, I was so fatigued I wasn't sure if my dick would even work right now, which was saying a lot. Especially around this woman.

"Thank you." She looked over at the bed, and I knew what she had to be thinking. She was wondering if I'd ever had sex there. The bedroom had racked up plenty of miles, all of which were from my teammates, though. Never from me.

"No," I answered the question she would never ask. "I've never here."

She let go of me and grimaced, the opposite of what I wanted her to do. "I wasn't thinking that."

"You were," I said, fairly confident I could read the

confirmation in her hesitant expression. At least she wasn't trembling anymore, nor panic-talking.

"You're confusing," she whispered as her hands walked up my chest, then up to the sides of my neck.

I nearly lowered my head to nuzzle her face, copying how Dallas was with her. Lucky dog. "I know, and I'm sorry, but it's your fault." Shutting my eyes, I leaned in and rested my forehead to hers instead of ravishing her mouth like I craved.

"My fault, huh?" she asked in that sweet, sexy tone of hers.

"Absolutely," I remarked, my voice deeper than I'd intended, rough with exhaustion and desire.

"Care to elaborate?"

"Not even a little bit," I said, shocked at the teasing territory I'd dipped into. "Let's get this over with then, huh? The nap."

"Sounds like torture," she commented, hitting me back with her own brand of playfulness.

Mission success in keeping her calm. Now to find out just how tired I really was. Would joining her in the bed calm my body and mind? Or would certain parts of me remain wide awake? "You already know sleeping next to you is not going to be easy."

"How hard?" More turbulence sent her pressing even closer against me, and sleep deprivation did nothing to tame my desire for this woman. She had to be feeling just how hard she made me.

"Bed," I grunted. "Now."

"You're better at giving commands than I am, I'll give you that." She smirked, then pulled away and trained her full attention on the bed, facing it like a problem she needed to combat head-on.

"You going to be good at taking them?"

She shot me a saucy look over her shoulder, but didn't reply, or give me any indication she'd comply with any of my commands—orders I needed to refrain from giving her unless it was to save her life.

My hand rested over my heart at the sad reminder that keeping her safe meant removing myself from her life after the mission was over. An idea that was too painful to think about, even if true. "Bed," I said again. "On top of the covers."

"And if I'm cold?"

I'll warm you up. I nearly rolled my damn eyes at my own thoughts.

I half expected her to crawl onto the bed on all fours with her ass in the air, just to tease me, but she had the good sense to walk around to the side and slide on that way instead. At least one of us was thinking clearly.

She really had been through a lot, and the fact we had any quasi-sexual banter going on after she'd witnessed war tonight spoke volumes about her. There was a hell of a lot more to this woman than met the eye. Maybe we were even more alike than I thought.

I took a moment to gather my thoughts as she curled up on the bed. She closed her eyes, resting her head on the pillow, her light blonde hair wild around her face.

No, you're an angel. It was up to me to keep her from falling, from joining me in hell. Which meant sticking to my original plan of not giving in to temptation.

I went around the bed and wordlessly removed her sneakers and socks before kicking off my own. I hated sleeping with anything on my body, let alone covering my feet.

She half frowned, half pouted. Too damn cute it hurt to

look at her sometimes. "Sorry, I didn't mean to get your bed dirty."

"I don't care about that." I climbed up next to her. "Just making you more comfortable."

"Oh, well, thank you," she said as I turned on my side to face her, maintaining as much distance between us as possible. Which was far too close—a mere three inches between our mouths. "Try and sleep. Like you said, they'll come for us if they learn something new."

"Roger that," I said with a smirk, propping my head on my bent arm while curling my other hand into a fist between us. It was a piss-poor barrier, but the best I could do to prevent me from reaching for her. A physical reminder to keep my distance.

"Carter?" My name floating softly from her mouth guided my eyes to her lips.

"Is it too much to ask you to hold me while we sleep?"

"You sure it'll help more than it'll hurt?" *Because it's going to kill me.* The last person I'd slept next to was Rebecca, and she hadn't been the snuggling type. Holding Diana in my arms while getting shut-eye would be unfamiliar. Dangerous to my control, too.

"I think it'll help more than it'll hurt," she said earnestly, drawing the breath from my lungs with that sad little expression.

I considered getting up to shut off the lights so it wouldn't shred me to see those beautiful blues, but being in the dark with this woman would lead my hands and body to temptation. "Okay," I agreed against my better judgment, another reminder I was anything but myself around her. "Turn around." I waited for her to do so, then scooted closer and drew her back tight to my chest. She parked her ass against my groin as if it belonged there, and I slipped my arm around her body, catching hold of her hand.

Our fingers laced together against her abdomen, and I rested my chin at the top of her head.

She was warm and soft and fucking A . . . she felt like home.

39

DIANA

"You're not sleeping." Carter's just-waking-up voice could compete with his deep, commanding one on the sensual scale.

How'd he know my eyes weren't closed? My back was to him. I'd done my best not to move a muscle while he'd slept, not wanting to disturb him. He'd needed to sleep, whereas I'd had plenty yesterday, and I wanted to cherish the moment of this man's strong arms around me. It was probably a once-in-a-lifetime experience to have him cradling me in a bed, and I wasn't going to miss out on a single second of it. I'd never felt so safe in all my life, even with the world crumbling around us.

"Diana," he prompted when I'd yet to confirm he was right. I expected him to pull away at any second, jump off the bed like it was on fire. But he didn't. He kept me hostage in his arms, our hands still together, resting against my abdomen.

"I'm not tired," I admitted. "You should go back to sleep, though." I doubted an hour had even passed since he'd closed his eyes.

"I'm good," he murmured, the fog of fatigue less prominent in his voice that time. So much so I almost believed him because I felt his erection on my ass. "Too good, in fact." His words were breathy that time, and at the feel of his mouth near my ear, I shuddered.

"You don't snore. For being over forty, I kind of expected that."

"Calling me old?"

"Mmmm. More like mature. Experienced. Kind of perfect." I turned my head, locking on to his eyes. They were close, and zeroing in on me as if there were a million things on his mind he'd never share.

"Not even close to perfect. I'll take the other two compliments, though." He smiled, and it wasn't so much forced as if he was trying to surrender to something, I just wished I could figure out what that *something* was.

Desperate to feel those lips on mine, but not desperate enough to beg, I shifted back around, an achiness filling my chest.

He unlocked our hands, and I felt the impending loss, expecting him to break apart from me. Instead, he moved his hand to the hem of my sweatshirt and slipped under it, resting his warm palm over my abdomen. The pad of his thumb smoothed in a circle around my belly button. "How long ago was this pierced?"

Shutting my eyes, I relaxed at his touch. "When my parents said no to getting it done at sixteen, I tried to do it myself."

"Ouch," he said with a light laugh.

"Yeah, it wasn't a pretty sight. The ring never made it in, but the scar seems to be with me forever."

"Scars have a tendency to do that," he remarked, his tone dipping low again. He had to be thinking about Rebecca.

And now, so was I. Maybe it was finally time to get the weight of my past off my chest. "Can I tell you a secret? One of those 'what we say in the air stays in the air' kind of things?"

"Is that a thing?" His palm pressed tighter over my stomach, thumb going still.

"Can it be?"

"If you need to tell me something, then yes, of course you can," he said almost somberly, which gave me pause.

Was this a need, or only a desire to unburden myself of guilt? What was I going to ask him to do, forgive me? Confess to him like a priest just because he had on a crucifix? It made me wonder why he kept it on when he continued to refer to himself as the opposite of holy.

"Don't leave me hanging now. I'm curious." There was a touch of playfulness in his tone, and it reminded me a bit of the man I first met at the embassy.

He resumed moving his hand, this time in small, sweeping circles over my abdomen. There was something about such soft, gentle touches from such a hard, strong man that had my heart racing that much more.

Here goes. "After you first saved me at the embassy, I developed a crush on you. So when I found out at the holiday party you were married, and to Rebecca, no less, I was devastated."

He slid his thumb along the center line of my body, stopping abruptly at my bra as if hitting more than just a physical barrier. "Go on," he said steadily, not pulling away. In fact, I was pretty sure he'd pinned his body tighter against mine.

"I, um, also felt guilty because I'd been thinking nonstop about you before that party. I tried to stop after I knew the truth, but it was hard to do." His thumb traced along the underside of my rib cage. "My one and only tattoo is because of you. My best friend insisted I get it, thinking it would help me get over my crush. To get over you."

His hand stopped moving. "Your tattoo is because of me?"

"Yes." Squeezing my eyes closed, I waited for my body to heat with embarrassment, but it didn't come. "When we bumped into each other at the restaurant Easter weekend, I was so shocked to see you. And to discover my body still reacted to you in such a way that . . . well, you get the idea. So, I've been carrying the weight of this guilt for years." Now I remembered why he needed to hear this, and it wasn't about me. It was about making him understand my words back at the lab—when I'd told Bahar I'd wished someone else had saved me.

"Diana."

I didn't let the warning in his tone stop me. "What I need you to know is that the time travel comment, it was because it's painful to want someone you can't have. To spend a third of your life comparing every single man you meet to that person." Shit, now I was going to cry, and I was as much of a fan of showing my tears as Carter seemed to be. "I've never been able to get you out of my head, so that's why I said that."

He was turning me.

Directing me to face him.

I kept my eyes sealed, unable to witness the rejection in his eyes, or see his mouth form the words to tell me to stop wanting what I couldn't have.

"Look at me." His voice was rough, demanding, but I refused to obey him.

I shook my head as the confession spilled out of me. "I just . . . I've felt tied to you since the day we met. Soul-tied, which sounds strange, I know. But now here we are. Despite you being stubborn and pushing me away, not to mention killing those two men in the shed regardless of my wishes, and enjoying tying people up—I still want you. I don't know how not to." When he said nothing, I filled the silence, continuing to ramble on. "I also saw what could be between us the moment you set your mouth to mine." My skin prickled from chills, goose bumps scattering across my body. "You kissed me, then our future played out like a movie in my head. It was so real I could've reached out and touched it. Touched us in the future. Our kids. Our—"

"Look. At. Me." He broke through my mess of words, silencing me as what I'd just said played back in my mind.

Did I really admit I could see myself having his children? *Did I actually go there?* That was kind of a big *there* to go to. But that kiss had proved time travel to the future was real. Because I got a glimpse, and it was freaking perfect.

"Diana." The plea in his voice was loud and clear, beckoning me to look at him.

How in the world could I do that after my confession? I hadn't meant to share that part. My awkward nervousness got the best of me. He must've thought I'd gone off the rails, mentioning the whole quantum jumping in my head to our future thing.

"Please." His gentle request had me opening my eyes, finding his glossy and his nostrils flaring.

Then again, I didn't have my glasses on, so maybe I wasn't seeing the truth. Just seeing what I wanted to see. Him returning my feelings.

"You saw *me* as a father?" His brows were drawn tight, and even without my glasses I knew he was sporting a steely look, eyes capable of penetrating to the deepest layers of my soul.

"Ye—" He captured my *yes* with his mouth, swallowing it with a kiss, taking both of my cheeks in his palms to deepen the connection.

Unable to stop myself, I worked my hands between our bodies and slid them beneath his shirt, aching to touch him. The hard ridge of muscles splaying beneath my palms contracted under my touch, sending shivers of electricity racing up my arms.

I gasped when he abruptly rolled to his back, pulling me on top of him. He gathered my face between his hands again as if he never wanted to let me go.

He matched me kiss for kiss. Tongue with tongue. Heartbeat for heartbeat.

Straddling him, my hands moved up his chest, our mouths finally breaking apart when I sat upright to take a look at this tough, gorgeous man beneath me.

His dark eyes were focused on me as he dragged his hands up the sides of my arms and held my biceps. The longing and desire were so intense, I wasn't sure how to handle the emotions pounding through me.

When I reached for the hem of my sweatshirt, he released my arms, allowing me to peel it over my head. I quickly removed my bra and it became a memory over my shoulder on the floor.

"Diana." My name floated from his lips, a rough sigh of exhaustion, like he was done resisting this thing between us. He reached up for my hair and twined the locks around his hand while palming my breast with the other.

I swallowed back a loud moan as I arched into his touch, elongating my spine while shimmying on his lap, feeling the pulse of need between my thighs. It was certainly between his. A *thick,* hard need impossible to ignore.

"Fuck," he said under his breath, dragging his hand up

from my breast to my throat, resting it there momentarily before hooking it behind my neck. Then he pushed up, meeting me halfway for another kiss. "Not now," he hissed between kisses. "I can't let my team hear you."

"I can be quiet," I promised.

"You won't be when I drive my cock inside you, trust me," he ground out.

All I could latch on to was the fact he wasn't saying no. Just "not here." I clung to that bit of hope, still unable to stop myself from searching for relief, rotating my pussy over his bulge, wishing away the bulky fabric between us.

"I need to see you come, though," he murmured.

Thank.

God.

"I've waited too damn long to . . ." He let his words trail off that time.

You've waited?

It was a flash of movement and muscle before he had me on my back, locked between his powerful thighs. His shirt joined mine on the floor. Then he removed the cross and set it aside, eliminating the last mental obstacle to taking what he wanted.

"Carter?" I wasn't sure what I was asking him, but he seemed to know before I did, and he nodded.

He cocked his head, eyes dropping from my breasts to the waistband of my yoga pants. He shifted back and palmed my center over the thin fabric. "Will you stay quiet if I touch you here?"

My hips lifted from the bed, aching for him. "Yes."

"You promise you'll be good?" He set a hand to my abdomen, urging my body back down, taking control of the situation and me, and every cell in my body complied. "Tell me you understand. Let me hear you say it. This room isn't soundproof. They'll hear you screaming. And then I'll have to cut off their ears for knowing how you sound when you come."

"Operators need their hearing," I reminded him, my brain apparently glitching, still a bit shell-shocked this moment was happening after he'd pushed me away earlier that night. My hands on the hard walls of his body offered more proof this was real.

"Tell me, angel, are you going to be good?" he rasped.

Angel? My panties were so soaked, more words like that and I wouldn't be able to hide how aroused he made me. "Yes, I'll be good," I confirmed. "Quiet."

He ran his thumb over the seam of the fabric. "How badly do you want this?"

"More than anything. I need it. Despite everything that happened tonight at the safe house that proved to be less than safe, all I can think about is . . ." *You tying me to that chair. Your commands. My desire to obey.*

"You're not selling me on this that well," he said hoarsely.

"No, please," I begged. "Touch me. I swear I'll be your . . ." I swallowed. "Good girl." Panting words was officially a thing. At thirty thousand-plus miles in the air. "Whatever you tell me to do, I will."

"Of course you will." A dark smile cut across his lips as he held himself up over me. He rotated his hips, letting me feel how hard he was, capturing the small cry from my mouth as he lightly thrusted against me. If only he was inside of me instead.

He was testing my ability to behave and stay quiet, and I was seconds away from failing. Probably would've had his mouth not trapped a deep moan with his kiss.

My breasts smashed against his chest, and my nipples

grew taut at the feel of his skin on mine. He dragged his mouth to my cheek, then over to my ear, shifting his weight to one arm.

He was going to touch me. Finally.

His rough hand traveled between our bodies, his palm slipping under the fabric of my pants and panties, and he hissed against my ear at discovering how wet I was.

"You have no idea how much I want to fuck your cunt with my mouth." I'd never had someone talk to me like this, and I never wanted it to stop.

He pushed two fingers inside my tight walls, dropping his mouth over mine at the same time, sensing I'd misbehave and cry. He was right. This man's skilled tongue in my mouth while he pumped his fingers inside me was beyond description.

"Oxy . . . fucking . . . tocin," I murmured against his lips, feeling a little drunk.

He eased his lips back, removing his fingers from inside me, but continued to send me closer to the edge, the heel of his hand rubbing soft, sensual circles over my clit. "You said fuck."

I bit my lip, hoping it'd come across as seductive and not goofy. "When the occasion calls for it." At the sight of his sexy side smirk, I added, "I've never felt this good in all my life."

His smile abruptly vanished, and he lowered his forehead to mine. "I'm a special brand of fucked up, angel."

The words "angel" and "fucked up" didn't exactly mix, and yet . . .

"Don't remind me anyone else has ever made you feel good before. It makes me . . . unhinged."

Ohhh. "I told you I want the wolf." I meant it, too. "I want you as you are. Possessive and all."

He lifted his forehead, and a haunted, almost sad expression was there. "Are you okay?"

"No," he answered earnestly. "I'm not." But then he kissed me again, stealing my ability to ask him to explain.

Distracted from my question by his tongue in my mouth and his touch between my legs, I kissed him back. Hard. Furiously intense, thirteen years of pent-up desire and guilt boiling over into passion and teeth and tongues.

His savage growl that fell into my mouth between kisses as he pushed his fingers inside me compelled me to take a chance and touch him as well. Hopefully, he'd let me.

I reached between us, our arms lining up alongside each other, the only barriers between our bodies, and I shoved my hand down his sweats.

Oh. My. God.

The man wasn't kidding about hurting me.

He was *thick.*

I felt his smile on my lips, letting me know he'd read my mind and my shock.

I did my best to get a firm grasp of him, to stroke his cock with the same glorious rhythm he finger-fucked me. He was huge, so our arms battled for space. Nearly breaking my promise to be quiet, I moaned in frustration when he stopped his ministrations, pulling his hand from my pants.

"One at a time, angel." He captured my wrist and removed my hand before going back to my pussy. "You first. Always."

"Is this . . . how you normally do . . .?" Why was I asking that while he fingered me? Maybe I was jealous, too.

He found my eyes, never stopping touching me, though. "No, it's not. Not at all."

The way he said it, the look in his eyes, it all came home to me. He felt the connection, too. He'd admitted at the house it was real. It was all happening so fast, but maybe the decade-plus of me wanting him meant this was the slowest of all burns and not instalove.

"Fuck it," he rasped. "I have to taste you." He reared back to his knees, peeled down my pants and panties to my thighs and stared at me for a moment.

"So pink and swollen for me. Fucking fuck, Diana." He tore a hand through his hair, chest heaving from deep breaths as his eyes raked over my body. I propped myself up on my forearms to see him better, to take in how he was looking at me. "You're so goddamn beautiful I don't think I can handle how you make me—"

I swallowed back my surprised squeal when he moved off the bed, gently dragging me to the edge as he went. He deftly finished removing my panties and yoga pants, hooked my knees over his shoulders, and buried his face between my thighs.

Holy.

Freaking.

Hell.

The moment his mouth fused with my pussy, I had to slap both hands over my mouth to hold in my scream.

He claimed my center with his tongue. Owned it with his mouth. Captured my soul with his achy need for me that went beyond sex.

I latched my ankles behind his head, lifting my ass off the bed, and gasped as his hand went around to my backside, squeezing my flesh hard while his tongue slid over me. In me.

Dizzy and breathless was my new favorite plane of existence.

But when this man's hand slid around to my *other* hole, and he applied pressure there with his thumb, it was sensory overload to the max. It took all my restraint not to bite my own hand to prevent me from yelling out his name.

Freeing one hand from my mouth, I grabbed hold of his head, clawing at his thick head of hair.

His moans against my clit nearly destroyed my ability to keep quiet yet again.

"I'm—I'm . . ." My nipples were painfully hard, and my entire body tensed as every nerve ending lit up. "Come-coming." I trembled almost violently. "Carter," I whispered, a piece of me breaking on the inside. A fragment I'd happily hand over to him to own forever. He seemed to know. To accept it. Savor it.

He kept devouring me even after I'd orgasmed, and I brought my hands to his shoulders, pushing gently to let him know I couldn't handle any more pleasure. It was so intense, I might die if he kept at it.

"I want you inside me, and I know we can't, but . . ." Barely down from the high, I begged, "My turn, and don't you dare say no."

He lifted his head from between my thighs, a sexy smile parked there as he traced the pad of his thumb along the seam of his lips. "I wouldn't dream of it."

So help me if anyone interrupted us, I might throw them from the plane myself, I didn't even care.

He leaned in and licked my pussy once more, his facial hair (and maybe I felt a naughty smirk from him down there as well) tickled my skin. I flinched, my sensitivity level a twenty out of ten.

He untangled our bodies and stood, huskily demanding, "On your knees, angel."

This man could give me commands in the bedroom every day and hour of the week. Forever and ever.

He shoved down his sweats and stepped free of them,

revealing black boxer briefs that could barely contain his hard-on.

I did as he instructed while he peeled down his briefs and took his cock in his hand.

The sheer size and girth of that man was both intimidating and awe inspiring. I stared at the crown of his cock, biting the inside of my cheek . . . wondering how in the world he'd fit in any of my holes, including my mouth. Nothing was ever understated when it came to Carter Freaking Dominick, was it?

"Angel?" The soft tone, such a break from his typical tough-guy voice, had my chest squeezing with emotion.

I could get used to that nickname, but part of me feared there was more meaning to that one word. A reminder to him I was off-limits to his self-imposed darkness.

I worked my attention up. From his hand slowly stroking his cock, to the slight dusting of hair along his happy trail, to his flexing abdominal muscles, and finally to his face. To his gorgeous eyes.

"I swore I'd never corrupt you like this." That little hitch in his voice was back. He joined me on the bed, resting on his knees in front of me, and cupped my face. "I keep losing my control when it comes to you."

I reached between our bodies to take his cock with both hands and taunted, "Then I guess you're really about to lose it now."

40

CARTER

FUCK ME TO HELL AND BACK AGAIN. SHE WAS GOING TO kill me.

Holding me firmly in the grip of her delicate fingers, Diana pressed against my chest with one hand, pushing me down onto the pillows. Settling herself between my knees, she lowered her mouth and circled her tongue around the tip of my cock before gliding her lips down around it. Stroking me while holding herself up with the other hand, she pulled more of me into that slick, wet heaven.

I watched as she varied her grip, her speed, how much of me she took into her mouth, finding a rhythm and pressure that pulled the reactions she wanted from me. *So fucking smart. Such a good fucking girl.*

But in truth, she wasn't my good girl. Or my naughty one. She really was my sweet angel. An angel with a sinful body and a mouth designed to send me over the motherfucking edge.

Because this woman. Damn this woman. She was going to make me come fast, hard, and deep into her throat with how much of me she'd managed to take in her mouth.

Choking and gagging didn't stop her. Hell, it seemed to encourage her to take more and more of me. *My overachiever.*

"Diana." Her name was a hiss of air from my lips as I tangled my hand in her hair. I didn't even need to guide her up and down, she was doing a superb fucking job all on her own, but I couldn't help but grab her blonde locks, pretending I had some semblance of control.

In truth, I'd never felt so out of control. So consumed by someone I couldn't think straight. Was she right? *Soul-ties?* How could that be? I didn't have a soul anymore. I'd never deserve her, and I'd only put her at risk, but—

My thoughts died when she swallowed even more of me, the head of my cock pressing into the back of her throat. As incredible as it felt, I wanted to be so deep inside her pussy, stretch her so wide around my cock she'd feel me for days after. I wanted to empty myself inside her, brand her, claim her as mine, and . . .

You saw me as a father? How could she ever see that? How could she look beyond the demon I was to see anything?

Something inside me had snapped when she'd confided she could see a future with me, her words stealing my ability to reason. To rationalize my way out of this moment.

My eyes glazed over and I dropped my head back to the pillows when she pulled up only to slam back down on me, her mouth meeting where her hand held my cock.

"Angel," I said under my breath, growing dizzy with all the blood rushing from one head to the other.

At the abrupt knock, Diana startled and stopped moving, but she didn't pull away.

"Hey, we have an update," Griffin called out. "You awake?"

"No, I'm asleep," I grunted, too blitzed to move. At the

same time, also too tense to walk out of this room without coming first. If someone pulled me from this bed before Diana got the chance to finish what she'd started, that someone was going to die. "Can you tell me through the door while I—" I lost my train of thought when Diana resumed her up-and-down rhythm, ignoring the interruption.

"Yeah, sure." I could hear the hesitancy in Griffin's tone, but there was no way he'd suspect this angel of a woman was fucking me with her mouth while he talked.

Now I was the one fighting to keep my mouth shut and hide the evidence of what was happening in here. "Just tell me the most immediate news," I ordered, using my hand tangled in Diana's hair to guide her.

She'd decided to torture me by slowing down, removing her palm from my shaft to cup my balls, drawing another hiss from my lips.

Such a bad girl for doing this with Griffin out there. Thoughts of her laid out across my lap, her perfect ass in view while I left my handprint there, filled my head.

"Yeah, uh," Griffin began, for sure finally clued in on his bad timing, "are you sure you don't want to come out here to talk?"

"Fine," I ground out, clamping down on my back teeth as Diana deepthroated me, working her mouth harder and faster. I no longer needed to control the movement with my hand in her hair. I kept it there anyway, twisting her locks tighter to try and retain some control. My other hand gripped the bedding beside me as she hollowed her cheeks and swallowed. I swore I heard the fabric tear as I pulled it tight in my fist. "Be . . ." I couldn't stop the grunt from leaving my mouth that time. "Be out in a second."

"Roger that." Damn the smirk I could hear in his tone.

I nearly roared out a litany of curses as Diana pulled her

mouth from my cock. "Your stamina is going to hurt my jaw," she teased, peering up at me, and I grinned.

She swirled her tongue along the head of my crown, and with those intense blue eyes fixed on me, I could've come then. The second she dropped her mouth down over me again, jerking me off at the same time, I gave her what we both craved.

Every muscle in my body tensed as I came in her mouth and down her throat. I let go of her hair and she lifted her head, meeting my eyes. She'd swallowed every last drop. At the sight of her pink tongue running over her bottom lip, I relaxed. The most relaxed I'd quite possibly been in far too long. At least since the day I'd seen her in the office in New York, and I'd wanted to pin her to the desk and eat her out.

"Was I . . . okay?" The tentative break in her voice had me hauling her into my arms, laying her out right on top of me.

With our naked bodies together, even with my dick fighting to recover after she'd sucked the life out of me, I'd easily lose track of everything but her. *That'd be a bad idea.* But damnit, I'd love nothing more than to forget it all and sleep curled up around her, then wake with her swollen cunt close to my cock, feeling her soft skin against my hard body. It'd be perfect. "More than okay, and you know it."

She smiled, but then winced and held her jaw.

Shit, it'd been painful for her to take me and that pulled me from my haze and reminded me of another issue. "Are you good? The bruises from jumping from the truck the other day, are you in pain?" I'd done my best to avoid looking at the little black-and-blue marks on her skin while we'd been together so I didn't lose myself to anger, but now my concern for her pain was at the forefront of my mind.

"Still have Advil in me, but pretty sure that orgasm you

gave me stamped out any lingering remnants of pain in my body." She gave me a sweet smile, then leaned in and kissed my cheek. It was soft and gentle, and somehow that moment had my heartbeat going even wilder than it had while she'd sucked me dry.

Fucked. I'm completely and utterly fucked.

"Let me have a look at you to be sure you're okay." I needed to get up and get dressed, knowing Griffin wouldn't wait too long before interrupting us again. I was sure whatever he had to tell me was important, but we were in the air, so it wasn't like we were going to be under attack. If we were in imminent danger, he wouldn't have let us be no matter what he thought—or knew—we were doing, so I was moving a bit slower than necessary. I could try to convince myself my pace had nothing to do with not being ready to face reality, but it was bullshit. That reality required me giving this woman up one day.

To hell with that. Not today, or tomorrow. I had to have more time with her after this. Just a little more taste of heaven before I let her go. Before I accidentally pulled her into my darkness and trapped her there with me forever. *But what a forever that'd be.*

"I'm really okay, I promise." She was blushing now when she hadn't been before. Was it catching up to her, that she was sprawled out naked on my bed and now remembering what we did with my team on the other side of the door?

"Roll over so I can check your back anyway," I ordered a bit gruffly. In truth, I wanted to see her like this. Naked on my bed from every angle. Needed to commit every inch of her to memory for when I'd eventually be getting off alone.

"Yes, sir." She smirked and rolled over, and my dick was already springing back to life at the sight before me. The line down her back. Her slender waist.

Unable to help myself, I traced her spine with my fingertip, racing it all the way down over the slope of her ass cheek, and she jolted when I curved it around to her damp center. "A few bruises, but you look perfect aside from that." I removed my hand and stood tall. "Turn over."

She did as I asked, then she propped her head up with her elbow and cupped her breast with her other hand, all the while staring at me with *fuck-me* eyes. The woman really did need her glasses. Needed to clearly see the man peering back at her. To understand what she was getting herself into with me, because what she'd experienced tonight barely scratched the surface.

"We need to go out there now, and you're making it hard for me to leave." I knelt on the bed and leaned in, taking her other nipple between my teeth.

"Very hard," she said, her voice husky as she reached between my legs.

My breath fanned across her nipple, coaxing chills. "Mmmm. Not always an angel, are you?"

"Because I'm distracting you while there's an important mission at stake. I'm being bad for not focusing on what's more important out there, right?"

I went still at the guilt in her tone I didn't want her feeling. I'd shoulder that burden for the both of us. She didn't need to carry it.

Witnessing the trepidation in her expression had me realizing there was nothing more important to me than her. Not even stopping an attack. That should've sent me back upright. The problem was, it didn't. I was hooked on this woman.

Lifting my head, I keyed in on the inside of her wrist, the tattoo she claimed to have inked there because of me. I considered opening up, confessing that the wings on my back were because of her.

I felt an unyielding need to give her something, to tell her some piece of truth that justified the way she looked at me. But instead of sharing the deeply intimate part of our shared reality, all I could bring myself to admit was, "Those two men in the shed are still alive."

Her eyes went wide, and she sat a bit, reaching for my cheek. I'd swear I was as bad as Dallas, yearning to lean in, to bop her face with my own, and beg her to touch me. To love me.

"You didn't kill them because of me?" She blinked and shook her head. "That sounded—"

"Exactly as it should." My shoulders collapsed, unsure what this all meant, and how messed up it actually made me.

"Thank you." She kissed my cheek again, and before she could retreat, I caught her wrist and dragged my lips over the tattoo and worked my mouth up her arm, kissing the inside of the elbow.

I wanted to kiss every part of her. Distraction was pitifully inadequate to describe what this woman was, and what she did to me. "We should get dressed. Focus," I finally pushed out, relenting to what I was supposed to say. "We need to see what they found out."

Appearing a little frazzled, she nodded. "Right."

I helped her to her feet, and we dressed quietly side by side, as if somehow it was the most natural thing in the world. Sharing the same space. Eyes on each other while putting on our clothes, hiding the evidence of what we'd shared in there.

We went into the bathroom next. I rinsed my face and hands while she used the toilet right next to the sink. No shyness or hesitation. I grabbed a paper towel to dry off my hands, making room for her at the basin without leaving the bathroom.

Combing her fingers through her hair, she met my eyes in the mirror from where I stood behind her. "Your cross. Don't forget it."

"It's not mine. Not really." I tossed the paper towel into the trash. "The priest put it on me back at the rectory. Said I needed it more than he did." *Guess he was right.* I went into the room and looped the chain around my neck, noticing how oddly weighed down I felt without it.

"I know we're short on time, but promise me we'll talk about what happened here."

I slowly faced her, finding her waiting by the door. Thank God I'd had the good sense to lock it, not that Griffin would've barged in. "I suppose it'd make sense to do that."

I joined her, intending to reach for the door handle behind her, but against my better judgment (that I clearly lacked around her), I shifted her hair to the side and leaned in to kiss her cheek as softly as she'd kissed mine.

And then I did the unthinkable—I let her know she wasn't alone in her feelings over the years. "I have a tattoo because of you, too," I confessed.

Before she could respond or react, I pushed the door behind her open and sidestepped her, trying to find a way to walk away from my desire to undo any damage our time together may have done. To her. To myself. To the whole fucking world.

41

DIANA

I HUNG BACK IN THE DOORWAY, MY BODY NUMB AS MY MIND processed what he'd shared. My legs were already weak from the orgasm, jaw sore, and now my head was spinning (for so many reasons). *Which tattoo? Why? When?*

Carter stopped in the aisle, leaned over an empty seat and picked up a black ball cap, pulling the brim down over his eyes as he put it on. Was he trying to prevent anyone from getting a read on his thoughts? Keep what went down in the bedroom strictly between us?

He stole a look back at me, the intensity in his stare going straight to my heart. He nodded, his eyes never leaving mine.

I swallowed and nodded back, giving him whatever reassurance he seemed to need from me.

Once Carter about-faced, my shoulders fell. Why'd the loss of his attention make me feel so alone? I was teetering on the edge. Skirting the line between the quiet sanctuary of the bedroom (and what had just happened in there) and a cabin full of people (working together to save the future). But without Carter at my side, I felt isolated. And my thoughts—

about him, us, everything—if not organized and focused, could be disastrous.

I peered over at the couch, catching Mya's eyes. She had to be wondering why I was braced against the doorframe, tense and wary, rather than jumping in to assist.

You can't stand like a statue in the doorway and be unproductive when you're at the center of all this. The little mental pep talk managed to get my hands down by my sides at least. Step two: walk.

An unwelcome thought pushed to mind, keeping me from budging. Rebecca's family money had paid for this jet, and I'd just given her husband (*ex-husband? widower?*) a blow job in the bedroom, and . . .

Damn the guilt. I couldn't handle that plus everything else happening in my life.

Carter turned to the side, checking on me again. Was he having similar thoughts? Regrets? Or maybe he'd dipped inside my head and plucked out my thoughts, knowing I'd been thinking about his wife.

Ex-wife. Had he really accidentally called her that back at the safe house? He'd clearly been surprised by his slip of the tongue, too. I'd witnessed his shocked expression when the words left his mouth.

Griffin was still talking to him, and although Carter's arms were locked across his chest, his attention was locked on to me. Was he hearing anything his teammate was saying?

Griffin slapped a hand over Carter's shoulder, physically redirecting him his way. The tense thread between us broke, finally forcing my feet to move.

I made it halfway through the cabin before Mya said, "Please tell me Carter slept for a bit. That man is broody enough, but without sleep, he might Hulk out."

"He slept a little." *Just before he gave me the best orgasm of my life.*

Mya closed her laptop as I sat next to her on the couch. With everyone in the cabin working, I felt utterly useless. This wasn't a problem I knew how to outsmart yet.

"I can fill you in, if you'd like?" She drummed her nails on top of her laptop. "Or you can wait for the Big Guy to do it," she tacked on since I was taking too long to answer.

"Big Guy" was the understatement of the year when it came to what he was packing below the belt. Adjusting my sleeves so they covered both my tattoo and my goose bumps, my attention cut back to Carter just as he was dragging his thumb along the underside of his lip. He'd done it in such a provocative way I found myself squirming on the couch.

I could stand in front of a crowd of hundreds and lecture on an attempt to merge quantum mechanics with Einstein's general theory of relativity without missing a beat. But try and have a conversation with Carter's smoldering eyes and enough brood to charge a nuclear reactor pointed my way? Not likely.

"I'm guessing you didn't hear me," Mya said with a little chuckle, waving her hand in front of my face twice.

I squeezed my eyes closed, chills peppering every inch of my skin like a suit of armor, a gift of invisible protection from Carter. Being in his presence did make me feel like I was cloaked in safety, though. The man exuded confidence and strength as much as he did sex appeal.

"You have news?" Those three words took far too much effort to say. "Please, go ahead and tell me."

"You sure you don't need another moment to, um, untangle those thoughts of yours?" Mya's tone was both teasing and surprisingly comforting at the same time. It did the trick and had me opening my eyes.

Hoping to ground myself in this conversation as opposed to mentally being back in Carter's arms in the bedroom, I interlocked my hands and rested them on my lap. "I'm ready now, I promise."

Mya peeked over her shoulder toward the distraction himself before offering me a kind smile. "You and Griffin are the only two people who knew Carter before . . ."

Before he became a pseudo criminal? Before Rebecca died? Before what? I kept those questions bopping around in my head instead of verbalizing them. I didn't need Carter to overhear us talking about him.

"I'm going to get back to the mission in a moment, but I'm curious now to know something." Her smile stretched. "Sorry, the former journalist in me." After a hesitant pause, she asked, "Was he different back then when you knew him? I never asked Griffin this, but I guess I assumed Carter was always Mr. Rough and Tough." Mya's tone was soft and lured me into the trap of distraction yet again. "Seeing the way he is with you has me rethinking that."

I flipped through the pages of my mind, recalling the few times I'd spent with Carter over the years. "He was sweet and kind," I whispered, my chest heating up as if my grandmother had given me a shot of her homemade grappa. "Funny. Charming, but in a way appropriate for a married man."

"Wow." Mya sighed. "Maybe you can bring that man back to us?" She lifted her palm from her laptop. "I mean, don't get me wrong, there's a time and a place for the scary version of him," she added with a chuckle, "but I'd like to see him happy. We all would."

"Happy's such an interesting word, don't you think?" When did Oliver join us? He raised his good arm up, bracing his hand against the ceiling. Leaning in a bit, eyes on Mya, the huskiness to his voice couldn't be missed as he said, "It's subjective like art. What makes one person happy is another one's misery."

"Oh is it now?" Mya challenged while drawing her arms over her chest as if preparing to play defense. "We were having girl talk," she added before he could adjust course and explain his random interjection into our conversation.

"Shouldn't you be discussing the mission instead?" Cocking his head to the side, he stared at her with such a sharp intensity, I felt the ripple of energy emitting between them.

"And shouldn't you be taking care of your bad shoulder and crying over your messed-up tattoo?"

Mya's words provoked a smile from him as they continued some type of staring contest.

Guess there's something between you two. Feeling uncomfortably like a third wheel, I accidentally blurted, "So, you two are exes or something?"

Oliver unlocked eyes from Mya's and pushed away from the ceiling, failing to hide a wince as he set a hand over the sling on his other arm. "No, Mason's her ex, and he's on the second jet."

"Where I wish you were instead," Mya sputtered, not so convincingly. "Also, we didn't date."

"Ah, no, you're right. You just—" He cut himself off from what I assumed would be a crude word, and I had a feeling Mya would've done it for him if he hadn't.

Great. Turbulence from within the plane. "News? You, uh, said there's news, right?" If there was ever a time to regroup, I supposed now was it.

"As you know, Secret Service checks your mother's home regularly," Oliver said, eyes still on Mya, but he'd dialed down his tone. The lingering effects of their showdown remained in the form of uncomfortable energy, though. "So, of course, after the incident with your glasses, they checked again. Also, swept your dad's place. Nada."

My shoulders slumped at the *lack* of news.

"Way to bury the lead," Mya grumbled.

"At least I'm talking about the mission and not about the key to happiness," he hissed back. Oliver had only joined the tail end of that conversation, but it'd clearly struck a nerve.

"So what's the lead, then?" I had to redirect these two before Mya tested the theory of gravity and threw this man from the plane. *I guess Carter and I aren't the only ones distracted by . . . well, feelings. The good and the bad.*

"Secret Service found no inconsistencies in your dad's security software, but Gwen did. She isolated two discrepancies in the footage that ninety percent of cyber experts would've missed. The security feed was placed in a loop on two different occasions, hiding about four minutes each time."

Not very comforting. "When?"

Still holding his injured arm, Oliver shared, "Wednesday night and two weeks ago."

"So, two weeks ago is when someone more than likely planted a device, and they hid the evidence they were in his home?" I asked, putting it together. "Then this Wednesday they removed it to cover their tracks?"

Mya nodded. "Your father met with Sydney's dad Wednesday afternoon. Archer passed over the tracker for your glasses and explained how to use it."

"That was the same night the President called Carter to the White House to task him with helping out," Oliver chimed in, "and your mother gave him the suitcase with your things. Your dad wasn't home Wednesday night, and someone must've known that was the case. So, presumably they broke in and took out the device, then hid the fact they were ever there by altering the footage."

"What about the neighboring homes? I'm sure most have Ring cameras in the front and back." *Of course, you're all smart. You checked already and clearly came up empty.* "Ignore me," I whispered, pushing at the tight skin on my forehead, exhausted. "You wouldn't have buried the lead on that one."

"Don't beat yourself up. It helps to talk through this," Oliver said, his tone much gentler with me than with Mya. "But you're right, no to the above."

"Our best lead from all of this is that someone knew your dad well enough to assume he'd go to extreme lengths to keep tabs on you even after a rescue," Mya shared.

"That leads us to believe the same person had prior knowledge that something would happen to you in the first place." Oliver and Mya made a great team at delivering intel when they weren't staring at each other like they wanted to murder one another. "Because otherwise, why your dad?" Oliver continued. "Why randomly start spying on him just before the lab attack? You know what I mean?"

After a few seconds to process, I admitted, "Yeah, I'm wiped out, burnt out, and, well, all the outs, but I'm following. Someone knew I'd be abducted because they were part of the hit. They figured a rescue attempt would be made. In case of success, they had a contingency plan to find me and take me back." I glanced at Carter, finding him deep in conversation with Sydney and Gray. "I'm guessing my dad wasn't home two weeks ago when they planted the bug either?"

"Your dad handles defense contracts for the Pentagon. Negotiates deals and the like." Oliver waited for my attention and shook his head as if in apology. "Sorry, surely you already know that." I didn't, actually, but I had no plans to admit that. "Well, anyway, he was in New York on business," he finished.

"And there's no way for Gwen to see the original footage from those two times? You said she's better than the majority of the world, so I'm just trying to be optimistic." *Pessimism will get me nowhere, so . . .*

"Gwen is the best. Like top five. The problem is, she thinks someone in the top four is responsible for a lot of what's going on. So, no dice on recovering the footage," Mya explained, frowning. "But that's another lead in itself, and the White House has people trying to track down those four hackers."

"Unfortunately, when you're one of the most elite hackers in the world, you're fairly fucking good at going ghost both physically and digitally." Oliver shook his head. "But between Natasha and Gwen, maybe they'll find the needle in the cyberstack. We find the hacker, and maybe from there, we find who hired them."

With all the names flying around, I was losing track of who was who. "Natasha is?"

"Ah, sorry." Oliver pointed to Gray. "Natasha's Gray's cyber genius sister. She's married to Wyatt, a SEAL working on this mission from a different angle."

Yeah, this is a lot. And I could really use Dallas right about now. I spotted him curled up asleep next to Jack. Well, pretty sure that was his name. He was talking to another J-named guy. *Jesse, right.* Okay, so maybe I would get all their names straight. Would be helpful in thanking them once this was all over.

"So, to recap, what you're both suggesting is whoever's behind all this knows my father, and they hired one of the world's best hackers to cover that fact and their tracks," I said, opting not to wake Dallas despite the comfort I needed from him.

"Basically, yeah. Whoever's fucking over the country must be fucking your dad, too." Oliver grimaced. "I mean, not literally . . . well, hell, hopefully not."

"Your delivery of shit news could use some work." Mya stood as if needing to be eye level with him, but he still towered over her. "After this is over, you need sensitivity training, or maybe obedience school. Ring the bell. Do the trick."

"Ah, if you want me to salivate like Pavlov's dog, buttercup, all you have to do is—"

Mya covered his mouth with her hand and gritted out, "Don't you dare lick or bite me."

"Enough," Carter rasped, and my spine straightened at the deep voice throttling all of our attention his way. "You two are exhausted, and turning on each other because of it doesn't help."

As Mya slowly removed her hand from Oliver's mouth, I spied a hint of his tongue catching her palm, but she didn't cringe or smack him. Maybe Carter's broody presence was enough to make them both behave. He was the bell himself, and he'd rung it damn hard.

Especially in the bedroom for me. Holy mother of all things . . . I sure as hell needed sleep if that's where my mind went.

Gray gathered everyone around in the cabin. The space was packed tight with bodies and energy, and it felt awkward to be the only one sitting. As I stood, I nearly stumbled back, nervous about what new fresh hell was about to be dropped on us all.

"Gwen just let me know she was able to track the source of the blackmail emails sent to Alyona to the Georgetown area in D.C.," Sydney spoke first. Hammer one of several I felt coming dropped.

Dallas finally stirred awake, apparently feeling the weight of that thud of news, too. He maneuvered around everyone in the aisle to get to me. He was a living, breathing, four-legged oxytocin booster.

"Not a VPN situation?" Mya asked. "Spoofing the—"

"No," Carter cut her off, grit to his tone that had my goose bumps returning in a less savory way. Not from desire, but fear. "Gwen's sure."

"Georgetown's my mom's neighborhood." I swiped my fingers along my lips, unable to compute what was being shared. Dallas nudged me, reminding me he had my six, so I could pet him and feel better. *Try,* at least.

"There's definitely an inside man on the project, no denying it now. Someone who knew I was sent to rescue you. Probably saw my personal security footage from Amsterdam as well. Even knew I planned to reach out to Alyona for help," Carter quickly stated, and I barely registered what he'd said.

Personal security footage? Instead of tackling that question, I wound up regurgitating Oliver's unpleasant words from before and mumbled, "Right, this traitor is the one fucking my dad."

Carter's eyes widened, his shock either at my use of the F bomb, or from the fact I'd alluded to that insider traitor hooking up with my dad.

"Sorry, that was all me there despite Diana being the one to talk," Oliver said, quickly coming to my defense.

I could kiss him for the save, but decided to leave that for Mya and save Oliver from getting decked by Carter.

"Based on the listening devices planted at Joshua Mackenzie's house, coupled with this new find," Sydney went on despite my train wreck of a statement, "we believe the insider may be Senator Craig Paulsen."

Hammer number two sent me back to the couch, but it did the opposite for Carter and propelled him forward and down the aisle. "Take it from here for me, I need a minute," he said without even a passing glance my way.

That lack of eye contact and his quick departure was hammer three. I was, for all intents and purposes, effectively nailed to the couch. My attempts to stand and go to Carter were blocked when Griffin extended his arm in front of me, a plea to remain seated.

At the door thudding shut with enough force to send a volt of electricity through me, I opted to take Griffin's silent request and stay right where I was.

"Give him a minute. He's pissed. Not just at the situation, but at himself," Gray was the one to verbalize the reason behind Griffin's outstretched arm.

"Why?" I pretty much breathed out my question.

When Griffin lowered his arm, Dallas hopped up onto the couch alongside me.

"We've been looking into the backgrounds of everyone connected to the project since we were read into the operation a few days ago," Sydney began. "From Pierce Quaid at The Barclay Group to the President himself. There was a photo that was meaningless to me, but when I showed it to Carter just now, it narrowed down our suspect list to potentially one main candidate." She turned the iPad to let me see the screen, and given Carter's words before jetting away, I assumed the senator would be there.

"That's Craig Paulsen, but who's the man with him?" The second guy resembled Brad Pitt. *Clearly, it's not, so who is it?*

"His name is Andrew Cutter. He was a celebrity treasure

393

hunter, but secretly an overlord of illegal trafficking routes," Gray revealed.

I knew Craig was an asshole, but this went beyond that. Could he truly be capable of planning or assisting in what was happening with the lab attack? "You think he hired the Serbians since he has a connection to trafficking? You're saying Andrew's working with Craig?"

"No, Andrew Cutter isn't tied to this. Carter and my brother-in-law helped take him out back in 2021." Gray's words pulled me to my feet as the dots connected. Carter hadn't reacted as though he'd seen a ghost before taking off for the bedroom because he believed Craig was a traitor, but because . . .

"Andrew Cutter's the man responsible for having Carter's wife murdered, and now we know Craig Paulsen knew Andrew. We think Craig might have been the one to introduce the two of them, which ultimately means Craig may also be connected to Rebecca's death."

42

CARTER

"I KNOW YOU WANT TO BE ALONE, BUT IS THERE ANY WAY I can be alone with you?"

My fists were planted on the wall near the door, my heart thundering up into my ears so loudly I barely heard Diana's soft voice outside the door. "You don't want to be near me right now," I warned.

"I both want and need to be with you."

The vibration of the engines hummed through my body as I set my forehead between my palms against the wall. Her soft, imploring tone called to something deep within me, but I had to shut it out. Had to remain on task. On target. Unmovable. To keep her safe.

Unable to bring myself to talk, or to let her in, I remained quietly standing there. Racing thoughts all leading one direction. On one target. Craig Paulsen.

Over the years, I'd come to the conclusion that someone connected to me, who had intimate knowledge of and access to my work with the CIA, had placed Rebecca in Andrew's line of sight. Never had I imagined it'd been someone

Rebecca had personally known who led her on that dangerous path.

But that photo of Craig and Andrew together was taken three weeks before Rebecca's first dinner with Andrew. Given Craig's job, he probably knew about my employment with the Agency back then. That or Rebecca had opened her mouth to him. At this point, nothing would shock me when it came to her.

The fact they'd stayed friends after I'd asked Rebecca not to wasn't surprising either. I knew that much based on what he'd said to Diana in that limo.

At that memory, my body heated again, and my fists went against the wall as I remembered Diana's story about Craig cornering her. He could've hurt her, and . . .

"Carter?"

Working to control my breathing, I finally pushed away and went to the door. Squeezing my eyes closed, I unlocked and opened up, not ready to look at her. She'd witness the rage inside me, glasses or not. I couldn't control it. Every muscle in my body was taut, tense, and focused on one need only: to kill.

At the feel of her arms looping around my waist as the door thudded shut, I went still. "I'm so sorry," she cried into my chest.

I remained unmoving, unable to hug her back while locked into that one dark mode.

"I need to talk to your mother. She knows something about Craig. She has to," I gritted out, finally opening my eyes, my fuse still lit.

"Okay." She was shaking against me, and I couldn't even hold her. Too afraid I couldn't be gentle. I might accidentally squeeze her too hard, and I'd never be able to live with myself if I hurt her.

"But why would my mother not warn the President about him if she had any clue he could be a threat to national security? And wouldn't the CIA, or whoever managed my project in Amsterdam, be super thorough in their background checks for all those involved?"

She had a point. Two, actually. I had to try and search the logical part of my brain to accept them both. To not assume Craig was guilty of being behind all of this until we had more proof. I didn't want to misplace my anger and lose sight of the true target *if* it wasn't him. Still, I was convinced he'd placed Rebecca in harm's way, whether inadvertently or not.

"Your mother knows something." I shook my head. "It can't just be that Rebecca and Craig were friends behind my back, and—" I cut myself off, the answer now surfacing through my anger. My shoulders collapsed from the weight of the truth. It was right there, in my face the entire time. How had I not seen it before? "*He's* the one Rebecca had an affair with, that's what your mom knows."

She pulled away from me, steadying herself with her back to the door as she worried the side of her lip between her teeth. She kept her hands at my sides, not breaking that connection as she lowered her chin to her chest.

"You know, too, don't you? You overheard. Eavesdropped. Because neither of them would ever tell you that."

Tears nearly blocked the blue of her irises as she looked up at me. "I'm so sorry."

I gently removed her hands from my waist and stepped back. I wasn't rejecting her touch, I just needed a second. Just one. Okay, maybe two, to wrap my head around it all.

I went over to the bed, dropping down next to my hat I'd already tossed there.

"She became friends with that asshole after I warned her

to stay away from him. She cheated on me with him, then stayed close with him even after that. Why would she . . ." I rested my elbows on my thighs and lowered my head into my palms, feeling betrayed all over again for so many damn reasons.

Almost two decades with Rebecca in my life, and she felt like a stranger. So many years I could never get back, spent with her while she was spending them elsewhere. I'd sacrificed my soul and became a criminal for her in the name of revenge, and she'd lied, cheated, and broken me.

If I'd left Rebecca, she'd probably be alive, and I'd be . . . *happy*. Not just with someone *like* Diana, but with Diana. Now I was too fucked up beyond repair, and too dangerous because of my past, to make Diana the center of my world.

I lifted my head, sensing her proximity to me, feeling the bed dip as she shifted my hat aside to sit.

"Is that why you never wanted to work for Barclay Energy? Why you kept turning down the offers when she was alive? Even after she was gone?" I couldn't help but ask, everything clicking now.

"Yes," she surrendered, her tone as fragile as my current mental state. "I was too upset over what she'd done to you. That she'd ever even considered doing that to you. Too angry she had a man like you and couldn't see how lucky she was." Those tears in her eyes . . . I didn't deserve them. "Do you hate me for not telling you? I didn't want to tarnish her memory for you. I didn't think you even knew what happened."

"I could never hate you, Diana." I clasped her palm and threaded our fingers together, resting our hands on my leg. "Rebecca told me about the affair a few years after it happened, but not who it'd been with. And now I can't help but wonder if it was more than once. Not that it matters." I let go of a deep breath, wishing the heaviness in my chest would go with it. "She lied to me so many times. Kept so many secrets. What does that say about me? What kind of man was I that she felt she couldn't tell me anything?" Hadn't I asked Camila that only this summer, too?

Camila. Shit, maybe we did need to pull her into this case now. Could she help somehow?

"My work was classified, I had my reasons for keeping secrets," I went on. "What were hers?" Why was I doing this now, damnit? Diana didn't need this shit from me.

I closed my eyes, wondering if I could erase the past if I tried hard enough.

"Look at me." Her sweet voice was still there, layered beneath the command.

But I couldn't follow the order. Not yet. If I opened my eyes, she might see the real me, not whatever image she'd had in her head about me all these years. I'd rather her remember that guy—the hero who'd held on to her at the embassy and kept her safe—than know the man next to her now.

"Carter Matteo Dominick, look at me."

Her use of my middle name—my father's name—had my attention. Not to mention the sexy librarian-teacher voice she said it with, momentarily pausing the pain and reminding me of what we'd done in this bedroom barely twenty minutes earlier.

"I saw your name written on a document once," she confessed the second I peered at her. "My middle name's Laurel, in case you were wondering." A tiny smile formed on her lips. "Now you know, too."

I reached up and slipped my free hand to the back of her head, tangling her hair between my fingers as I swallowed back the thickness gathering in my throat. "I already know that. And pretty much everything about you."

She leaned closer, our mouths nearly brushing as she whispered, "Then you should know you can trust me. I don't know why she kept things from you, but I won't. I'll always be honest with you. Sometimes the truth hurts, but—"

My mouth dropped over hers, catching the rest of her words with it. Cutting off everything after *but*. Everything after but was usually bullshit anyway.

I released my hold of her so I could guide her around to sit on my lap. She didn't hesitate, straddling me easily as she rested her arms over my shoulders. We kissed like we didn't have a care in the world. As if it was only us up there. No burdens. No fucking problems.

I wasn't sure how we went from talking about Rebecca's betrayal to my tongue in her mouth and my cock pressing against her, but I wouldn't have changed it for anything.

She was taking away the pain and anger inside me with more than just her kiss. It was her honesty. Her trust in me.

But I hadn't been truthful with her.

I went still. Stopped kissing her. Pulled back to capture her face between my palms. "I have to tell you something." *Am I doing this? Now?*

"What is it?" she whispered. Her eyes were so expressive. The way she peered at me I'd swear she had the mysteries of the universe in that head of hers. And she was offering me the key. An invitation to be in heaven with her.

I brought my forehead to hers, closing my eyes while keeping hold of her face. "There was other security footage hidden in Amsterdam, and it was mine. I broke into the lab while it was being constructed and hid it there before your team arrived. That's how the President and my people knew what happened to you even after the main security cameras were destroyed."

"I don't understand. What are you saying? Why would you do that?" She didn't pull away, sounding more confused than angry.

"You." The word barreled from my mouth like I was a dying man taking his last breath. My nerves were stretched thin, and I was worried I'd lose her, even while knowing I couldn't ever truly have her.

"Me?" The little word punctured the air between us, but she'd yet to move. To resist.

"Yes, you." I finally opened my eyes and leaned back in search of hers. She stared at me, patiently waiting for me to explain. "After I saw you in Pierce's office in New York that day, I was worried about the sale and what might happen to you. I wanted the ability to watch over you."

Her mouth rounded in surprise and she blinked a few times, putting it together. "You were checking in on me? That's . . . well, sweet."

That wasn't what I'd anticipated as a reaction, but then again, Diana wasn't like anyone I'd ever met before. Definitely not like Rebecca. "Not sweet." I frowned, unsure how to make the word stalker not sound so horrible, but I doubted there was a way to sell this as anything other than what it was. A man obsessed. "I—"

The knock at the door may have saved me from losing her before I was prepared to. Then again, I doubted anything would truly prepare me for the moment we'd have to part ways.

"Yeah?" I called out.

"Gray let POTUS know there's a possible traitor among his people," Griffin shared. "The President wants a word with you. He's in the Situation Room. We have him on a secure line for a video conference."

"Be right out." I returned my attention to the angel on top of me. "I guess this conversation will have to wait." It wasn't exactly the time or place for it anyway. Then again, neither was burying my face in her pussy in this exact spot not that long ago, and that hadn't stopped it from happening. *No control. I have none when it comes to you.*

She shifted off the bed to stand, and I forced my heavy legs to hold me up as well. "We'll talk later, okay?"

Worried she wouldn't want to kiss me after learning the truth about my unhealthy fixation with her, I leaned in and set my mouth on hers.

Her moan and how incredible her lips felt on mine made me lightheaded and hard again. "I should probably not have an erection on the call with POTUS," I said after groaning from the loss of her mouth.

"Probably not." She wet her lips, and I hooked my arm behind her back, drawing her against me.

"You're going to be the death of me," I rasped before catching her tongue with mine, arching into her so she could feel how turned on I was even with the fate of the fucking world hanging in the balance.

That alone should've let her know I wasn't the good man she thought I was. Because I'd let the world burn for just one more minute with her.

43

DIANA

THERE WERE SO MANY THINGS GOING THROUGH MY HEAD, BUT I really needed to direct my attention to our video call with the President. What time was it in D.C.? *Hell, what time is it here?*

Carter and Gray were standing in front of the flat-screen TV in the main cabin. I kind of loved Carter had his ball cap on backward and was wearing sweatpants while talking to the Commander in Chief.

Deciding it'd be best to let Carter and Gray handle business, I hung back and peered around the cabin, not sure who to sit next to. Mya and Oliver appeared to have picked up where they left off in arguing, and since I had no interest in third-wheeling it again, I made my way to my new furry friend on the couch.

Dallas licked my cheek, then bopped his nose against my jaw as if telling me to calm down. I was glad Carter had him in his life. From the little my mother had told me about Carter back in the day, his Southern accent was thanks to being born and raised in Texas, and I loved how he'd named him after his hometown.

"I understand you *think* the CIA's ruled Paulsen out as a security risk or traitor, but we have concerns that have bumped him to the top of our list." Carter's declaration was loud enough for me to hear him word for word, even over the noisy thoughts still circulating in my brain.

I angled my head, searching out the President through the space between Carter and Gray. President Bennett was leaning back in his chair, tapping a fist at his mouth as if unsure what to say or do. Fate of the world and all.

"A photo and tracing an email to Georgetown isn't enough for me to go ahead and convict the man of treason," the President responded. "Give me more than that. It's also possible Gwen was able to retrace the blackmail emails to Georgetown because someone wanted that information to be found."

I wasn't a cyber-special-anything, but if these mystery people behind everything were that good, I was with the President on that. Wouldn't they throw us off on purpose?

Then I remembered some of the other details laid out before Carter took his walk down that dark alley of memory lane. How so much uncertainty still swirled around Rebecca and Craig. Maybe the world's best was arrogant enough to think no one could outsmart them, so there'd be no need for a misdirection ploy.

"Gwen would know if she's being played, and *only* Gwen was able to find what she did. Our enemy may have one of the world's best hackers working for them, but so do we," Gray said, echoing my last thoughts.

"Gwen traced the signal to a server farm," Sydney joined in, offering more concrete details that'd probably go over my head the way physics equations did for most. "From there, she navigated through a complex web of, well, if you'll excuse me, sir, fuckery, to isolate the exact origin of that email. Throw in the fact there was a freak power outage—that same day, and twice within the hour—on the same block where the coffee shop was located, and I believe we have enough to confirm the hacker was there."

"So, they messed with the power grid to destroy evidence they'd been there on the off chance someone did track down the coffee shop," I said, somehow following along despite exhaustion. *Like a practice run of what's to come. Take out the power and Wi-Fi.*

Sydney turned toward me and nodded. "Exactly. And there were no internal cameras at the coffee shop, which was probably one reason he or she selected that location."

"Rewind back to Craig Paulsen for me," the President said, drawing Sydney's eyes once again. "I'm still waiting for you to convince me of his involvement in all of this."

"You have a traitor in your circle, sir," Carter responded, his tone dropping lower that time. "Of those few people, who do you not trust with a loaded weapon in the same room with your family?"

"Paulsen has nothing to gain from sabotaging this project." A different voice came over the call before POTUS could answer, and I leaned to the side to see who else was on the screen. Ah, Gray's dad, the Secretary of Defense.

"Then why was Paulsen spending time with a man like Andrew Cutter in 2018? I'll remind you this is the same man responsible for blackmailing Rebecca and forcing her to break into my files so he could manipulate the illegal trafficking trade routes and eliminate his competition. The man who had Rebecca killed. *That* motherfucker," Carter hissed.

Wait, what? That's why she died? I stopped petting Dallas as every voice in the cabin went silent.

"Andrew Cutter?" Now that was a voice I knew well.

"*He's* responsible for Rebecca's death?" Mom asked, seemingly shocked to hear that name.

"You knew Andrew Cutter?" Carter's arms fell to his sides, weighed down by information more powerful than the earth's gravitational pull. "But of course you did," he added a heartbeat later. "Because you're all connected." He stepped so close to the screen I had to wonder if he'd try to reach out and throttle someone directly through it.

"It's not what you think." There was a touch of panic in Mom's voice I wasn't used to hearing.

"Then by all means, fucking enlighten me," Carter snarled back at her. His words elicited a little yelp from Dallas, who must've heard his dad curse quite a few times and knew the F word meant business.

Thinking of Dallas being constantly at Carter's side brought another pet to my mind. "They didn't kill Pierce Quaid's dog," I murmured at the memory. "The men who took us let Pierce keep him. That's weird, right?" I hadn't meant to interrupt the showdown between Carter and my mother, nor voice my thoughts out loud, but all eyes were suddenly on me.

Carter and Gray turned to the side, peering my way, and placing me right in the President's line of sight. My mother's, too. She was standing behind the President wearing her favorite pink three-piece suit, an odd choice for this type of conversation.

"Diana." Mom had said my name as if she'd forgotten I was there. My comment also appeared to shock her back to her normal state of calm, cool, and callous. "Your father sends his apologies about the tracker. I had no idea he did that, and he—"

"Diana." Carter's voice was a whip-crack in the small

space, giving me the floor and her no chance to argue. "You were saying . . ."

All eyes remained on me. I even had Oliver and Mya's attention. There was no way to backtrack that information now that it'd escaped my brain. *Here goes.* "Pierce Quaid, the head of The Barclay Group, and part of the whole secret hostile takeover with the CIA," I began, throwing a little inflection in my voice to let the President know I wasn't a happy camper about that whole plan . . . "Well, Pierce had a very yappy and annoying Chihuahua. What if Pierce got to take his dog with him because he was in on the plan? He was the first one separated from us. What if he's not a hostage at all, but was an insider at the lab?"

Sydney opened her laptop and said, "We've already been looking into everyone connected to the project, but you may be onto something. We'll dig even deeper into his background."

"Pierce Quaid's friends with Craig Paulsen. They could be in on it together." I stood and folded my arms, my nervous chills unrelenting. "Pierce was also close with Rebecca. Then there's your Secretary of Energy boyfriend to consider." I pinned my stare directly on my mother. "You and Jared started dating before Rebecca was killed. Pushed me to work at Barclay in the first place. Now it appears you know Andrew Cutter, too. Seems to me, Mom, *you're* at the center of everything." *Right along with Rebecca.*

Carter gave me a little nod of approval or thanks, maybe both, as I sat, not eager to remain the center of attention.

"First of all, if you're implying I was aware of the project in Amsterdam prior to you being taken hostage, no, sweetheart, I wasn't." That *sweetheart* was delivered with the perfect amount of bitterness only my mother could pull off. "Secondly, there's no way anyone I know is behind what happened. Not even Craig." She stepped closer to the camera, lowering herself into the seat alongside the President, and I wished I had my glasses to get a better read on her. There was something simmering beneath the surface, and she needed to hurry up and share whatever it was.

"How did you know Andrew Cutter? Connect the dots for us," Gray said, his tone as icy and firm as Carter's had been.

"I should've been informed Andrew was behind Rebecca's death a long time ago," Mom said, her tone hesitant.

"His death involved classified details, and you didn't have the clearance back then," Secretary Chandler told her, his voice deep but steady. Like father, like son. "Now, tell us what you know."

Carter stepped to the side, giving me a clear view of my mother as she shared, "Back in 2018, someone anonymously sent Rebecca information that suggested her parents' plane crash wasn't an accident."

"Why the hell wouldn't she tell me that?" Carter barked out, his hands tightening into fists at his sides.

Dallas jumped down from the couch and raced to his dad, whacking his tail against Carter's leg to let him know he was there if he needed him.

"Andrew Cutter was a salvage expert," Carter grated out before Mom could answer him. "She went to Andrew, not the other way around. She wanted his advice about the plane wreck since it'd crashed in the sea, and Andrew . . ." He removed his hat and tore a hand through his hair. "I believed a dying man's word. But Andrew didn't tell me the whole story. Why would he?"

I wanted to rush to him the way Dallas had, but I was anchored in place, buried beneath too much information. We needed a freaking commercial break. Time to recover between what felt like strikes from the god of thunder's hammer itself. Bit by bit, each new reveal whacked me harder than the last, thrashing Carter with even more force.

"I clearly didn't know Andrew was responsible for her death, and if he did what you're implying and blackmailed Rebecca, she never told me about it," Mom shared, her reading-from-a-teleprompter voice confidently projecting throughout the cabin. "I never met Andrew, nor did I set the two of them up. Rebecca did tell me she shared the anonymous photos and intelligence sent to her about her parents' crash with Craig Paulsen, though. As you seem to now know, they were close friends. Shortly after that, Rebecca met with Andrew. I don't understand how that dinner turned into Andrew blackmailing her, or eventually having her killed. And why would Rebecca keep things from that point on a secret from me? She shared everything with me."

Mom had the nerve to sound offended at that part, driving home the point that Rebecca shared more with her than with her own husband.

"Andrew Cutter was far more than a salvage expert and treasure hunter. He was The Italian." The President's words were meaningless to me and carried no weight, but apparently they were yet another big reveal for my mother.

"The Italian?" Mom repeated. "The overlord for the illegal trafficking routes?" So, she was familiar with what I assumed was a moniker but not his true identity as Andrew Cutter?

At the President's nod, I couldn't help but ask for a little clarification. "Wasn't the Barclay jet recovered after it went down in the water? Rebecca wouldn't have needed Andrew's help locating it." Eyes on my mother, I continued, "You're saying Craig suggested Andrew could examine whatever new evidence Rebecca had received to determine if the crash was really an accident? To help prove her parents were murdered?"

"Yes, exactly, but didn't The Italian disappear in 2021?" I wasn't sure who she was asking, but then Mom abruptly whipped her focus to Carter and muttered, "Oh. Not missing. Dead."

Dead. Carter's vengeance. We were circling back to it, and to Rebecca, all over again.

Carter placed his hat back on his head, face forward, tugging the brim down to shield his eyes. "Why would Rebecca go to Craig Paulsen instead of her own husband about all of this?"

"I don't know," Mom said, speaking surprisingly softly. "But when she received the alleged evidence her parents were murdered, she sold off the rest of her family's business holdings. She wanted to focus on Barclay Energy. She believed if her parents were killed, there had to be a connection to her father's work in clean energy and someone was trying to stop him from being successful. I'm sorry I didn't tell you before, but she asked me to never mention it to you. I wanted to respect her wishes, even in her death."

"You didn't think for one fucking second maybe looking into her parents' death got her killed, too? The day I asked you at her funeral if you knew anything, that thought never crossed your mind?" Carter seethed, emotion heavy in his tone, anger laser-focused on my mother.

I hated sitting back and watching the scene unfold, feeling helpless, but I doubted interjecting myself into their conversation was the right move.

"I did. Of course I did. I told the CIA and FBI everything I knew. They found zero connection between her murder and the crash," Mom shared. "I also didn't tell you, because I wasn't certain you didn't—"

"Kill her for eleven billion dollars?" Carter shook his head. "Or for that matter, kill her parents to set plans in motion long ago." He reached around and held the nape of his neck as if his mental anguish had manifested into physical pain.

It was taking all of my restraint not to go and rub his back for him. To soothe him the way he'd taken care of me yesterday.

Carter sighed, defeat encapsulated in the simple sound. "Someone must've made Rebecca doubt me. Planted those seeds of uncertainty in her mind. There's no other reason she wouldn't tell me. Then she got sidetracked by Andrew's blackmail."

Griffin did what I wasn't yet prepared to do in front of everyone—go to him. He nudged him in the side with his fist; not exactly what my approach would've been. "We'll figure this out. If we left a loose end back in the day, we'll wrap it the fuck up, don't worry."

Loose end. Back in the day. The phrases were clunky and unfamiliar, and they left a bad taste in my mouth. Did Griffin just imply he'd help Carter resume his quest for vengeance? Kill anyone still alive who may have had a hand in Rebecca's death? Including a senator. Serve life in prison for it unless he could make it look like self-defense. Even then, it depended on the state where he murdered Craig.

Shit, I had to stop my runaway thoughts before I wound up on a collision course with panic and anxiety. Wild enough, two states I'd rarely seen my parents in growing up. They'd just been the original cause of mine.

"I've been quiet so far." Oliver stood and took a step forward as Mya tugged on his shirt, trying to get him to park his ass back down and stay out of it. He shot her a backward glance none of us could see, but I assumed it was a dirty look. "Buttercup, let me go."

I barely heard that one over the engine noise and murmuring from the rest of the team. I did easily catch Mya's eye roll as she released him, though.

"What doesn't she want you to say?" Carter asked, moving toward the back of the cabin.

Oliver now had the floor. All eyes on him. Holding his bad arm, Oliver's gaze swept around the room before landing on Carter. "Is it possible that while hunting Rebecca's killer, you may have had a bit of tunnel vision? You were so focused on believing she died because of your work with the CIA, maybe you missed the bigger picture."

Carter's hand shifted to the back of his neck. Was he bracing for impact? Or doing his best not to cross the cabin and charge the man who'd told him he may have fumbled the ball in regard to his wife's killer.

"I believe Andrew had her killed, I really do." Oliver lifted his free hand in the air in surrender. "But maybe that was all predesigned. What if someone placed her in Andrew's line of sight knowing what'd happen to her? Andrew may have been an unsuspecting pawn himself." A few cautious steps toward Carter had Mya on her feet. Considering how much she supposedly couldn't stand the man, it seemed a little odd she also wanted to have his six.

"Sounds like a conspiracy theory to me," Secretary Chandler tossed out, breaking the awkward beats of silence pulsating through the cabin.

"But is it?" Jack stood and joined Oliver, hands going to his hips. "What if the Barclay crash really wasn't an accident. Rebecca's father was the main vocal advocate for making cold fusion a reality, and he had the financial means to go after what most considered a pipe dream back then. It's possible someone didn't want him to be successful."

"Then years later, for whatever reason, someone decided to tip off Rebecca about the crash, and she turned to Craig Paulsen for help," Oliver said, continuing with Jack's train of thought. "The senator may have been planted in your lives to keep tabs on her. When she came to him, Craig panicked, thinking she'd find out he was connected to the crash. Also, those photos prompted Rebecca to focus on clean energy herself, trying to make her father's mission her own."

Carter's silent stewing had me growing even more nervous, but I was also impressed with how brave these men were to present their uncomfortable theories to a man who was the archetype for the term dangerous. *Except* when it came to me.

"So, you're saying when Rebecca picked up where her father left off with cold fusion, Craig found a way to distract and divert her attention?" Sydney asked, her eyes never leaving her computer screen as her fingers flew across the keyboard.

"I just don't think Craig would want Rebecca dead." Mom's statement succeeded in cutting off any answers to Sydney's question. It also diverted my focus to Carter, who now had his hands braced against the ceiling, back to us all.

I had to chime in, and speaking up had my stomach banding tight. "That night in the limo, Craig seemed pretty convinced Carter killed Rebecca. And if he was knowingly responsible instead, he's one heck of an actor. He was upset in a way that, well . . ." I couldn't finish that line of thought so publicly, but I knew Carter understood my point. Craig had cared about Rebecca.

Carter's arms tensed so dramatically, even I could easily

make out the hard cuts of muscles tightening. I'd definitely hit a nerve.

"What night and in what limo?" Mom asked as that part of my statement registered.

Carter slowly lowered his arms and faced not the room, but me. Dead on. This had to be overwhelming, even for a tough guy like him. He wore the cloak of *I'm just fucking fine, don't worry* like it'd been tailor-made for him, but the fabric was fraying with each new piece of information thrown at him.

I knew Carter wouldn't want to hear this part about the limo again. He'd snapped the first time, and in his current agitated state, I had no clue how he'd react. I had to make this bullet point quick since it'd only just dawned on me that only Carter (and Sierra) knew about that night.

"Craig found out through Pierce Quaid that Carter visited me at the office in New York the day of the so-called hostile takeover. Craig forced me into his limo, demanding I tell him about my conversation with Carter. He was also curious to know if I shared anything with Carter about my work in cold fusion."

"Well, hell," Jesse drawled, joining in now, "that sounds like guilt to me."

"You should've told me about that," Mom was quick to snap out, like I was guilty of something. "I could've done something."

"Like what? You and Dad thought we were a match made in heaven. You were happy to marry me off, or at least try and get me to date Craig, even knowing his dirty secrets. You'd have believed him over me." Shit, if my mother hadn't already been in Carter's crosshairs, that planted the bullseye squarely on her head. I didn't have to see him to know he was a bull ready to charge. In this case, maybe whisk me away from all the Craigs of the world.

Turning to face him, I let my eyes tell him what my words couldn't. *I'd let you if I could.*

"Don't forget," Secretary Chandler spoke up, rudely intruding upon my telepathic efforts to communicate with Carter, "Craig was part of the hostile takeover involving a highly classified project. He could've been concerned Carter might try to sabotage our efforts. He was covering his bases, just not in a way I approve."

"Covering his bases, huh?" Carter's dark tone slipped under my skin, the implication of what he wanted to do to Craig loud and freaking clear.

"I'm assuming, like myself, Craig wasn't given access to the case details involving Andrew's death and how it related to Rebecca," my mom interjected, peering at Secretary Chandler in the Situation Room.

"Definitely not aware," Secretary Chandler confirmed.

I blinked a few times, remembering I never did finish sharing why I'd alerted the cabin and the White House to my unsavory confrontation with Craig back in June in the first place. "I don't think Craig led Rebecca to Andrew knowing he was that Italian guy. He wouldn't have knowingly connected her with someone who would have her killed." Carter quietly stared at me, but since he wasn't stopping me from continuing, I added, "Doesn't mean someone wasn't pulling his strings then or now, and Craig just doesn't know he even has a puppet master." Not exactly the type of string theory I was used to dealing in. *Also, back to Oliver's original theory.* "And by the way, my mother and Rebecca not sharing anything about the plane crash with Carter didn't make it easy for him to think outside any other box than the one he had to work from." Based on what I now gathered, that was smugglers and traffickers.

Mom's shoulders collapsed, and she tossed her hand in the air. "How about we just bring Craig in and clear up this whole mess?"

"And give him the chance to pony up whatever bullshit excuse he has preplanned for this exact moment?" Gray locked his arms over his broad chest, standing his ground alongside Carter. "Maybe he does have someone pulling his strings, but whether he knows about it or not, someone may get tipped off we're onto them."

"Onto what? We don't know a goddamn thing." Mom slapped a hand over her mouth and closed her eyes. Not only had she just swore publicly, but she'd have taken a wire hanger to my ass as a kid if I'd ever used the Lord's name in vain like that. "My apologies," she whispered for losing her cool and for her brashness.

"I need more conclusive evidence Craig Paulsen or Pierce Quaid are tied to what's going on. Now if you'll pardon my language," the President said while standing, pointing at the table, "fuck the *ifs*, and get me concrete proof of who I can or cannot trust in my own damn house."

"Craig's behind all of this one way or another," Carter began steadily, "and his head is mine."

"To question, you mean?" POTUS asked him, drawing his hands to his hips, his patience as worn thin as all of ours.

Carter huffed out a laugh, but his voice turned grave and his next words rocked me to my core. "You asked me to be the man I once was for the sake of this mission. No sense in turning back now, is there?"

44

DIANA

THE SECOND THE CALL ENDED WITH THE WHITE HOUSE, THE floor rumbled beneath my feet, sending me straight into a brick wall of muscles.

Carter slammed one hand to the top of the nearby seat and looped his other arm around me, pinning me to his chest, keeping us both from going down.

"Buckle up, buttercup," I overheard Oliver say somewhere in the background, but I couldn't pull my attention from the man staring down at me.

"It'll stop soon," Carter said steadily, eyes still riveted to me as his hand slid a bit lower to the small of my back.

The man had control of both my body and the sky, so it would seem. We stopped shaking, but he didn't let me go, and I had to wonder if he realized how close his palm was to my ass. Was it gravity pulling it lower and lower? Or something much more powerful.

"A word, please," I whispered. "In the bedroom."

His eyes darkened and his arm tightened around me. *Is that a yes or no?* "Get Gwen back on the phone," he ordered a beat later, still not taking his eyes off me.

"On it," Jack answered him.

"See where Gwen's at on decrypting the text you pulled from the phone in Poland." He finally let me go and turned to Gray, gesturing toward the cockpit. "In the meantime, tell the pilot to head east until we choose where the hell we're landing. We can't stay in the air much longer."

"And what are you planning to do?" Gray asked him.

"Apparently," Carter ground out, "I'm off to the bedroom to have a word." He gently secured a hold of my arm as we walked. Was he worried the sky wouldn't heed his command to behave, and I might tumble into someone else's lap?

Once in the bedroom, with the door closed and locked, he turned and pinned me against the wall. Hands over my shoulders, he caged me there, eyes on eyes.

"Worried about turbulence again?"

A dark smile came and went. "Maybe." *Hooded eyes and doubling down on the brood? Check and check.* "You finally come to your senses about me?" One hand shifted to my face, and he dragged his thumb along my lip to my cheek.

Distracted by the intense energy between us, it took me a minute to internalize and translate what he was saying. "Because of what you said to the President at the end of the call?" Talk about a mic drop moment.

Met with only silence, he threaded his fingers through my hair, the pad of his thumb gently catching my temple in the process.

"I understand you're upset that your justice might be . . . *incomplete?*" That didn't feel like the right word.

He leaned in closer, arching into me, letting me feel his arousal. There appeared to be a fine line between anger and desire when it came to this man. Confirmation he used sex to help ease the burden of his wrath.

"You think that's why I'm in a murderous mood right now?" He cocked his head, gripping my hair a bit tighter.

"Isn't it?" I whispered, my body mirroring his energy. Responsive. Ignited.

"No, angel." That "angel" felt rich and indulgent, like dark chocolate icing on top of my favorite kind of cake. My guilty pleasure was Devil's Food—the freaking irony.

"Then what is it?" My hands slipped beneath his shirt, taking a sweet and decadent journey over his rippling abs that flexed beneath my touch.

The tug of my hair had my chin tipping up, and I swallowed back a moan. He wasn't hurting me. Just creating some primal urge I didn't know was inside me. A craving to be dominated.

His forehead tightened as he hissed, "If I killed Craig Paulsen, would you forgive me?" His hips rotated ever so slightly, his sweatpants a weak barrier between us.

Despite his question, I found myself copying his movement, desperate to feel all of him but inside me. "I know you're trying to scare me, but it's not working." My palms skated around to his back beneath his shirt, as I visualized the feathers and arched wings there.

Angel wings on his back, and he called me his angel. It was rather poetic.

He dropped his eyes closed, his lips hovering over mine. "I need your answer," he said gruffly, going still. "If Craig's connected to what happened to you this week," he began in an eerily even tone, "I will kill him. Not a merciful death either. A slow and excruciatingly painful one."

"Wait, you want to murder him because of me? Not Rebecca?" I'd meant to keep that as an internal thought, damnit.

Eyes flashing open, his other hand cut straight to my

waist, his fingers digging into my side over my sweater. "Of course." The lilt in his tone made me wonder if I'd insulted him.

Before I could make sense of that, he set his mouth to mine, kissing me with such fervent intensity I wasn't sure if my trembling was from this moment or more turbulence.

Letting go of my hair, he shifted his mouth to my ear and grated out, "I want to fuck you so bad, you have no damn idea. I'm almost willing to risk my team hearing you just to have you." He resumed kissing me again as if he hadn't just dangled the idea of plunging his cock inside me as a way to relieve his tension, and probably my own, too.

My hands moved up his sides and to his arms, holding on to him as if I might fall through the floor and join the sky if I let go. Guess I'd find out if this man could also fly, knowing he'd jump after me.

"Your teammates need to concentrate out there, remember?" I reminded him.

"They'll figure it out." A brief smile touched my lips before his tongue rejoined my mouth, stealing my ability to keep my legs steady.

The man didn't miss a beat. Even with my back to the wall for support, he didn't take any risks. He kept a firm hold of my side, clearly feeling my knees buckle.

"You want to punish me for making you lose control again, don't you?" I wasn't sure if I meant that as a sexy tease to do exactly that, or in concern for the soft flesh of my ass cheeks.

He nipped at my bottom lip and his "yes" floated between us before he spun me around. My breasts hit the wall, and he flung my arms up, cheek turned and palms to the wall. For a moment, I was lost to thoughts of his handprint on my ass.

Sweeping my hair away from my ear, he held me tight

and positioned his hard cock up against me. "You want to know how I'd do it, don't you?" That dark promise had my body exploding in goose bumps.

"Yes, please." Should I have followed that please with "sir"? God, this was foreign territory to me.

Accepting my permission to have his way with me, he shoved my yoga pants and panties down to my thighs. I arched forward in anticipation of a stinging sensation to my ass cheeks.

I'd officially forgotten the reasons we'd come to the bedroom in the first place. My every thought, instinct, intent was on pleasing this man. Letting him please me.

"Tell me, angel. I have to get your answer first." He smoothed his palm over my ass cheek, caressing in small circles as if he'd already spanked me and was helping ease the lasting sting there.

When his hand curved around to find my sex instead, his fingers sliding through my arousal, I bit back the cry of ecstasy. "An answer to what?"

"Will. You. Forgive. Me?" Each word punctured through me, tearing a hole in my lungs that were working overtime to breathe normally.

For murder, I finally remembered. *That's what you want to know.* "Carter." His name was a broken cry from my lips. A painful sound. "What if I ask you not to kill because of me instead? Can you do that for *me*?"

His fingers went still over my clit. "I don't know."

I fought back the tears as I admitted, "Then I don't know either." How could I help this man see his soul was worth saving if he was so hell-bent on sacrificing it *for* me? "I do know I want you." My voice broke, and at the feel of his chest heaving from deep breaths, I added the promise, "No matter what."

He placed his hand on the wall near my face, right in my line of sight. His golden-tan skin in view as he resumed touching me with the other. I squeezed my eyes closed again, losing myself to his touch, to the fact he hadn't backed away.

His thumb caught the sensitive spot at my center, drowning out the noise in my head with every flick of his thumb. He sent me higher and higher. Flying took on a completely new meaning—forgetting all over again why we were thirty-plus thousand miles up in the sky—and I broke.

An orgasm ripped through me, and as I came down, he set his mouth to my ear and rasped, "Have you ever had a safe word before?"

"Definitely not." My stomach was still fluttering from the release he'd given me, and now my ass cheeks tightened in anticipation of that spanking he'd yet to give me. "But your name is the first thing that comes to mind when I think of safe," I confessed.

"My name should be the last thing you consider safe with your ass exposed and my palm fucking twitchy." Not even a split second later, a gruff breath fell from his lips, hitting the shell of my ear. "I'm . . . so sorry." There were so many layers to his tone and that apology, it'd take me all morning to peel them back.

He pulled his hand away from my sex and guided me around to face him.

"What's wrong?" I took hold of his shirt, anxious for him to explain the apology so I didn't have to cut through the context and find the meaning myself.

"I don't think I can be *that* guy with you. Safe is what I want you to feel with me, and I lost my head. Became angry and tense, and wanting you so damn bad it hurts everywhere."

The rawness and sincerity had me choking up as I

tightened my hold of his shirt, worried I'd lose him again. To the darkness. To death, too.

"I knew what you meant," I said as fast as possible. "And I need you to know I understand the difference between you keeping me safe and you making me feel safe. I understand consent, and you have mine." I needed his eyes back on me so he recognized I'd meant every word. "But are you saying you can't be yourself with me?" *And is it only because I'm unsure I can forgive taking a life when it's not in self-defense?*

"I can't be like *that* with you." He straightened but seized hold of my waist. "Correction, I don't *want* to be like that with you. I just don't know how to be any other way." He shook his head. "You don't want me killing that asshole, and I can't promise that any more than I can make your parents like me." His brows slanted, and my heart hurt all over again. But for him.

"My parents don't even like themselves." Even as the words left my lips I recognized the read-between-the-lines message he'd given me. He was thinking about a future with me. There was hope he wouldn't run after this. That he wouldn't try to push me away?

"What if that guy was just a temporary placeholder while you found your way back to being who you really are?"

He opened his mouth, only for a knock at the door to rob me of whatever he'd planned to share. "If it's Griffin, go away," he barked out.

"And if it's not?" That was definitely Mya.

He muttered a few choice words and grumbled, "What is it?"

"Gwen's about to reach out with news related to that encrypted text, thought you might want to join us." Mya's words were fast, as if realizing she was on borrowed time with Carter.

"Be right out." He pushed away from the wall and reached down to return my yoga pants and panties back in place.

At his frown, I palmed his cheek, directing his attention back to me. "Maybe that was the universe's way of telling us now isn't the time to finish that conversation."

"Fair enough," he said in a less than convincing tone.

I leaned in to kiss him, intending on letting him know everything would be okay, but he stopped me and warned, "You put your mouth on mine, and we won't be leaving this room. I'm still riled up and tense." He brought my hand between us to feel his hard length, and his jaw locked the moment I tugged my wrist from his touch only to send my palm beneath the fabric instead.

He swore at the skin-on-skin contact, my hand gripping as much of him as possible. "You being this tense could be dangerous." I arched a brow, but his eyes were laser-focused between us, staring at where my hand was, slowly sliding up and down his length. "How fast can you get off?"

A smirk cut across his mouth, and he wet his lips, eyes finding mine again.

I didn't wait for a response, dropping to the floor and dragging his pants and briefs down with me.

He grunted and bent forward, planting both hands on the wall. On my knees, my back flush to that same wall, I peered up at him, holding his eyes as I licked the crown of his cock, relishing in the way he stared down at me, harsh breaths leaving him as he waited.

Not willing to waste another second, I hollowed my cheeks and took him fully into my mouth. He went from groaning to murmuring my name, and not even a minute or two later, he rasped, "Fuck, that's my—"

The "good girl" I'd felt on its way died in the air as he came hard and deep in the back of my throat.

Satisfied with myself, and after swallowing every drop, he helped me stand and did what I had no clue I'd ever needed. He drew me into his arms and hugged me.

Orgasm oxytocin was great. But Carter holding me like I was his whole world, well, it was a whole other level of amazing. This man could easily be more than just my world. He could be my entire universe.

45
CARTER

Fucked. There had to be a better word than that to describe my current state as I listened to my teammates pitch ideas back and forth about what to do next, and where to land while we waited for Gwen to call. At least the Secretary of Defense had given NATO the heads-up not to shoot down my two jets since we were in foreign airspace without a set LZ.

"Wait, what'd you say?" My angel's sinful mouth was my new favorite distraction with it parted open like an invitation for me.

I must've tuned out whatever Jack had said, too busy stressing over the fact I was—for the lack of a better word —fucked.

"The Sapphire would be a place no one would expect us to go, being a hotel haven for criminals and all," Jack said, presumably repeating himself.

"Oh, I heard that." Diana leaned back in her chair across from me, the distance between where she was and my lap where I'd have preferred, entirely too far away. "The, uh, other thing."

What thing?

"Ah, yes. Carter's use of cutlery is impressive. I thought he was good with a knife, but you should see what he can do with a fork." Jack and his fucking timing.

Diana had just been trying to walk me off the cliff of being a psychopath, and there was Jack telling her what a great killer I was. I mean, he wasn't wrong. *Fuck.* Yeah, I was as married to that word as I was to my sins.

Diana narrowed her eyes on me, her cheeks becoming as pink as her ass would've been had I spanked her like I'd wanted to.

The fact I hadn't been able to do it, worried even a small sting might hurt her, was . . . unexpected, to say the least. After years of believing I could only take a woman one way, all my rules went out the window when it came to Diana. I was at her mercy, not the other way around. Al-fucking-ready. How many hours had even gone by since I'd rescued her?

Maybe I could just continue to be the selfish bastard I was. Keep her. Go ahead and taint her with my filth and darkness. Then her words came back to me. *"What if that guy was just a temporary placeholder while you found your way back to being who you really are?"* Could she do the impossible and bring me back into the light?

Lost to my thoughts again, staring so deeply into Diana's eyes I was pretty sure I saw my own reflection, I barely heard Oliver when he commented, "You weren't even up there when he forked that dude to death. What do you know?"

"No, but I was." Gray was off to my side in the aisle, using the remote to drop the screen back down. Hopefully that meant Gwen would be calling with news. "And stop bullshitting around with stories that don't help us. We need real plans."

"Roger that," Jack snapped back at his best friend, earning him a scowl from Gray.

Yeah, we all needed rack time before we killed each other.

Reminding myself this sweet woman across from me didn't want more blood on my hands, I reached into my pocket for one of my disposable phones and did a quick search to ping a contact of mine in Lithuania. I needed to let them know to save those two traffickers from becoming victims of the wild boars roaming the area. Not a pretty way to go. I added one last quick message.

> Me: Make sure they're behind bars, though. With a forever kind of sentence.

I didn't need to tack on the words, "or else." They already knew what would happen if those traffickers were ever to make it to the streets again.

"Who was that?" Diana asked, drawing my eyes as I powered off and pocketed the phone.

"Preventing those animals in that shed from being eaten," I grumbled, and she couldn't hide her smile at that. A small victory in her desire to help me find my way back to that guy I'd once been. The operator in the Unit who followed rules of engagement to a T.

"Maybe Bravo will turn something up while on the ground in Norway." Sydney's comment to Mya from the other side of the aisle briefly stole my attention.

"Don't forget, you're still a wanted man with your face all over the news. That puts a bit of a target on our heads."

I cracked my neck as I stared at Mya, silently cursing her equally for-shit-timing reminder. Wanted or not, there'd always be a bullseye on my head. And that right there was a perfectly justifiable reason to stay away from Diana when this ended. Her safety would trump my wants and my needs. Always.

"Oh God, I forgot about that." Diana's eyes widened. "Can't they pull that news story? Take you off the list?"

"The line's connecting with Gwen," Gray shared, saving me from having to tell Diana I was a threat to her safety regardless of the news or the wanted list. "Hey, what do you have for us?" he cut to it as Gwen's face filled the screen.

"I have news," Gwen opened up with. "I decrypted the text you pulled from the phone in Poland. It's a location for Port Leith. That's it."

"Edinburgh?" Griffin asked, standing alongside Gray, but not blocking the view of the screen.

I reached for the crucifix, nearly forgetting it was there, as I thought back to the day I'd nearly tripped over Dallas. Looking over at him brought me back to the night I'd seen a priest for the first time.

"My assumption is those men were supposed to bring Diana there if they were successful in taking her from you all," Gwen shared. "It's possible the other hostages from Amsterdam are there as well."

"But?" Gray prompted, and damn that pause from her.

"Whoever's handiwork is behind this encryption is a match to the person who emailed Alyona from Georgetown, but it's not a match to whoever encrypted those files sent to the traffickers with information to take Diana to Oslo." And there was that "but" loud and clear.

"Two different hackers working for the same group?" Gray spoke before I could. "Or two different groups targeting Diana?"

"Definitely two different hackers," Gwen said with confidence. "The one coordinating with the Serbians was good, but the other hacker is better-than-me good."

"If you have one of the most skilled hackers on your team, you don't bench your quarterback and put in your backup." I smirked at Gray's analogy. Once an athlete, always an athlete. That West Point ball player was alive and well in some capacity in Gray. "Maybe we're dealing with two groups, then?"

"Isn't it always two?" Jack said under his breath while rising alongside where Jesse was already standing, hanging off to the side of Mya's seat.

"If the group responsible for the hit at the safe house in Poland is also the one who sent the blackmail to Alyona, then I'm thinking," Mya began, tapping the closed lid of her laptop, "the blackmail was a distraction from their plans to hit us in Poland. Or a secondary backup if they failed in Poland in hopes they could get Alyona to turn on you."

"Considering Alyona hasn't reached out to you with an update since she cut and run," Jack said while peering at me, "my guess is they were only using her, and they never actually thought she'd double-cross you."

"There are only a handful of people who had access to Carter's private footage from Amsterdam who also knew he reached out to Alyona for help. It's not us. Not the President's SEALs." Gray rehashed what we already knew, keeping his eyes locked on me. "It's not Diana's parents, my dad, or the President himself. And I can personally vouch for the CIA director."

"So, that leaves us with the Secretary of Energy and Craig Paulsen as the only possible traitors in the group. They know we're working this case, and that we were planning to turn Diana over to Bravo at zero three hundred." Jack had said what we already knew, but would it be enough evidence to convince the President to bring both men in for questioning regardless of who was pulling their strings?

"Jared and Craig didn't know you were taking me to Poland, right?" Diana asked. "So if it's one of them who's helping the enemy, that's why they had to rely on the tracker."

I nodded, unable to join the conversation yet, still trying to work through the best course of action. I wasn't used to my focus being so thrown.

"Now that we know there's probably two groups, what does that mean? If Jared or Craig is the insider in the second group, then how'd the first group know about the lab?" Diana asked as she stood to get a better view of the screen.

I was at her side in an instant. Pure instinct, and maybe something else taking over. What if turbulence hit? I'd rather her fall against me than land in Oliver's arms. He was entirely too close and convenient.

"And for that matter," Diana continued, pushing at the skin on her forehead as if doing advanced calculus in her head, "how'd the second group know there'd be a hit by the first?"

"Those are very good questions," Gwen spoke up. "We'll figure it out. In the meantime, where are you all headed? Scotland?"

Gray and I exchanged a passing glance before I tipped my head in request to take point. He'd needed me to run the show when it came to the woman he cared about being in danger during a mission, and now I understood why. Same boat. *Well, in my case, a plane.*

"We can't stay up here forever," Gray said, turning back toward the others. "Let's head to Scotland. If Pierce Quaid is also an insider, for whichever group, he may be walking around as a free man. It may be faster to get intel on the ground. We'll hack all the local CCTV footage there and try and get a match for him or one of the other hostages."

Diana stepped closer to me, and without thinking it through, I reached for her hand and locked our fingers together, not caring who saw.

I barely heard Griffin's casual comment as he said, "Did I ever tell y'all about the time we had to wear kilts, and how that op was weirdly connected to your sister, Jesse?"

Diana and I stayed locked in that moment, hand in hand, as Jesse commented back to Griffin, "Don't tell me."

"Who do we know who can help in Scotland? You still have your contacts there?"

I couldn't take my eyes off the brilliant blue ones before me to register who the voice belonged to. Didn't matter, the conversation continued around us, our little bubble safe for the moment.

"Don't those billionaires, the McGregors, have cousins in Scotland?" another someone asked, hell if I knew who.

"They're Irish, not Scots." Mya that time maybe?

"What are you thinking?" Diana mouthed, and I drew her closer, allowing the background noise of my teammates to fade away.

"Energy doesn't lie," I whispered back. "Matter can neither be created nor destroyed."

She blinked, replaying my words as if surprised I'd thrown science at her. I was a little surprised, too. "Oh." Her little wide-eyed look and nod had me believing she'd landed in the same physics textbook as I'd just stumbled into somehow. On the same page, she murmured, "What if one group wanted us to help create an EMP weapon?" I squeezed her hand, encouraging her to keep going with that thought. Her eyes fell shut as she acknowledged the truth I felt in my damn bones. "And the other one already has a weapon . . . and they're worried I can stop them from using it."

46
CARTER

"I'm just not sure how we're going to pull this off." Oliver's less than optimistic tone as we rolled up to the gates of our new place had me squeezing Diana tighter to my side in the back of the stretch limo.

The last time I'd been in a limo was in . . . *Shit*, I didn't want to dredge up memories of fancy parties from the past—parties Rebecca had dragged me to—any more than I wanted to relive the details Diana had shared about Craig cornering her in his limo in New York.

She rested her hand on my leg, giving me a squeeze, somehow knowing I needed her to ground my thoughts before I lost myself to anger.

Dallas was on the other side of her, and he lifted his head and licked her cheek.

Jealous, boy? That her hand is on me, not you? I get it.

Not missing a beat, Diana scratched behind his ears, giving us both the attention we needed.

Dallas yelped his thanks as my eyes fell back to where her

435

hand rested on my jeaned thigh. I'd changed before we'd landed, but Diana, and her love of being cleaner than a bar of soap itself, had showered again. I'd opted to stay outside the bedroom that time, knowing well enough by now I had zero self-control around her when we were alone. That would also be problematic in our new temporary headquarters when we could be there for days or even weeks.

"I have no clue if I can stop an EMP weapon, but I'll do my absolute best to try," Diana answered the question Oliver hadn't technically asked her. She had to be feeling the weight of the entire mission on her shoulders now.

"And we'll all be here to help you," Mya promised, sitting across from us.

I had a feeling Griffin had purposefully chosen to sit in between her and Oliver, hoping to be a barrier and prevent their typical married couple-like bickering from happening.

"Maybe we'll also find your colleagues, and we can convince them to assist you." Griffin may have been speaking to Diana, but his worried eyes were pinned on me. I knew that look. A warning or lecture of some kind was coming, and in this case, I deserved it.

Diana's shoulders fell, and she turned her attention out the side window as we approached the home. Two other limos with the rest of Falcon and my second team trailed behind us, followed at a safe distance by an SUV full of our weapons.

I'd wound up calling the Irish billionaire family, the McGregors, for help securing a location and extra artillery. POTUS also made sure my jets weren't intercepted by law enforcement upon arrival. After landing, thanks to the McGregors' wealthy and well-connected Scottish cousins, we now had transport and a new home.

My path had first crossed with the McGregors while

taking out Andrew Cutter. Apparently, I couldn't escape my past no matter which way I turned.

"This place feels too pretty for what we're here for." Diana's free hand settled on the window as we neared the front of the coastal estate.

"It could also double as the set for *Outlander*, minus the modern upgrades," Mya said, taking in the view as well. "God help me if I have to see you in a kilt on this trip."

"From what I remember overhearing on the jet," Diana began, a sly smile crossing her lips, and I knew where this was going, "is that the only two people in this limo that have ever worn a kilt are Carter and Griffin."

I smirked, and spied a grin tug at Griffin's lips, too.

She was going to fit in quite well with the team and our awkward humor.

"So, back to this place, how'd we acquire it?" Diana asked as we waited for Teddy to manually open the five-car garage so we could park inside.

"A contact we've worked with before arranged it. The homeowners aren't living here because it's undergoing renovations to be placed on the market," I told her. "The property already has a state-of-the-art security system, not to mention the choppy and rough waters as a backyard make it harder for an enemy to infil from that way."

"Are these people famous or royal?" she asked, her curious beautiful blue eyes on me.

Teddy was back behind the wheel now, pulling into the garage as I shared, "Billionaire family, and you know how billionaires are"—I grinned, unable to stop myself—"they tend to be a bit paranoid." The smile that pulled from Diana was worth every ridiculous word.

Once everyone was parked in the garage, the team

quickly split up. A few guys to do a perimeter check, and the rest of us filtered in through the side door to enter the home.

The exterior of the estate mimicked a thirteenth-century castle, but on the inside, the interior was as modern as any other twenty-first-century home.

Inside the main foyer, Diana did a three-sixty spin. All that was missing from her twirl was a skirt to hold on to. Or our daughter's little palm tucked inside hers to share the view.

What. The. Fuck. I rubbed my eyes, trying to will away the painful thought. And it was painful, because how in the world would I ever have a future with someone like her, knowing I could be the death of her and our future kids?

I couldn't be a world away on a mission and hear Diana on the phone while someone . . . I nearly dropped to my knees at the brutal vision searing right into my skull.

"You okay?" At her words, and the feel of her hand on my bicep, I jolted and pulled away from her.

"Tired," I hissed, hating the gruff tone I'd taken with her. Opening my eyes, I motioned to Mya. "Can you find a room with two beds for now that you can share for a nap?"

Diana lifted her hands between us. "Wait, you're not going to stay with me?"

Could I share a room with her? Yes.

Would we have sex? Also yes.

Would I then break her heart when I walked away to save her life? I knew mine would split in two, that was for damn sure.

"We'll figure that out later," was the best I could give her. "Dallas, go with Diana. Stay by her side," I ordered, then waited for Mya to give me confirmation she'd heed my unspoken request to also keep any eye on Diana.

Mya nodded, then set a hand on Diana's back. "Come on,

let's explore this palace together. Maybe it has a library with a rolling ladder."

"Stay off ladders. And don't trip over any paint cans. Or inhale paint fumes. Or—"

"Easy there, Dad," Mya said while peering back at me over her shoulder. "She's a scientist, and I'm, well, whatever I am now. We're good, don't worry."

Oliver jerked his thumb toward them. "Want me to follow them?"

"Not on your life, Lucas."

Mya's use of Oliver's last name inspired a devilish grin from him. They needed to screw already and save us all the headache.

"I'm too tired for them," Griffin said, coming up alongside me. "Seems like Mason's idea to stay outside was the smarter choice." He gave me a quick pat on the shoulder, his way of letting me know we'd catch up on that lecture later.

"Go. Sleep," I told Diana since she'd yet to budge.

"Okay," she only mouthed back.

I waited for her to leave with Mya and Dallas before I faced the rest of my teammates who were still hanging back.

"After Diana wakes up, I'll get a list from her as to what she needs for a lab," I said, barely able to keep my head up at this point. "I don't want to have to resort to relying on Diana as a backup plan if an EMP weapon is detonated. She doesn't deserve that kind of pressure or guilt. Let's find the bastards before they can set one off."

Easton stepped forward, breaking away from the others. "Fucking PACE. I'm with you on this. Primary over emergency every day."

"Speaking of plans," Teddy piped up. "Alyona ever reach out? Nothing new from her blackmailer?"

"No, but I have a guess where Alyona took off to. I'll get a hold of her soon." *Sleep first.* "Go secure the property while I shut my eyes for a second." I wasn't even sure who I was talking to at this point. "You think you can handle that?"

Gray stopped whatever conversation he'd been quietly having with Sydney near the French doors leading to a room off the foyer. "We're good. Go rest. We could use Carter Dominick again."

"And that means?" I waited for Gray to hit me with the blow I already felt coming from two countries away.

"You know exactly what I mean," Gray said casually before resuming his private conversation with Sydney.

Easton caught my eye next. "If we've got a shot in hell of stopping an attack and preventing the outbreak of wars, then we gotta do what we gotta do, man. And in your case, that means becoming the man everyone fears, doesn't it?"

"Or better yet," Jack tossed out, dropping a duffel bag by his boots, the thud echoing around the foyer, "just be the devil yourself."

47

CARTER

Nᴏᴡ Nɪɢʜᴛᴍᴀʀᴇꜱ ʟɪᴋᴇ I ʜᴀᴅɴ'ᴛ ʜᴀᴅ ɪɴ ʏᴇᴀʀꜱ ʜᴀᴅ ᴊᴏʟᴛᴇᴅ ᴍᴇ from sleep, and I'd woken in a sweat. Sitting on the edge of the bed, I slipped on my Apple watch, checking the time. It was already the afternoon, which meant I'd been out for four hours.

Shit sleep was almost worse than no rack time at all. Visions of Diana screaming and reaching for me while I'd been chest-deep in quicksand, unable to help her, had played on some sick loop in my head during those four hours.

Noticing one of my two disposable phones was lit up with a notification, I picked it up from the nightstand. A text from Gray.

> Gray: Bravo was rerouted here. Meeting up with them to chase leads on the other hostages.

I sent him back a quick message, then peeled off my sweat-soaked shirt while catching sight of my duffel bag by the door. I had no clue who'd dropped off my things while I'd slept, but hopefully they hadn't witnessed me clawing at the air, trying to escape the lethal mud my subconscious was mired in.

After a shower and change of clothes, I placed a call to Alyona, wanting to get it over with so I could find Diana and check on her.

"Was expecting you to reach out sooner," she answered, her voice sounding as tired as I felt.

"Since you haven't made an effort to call me, I'm guessing no more threatening emails?" I leaned off the edge of the bed, holding the phone to my ear with my shoulder while sliding my boots over from where I'd left them before passing out.

"Nothing. But since I don't have the package, I'm working on safe transit for my parents and sister to a secure location. I've already funneled my money to new accounts."

"It's good to be prepared, but I think you're safe. We have reason to believe you were a decoy so we wouldn't expect the attack in Poland." I knew that would be good news for her, not that she'd take it at face value and relax. Not that any of us could relax until this was over.

"You're going to owe me a lot more than that three million for the shit storm you've pulled me into." Her tone had less bite to it than I'd expected. "*But* I am sorry I bailed on you in Poland. We both know you'd never have done that to me."

Lacing up my boots, I reminded her, "You had to put your people and family first, I get it." I wasn't this woman's greatest fan, but at the end of the day, she brought me to Diana, and that was all that mattered to me right now.

"Maybe that girl isn't your weakness after all. I may have had that wrong." Another curveball. Where was she going with this? "Rebecca, *that* woman was your weakness. But Diana, maybe she'll turn out to be your strength."

"You okay? Hit your head?" I stood, unsure what had come over her. She was acting as out of character as I'd been lately.

"I've always had a soft spot for you, Dominick, you know that." A sigh fell across the line. "Also, maybe if you can be happy again, there's hope for me, too."

Unsure what to say to that, because I had no clue how to handle this Alyona, I went for my cross on the nightstand, buying myself time to think.

"If you learn anything, let me know," she said before ending the call, saving me the trouble of a follow-up.

I stared at the phone, still thrown by her words, but as long as she didn't have issues with Diana, I wouldn't have issues with her.

With both my phones and my wallet back in my pockets, I went out into the hall in search of Diana. Since I'd seen her and Mya head toward the back stairs earlier, I dodged scaffolding and cans of paint and headed in that direction.

On the third step up, I paused as Easton let me know, "The boys are about to head out to go on their errand run for Diana." I swiveled around to face him, and he lifted his chin toward the upstairs. "Griffin's just double-checking a few items on Diana's list. He's with her now."

She's awake? Already wrote the list? I shouldn't have slept. "What about the other list? Mine?" I'd jotted down a few other things I thought Diana might need as well, like glasses.

"Mya and Oliver are at a pharmacy now. Oliver needed new supplies for the medkit and his shoulder injury, and Mya was worried he'd get lost out there on his own." Easton rolled his eyes. "Those two fucking yet?"

I could've laughed at his accurate assessment of their relationship despite not really knowing either of them, but I was too anxious to get to Diana. "Not that I know of." I lifted my hand. "And to be clear, I never want to know."

"Gray's with Bravo. POTUS had them fly here from Norway," he said, switching gears, thank God.

"Yeah, he texted." I nodded. "How's the security looking here?"

"As it should."

Good.

"With any luck, we'll find the other hostages quickly." He swiveled his ball cap backward, grimacing. "Sorry, I hate using that word. Luck."

"Yeah, don't I know it." I angled my head toward the stairs. "Anything else?"

He smirked. "Anxious to get to her, huh?"

"I'll take that as a no, boss, there's nothing else." Not waiting for him to give me shit, knowing I'd get plenty of it later from Griffin, I continued upstairs, hanging a left down the first hall, checking each room one by one.

"What are your thoughts on soulmates? You think they're real?" At overhearing Diana's question, I halted outside the next doorway, flattening my back up against the wall. Where was she going with that? Was she still with Griffin, or talking to someone else?

"I'm not sure." That was definitely Griffin. "My wife was married to someone else before she met me, and he, uh, died. He was a really good man. Big shoes to fill. I, uh, won't ever be able to fill them the way he did, if you get what I'm saying, but . . ." He was struggling to get through this, and I didn't blame him. "I'd like to say I'm Savanna's soulmate, but then was Marcus not? Doesn't seem right, so maybe a person can have two?"

Shit, I knew Griffin, and he must've slept as badly as I did if he was answering her question so directly. Then again, maybe his honesty was a credit to his wife and her effect on him since they'd married. The man became butter around Savanna, just the way I—

Am I butter now? Is that what's happening?

"I'm so sorry. I had no idea, or I wouldn't have asked you that," Diana apologized.

"It's okay. But, Diana, if you're trying to ask if there's room for someone else in Carter's life to, well, you know, be his 'the one,' then . . ." He let his words hang, and there I was taking a page from Diana's playbook and eavesdropping, unable to stop myself from listening in.

Did she really want a future-*something* with *me?* She'd alluded to that on the jet with her comment about children. *My* children.

I'd tried to push her away by letting her see my darkness, and how easily I could uncage the beast from within if provoked.

Then, at the ass-crack of dawn, in that jet bedroom, I discovered I was capable of reining in the wolf when necessary.

"What is it?" she asked Griffin, her tone so soft it could break.

"If you only get one soulmate in life, then Rebecca wasn't his," Griffin shared somberly, his voice growing closer.

I needed to back up and do my best to appear as if I was only now arriving. But when he stepped into the hall, he immediately grimaced, clearly reading the look in my eyes. He knew I'd heard him, despite my efforts to play off I'd just shown up.

Spying a folded sheet of paper in his hand, I pointed to it, hoping I could pivot in a different direction. "You think you can get everything from the list?"

445

Diana peeked into the hallway, setting her hand to the interior frame while meeting my eyes.

"It's not like uranium is on there, right?" God help me, I was joking now. I *was* butter. Melted, and a fucking mess.

"No, but it'll take a lot of your money to keep people silent and not ask why we need what's on here." Griffin waved the paper between us, and my attention skated from it to the woman I was obsessed with.

Obsessed. I'd only ever understood that word relating to my mission for revenge. It'd taken on new meaning when it came to her.

"We need to talk before I head out, though. Alone," Griffin said, *not* asked.

The lecture. Right. "Stay put," I told her, not sure where she'd go, but I didn't need her wandering around the place alone. Or following us and eavesdropping on whatever Griffin was about to drop on me.

"Sure," she answered, and I followed him into the neighboring bedroom.

Once inside, he pushed the door closed and pocketed the list.

"What's up?" I set my shoulder against the wall, exhaustion quickly setting back in.

"I can't believe I'm asking you this, but did you two have a thing in the past? You said you knew her then, but . . ." He shook his head. "I'm not suggesting you hooked up while you were married, because I know you're not a cheating piece of shit, but I've never seen you like this before. Not even with Rebecca. And no way all that came about since we rescued her."

Way to lay it on me. Of course, I knew Griffin's brutal honesty was because he gave a damn. He and Camila were also the only ones capable of laying the hammer on me like this without fear I'd strike back.

I straightened to stand tall so we were at eye level and swiped a hand through my wet hair. Sometimes it was like looking in a damn mirror with this man. Not just because we had the same dark hair and eyes. Or because we both had Brazilian ancestry on one parent's side, not to mention similar tattoos (which Delta used to give us shit about). More so because he understood pain and tragedy, and he'd been at my side every step of the way during my hard times.

"You going to talk or just keep staring at me like you're seeing an apparition or something?" he pressed.

Playing dad now, huh? "I never cheated, no. Nothing happened with Diana before this week, either."

"So, something happened on the jet? I swear that bedroom needs a cigarette after all it's witnessed in the last two years." Griffin managed a smile that time, and I was tired enough to smile back.

Relenting, I finally shared, "After I saw Diana at the office in New York in June, I lost my head."

He frowned. "What do you mean?"

"I haven't been able to fuck anyone," I cut to it, channeling his bluntness as my voice dug a bit deeper at the confession.

"Well, that explains why you've been a serious asshole for months, even more than normal. So, the rumors about you and Gwen hooking up this summer are just that? Gray and Wyatt don't need to fight you? That's a relief. I thought that was why she stopped working with us."

Rumors? For fuck's sake. "God no, but Gwen may have developed feelings for me that I didn't return." *And that's on me.* "Why are we talking about this right now?"

"Because I've never seen you operate at anything less

447

than a hundred and ten percent, not even when searching for Rebecca's killers. And from what I can tell, you're working below fifty now. Fifty makes it a coin toss whether you live or die." He reached for my shoulder. "I don't want to lose you, brother. Especially not when I've also never seen you look at a woman like you look at Diana. Not ever."

Not ever? Not even with Rebecca?

"Jesse told me what Jack said to you downstairs earlier. That you need to be the man you once were if we're going to be successful."

The devil. Yeah, I remember.

"Well, I disagree. That man had nothing to lose." He pulled his hand back and folded his arms. "I'd rather a man with everything to lose have my six."

Something was getting lost in translation. "Spit it out. What are you saying?"

He leveled me with a hard look. "Don't be the devil again. Be the man you were with Delta. That's the guy I want to roll with on this. I'm a father now, and if we don't stop whatever may go down, my wife's and son's lives could be at stake. I need a Tier One operator at my side, not a man criminals fear."

I closed my eyes, registering his words one by one. The message, and the *but* coming, knowing in this case it wouldn't be bullshit with the follow-up.

"You're distracted. From personal experience, I know what that can do on an op."

I opened my eyes and nodded in understanding. *Message received.*

"But, Carter, when this is over, don't fuck things up with her because you're worried you're bad for her, or too dangerous. Everyone's entitled to forgiveness and second chances, so my wife says, at least. Not that I think you need it." He opened the door, then faced me. "That girl in there deserves to be happy, and my guess is you'd make her that way. You owe it to yourself to be happy, too."

"I'll always have a target on my head, wanted list or not," I reminded him of my harsh reality.

"Yeah, well, just because I need the old you back for this mission, doesn't mean your persona as an intimidating motherfucker everyone fears has to change. And no one, and I mean *no one*, would touch *that* man's girl."

48

DIANA

"Did you hear us?" Carter asked as he locked the door. "I wouldn't blame you if you were listening in."

"No, I didn't eavesdrop." I sat next to Dallas on the king-sized bed, waiting for him to face me.

When Mya and I couldn't find a room with two beds earlier, she'd said, *"Carter will want to sleep with you tonight, anyway. You two should have the biggest room and also be far away from everyone."* I didn't mind her implication one little bit, either.

A girl could only hope.

"I trust if there's something important for you to share with me, you will," I added when he'd yet to respond or turn.

As much as I wanted to get up and go to him, I was too weighed down by worry. Could I truly stop an EMP weapon if it was detonated?

Continuing to pet Dallas, I waited as patiently as possible for Carter to give me his attention. Something new must've been eating at him, and I wasn't so sure I could handle any more bombs being dropped. I was also reconsidering my thoughts on if time travel was possible, because we kept dipping into too many "yesterdays" for it not to be.

Finally pushing away from the door, he raked his hands into his hair while turning. "Maybe trusting me is the last thing you should—" He bowed his head. "That's the shit I need to stop saying if I'm ever going to change, damnit."

Those words sent me springing into action, propelling me to my feet. I slowly ate up the space between us, waiting for him to go on, wondering if we were about to pick back up on one of our unfinished conversations from the jet.

He appeared to have showered since we'd arrived. New clothes as well. His short sleeves gave me the opportunity to appreciate the tattoos on his arms. I hesitantly reached out and traced the outline of a dagger inside his right forearm.

"I want to be a better man for you. Maybe for me, too." Eyes slowly journeying to my face, he added, "I'd say what I'm feeling for you is too soon, but it also feels like a decade too late." That deep tone grounded me in place, and my fingers went still on his arm.

I tucked his words away somewhere safe so I could hold on to them forever, in case he did abandon me someday. I hated to think like that, but he was right. These feelings were as new as they were old, and I wasn't sure how to articulate how I felt either. Maybe there'd never be an explanation because our connection wasn't of this world.

"Not too late." I slid my fingers away from his arm and over to my own wrist. I pushed up the sleeve of my sweatshirt to reveal the double helix intertwined with the tree of life tattooed there. "Time in the grand scheme of things is limitless. Eternal."

In one swift movement, he captured my waist and brought me flush to his body, the floor momentarily falling away beneath me. The man could literally sweep me off my feet.

Hands to his chest, chin tipped up, I asked, "What's going on in your mind? Where does it hurt? What exactly *is* hurting you? How can I help make it better?" I hadn't meant to unleash a flurry of questions, but I could feel his pain radiating through and from him like an electric current.

"Everything hurts, all the time." His brows pulled together. "Except when I'm with you."

His raspy confession pulled the air from my lungs, and when I pressed up on my toes to get even closer to him, he met me halfway.

Our lips fused. Tongues met. Souls interlocked. Forget a prince waking a princess with a kiss, this man made me feel like an immortal with one.

"Diana," he grated out, breaking away too soon. "We can't. Not now." He held on to my arms, meeting my eyes.

I didn't press for a reason. It was obvious. We had a mission, and I was very much part of it.

"My teammates have families. I made a promise to Griffin I'd keep focused. I can't be reckless." He held on to my arms as if worried I might fly away. When would he understand, the only place I'd go is back to him. "After this is over, I'd like to try, though. I never thought it'd ever be possible for us, but maybe it is?" He steadied his gaze on me and chills coasted over my skin.

"You want to try to be with me?" *Not try to push me away again. No more talk of how you're too dark, too dangerous?*

"I obviously have issues, but if you think there's a chance you may . . ."

Oh God, sensitive Carter was even better than the broody, sexy version. "I want you," I said as clearly as possible. I needed him to hear me, loud and clear. Know it in his heart. "I have no conditions."

He set his forehead to mine, his breath fanning across my face. "Where the fuck have you been all of my life?"

"It wasn't our time then. And I suppose it won't be until we finish the mission." I hated that part, but if something went sideways, and he blamed our relationship as a distraction, I knew he wouldn't be able to live with himself. Maybe I wouldn't be able to either. "I just need to figure out a way to either stop an attack or reverse its effects if used." I forced a shrug. "No biggie."

His smile touched my lips. "Whatever you need, I've got your back. I'm here for you. I'm not so great at physics, but if you need me to crunch some numbers or throat punch a guy, I'm your man."

My tongue peeked between my lips to catch his before I could stop it from happening. He captured my tongue right back, and the light groans from each of us mingled as one.

"I'm too tired to be this close to you and not kiss you."

"Hence the kisses now?" I murmured, almost dreamily, swept up in the seductive haze of our desire.

"Mmmhmm." I melted into his touch as his fingers tangled up my hair, drawing me in closer. Another hot kiss before he said in a husky voice, "I'm not leaving you in this room alone tonight. But can we share a bed without my cock sliding inside you?"

"Talk about missions being impossible." The fact I could make a joke at a time like this was as comforting as it was concerning. I was also soaking wet and aching for him. One touch and I'd go off like a bottle rocket. How would we survive the week (or God forbid longer) without having sex? *Fate of the world,* I had to remind myself. *Fate of the freaking world hanging on my very tired and tense shoulders.* "We should stop kissing, then."

"Yeah," he said against my lips, not backing down yet. "I

just don't have the energy to stop myself from taking what I want."

I rotated my hips, feeling how hard he was, and he arched into me, pulling my hair even tighter. "You're not too fatigued below the belt, so it would seem."

"I have a permanent hard-on around you, angel." We were already failing miserably at our plan. "We *should* work, though." He let me go and backed away, tearing a hand through his hair while dragging his thumb along the line of his lips with the other.

Dallas's little yelp reminded me we had company.

"I should call Zoey and Camila, then I need to check in with Secretary Chandler to see about the old case files surrounding Rebecca's death." His tone turned more reserved, clearly doing his best to regroup, likely hoping it would help me do the same. "I doubt their files will connect Rebecca's death to the plane crash, or I would've heard about that long ago. Doesn't mean it's not true, just that they didn't find anything."

I nodded, then realized . . . "Wait, who's Zoey? Camila?"

"Camila's the only family I have outside the team. Not by blood, but she's like a sister. You, uh, may have met her at the funeral. She helped your mom organize it for me."

"Ohh, I think I do remember her." Super sweet. Kind eyes. Gorgeous.

"Camila's off-the-grid right now, but we have an emergency method of getting ahold of one another. It'll probably be twelve or so hours until she gets the message, but she may be able to help us. She's not only in the security sector herself, but she has . . . visions."

"Visions?" I arched a brow, curious for him to elaborate.

"Sometimes she can see things that haven't happened yet." He ran his hand along his bladed jawline, smoothing a palm over the facial hair that'd deliciously prickled against my skin when he'd kissed me. "Sounds wild, I know. Not sure if I even want to know the future, though."

It isn't wild to me, and it sounds like we could use her help. "Why don't you want to see the future?"

"Because what if you're not in mine," he said bluntly.

I closed the gap between us, lacing our fingers together and brought our hands over my heart. "That's for us to decide, not someone else." I wished he'd smile, or show me some indication he believed me, but the worried expression I could see even without my glasses didn't fade away. Assuming he'd prefer to move on to a new subject, I asked, "What about Zoey?"

He squeezed my hand.

Okay, not the best sign.

"She was MI6. We worked a case together, and her fiancé was killed." He lowered his eyes to our locked hands. "I was searching for his killer the night Rebecca was murdered."

I remembered him telling me he'd been on the phone with Rebecca when she'd been killed. Now I knew why he'd been away. Everything kept clicking together like a puzzle I wasn't so sure I wanted to solve.

"Zoey and I stayed in touch over the years. Not exactly friends, but we've worked together here and there since," he went on when I'd yet to formulate the right words. "She should know what's going on, and maybe she can help." He returned his attention to my face, and there was something in his expression that felt almost apologetic as he studied me.

What are you sorry about? Then it hit me. The stab of jealousy. More pieces locking into place. *You were with Zoey. With her, with her.* "Zoey. Alyona. Gwen, too?"

He frowned in obvious understanding of what I was asking. "Not Gwen, no."

My stomach remained a pretzel as my thoughts swirled in my head. "Gwen reminds me of a younger version of myself." I hadn't been able to miss the uncanny resemblance on that screen earlier. Same hair and eyes. And not to be cocky, but I was smart, and she clearly was as well. "We're alike in more than a few ways," I added under my breath, not letting go of his hand. Something told me he needed to know I wouldn't bail on him at the first sign of stress.

He cupped my cheek with his other palm. "You're your own person, Diana. You're the only one I see. That's all you need to know."

That was all I wanted to hear. I didn't need to know about the women before me. None of that mattered. No more dips into the deep end of the past. "I know you're worried about me, but you should also get a little more rest at some point today. You don't seem well-rested. If you're too tired, we just might slip up later."

He grinned. A full-blown one, too, not the side smile I'd grown accustomed to seeing. "You have a point. I'll try and rest later. If I'm too tired, I'll wind up doing all the things I've been dying to do with you."

My pulse fluttered. "Like what?" Wrong question to ask when we needed to behave, but I couldn't help myself.

Mouth to my ear, his voice sinfully dark, he whispered, "Here I am, trying to be a changed man, and it's an angel attempting to provoke the devil to come out and play."

49

DIANA

"You believe in me, Dallas, don't ya? Think I can pull off a miracle and save the world?"

Dallas tipped his head to the left, then to the right, staring at me as if I'd asked him to solve quantum gravity. We'd need a particle accelerator larger than our whole galaxy to test that out. Yet, what I was being expected to do felt somewhere along those lines.

Trying to block an EMP weapon, or reverse its effects, would more than likely require way more than my brain. Not to mention I'd had a half a billion in equipment ready to be assembled to test my theories back in Amsterdam.

Would my laundry list of items I'd asked Griffin to procure really amount to anything more than me pulling out my hair as I failed?

Fail: first attempt in learning. I didn't have time to learn, though, that was the problem.

"No pressure, right, Dallas?" I resumed scratching behind his ears, and he made a little yodel-like singsong sound. "I'll take that as a yes. I'm glad you believe in me, that makes one of us."

I sighed, unsure how long it'd be until Carter returned from the calls he had to make. I contemplated killing time with music while waiting for either him to come back or Griffin to return with the supplies to set up a lab. Considering some of my best work came from listening to the same beats downloaded on that MP3 player Carter had given me, maybe tunes weren't such a bad idea.

"Be right back," I told Dallas, and he bopped me with his nose as I went to stand. "Not leaving the room, just getting something from my bag." *Overprotective like your dad.*

Carter, of course, had the bag my mother had packed thoroughly checked for other transmitters before we'd boarded the jet in Poland, and thankfully it'd been clean. I still couldn't believe my father had thought to sneak a tracker into my glasses but couldn't remember I hated jewelry every year on my birthday.

Ironically, the glasses were the first accessory he'd given me in years that had actual meaning.

Sighing, I faced the connecting en suite, headphones now procured from my bag. *Maybe I should clean up first, then the music.* I'd only taken a quick shower on the jet, and I had a feeling the en suite in a castle-mansion would provide a much more pleasurable experience.

I shook my head, realizing I really did have issues with needing to be cleaner-than-clean. Since that "issue" didn't hurt anyone, only gave me dry skin in the winter, I set aside the headphones, deciding to take another one. I earned it with all I'd been through.

After removing my sweatshirt, I reached for the hem of my tank top, but Dallas went to all fours, stopping me. His ears were pointed and tail whacking around.

When the door opened, I should've known it was Carter

coming. Dallas would've given me a much louder and more aggressive heads-up if there was a threat.

"Stand guard outside the room," Carter directed to Dallas, and Dallas's command of the English language kept impressing me hour by hour. Not to mention how he often used his teeth like a human hand.

I checked the time on the nightstand while Carter closed the door. He'd been gone for maybe fifteen or twenty minutes. Quick calls.

"You're testing my patience, I see." That deep tone throttled my semi-dazed state to wide awake.

I dropped my eyes to follow his gaze, finding my nipples piercing the ribbed tank top. "Bras are annoying, and I was about to shower."

He angled his head, remaining by the door. "You really don't like to be dirty, do you?" There was a hint of a tease there that inspired me to respond in kind.

"Not unless it's you making me that way." I'd never played with fire before this man, and now it happened on autopilot.

I watched as he began mentally undressing me. Really taking his time, too. Bonus points for his knuckles kissing his jawline, stroking up and down as if contemplating all the ways he'd make me come.

That belt around his waist was going to forever intrigue me as I wondered how he might use it. He'd already confessed on the jet he didn't want to be rough with me, but maybe bondage would be . . . *fun*?

I tapped my fingers against my mouth as he stared at my lips, looking like he might break his decision to abstain and ravish me. "You're going quiet on me."

"Not for the reasons you think."

"Oh, I think I do know." I wasn't able to hold back the

seductive tone in my voice any more than he was able to stop himself from coming for me.

He captured my waist, his strong palm curving around my body, and he spun me so my back was to his chest. We were like quantum entanglement ourselves—when two particles linked together, no matter how far apart they were in space and time.

Basically, a match made in heaven.

Pushing my hair to the side, he dropped his mouth over my ear. "I can't share that bed with you." His free hand went to my abdomen in a possessive hold, then he slipped his rough palm under my tank top and cupped my breast like he owned it.

God do you ever. "I can put my sweatshirt back on if that helps?" He pinched my nipple, then rolled it between his fingers, making it even harder. And with his dick pressing against me, I had to bite back a moan. "You've already seen my breasts. Nothing new. We should be okay."

"You're funny." He squeezed my tit again, his hand capable of holding all of me.

This man was so much bigger than me and larger than life. Yet, he made me feel like I wasn't just the center of his world but his entire galaxy.

"I'll never grow tired of seeing you. Touching you. But no, it's not your top that'll make sleeping next to you impossible." He let go of my breast and whirled me around. Capturing my face between his palms, he drawled, "It's your mouth."

He kissed me hard, and I kissed him right back.

So much for restraint and being mission-focused. The world was screwed.

The sound that came from this man as his lips made love with mine could only be defined as a snarl-like growl. *My wolf.* He matched my passionate kisses and upped the ante, giving more than I thought possible.

"Fucking fuck," he hissed.

Two things I knew for certain: my mother was wrong about the word *fuck*. It wasn't unbecoming. When Carter said it, it could, in fact, make me come. And secondly, I wished more than anything this man would go ahead and do exactly that right now.

He'd already penetrated my metaphorical walls. Why not my other ones? Maybe sex wouldn't be a distraction, but a very welcoming reboot to our energy and focus?

"How do you keep doing this to me? Making me lose control?" His voice was barely a murmur as he continued to hold my face, keeping me close to him—a place I could easily stay forever.

"I suppose there really must be a physics explanation for what's happening between us," I whispered, eyes shut in anticipation of the *more* I wished he'd give me.

"Physics." The word fell from his mouth, both a question and heavy with disdain for the subject matter, as he untangled our limbs from our intertwined state. "I suppose I should've let Dallas stay in here to protect you from me."

He returned the little smile that'd snuck up on me, and seeing him wear it did wonders for my overall state. That smirk gave me hope that maybe I could pull off a miracle and come up with a solution to a seemingly unsolvable problem.

"We're supposed to behave, I know." I did my best to mask the reluctance in my voice. "Your team needs us. Their families and everyone else's families are relying on us." I surrendered a nod to let him know I was back on track.

It was impossible to deny how effortless it truly was between us. Heck, even all the way back to 2011 when we first met, we just clicked. Wrong time. Right people.

He cocked his head, quietly staring at me. His eyes turned impossibly darker, his voice husky, as he claimed, "To be clear, I want to take you on this bed right now. Spread your legs open and lick that sweet cunt. Fuck you against every wall in this room. Impale you on my cock and watch you ride me. Then take your ass. And after that, we shower together. Preferably without our clothes this time."

I faltered. Not just one step back, but a few. Turned on but also hung up on one particular part. *That* dick in my ass? *Ouch* didn't even begin to describe how painful that sounded. Yet, there I was, growing even wetter at his speech. Distracted yet again.

"But you're right, we have to behave. I already forgot I came here to give you an update, not a twisted fantasy script." He swallowed those three steps and crowded my personal space, stealing my breath, too. "When this is over, and you save the world, I'll give you anything and everything you could ever want from me in the bedroom, got it?" He tucked his fist below my chin and urged me to meet his eyes. "Tell me you hear me."

I did, but . . . "And out of the bedroom, too, right?"

He expelled a deep breath that coasted over me. "I'll do my best. It's been a long time since I've known the difference between right and wrong. I'm trying to do the right thing now, but all I want to do is be with you and say fuck everything else."

Oh God. "The last thing in the world I want is to be the one to corrupt you."

A low, deep laugh rumbled from him, and the sound was as sinful as his smile. "You can't corrupt me, angel." He leaned in and brought his mouth over mine. "Save me, though, maybe."

He kissed me softly that time. An until-next-time kiss

embedded with a promise there'd be another time. I opted to convince myself of that, at least.

"Okay, then," I whispered once he finished making me dizzy, and did my best to remember what we'd been talking about before he mentioned putting his could-win-trophies-sized dick into my ass. *Talk about defying physics.* "What's the news?"

"First, cover up. Not only for my benefit, but so I don't kill my teammates for seeing your nipples when we leave this room."

My eyes landed back on his belt, and I forgot all about his request, my mind once again entertaining those dark and dirty thoughts about the leather wrapped around his waist.

"I won't use this on your ass, angel. Not opposed to tying you up with it or having you bite down on the leather while I make you come, though."

"I feel like that'll wind up being a death-by-orgasm kind of experience regardless of how you use your belt on me. But, if I'm going to die, at least I'll be happy and satisfied." I blinked, trying to recall yet again what in God's name we were supposed to be discussing. The theory of relativity, perhaps?

At the sight of him walking back a step, tearing a hand through his hair, I realized my poor choice of words.

Rebecca. Her name was a whisper on my lips as I looked down at the floor. "I'm sorry." I lifted my face and held my hand up. "That was so inconsiderate of me . . ."

He grimaced. "The thought of you dying in any way, shape, or form is something I can't ever allow myself to picture happening. I wasn't thinking about her. Just you."

His solemn tone punctured through me, and I might've fallen to my knees from the meaning packed into his words had he not banded his arm around me, keeping me steady.

"When the President told me the lab in Amsterdam was hit, and I knew you'd been there, and I thought I lost you, my world stopped. It stopped spinning. What I'd planned to tell you on the jet earlier . . ." He closed his eyes, and I waited for him to go on, my nerves eating at me in anticipation of what he seemed scared to reveal.

"It's okay," I promised. "I'm not going anywhere. You can tell me."

He dropped his forehead to mine. "I've been watching you, Diana. Before the lab was hit, I didn't just check in on the site to make sure the new owners were . . ."

My hands slipped between us to rest on his chest, and his heart beat furiously beneath my palms. "I don't understand."

He lifted his head and peered at me. "I couldn't take my eyes off you once I saw you on camera. I kept checking on you to the point it became *unhealthy.*" His brows snapped together as he waited for me to process what he was trying to tell me.

Obsessed with me? Watching me? Goose bumps flew over my arms as I kept trying to add up the sum of the parts to get the whole. To get the truth he was trying to lay out for me. An error message kept flashing in my mind, and I couldn't make sense of what he was telling me.

"Since I saw you in New York, I haven't been able to stop thinking about you. I was the one who loaded the music because I knew what you listened to while working. I know more about you than I should. I've been stroking my cock to thoughts of you since that day in the office, unable to want anyone else but you."

Oh. My. God. My knees buckled, and he pinned me even closer to him as if worried I'd collapse.

"I stopped checking in on you five days before the lab

was hit. I was trying to get over you, and that's why I didn't know what happened until POTUS told me."

Trying to get over me? "You've wanted me for that long?" My trembling hands remained fixed to his chest, and he gave me a firm nod. I lifted my eyes to the ceiling, still trying to understand. "The tattoo because of me was recent, then?"

"No, that was years ago. The angel wings on my back."

"Angel . . ."

He let go of me, the fear I was about to reject him vividly clear in his haunted expression. When he turned away, I couldn't help but push up his shirt to study the wings on his back.

"You've been carrying me around with you for all that time." I traced the arch of one beautiful wing. "Literally, so it would seem."

His back muscles flexed, making it appear like the wings were moving inward, meeting in the middle. So stunning, and because of me.

"I'm sorry." I dropped his shirt at his pained apology, urging him to face me.

Tears pricked my eyes at what this all meant. "So, we're both obsessed with each other." My heart was still in overdrive knowing he'd been thinking about me all summer and fall. "That explains a lot." I pointed back and forth between us. "It's why we've spent less than forty-eight hours together, but we already feel the way we do."

"I don't understand. You're *not* mad?" He appeared genuinely confused. Had he really expected I'd be upset?

I hooked his belt buckle with my finger. "Only upset we didn't reach out to one another sooner. But everything happens for a reason, and the wait was worth it." Cue the tears. What I felt for this man was just . . . "For you, Carter, it's all worth it."

467

50
CARTER

"You're not real, are you?" I stared at her, uncertain I'd heard her correctly. Was I so tired and disoriented I'd also become delusional?

"I guess you should kiss me to find out," she whispered, and I forgot all over again about the news I needed to share, right along with the mission itself.

I gathered her in my arms, lifted her from the floor and carried her over to the bed. I couldn't have her now. But fucking hell, I'd have her for just one more minute. The theme of the last two days when she was near me.

Holding myself over her, I felt the heavy weight of the cross slip between us, settling between her breasts. Shifting my eyes to her face, I'd swear it was as if she saw the man I was at thirty looking back at her. The man I'd been before I'd become corrupted by the world.

She saw someone worth saving, and it gave me . . . well, fuck, it gave me hope.

I dipped in and sucked her bottom lip before catching her tongue with my own.

At her moan, I closed my eyes and gave her as much of myself as possible in that kiss.

The parts of me I'd locked away as a kid—seeing my dad hurting from fighting with my mom, all the way to the parts of me that had become broken from fights with Rebecca. All of it. I wordlessly gave it to Diana through that kiss. A kiss that seemed to free something in my chest, hoping she'd understand me in a way I doubted anyone else ever had.

I could love this woman. Maybe I already did. Maybe she was right, and people were destined to be together, not only in this life but in whatever came after.

I ignored the scars of the past, and their horrible timing, trying to manifest into physical pain. Trying to steal me from this moment and this amazing woman.

"Carter," she whispered.

"Yeah?" I asked, somewhat in a daze, pushing myself up on my forearms to better see her.

"I think I might know how to protect us from an attack."

Not what I'd been expecting from our kiss. Her words also reminded me I had an update to give her.

Her smile reached her deep blue eyes, excitement lighting her up. "Music is usually what inspires my best ideas, but apparently your kiss just did instead."

"I'll take that as a compliment." I rolled to my side, and she turned toward me, resting her elbow on the bed and her cheek on her palm. "What's on your mind?"

"Newton's first law of motion to be exact." Another sweet smile from her, and I had to resist the impulse to lean in and kiss her.

"Oh really?" I arched a brow, curious where my little genius planned to take me next. My heart was still racing, my head and the rest of my body not yet catching up.

"An object in motion stays in motion with the same speed

and in the same direction unless acted upon by an unbalanced force."

"I'm familiar with that law." I reached for her hair, threading my fingers through her locks. Getting turned on by science was a first. Not that I'd yet to "shut down" from our kiss. Talk about an object in motion . . . *And I'm smiling again. Probably a goofy one, too.* This woman was changing me faster than my heart was beating.

"It came to me because of us. We can't seem to stop ourselves no matter how much we try to behave. We keep staying in motion, you know?"

That's one way to put it. I narrowed my eyes. "I definitely get the part where we're struggling to keep our hands off each other no matter how much we try, even with . . ." *Ahh.* I finally caught on. Damn, this woman was smart.

"What if we don't need to recreate the wheel here to stop the attack? With the right *cyber* minds helping me, I think we just might be able to counteract an attack. At the least, stop the damage an EMP weapon would inflict. Aka, no fallout. No chaos."

"Cyber minds, huh?"

"Gwen. Maybe Gray's sister? Anyone else you know and trust would be great, too."

Some of the President's people could help out, like Harper Brooks. I'd worked with her not only on an op with the Agency, but to take down Andrew Cutter. It helped she was also married to one of POTUS's off-the-books SEALs.

"If we combine my expertise with theirs, I think that's how we stop an attack from causing mass devastation. No need to go hide out in a bunker when all hell breaks loose."

"Because it won't break loose," I finished her line of thought, liking where she was going with this. I let go of her hair, and we both sat upright. I bent my knee and hooked my arm around it. "And Newton's law can help, huh?"

"Since we can't exactly create a Faraday shield to enclose around cities, we need to stop the pulse at the source," she explained, eyes wide, clearly invigorated and energized. "We need to create an unbalanced force to stop the motion from happening. And by motion, I mean the electromagnetic pulse. Electromagnets only work when an electric current is turned on. We need to find a way to jam the signal so it can never transmit."

"Guessing we can't just find the power source and shut it down that way?" It was probably a ridiculous shot in the dark, but I had to try. Direct targeted hits were easier for me to work with than theory.

"The whole 'just unplug it' concept," she said with air quotes, pulling them off as adorable and not condescending, "would be great if you can locate the source, and shut it down without causing a Chernobyl-style disaster." Not taking a breath, she kept going, talking with her hands, her entire body animated and involved. "The only way to sustain fusion is to have tremendous amounts of pressure and temperatures. If you release the pressure on a plasma-fuel mix, you stop the fusion reactor from operating."

This was a little over my head, but I trusted her to know her stuff. Most sought-after mind in science, after all. "Sounds like I could only buy us time that way, until someone flips the pressure back on once I exfil and they go for round two in an attempt to turn the weapon on a target." I finally put together her words, getting two and two to equal four. "And obviously blowing up a nuclear reactor would have devastating consequences across the board."

"Yeah, and although you could use magnetics or maybe even liquid nitrogen to rapidly change the pressure and decrease the temperature on-site, there will be nothing to stop them from rebooting and starting all over again."

"And that's where you and your genius brain come in. Why you want to partner with cyber on this," I said, still doing my best to follow along with how fast her mind worked.

"Right, so we need our own type of defense system in place to intercept and lock on the target once it's fired. To block it like a shield." She hopped to her feet, pacing the length of the bed in thought. "We could divert the electromagnetic pulse into space." Facing me, she dragged her hands through her long blonde hair. "I mean, we may accidentally knock a satellite out of orbit, but that'd be a best-worst-case scenario."

I stood along with her, holding on to her arms, feeling hopeful, and it was a damn good feeling.

"The only type of electromagnetic pulse I couldn't stop is if someone actually set off a nuke in space, and that'd have the same effect as an EMP weapon."

Like we needed another reason to keep nuclear weapons from terrorists. Thank God the EMP weapon only required a nuclear reactor to set it off but wasn't nuclear itself.

I stared at this woman, blinking in shock at how easy she made all of this sound.

She reached between us, tapping her fingers against her lips, her mind clearly still working overtime. Solution-oriented. If our kiss helped spring these ideas to life, what would sex do? Fucking A, the fact my brain went there . . .

"And you can really do this?"

"I obviously can't construct and build a laser myself, and we'll need several of them. Plus, we're probably short on time. The U.S. military can reconfigure some of their existing laser missile defense systems based on the formula and code we come up with here, though." She pinched the bridge of her nose, eyes closing as she continued, "With the size of our country, we'll need three locations. Both coasts and somewhere central. Between those three ranges, the lasers can cover enough territory to stop a pulse, or even a solar flare, from destroying any mainland city. We'll need to create something smaller and more remote for Hawaii and Alaska." She was speaking so fast I was shocked that in my current state I could keep up with her beautiful mind.

"If our insiders have connections at the Pentagon, that could be problematic. We can't tip off whoever's behind this. They'll likely move up their planned attack," I said, remembering the Craig Paulsen problem all over again. "We need to get Craig and Jared behind locked doors until we can determine which one of them is behind betraying our country."

I let go of her and reached into my pocket for my phone. I texted Secretary Chandler to call me back on a secure line, no time to waste, and the moment the call connected, I laid out the plan.

"Yeah, got it. Let me know when you have them in your custody," I said at the end of our quick but productive call. Turning back to Diana, I told her, "He's going to fill in the President, but he believes he'll be on board." And why wouldn't he be? Diana was offering to save the country, and by extension, save the world.

"How would someone know I could do this, though?" She dropped her forehead to her palm, applying pressure there in small circles. "I didn't even know I could do this."

"It must be someone who's been watching you for a long time. Knows you well. What you're capable of."

"Great, a stalker." She lowered her hand to cover her

mouth, her words mumbled as she rushed out, "Not like you, I mean."

With no energy to remind her that term still fit me to a T, I instead reminded her, "Pierce Quaid would be pretty familiar with your capabilities."

"Right, I nearly forgot he may also be a traitor. I mean, we're assuming he's guilty because of his dog, which wouldn't exactly win over a jury as the nail in the coffin." The corner of her lip hitched, and I leaned in, kissing the edge of her mouth.

"What was that for?"

"For being you." Realizing I was seconds away from falling victim to the need to kiss or touch her more, I stepped away and crossed my arms. "I should bind my wrists when we share a room if we ever want to get any work done."

She smiled. "Even then, you'd surely Houdini your way out of any obstacle to get to me."

"You better believe it." I swallowed, trying to get back to the mission, but it was hard to do when she looked like a ray of fucking sunshine after devising a plan to save the country.

She blinked a few times, that familiar pink she often wore around me returning to her cheeks. "The news. Oh jeez, we got distracted. What updates do you have for me?"

"You kind of stole my thunder by coming up with a plan to save us all." I smirked, locking eyes with her.

"Ah, maybe a little." She shrugged, and the little movement drew my eyes toward her breasts. More specifically to the fact she'd yet to cover her nipples poking through her tank top.

"Sweatshirt," I damn near begged. "Then we talk."

"So bossy." She rolled her eyes in a playful way but did as I asked.

Once she had on her sweatshirt, I rummaged through my

memory, trying to remember what the hell I'd been planning to share with her in the first place. "Zoey," I began, hating how much she now knew about our past, "already knew about the lab hit in Amsterdam. Even though she's not MI6 anymore, they called her in for help. England was part of the joint project, and she was one of their best."

"I planned to reach out and give you a heads-up. You beat me to it," Zoey had said after I'd shared the shit news about a possible attack. *"I knew about Amsterdam, not about a second lab being hit. Their secondary site here wasn't compromised, but after the attack in Amsterdam, they're on alert."*

"What'd she say? Does she know anything?"

"England's second lab is secure. They weren't attacked."

"I suppose if the original bad guys who first hit the labs were only after the scientists to develop a weapon, they wouldn't need to hit every country's secondary sites."

"It's also possible only the U.S. had insiders, which is why they could only hit those two labs," I reminded her.

"I'm guessing we're definitely not ruling out American cities as targets despite the traitors probably coming from within. So, if our theory is right, and the first group wants to create a weapon, which will take a long time, they're not an immediate threat." She cringed as if hating her choice of words. "My friends, of course, are in danger."

"The second group is the clear and present danger for our country," I said in agreement.

"They're why we need to quickly reconfigure the lasers to stop an attack, and we're assuming it's coming soonish considering the lengths they're going to in order to get ahold of me."

"Right," was all I could manage, hating how much she was at the center of all of this.

"Then if the second group's responsible for the hit against us in Poland, why not just blow up the place while I was in there? Why send all those men to die? Kill me, and they reduce the risk an attack can be prevented."

My hand whipped to the back of my neck, the tension returning in the form of real pain. "They must know it'll only be a matter of time before another country creates an EMP weapon, and once they use theirs, a counterattack will be launched." It was the only logical thing that came to mind. "They must believe you're the closest to making that happen. And having their hands on someone like you could be beneficial to other projects of theirs, too." *Not that I'll let them, or anyone, get a hold of you.* Once our two immediate threats were expunged, I'd make sure the world knew this woman was off-fucking-limits.

"A lot of people believe I can do this, so I guess I better believe in myself."

I nearly took her in my arms at the sound of her small, fragile voice, but I refrained, infusing the support and confidence into my voice when I told her, "You're damn right you should."

"And we're making progress, aren't we? This is good."

I nodded, but couldn't stop working the knots forming at lightning speed at the base of my skull. "China," I sputtered. "They're the only ones anyone knows of who are close to having a weapon, or possibly already has one." That reminded me of what else I'd yet to share about my call. "Zoey's in Beijing. She has assets on the ground there, and she's trying to determine if the Chinese government is behind any of this. If that's the case, their government must be working with the American traitors. The British PM isn't talking to President Bennett right now, but Zoey will provide me with intel so I can let POTUS know."

"That's something, I suppose. Thank God for your contacts." Her gaze fell to the floor, and I sure as hell hoped she wasn't thinking about my past.

She had nothing to be jealous about. Not even when it came to . . . I cleared my throat. *Rebecca.* Guilt was a fickle fucking thing, and it had its moments when it liked to beat the shit out of me. And now wasn't the time for it.

"Guess it was smart to call her."

"Yeah, that's what Secretary Chandler said on our earlier call. Of course, he'd lectured me on doing it before thanking me." *Typical.* "Hopefully Camila touches base by tomorrow. I left her a message using our emergency protocol."

"Good . . . and wasn't there one more thing you looked into before I distracted us with Newton's first law of motion?"

Rebecca's death, yeah, that news. I thought back to what the CIA director had told Secretary Chandler, that had then been relayed to me on that ass-chewing-appreciation call. "The CIA had nothing tying the Barclays' plane crash to Rebecca's death. At least, there's no records with any law enforcement agency that'd investigated her death. Aside from Andrew, the only person your mother claims Rebecca shared the evidence with was Craig Paulsen."

"I guess it helps we'll get a chance to talk to him, then." She narrowed her eyes, clearly waiting to find out whether or not I'd be able to resist murdering him if I found out he was connected to endangering Diana.

I wasn't sure what to say, so I opted not to answer the question she hadn't officially asked.

Her long lashes fluttered a few times as she waited for me to pick the conversation back up.

"Gray and Bravo Team are working together right now to locate the other hostages that were with you before you were split up." Misdirection. My specialty. "If Pierce is walking around as a free man because he betrayed the project, they'll also find him."

With her free hand, she reached for my chain, taking the cross in her hand.

"And I hope William's still alive, so I can—" I cut myself off two seconds too late. I'd so easily wound up in murderous territory again.

"I get the feeling I'm not going to like why."

Probably not, but I was going to say it anyway. "William didn't even try to protect you that night in the lab. And since he knows how your lips and body feel," I explained, leaning in closer as she closed her hand around the cross like she might be able to save me from future sins with it, "I may just have to kill him, too."

51

DIANA

"Old habits," Carter grunted.

"Yeah, I know, they die hard."

After a resigned sigh, he said, "How about just a word with William, then? That allowed?"

That was a huge step at meeting me in the middle. Although, he'd already taken quite a few steps, including not killing those men in the shed the other day, and ensuring animals didn't turn them into food. Maybe I needed to do a little moving myself. I could budge, I supposed. "A *few* words."

At my meet-in-the-middle offer, he smiled.

I was on the verge of asking, *What about Craig?*—but a knock at the door saved him from having to hear it. I had a feeling an answer of, *No, I won't kill him either,* would be harder to pry from him than food from a gator's jaws.

"You guys decent?" Mya called out.

"Funny," Carter grumbled, probably too low for her to hear. "Come in," he hollered, then stepped back, placing distance between us.

Mya opened up, holding two shopping bags in one hand.

"Big Guy here had me run errands for him. Prescription glasses and a few other things for you, too." She entered, but Dallas remained in the hall, peering at his dad for the OK to head inside.

Carter slapped the side of his leg, and Dallas eagerly ran over to him.

Seeing Carter smiling while petting Dallas made me forget his thirst for vengeance. All I saw was a sweet, kind man with his best friend.

"I picked up a few other things I thought you might want as well," Mya went on, setting the bags on the bed. "I couldn't help myself."

"Like what?" Carter stood tall and went over, reaching into one bag only to drop what appeared to be a red lace bra. "Mya." He dragged out her name while glaring at her.

"What? You told me to get her more clothes. She needs undergarments, too. A girl can look good while saving the world, can't she?" She pointed at her chest. "Case in point." She casually winked, letting me know she enjoyed getting under the "Big Guy's" skin, just not nearly as much as getting under Oliver's.

Carter gripped the bridge of his nose, sighing. "Did you wash everything, at least?"

"The machines downstairs had a sanitize mode, so yeah. Tags are removed and everything is set to be worn," she shared.

The fact Carter had thought to appease my need to be "clean" in the midst of chaos warmed my heart and had me sending him an appreciative nod. He really did know me well. His "study" skills had definitely paid off.

"Thank you," I said to both of them.

"I'm going to go make a few more calls. See where we're

at on POTUS agreeing to this new plan and getting Craig and Jared brought in for holding."

"Great." My attention skated to the bags, curious what else Carter had Mya buy, as well as what she'd bought without his knowledge.

"New plan? Did I miss something?" Mya asked.

Carter gave me a go-ahead nod to share, and so I did. I rambled away, offering her the bullet-point version of my laser plan. "Will you be able to help out with this?"

"I'm not Gwen or Natasha," Mya began, "but I can hold my own. I mean, God forbid we lose the ability to use Snapchat, right?"

"Real funny," Carter said under his breath, then gestured toward the door. "Why don't you give me thirty minutes to talk to the President and the others, then join me?"

"Sure." I followed his line of sight as it wandered back to the bags. *The red bra.* Tonight would be torture if we attempted to share a bed. Doubtful Carter was the pillow-wall type. Knowing that man, he'd sleep on the floor and let Dallas take the bed.

"Thirty minutes," he said again.

If he didn't see me by then, he'd probably come up and toss me over his shoulder, carrying me down. Not a horrible idea, but bad for his back.

He called Dallas over to him, and without another word, they both left, the door thudding shut behind them.

Mya went over to the bed and dumped the first bag, then the second. "I never thought I'd see the day that man falls all over himself about a woman. I can't tell you how happy that makes me."

I blinked, replayed her words, then did the only thing I could think of and grinned.

She lifted a box of condoms. "I couldn't resist buying a few extra things for you."

I stared at the letters XXL on the box, and my heart broke free from its cage in jealousy. "How do you know that?"

Mya dropped the box and waved her hands in the air as if pushing away whatever ideas were now in my head. "*Not* what you might be thinking. We were undercover for a dating game show not that long ago. Carter had to strip, and well, let's just say when they offered him a leaf for coverage . . ." She started chuckling, her cheeks going red. "I didn't see him, no worries. But the implication he'd be in need of something bigger than they'd planned to provide was obvious."

I couldn't begin to imagine Carter holding a leaf over his crotch. Or consider any leaf, for that matter, doing the trick at covering him up. "I guess at some point I'll need to hear that story in full."

"Absolutely." She tapped her nails on the condom box before tossing it aside. "But anyway, I just thought maybe you'd need some protection."

"You're probably the only one here who thinks we should use any. I mean, no, the team didn't have a group meeting and decide Carter should screw me bare. Although, the idea is nice. Not the team meeting, the other part." Mya's smile brightened, and it dawned on me none of that had stayed trapped in my head. I'd expressed what was supposed to be an internal rambly monologue.

"I like you," she said with a nod, ending the discussion instead of making me recant my words, or at the least, explain them.

I rubbed the sides of my arms, trying to chase away the goose bumps beneath my sweater my awkwardness had inspired. "Carter thinks we should behave during the mission and refrain from being together. I guess Griffin got into his head, but I suppose he's right."

This was a conversation I could see myself having with Sierra, not someone I barely knew. Then again, considering her husband had planted the idea in her head that Carter was evil, Sierra would hate that I was with Carter at all.

Sierra was on vacation right now, or she'd be panicking as to why she hadn't heard from me in days. She always went technology-free when she traveled, wanting to disconnect and truly relax. She wasn't an Instagram girl, so she never posted about her trips. Probably her paranoid husband's doing. Now, I was thankful for that. I didn't want her knowing what was going on, or worse, getting dragged into danger.

"Let me get this straight, you're saying *Carter* is heeding advice from *Griffin* about *abstaining* because of a mission? That's rich." Mya *tsk*ed. "Griffin's no one to talk. I wasn't working with him on the mission related to his now-wife, but suffice it to say, I heard Griffin was incapable of abstaining himself."

"Was the fate of the world on the line? Could our country explode into civil war if we had a nation-wide blackout on our hands that could last years?"

Mya closed one eye and tipped her head side to side for a beat. "Not quite this Armageddon-like, but no picnic either."

Unsure what to make of her words, I went ahead and sat on the bed next to her, combing through the clothes and other items she'd purchased.

"Just so you know, though, none of the guys, nor Sydney, 'behaved' when missions brought them to their loved ones." Her use of air quotes was somehow as comforting as was her implied message not to feel bad for desiring Carter at a time like this. "If Griffin's giving Carter shit, it's because he's a nervous father now, and he's not used to seeing Carter operate at less than a hundred percent. I guarantee, if a lecture did happen, those were even the words he used." Before I could share my concerns about distracting Carter, she read my mind and waved her hand again. "Don't think that. The man's going to be a little less focused regardless because he's got feelings for you. That's clear. Sex won't change a thing."

"I mean, true. And considering a kiss just inspired my idea as to how to stop an EMP weapon. . ." I had no plans to finish *that* thought out loud this time.

"Well, there you go. If I were you, I'd relieve tension in your off time. Not like you can work twenty-four seven. Your mega brain will need a break." She gave me a small smile as I picked up an eyeshadow palette. "Oliver and I were at the pharmacy, and I know this is probably the last thing on your mind, but I couldn't resist the makeup aisle. If you can't tell, I'm a makeup girl, and something about a smokey eye, blush, and lipstick make me feel a bit more alive and fresh. In case you're the same, I grabbed a few things for you, too."

"I could hug you right now, and the dark circles beneath my eyes are already thanking you." I traded the eyeshadow for the travel-sized bottle of perfume. "You thought of everything." Surely Carter would appreciate me smelling like more than just plain soap. Then again, it might be a bad idea to intoxicate his senses when we're already struggling to refrain from touching one another.

"I couldn't find anything decent I liked at the store, and Oliver rushed me—such a pain in the ass—so that's one of my travel-sized ones."

Kilian? I hadn't heard of that brand. I read the label out loud: "*I don't need a prince by my side to be a princess.*"

"From the sounds of it, you found your king."

Touché. Carter was certainly that. "And have you found your king yet?"

486

Mya's eyes shot to the door, and I wondered if Oliver was out in the hall. "I'm beginning to wonder if he'll ever make a move. He's stuck in his own head, and I haven't made it easy on him. Surely you noticed." She patted the bed at her sides, then abruptly stood. "Well, I should go talk to Sydney about the plan. Play the phone-a-friend game and call Gwen. It's nice we have one of the world's best hackers on our side. Maybe we'll also track down the elite hacker who's working for the enemy, too. That'd be another win."

"What about Camila? Is she tech or science savvy?" I slipped on the gold-framed glasses to test them out next. They were nearly perfect for me, which was probably thanks to Carter.

"Camila's decent at tech stuff, but she's more like Carter. Go undercover. Kick ass. Take names. Basically, a female version of him. It shocks me they're not actually blood related. I mean, sometimes I wonder." She folded her arms, continuing her train of thought out loud, and I wondered if she had the same issues keeping some thoughts in her head, too. "Camila's mother went to school with Carter's dad in Brazil, and they dated back then. Camila doesn't know who her father is, but Carter's dad and her mom stayed friends after they broke up." She rubbed her eyes, shaking her head. "Shit, I'm not trying to be the girl who starts rumors. I have no idea why I just said that to you. I didn't mean to imply Carter's dad cheated on his mother." Hand back at her side, she cringed as if she'd eaten a habanero pepper or something sour. "Must be the former reporter in me coupled with exhaustion causing me to open my mouth like that. I'm sure Carter's told you all about Camila by now."

I let go of the perfume, feeling an achy pain in my stomach at the idea I barely knew a thing about him outside of our limited time together. I didn't want to translate that to meaning what we felt for each other was only lust. Sure, it was combustible what happened when we shared the same air, but still. "Carter's dad's Brazilian? My mother never told me."

Mya sat alongside me again, nudging me lightly with her elbow. "You've been busy. I'm sure he'll get around to telling you everything about himself. Don't overthink this."

"Okay." *Real* convincing.

"It's not like Carter told me any of this. What I know is from Camila." She uncrossed her arms. "Well, Camila didn't bring up the theory about her being related to Carter. That's all me." Back on her feet again, she sighed. "I should sleep at some point. I only managed an hour today before shopping."

"Well, I agree with the sleep part. I'm going to blame being tired on my desire to wash up again and maybe put on some makeup."

"I'm no one to judge. Trust me. Plus, Carter said to give him thirty minutes." She started for the door, then stopped and faced me, zeroing in on me as if a thought had come to mind. "Do we need to change the list you gave Griffin because of your new plan?"

I quickly went over everything I'd requested for my lab. "No, we should be good." It wasn't like I'd be sending him out to buy parts to build a nuclear reactor. "The only thing I'll be lacking on my end is the cyber expertise."

"Well, we've got that covered, don't worry." Her eyes landed on the bed, more specifically on the red bra at the top of the pile of clothes. "He's not going to last another twenty-four hours, just so you know. Be sure not to let him feel bad about it after his control snaps. The last thing he needs is more guilt."

52

CARTER

Shrugging on my leather jacket, I peered over at Dallas curled up on one of the plastic-covered sofas we'd pushed off to the side of the media room. "Ready for a walk?"

Dallas's ears perked up, but he didn't jump down in excitement.

"Tired, huh? I know the feeling." I patted the side of my leg. "Come on. We'll go look around out there. See what trouble we can get into."

"Can I join you on your walk?" Diana asked from behind me, and now Dallas was motivated to get up. His paws slid across the hardwoods in his race to get to her.

Traitor. I slowly turned to see Diana hanging back in the doorframe sporting her new glasses and a sexy-as-fuck smile.

She took a knee alongside Dallas and nuzzled her face against his nose.

God help me, this woman was already destroying me— albeit in a good way—but whenever I saw her with my best friend, I had the urge to surrender to her. Kneel and offer myself up the way Dallas was doing now.

489

I shifted up the sleeve of my jacket, checking my watch. "Twenty-four minutes. You're early."

She pushed upright and Dallas sat at her side, waiting for the walk he'd been too tired to take before. "Good thing, too. Or I'd have missed the walk. I could use some fresh air."

"You need something warmer if you plan to go outside with us." I studied her outfit, assuming her ripped jeans and nude-colored, fitted, long-sleeved shirt were courtesy of Mya. "Bet Mya paid extra for the jeans to have a hole in them." How would I be getting any work done with her dressed like that with her curves perfectly outlined and begging to be touched?

"Uh-oh, is grouchy Carter back?" She smirked. "Such an old-man thing to say, by the way."

"Do I need to remind you I'll be forty-six next June?" I did the math. With her birthday in January, that made me eleven and a half years older than her. *Screw the age gap.* "I'm as old as I am stubborn, I suppose."

"By those calculations, you're ancient, then." She slid her tongue across her glossy pink lips, the color a perfect match to her nipples. The little tease. "Way older than four and a half years shy of fifty."

Fifty. Don't remind me. Although, in truth, being around her made me feel like a twentysomething-year-old. It was as if she was giving me a second chance to be the man I couldn't be in my twenties, mired in the trenches of war. "I have another jacket. Hold on."

I went over to my rucksack and retrieved my other jacket sitting on top of it. Clutching it between my palms, I slowly cut across the room her way, never taking my eyes off her. Beautiful wasn't a word I usually threw around, but when it came to Diana, she was the fucking definition of it. She was stunning no matter what, but tonight, she'd accentuated her

490

blue eyes, high cheekbones, and full lips with makeup, making everything I already loved about her pop that much more.

"Here," I grunted, pushing the jacket her way, feeling a little dizzy as I inhaled her scent. "Perfume?" *Damnit, Mya.*

"Mmmhmm." Her eyes fell to the jacket from my Army days. "This feels . . . special?"

It was nearly as old as I was. "It's been with me a long time." I swallowed. "Once I hold on to something, I don't let go."

She peered up at me with those big blues that thankfully her glasses didn't hide. Her lips parted, but no sound escaped.

Clearing my throat, I stepped back before I hauled her against me.

She shook her head as if trying to break from the same spell I was under and put on my jacket. It was far too big for her, but when she brought the inside of the collar up to her nose and inhaled, it took me a second to catch my breath. The zipper was on the opposite side than she was probably used to, and when her fingers hesitated the slightest bit, I gently nudged her hands away and took over.

Her eyes fixed on me as I slowly zipped her up, and we were caught in another moment, until Dallas's howl reminded me of where we were and what we were supposed to be doing.

"This is cozy. I could sleep in it. Snuggle right up. And it smells like you. All masculine and rough."

"What does rough smell like?" I smirked, stepping away.

"Mmm. Easy. Like you." She stuck her tongue out at me, and that was all it took for me to snap.

In the space of a second, I had her pinned to the wall with my tongue inside her mouth. The details of my call with the President were lost. So was my sanity.

She moaned, holding the collar of my jacket while I held her face.

"Ohh, well thennn . . ." Was that Mya? "I'll come back."

Diana's glasses were a mild inconvenience, but I didn't give a damn. I kept kissing her. I let myself be reckless for a few more seconds, becoming that twentysomething-year-old who never had to watch his friends die in the war.

The reality of our situation finally settled back in, and after a few more heated seconds, I forced myself to let her go. I tore my hand through my hair, doing my best not to stare at her swollen lips, satisfied at the fact that was my doing.

"The President is on board," I finally told her. "As long as you can relay information to the teams he's organizing to outfit their existing missile defense system from here, we're all set."

"Wow, they'll take orders directly from me?" She brushed her fingers across her lips. "No pressure, huh?"

"You'll do great." Now for the part I didn't want to share. "New intel suggests if a hit is coming on U.S. soil, it'll take place on election day. So, it's a tight timeline."

"*Really* tight." She dropped down alongside Dallas, clearly in need of his brand of comfort.

Which is why these people are hell-bent on getting to you. Only now, they may not care if you're brought in alive, just as long as you can't stop them from their attack. She didn't need to know that, though. "Still doable?"

"I, um, hope so." She kept her eyes on the floor and her hands on Dallas. "Did you update Gwen and the others?"

I nodded, then gestured to a table set up across the room with five laptops lined up. "In about thirty minutes, Gwen and the others will be joining you virtually to get to work."

"Okay," she said softly. "So, who's on my team?"

"Aside from Natasha, Gwen, Sydney, and Mya," I started,

"there's Harper Brooks. She was with the CIA, but now she works with one of the President's SEAL Teams, and she's married to one of the Teamguys. And then there's Jessica. She co-runs Bravo with her brother. Another genius, and she's also married to—"

"One of the Teamguys?" She smiled.

"Yeah, her brother's best friend."

"Ah, bet he loved that."

I smiled. "Eventually." Well, from what I'd heard.

She peered around the room cluttered with our equipment. "Too bad Bahar isn't here. She's one of the best physicists in Turkey." Her smile evaporated. "I hope she's in Scotland and okay."

"Gray's with Bravo following leads. If she's in Scotland, they'll find her." I just wasn't sure if they'd find her alive. Needing to change the subject before she read the worry in my eyes, I added, "Some of the guys are also working on clearing out a space down the hall for your lab in preparation for Griffin to return with your supplies."

She stopped petting Dallas and stood, and I did my best not to lean in and kiss away her nerves. "Guess that means the sands of time get flipped and the countdown officially begins." Her gaze snapped to my arm, covered by the jacket, where the same image was tattooed there. "Anything about Craig or Jared?"

Even hearing Craig's name felt like a whip cracking between us, and I sure as hell hoped that man wouldn't be an issue for us. I supposed one way for Craig not to cause problems between us would be for me to agree not to kill the bastard. "Secret Service should be picking them up soon."

"Good." She peered around the room, drumming her nails against her outer thighs. "And what happens if I fail?"

Not an option, but I did my best to mask my own worries

and said as steadily as possible, "Plenty of contingencies and backups." *Only one, actually. The emergency plan.*

Her eyes narrowed. "Like?"

"Sending you somewhere safe before all hell breaks loose." I wasn't sure where that'd be, but the bunker in Montana was no longer safe if we had a traitor in the White House.

"You won't be coming with me." Her small, sad voice gutted me. "You'll stay out and fight?" Before I could answer, she held up her hand. "I would never ask you to choose me over the country. Don't worry."

Chills beat down my back. "The thing is," I began, slowly meeting her eyes, "I'd choose you."

53

CARTER

MYA AND SYDNEY'S INTERRUPTION STOLE DIANA AWAY before we could finish our conversation, which was probably for the best. Sydney was anxious to get a head start before the others joined in over the secure web call, so I'd gone ahead and walked Dallas alone.

After Dallas wrapped up his business, I found an old Land Rover Defender in a shed tucked away in the wooded area of the property. With Dallas exhausted, I opted to use the Defender instead of walking to do a perimeter check. On our drive, we also stumbled upon the owner's helipad and Bell JetRanger helicopter. Easton was a pilot, so although the helo wasn't exactly designed for special operations, it'd make do if we were in need of a quick flight anywhere.

Before heading back to the house, I found myself parking near the cliffs overlooking the water at the back of the property. "I need some fresh air. Staying in here or coming with me?"

Dallas barked and scrambled to stand in the passenger seat, letting me know he'd join me outside. I went around and opened the door to let him out, and we headed over to the edge of the cliff. He stood beside me as I took a knee, staring off in the distance at the water.

Barely a minute later, one of my two disposable phones vibrated in my jacket pocket. An unknown number from Bali. *Camila?* "Hey," I answered, relieved to hear from her so soon. "I didn't think I'd hear from you until tomorrow."

"A gut feeling told me to check early." Based on the background noise, she was in the city. It wasn't quite morning yet if she was in Bali, though.

"Do you know what's going on?" Was it possible she'd felt something? Seen it? Or was Bali safe from our current problem, so she'd be in the dark about what was happening?

"I don't know anything. I've been off-grid. What's happening? I'm on an untraceable line, so you're clear to tell me."

Where would I start? With Diana? With Rebecca? I scratched Dallas behind the ears, then began petting him, needing oxytocin myself to get through this. I decided to switch over to Portuguese. Talking in my father's native language always made it easier for me to express myself.

After going over everything I knew, I switched back to English. "Are you still with me?"

"I'm processing. It's a lot to take in. The fact I didn't see any of this coming has me thrown. I have your back, you know that. Just tell me what you need me to do. Want me to try and get a read on what might happen?"

Did I want to know the future? What if Diana wasn't in it? "Since you're in Bali, maybe first meet up with Zoey in Beijing. I need to know if the Chinese government was successful in creating an effective EMP weapon. And if so, if they're the ones planning to use it and where."

"On it. I'll reach out to Zoey now to coordinate. Based on what I find out, we'll figure out next steps after that."

"Thank you." I set a hand over my chest, relief swelling there now that I knew she was joining in.

"And, Carter," she whispered, "I don't want to talk down about the dead, but . . . Rebecca didn't deserve you, but *you* deserve Diana."

The call went dead before I could respond. First Alyona. Then Griffin. And now Camila. All telling me what I already knew deep down. Diana was mine, and I'd go to the ends of the earth to fight for her to stay that way.

I swapped my phone for my wallet, knowing there was another hurdle in my way of truly moving forward. I retrieved that obstacle from where it was hidden between credit card slats.

Closing my hand around the wedding band, I let the wind whip my face as I shut my eyes. I couldn't hang on anymore. It was time to let go, and there was only one way to do that. Even with unanswered questions still out there, I had to move on.

Opening my eyes and unfurling my hand, I rasped, "I forgive you."

Intense emotions choked me up as I threw the ring over the ledge. A weight lifted from my chest as I added in a strained voice, "Goodbye, Rebecca."

5 4

CARTER

I GRABBED HOLD OF THE INTERIOR DOORFRAME AND STUCK MY head into the command center, checking to make sure everyone had eaten after I'd sent Mason out for food. In truth, I'd use any excuse I could get to put eyes on her. "You all eat?"

"If you call five slices of pizza eating and not overindulging." Diana swiveled around in her desk chair to face me. "Guess I made up for the past week."

"You deserved each and every piece," Mya said with a chuckle, her back to me as she worked on something alongside Diana.

Gwen and the others weren't currently on webcam, so I assumed they were taking a break, too. Dallas was resting as well. More like snoring under the desk by Diana. He hated being away from her as much as I did.

"Thank you for the dessert, too." Diana removed her glasses, shooting me a bold, seductive look. Yeah, she was onto me.

Devil's Food. My angel's favorite. One day, I'd have a chance to learn more about her in the right way, but the little appreciative glance from her at my dessert choice meant my stalking had once again paid off.

"I can't wait to overindulge on that soon, too," Diana teased, and Sydney grabbed hold of her chair, spinning her back toward the table to face the laptops.

"We're about to jump back on our call, and you're distracting her." Sydney flicked her wrist over her shoulder, letting me know to beat it.

"Fine," I grumbled, but now eating cake with Diana while naked was at the top of my one-day-we'll-do-it list.

Returning to the hall, I shook my head, shocked that I'd become a man with a to-do list. I also knew if Diana and I were to marry one day, smashing cake against each other's faces during the reception would be one of my favorite memories. Another thing Rebecca had never let me do.

I stopped walking, surprised by where my thoughts had drifted.

A pair of boots heading my way pulled my attention back to reality and up to see who they belonged to.

"You're back." I frowned. "That mean you didn't find anything?"

Gray tipped his head, motioning for me to step into the closest room. I followed him, and he shut the door and reached for his phone. "Hopefully you didn't eat. The photos I'm going to show you might even make a man like you lose his lunch."

A man like me, huh? Fair enough. Also, not the best way to start the conversation. I needed good news, and clearly he wasn't about to give me that. "Way to kick things off," I said while accepting his phone.

Swiping through the photos, the phantom smell of burnt flesh filled my nose, and my stomach turned. I was used to death and destruction, and had lost count of how many lives

I'd taken, but if the images were what I thought they were, and Diana's colleagues had been burned alive, I had no clue how I'd tell her.

Forget those words I'd planned to have with William. Dead men didn't talk.

"I was just at the coroner's office here in town. Three unidentified bodies were recovered from a building that'd been on fire at Port Leith. Two women and one man from what they could tell. There's too much damage to make out their faces, but there are rope-like fibers burned into their skin on their wrists and ankles, suggesting they'd been tied up."

"Fuck." *Bahar? William? Another female colleague of Diana's?*

"Forensics indicates they were killed before the fire, which happened about one hour after we were attacked in Poland. Still not the news we were hoping for, but at least they weren't burned alive."

Processing that information, I swiped to another image. "Pierce Quaid," I said under my breath. "He's alive? Where?" The photo on Gray's phone showed Pierce outside a BMW sedan on a city street. The next image showed that same BMW on fire.

"Not alive anymore. That footage is of Pierce taken in Antwerp this morning. Thirty seconds after he got behind the wheel, it blew up. The Agency's sending someone to Belgium to get a positive ID and ensure it's really him."

"Someone wanted us to see this."

Gray nodded, shoving his phone back into the pocket of his fatigues. "Looks like Pierce was an insider, but someone's tying up loose ends."

"If Pierce was on camera in Antwerp, that's a false lead they want us to chase. Another diversion." I folded my arms, searching through the facts in my head of what we already knew to piece together what this new information meant.

"More than likely, but what I'm trying to figure out is if those three people were Diana's colleagues, why kill them? If they thought their location here was burned"—he grimaced at his choice of words—"why not relocate them elsewhere. They needed the physicists for help, especially since they don't have Diana."

"Because maybe it was never about the hostages or the research?" I dragged a hand down my face, mulling over the facts. "What we do know," I began, "is that someone outsourced the attack in Amsterdam to the Serbians to keep their own hands clean. What if their plan all along was for us to think the lab was destroyed to stop the project, as well as steal the research and the best minds to create their own weapon, but it was actually to hide some other underlying motive?"

"Thwart our efforts to have a weapon so when they use the one they already have against us, we can't counterattack," he said, following along. "But what they didn't anticipate was you being brought in and having the security footage that fucked with their plan before they had a chance to finish it."

"Judging by the fact they probably murdered the other hostages and have moved mountains to try and get to Diana, she's the only one they ever gave a damn about." *They just didn't want anyone to know she was their main target during the lab hit.* "They had every intention of pinning this mess on the traffickers and the unsuspecting target who allegedly hired the Serbians, which is why there was a different hacker tied to the encrypted USB in the first place."

"And that lead is what had us thinking we may be dealing with two threats." Gray grunted, mirroring my frustration. "More like the first one being an artificial fucking construct.

The government would blame them, wrap up the case, and drop their guard, just to get blindsided by an attack."

I walked through the details in my head over again, trying to make sure we weren't missing anything. "But because I was brought in, which was the curveball they didn't count on, they had to change gears and fast. They couldn't try and block Diana's rescue from the Serbians or it'd draw attention to the fact they have a man in the White House. And thanks to Diana's father, they didn't have to because they had a backup plan to get her back post-rescue." Thank God for my obsession.

"Only, the group never anticipated we'd win that fight in Poland and learn about the tracker in the glasses. They underestimated our team, including Gwen. If they're tying up loose ends now, that means they know we're onto the fact the original plan was a distraction, and they're short on time. They must also be getting nervous that they can't get their hands on Diana, which has me wondering if Diana has value to this group beyond her ability to create a way to stop the attack," Gray theorized. "And if Pierce Quaid was also an insider, it looks like he just became their first sacrificial lamb."

"And they'll need a second one," I said under my breath as Gray's phone began ringing. "Whoever winds up dead next is either the traitor and another loose string being eliminated, or the alibi for the real one."

Gray waved the phone between us. "It's my father," he let me know, then placed the call on speaker. "Carter's on the line, too."

"Craig Paulsen's been brought in, and he denies any involvement." Not wasting time on pleasantries, the Secretary cut straight to it. "He's willing to take a polygraph and have his home searched as well. But Jared Felsely is MIA. The

Agency located his Navigator down the street from his office, and right after he exited the vehicle—"

"The power went out on the street?" I took a chance and guessed.

"An unexplained surge in the power grid took down three blocks for five minutes," Chandler confirmed my hunch. "We can't track Jared anywhere from then on."

My mind wrestled with what it all meant. Was Jared being set up to cover Craig's ass? Or was Jared the traitor? And why did the idea of Craig being innocent disturb me so much?

"We'll touch base after the interrogation with Craig. Carter, I know you'd like a word with him as well, but in light of the situation with Jared, the President would like to hold off on you speaking with him until we have more intel." His remark added more fuel to the fire, and my fuse had already been lit by the news that Craig was either not guilty, or he was going to *try* and walk away a free man by framing Jared.

"Fine." It wasn't like my standard questioning techniques would work over a web call anyway. "But I *will* speak to him at some point." I sure as hell hoped I'd made myself clear to both men on the call.

After a quick update about Diana, Gray shared the conversation we'd had prior to the call.

"If China's not behind any of this, and it's not sounding that way based on intelligence, we need to narrow down our suspect list to who has the means and motive to pull this off," Chandler said at the end of our back-and-forth speculating.

"Narrow it down?" I scoffed. "We don't have anyone other than China on the list." Which was a problem, because I was with the Secretary on doubting this was the Chinese government's doing. They'd have gone in for a clean and precise hit if they knew about the labs. No evidence left. No leads to track down. No one left alive.

"Then I guess you better do what you were tasked to do. Use your contacts with the underground criminal world and get me a goddamn list," Chandler shot back, exhaustion heavy in his voice. He more than likely had as much sleep as we had. "Be in touch." He ended the call, and Gray apologized for his father's tone, not that he'd needed to.

When Gray started for the door, presumably to fill in the others, I wrapped a hand over his shoulder to stop him. "Diana can't know about the fire. If those three people were her friends . . ." We still needed positive IDs on them, so why preemptively put her through hell?

"She'll be distracted and in mourning if she knows. I hate keeping this from her as much as you do, but you're right."

"There's a lot of people counting on us, and you have a pregnant wife back home on top of things. We have to pull this off."

Gray's shoulders fell. What was it now? "Jack's wife called him earlier today to let him know she's expecting as well. She was planning to wait and tell him once he got home, but with the news we'd be here for a bit, she was too anxious to wait. He may be a bit tense now. Just thought you should know."

I scrubbed a hand along my jawline, happy for them but now also worried about his focus. "That's good news for them, though."

"Yeah," he said with a sigh. "We should fill the team in on everything else."

"I'll need you to do that without me." I couldn't face Diana right now and lie, knowing at some point later she might hate me for it.

DIANA

I SAT UP IN THE BED, RESTING AGAINST THE BLACK LEATHER headboard. Dallas was curled up on top of the covers by my feet. It was three in the morning, and we were way past due to sleep, but we were making so much progress, so I didn't want to stop. I had a top-notch team, and after tonight, I had the confidence to believe our plan was truly doable.

Although, my confidence was going pound for pound in the heavyweight department with my anxiety. After everything Gray had shared that evening, while Carter had been curiously absent from the meeting, how could I not be even more anxious?

Not two enemies. Just one and a fall guy (or guys).

Then there was the fact I'd more than likely been one of their main targets all along. And not just because I was the Secretary of State's daughter, but because they believed I was capable of shutting down their real goal: launch an attack with a weapon they—whoever "they" were—already had on U.S. soil. So, that's why they'd been spying on my dad weeks before the attack. They had contingencies for their contingencies, including making use of their insiders planted inside both my lab and the White House.

They just hadn't counted on Carter Dominick, or his obsession with me.

Now that same man—who'd practically dragged me from the room to force everyone to get some sleep—was standing on the other side of the bed, shirtless, staring at it as if it were made of nails instead of the fluffy cloud of heaven that it was.

His thumbs rested on those sexy slanted lines that disappeared beneath the waistband of his black sweats. "Dallas doesn't normally sleep on the bed. This is going to create a habit I'll have to break." I highly doubted that gruff tone had anything to do with the sleeping arrangements for Dallas.

"I think having him on the bed will help us behave and actually sleep, don't you? I mean we're both probably too wiped out to cross the lines, but just in case, he could play defense." Carter's brows drew together, his eyes cutting back to me as I added, "I do want you to hold me, though. So, on the bed, but without him between us, is what I think is best."

He lifted his hand, sliding the pad of his thumb along the underside of his lower lip. "You do, hmm?" I nodded my answer since his gaze, so intensely pointed at me, rendered me mute. "I am tired. Wrecked, to be exact. Frustrated on top of it. Hating that Craig's lying through his teeth, and your mother's boyfriend is being tossed under the bus, and—"

"We don't know for sure if Craig's lying. He could be innocent."

That comment had his jaw ticcing. He wanted a reason to kill him, didn't he? Of course, in Carter's mind, he probably already had a hundred. Just touching me that day in the limo seemed to be enough. We still had to circle back to the whole him-murdering-Craig thing at some point, but we'd cross that bridge when we had to, I supposed.

"Let's not talk about Craig right now," he bit out.

Yeah, good idea.

"My point is, my head and body might be drained of energy, but my cock doesn't care. You put your ass up against me while I hold you, and it's getting fucked. At least, one of your holes is." He shoved down the sweats, showing me how hard he already was. His dick strained against the fabric of his black briefs.

I gulped, trying to register what he'd said. Backdoor access was something I'd never considered, and there I was, tightening my ass muscles in curiosity if such a feat was truly possible.

"I'm not in the best state of mind, and you know how I get when I'm tense and wound up. I don't want to lose control the way I almost did with you on the jet."

"When you almost spanked me, you mean?" There went my ass cheeks again, this time in anticipation of his hand swatting my soft skin. That I could handle, though. Well, I assumed I could. I trusted this man to take me only to a safe limit of what I could tolerate, limits that'd result in way more pleasure than pain. When he remained staring at me, jaw as tight as his muscles appeared to be, I broke the silence. "Seems to me you need some tension relief so you don't snap."

"Diana." His shoulders were the only part of him now relaxed. "I just . . . can't be with you right now."

"I know. The mission has to be the priority. You're also upset with how much you don't know yet, I get it. We have to stay focused. That doesn't mean you can't go in the shower and jerk off."

He dropped his head, but I doubted he was taking in the sight of the massive erection he was sporting. "It's not that. I mean it is, but it isn't."

"I'm not following."

Instead of explaining as I needed him to do, he said, "The only way I'm not sleeping on the floor is if you can promise me you'll keep to your side of the bed, and not torture or tease me."

Could I promise that?

Before I could surrender an answer, he dropped a few more colorful expletives under his breath, garnering a howl from Dallas. "You toss and turn in your sleep, don't you? You'll wind up on top of me or *under* me." His scowl was almost cute that time, then it transformed to a sharp wince. "No, I didn't have cameras installed in your bedroom in Amsterdam," he quickly added, as if worried I'd think he'd taken "checking on me" to another level. The thought hadn't even crossed my mind.

"I do move around a lot." I clutched the bedding to my chest, knowing he wouldn't be pleased with my nightwear. Mya had bought me cute oversized tees to sleep in. Those shirts gave Carter direct access to between my legs. He'd waited for me to get under the covers before coming into the room from the en suite, so as far as he knew, I had on shorts or pants.

"I'm sleeping on the floor." He went to the closet and returned with two blankets, took a pillow from what would've been his side of the bed, then rolled the blankets out, smoothing them across the floor. His movements were methodical and efficient as he prepared his bed. Once he was done, he petted Dallas on the head and told him goodnight.

I wanted the same little pat, too. A kiss would have been even better.

When he stood tall, he came closer and removed my glasses, setting them on the nightstand. "Get some sleep." His sweet tone was quite the contrast from before. Same with the soft kiss to my forehead. When our eyes connected, I became lost to both time and space. His breathing picked up, and I noticed he'd removed the cross at some point, probably in the bathroom when he'd taken off his shirt before joining me in the bedroom. "You won't roll off the bed and fall on me now, will ya?" he teased, that sexy Texas accent I loved sliding through.

"I'll do my best not to toss and turn *that* much," I whispered as he pushed away from the bed, taking a knee on the temporary bed beside me. It pained me that he'd be sleeping down there. "You're sure you can't be up here and hold me?"

He stretched out but didn't cover himself with the second blanket, his desire tenting his briefs obvious even in the low light of the room. "I'm sure."

I lay down and switched to my side so I could better see him. "I'm not sure I'll be able to fall asleep yet. Maybe you could tell me something about yourself? Distract me from the negative energy and my anxiety. Also, you know so much about me, and I barely know anything at all about you."

"What would you like to know?" he asked, and to be honest, I didn't have a ready answer. I'd been expecting a get-to-sleep brush-off.

"Basics for tonight. We can peel back a few layers every night we're together. How about that?"

His forehead creased, but he relented with a nod.

"Favorite color?" That was as basic as it could get.

"Black." He rested a hand over his heart, one finger tapping as if in time with his heartbeat.

"Do you like ice cream?"

"There are people who don't?" He cracked a smile. "Rocky road."

"Mm. Good choice. Do you know mine?" *Of course you do. You know how I like my pizza, not to mention my favorite dessert.*

He closed one eye and admitted, "I do. Equal scoops of strawberry, vanilla, and chocolate. But you pour so much hot chocolate on top, you wind up with all chocolate anyway."

This was already helping ease the tension in my body, and hopefully I'd sleep better because of it. "My questions sound like I'm giving you a survey, when in reality, I'm a bit rusty when it comes to communicating with the opposite sex." His smile evaporated at that. *Right. You hate thinking about men from my past.* "Okay, one more survey question for now, then we can shut off the light and sleep."

Since I hadn't been prepared for him to let me ask him anything, I had to think of another one on the fly. Sierra hijacked my brain, and I asked what she would've. "Celebrity crush?"

He let go of a deep breath, as if the question had pained him. "I don't have one."

"Really?" *Why'd that make me happy?* "Neither do I. Celebrities don't do anything for me, but I thought I was the only one."

His grouchiness vanished almost immediately, and there was something more there I couldn't read.

"You okay?"

"You just keep taking my breath away. Not sure how else to put it," he whispered.

There goes my heart. He seemed to power it up like nothing else could. And comments like that proved he wasn't a devil. Far from it.

"Sleep, angel." He lifted his chin and tilted his head, hinting it was time to kill the light on the nightstand. "If you're good, I'll give you three more answers tomorrow night."

56

DIANA

From inside my makeshift lab, I stared at the rolling whiteboard, headphones on and music blasting in my ears, as I studied the equations scribbled in blue ink. My eyes were a bit blurry from fatigue, and the numbers were starting to swirl and become 3D in front of me.

It'd already been more than twenty-four hours since I began working in coordination with the Department of Defense.

I dropped into my chair, exhausted. I could only do so much thinking before my creativity tapped out. I swapped my MP3 player for the disposable phone Carter had given me. He'd programmed two numbers into it—a secure line for my mother and his.

Based on the time, I had a few more hours until Carter would track me down and force me to take a brain break by way of sleeping.

It'd be our second night sharing a room there, and I was a little curious if it'd play out the same as last night. Would he let me ask him questions before he dozed off on the floor like he'd promised? Had I been a good enough girl?

He'd kept his distance from me all day, more than likely to refrain from distracting me. He was busy as well, trying to figure out who'd orchestrated this plan from the get-go.

If only Craig would talk. Share something. Unless he's really innocent, so there's nothing to share?

At my stomach growling, I took a granola bar from the pile Oliver had dumped onto my desk.

Oliver had also been responsible for making sure I ate dinner. Carter had given Oliver explicit instructions not to leave my side until I cleaned my plate.

I couldn't help but return Oliver's orders with one of my own. *"Well, please tell Carter I would've thought he'd know me better than to worry I'd go hungry. I'm a stress eater."* That was something Carter would've known since he'd been watching me in Amsterdam. He clearly just enjoyed being bossy.

"Orders are orders, ma'am," had been Oliver's response.

"Afraid to get on his bad side, huh?"

"Absolutely," he'd returned with a laugh.

Finishing half the granola bar, I kept staring at my phone, wondering if I should text him. Despite being in the same house, maybe he'd given me his number in hopes I'd reach out?

Going for it, I typed a quick message.

> Me: I miss you.

I stared at what I wrote, then quickly backspaced the words, deciding it wasn't the best first text to send him.

Before I could think of another message, my phone vibrated. Unfortunately, it wasn't Carter. Nope, it was the second number in my phone. *Susan.* Considering Carter had programmed the contacts, I was surprised he hadn't gone with something a bit more colorful to describe her.

I'd already spoken to "Susan" twice today in light of her boyfriend being missing. I'd been worried how she was coping with everything, because I would have lost my mind if I'd been in her shoes.

Nope, not Mom. She was handling it in stride. Emotions buttoned up. Calm and resolute. She really had been tailor-made for the role of Madam Secretary.

> Susan: This might be the first (and only) thing Carter and I ever agree on . . .

That had me sitting up taller and tossing the uneaten granola bar on my desk.

> Susan: Jared can't be guilty. He's being set up, which means Craig's the traitor. I don't know how to prove it, but I will. And if Craig could do something like THIS . . . then what if he really knew who Andrew Cutter was back in the day, and he's why Rebecca died?

I blinked, then reread her message. My heart was officially racing. Mom showing emotions? She'd never be able to say those words out loud. Hence the text.

> Susan: I have a bad feeling. What if Jared's dead?

Finally remembering I could respond back and not be passive to this conversation, I answered her, not providing the most enthusiastic response, because I honestly had no clue what to say.

> Me: He may still be alive.

I blamed the exhaustion for my award-winning response.

> Susan: I'm getting pulled into the Situation Room, I have to go. It's late where you're at. Don't forget to sleep. Dad sends his love. He's proud of you.

"Just Dad, huh?" I groaned, needing a palate cleanser after that brief conversation, and my thoughts landed back on texting Carter. Talking to him would help me reset before getting back to work.

At the sound of the door opening, I turned to see Dallas creeping on me. I leaned forward and motioned for him to come in.

He hurried over, planting his paws on my lap to lick my cheek, and seeing him gave me an idea.

"I bet you've never taken a selfie before." I opened the camera app and held the phone out. "How about we send your dad a picture?" Dallas nudged me in the face with his nose before I snapped a few photos of us together, including one where he'd had me laughing.

Once Dallas was parked alongside my chair, I swiped through the pictures, and he howled as if pleased with how they turned out. At this point, I'd begun to wonder if he was part human. He lifted a paw up, swatting the air as if letting me know that was his favorite.

"That one? All right. I'm hitting send." He curled up by my chair, and I interpreted that as him being content with my choice.

After a few minutes passed and no response, I did my best to focus back on work and not be disappointed. Headphones back on and music playing, I stood and went to the whiteboard to study my calculations again. I did my best to lose myself to the beats playing, but startled when Dallas abruptly hopped up to all fours.

I whirled around to see Carter in the doorway, standing there like a Titan, a man capable of ruling the cosmos. Those strong arms were encased in dark sleeves that showcased the ridges of every muscle.

Unsure why he kept still, quietly staring at me, it dawned on me he was probably waiting for me to pause the music. It was hard to think straight with those dark eyes fixed on me and all that intense brood pointed my way. *Which* was exactly why he'd avoided me all day.

Music off and headphones and the MP3 player on the desk, I waited for him to speak.

Still nothing.

Dallas began whacking his tail excitedly against his jeaned leg while Carter's intense gaze magnified. Pupils taking over the dark brown of his eyes, turning them nearly black.

Wringing my hands together, nervous he'd never answered me because he had bad news, I sputtered, "What's wrong? Something about Craig? Jared? News from Zoey and Camila?"

He shook his head no in response, then pushed away from the doorway, standing tall as his eyes flew to the table. "Is that the only photo you took?"

Pivoting to the side, I followed his gaze to the phone. "There are a few more. Are you upset with me?" Why in the world would a selfie piss him off?

He went over to the phone, wordlessly picked it up, and knowing him and his overprotectiveness, he probably deleted my photos.

Facing me, the phone back on the table, he surprised me by drawing his fist beneath my chin. "I should go now."

Those four words came out hard and rough, and I felt them scrape over my skin.

I swallowed. "Do you have to?"

My lips parted as I tried not to moan at his hard-on now pressing into me. "Yes," he gritted out. Cupping the back of my head, he brought his mouth to my ear. "I have to relieve my tension, angel. You told me to do it last night, and I didn't. But if I don't do it now, I'll kill someone."

Closing my eyes, I whispered, "I do like your teammates, so I'd hate for you to have to do that because you're tense. Plus, we need their help to find my colleagues, not to mention wrap up this case so we can have our shot at forever." *Shot at forever?* Yeah, I said that, and his eyes narrowed on my mouth the moment those words dropped.

Drawing his face back to mine, feeling his lips brush across my cheek in the process, I met his gaze as he rasped, "I'm too damn tense to be this close to you, because I want that shot now."

"And yet, here we are again, not backing away from each other."

With grit to his voice, he warned, "Do you have any idea how much I want to set you on this desk and eat you out?"

Well then. "But let me guess, if someone walks in on us, you'll have to kill them for seeing me." The moment those sassy words left my lips, he dropped his mouth over mine, stealing my lower lip between his teeth.

"Precisely." He let me go and backed up. "This is your fault. You sent me that photo." There was a hint of a smile tugging at his lips.

"You're acting like I sent you nudes," I teased.

He cocked a brow. "Angel?"

"Yes?"

"If you ever take a nude photo of yourself, risking someone else possibly seeing it, I will take you over my knee." The dark edge to his tone inspired chills to fly over my skin. "I don't want to be that guy with you, but don't test me."

I squeezed my legs together, very much wanting him to be that guy with me. Right now, in fact. His handprint on my ass cheek. He didn't seem to get that I didn't equate that action with him being "that guy."

Unable to stop myself from provoking him, I noted, "So, what you're saying is, if I want you to bend me over and spank me, I should take a nude."

The space between us became a distant memory as he guided my arms over his shoulders to pull me against him. "I've had a shit day, and I've missed you," he admitted before kissing me. "I was trying to give you space," he added, his mouth lingering at my ear, as if struggling to look me in the eyes.

"I'm sorry you had a bad day," I said before his mouth returned to mine, stealing away whatever else I'd planned to say as Dallas crooned in the background.

"It's getting increasingly better," he murmured once he pulled back to find my eyes. He threaded his hands through my hair before holding my cheeks. "I should go, though."

"Do you have to?" I chewed on my lip, hating the thought of him leaving and satisfying himself alone.

"Did you get yourself off in the shower you took today?" His brows tightened as he studied me like a human lie detector.

Closing one eye, I revealed, "Maybe."

He framed my face with his hands again. "Of course you did," he said before finding my tongue, letting the heavy weight of his cock press against me.

When our lips broke, I gave in and admitted, "I guess it's only fair you do, too."

Stepping away from me, he dragged a hand down his face, shaking his head. "You have three more hours to work, and then you need to sleep." He'd flipped a switch. Somehow managed to reset despite his cock still pitching his jeans. "I'll come get you when it's time." Then he shot out an order for Dallas to stay put, and left.

Hot, bothered, and unsure how in the world I'd come down from this high without an orgasm, I picked up my phone to confirm if he'd deleted my selfies with Dallas.

My hand slipped to my mouth when I realized he hadn't erased them from the phone. No, instead, he'd texted himself every single one.

5 7

DIANA

The bedroom door was unlocked. Maybe he'd subconsciously left it that way in hopes I'd follow him? *A girl can hope.*

Inside the bedroom, door closed and locked, I stripped down to my red bra and panties. Never had I been more grateful for the matching set, not to mention the razor Mya had purchased for me to use during my shower earlier.

Staring at the connecting en suite door, my heartbeat was still ramped up and pounding in my ears. Nervous, but excited, I slowly crossed the room. Would the bathroom be unlocked, too? It wasn't like he'd expect anyone from his team to enter the bedroom. They knew better.

The doorknob twisted easily in my hand. In his hurry to get off, he'd left it unlocked as well.

Slowly pushing open the door, my breath froze in my lungs at the sight before me. Steam had yet to crawl over every inch of the glass shower, and I could clearly see Carter stroking himself beneath the spray.

He could also easily see me.

"Diana." His deep voice cut through the glass and the noise of the running water.

"You can't just leave me hanging like that." Such a flimsy protest, but it'd been the best I'd come up with on my way up the back steps. I tilted my head back toward the bedroom. "So, I'll be on the bed. If you'd prefer to join me out there instead, we could relieve some tension together."

Before I lost my confidence, or gave him time to shut me down, I turned and sashayed toward the door, giving him a nice view of my ass in the skimpy, cheeky panties.

Back in the bedroom, I dragged down the heavy comforter and positioned myself at the center of the bed. Drawing my arm up behind me, I bent my elbow to prop up my head, and set my hand between my legs. My arousal was already soaking the panties thanks to this moment amping up what Carter had started downstairs.

The water turned off, giving me hope we'd chase our relief together. Maybe we'd both think even better afterward.

Carter filled the doorway, resting his hands overhead on the frame, taking my breath away. His golden-tan skin glistened, and I wanted to kiss away the water droplets covering his corded muscles. His chest lifted from a heavy breath, and as he let it go, his arms dropped to his sides along with it.

His decision to join me, coupled with his rigid cock on display, had me hoping he wouldn't reject me. Yet, he wasn't coming closer. Something was still holding him back. "What's wrong? I mean, aside from the obvious."

The tight draw of his lips sent an unsettling feeling in my stomach, but Carter was quick to read my nerves and broke his silence. "Nothing you need to know yet."

Yet? I ran through horrible scenarios of what that nothing might be. I flipped through the pages of possibilities at lightning speed, and landed on the decision I wanted him regardless.

Sitting upright, I took off my bra and tossed it, then wiggled my panties down my legs, kicking them off the bed as well. I went to my knees and sat back in prayer position, offering myself to him in a way I'd never done in my life. Completely exposed with the lights on, all flaws on display.

His fingers curled inward at his sides, fighting hard to keep away from me. He squeezed his eyes shut and gritted out, "If relieving tension will make you feel better, you'll need to touch yourself. I can't . . ."

"Because of the 'nothing I don't need to know yet' still between us?" I whispered, and he nodded, still refusing to meet my gaze. "Will it hurt me when I find out?" Chills hit me with vicious force, twining around my throat like ivy as he surrendered another nod.

"If it's confirmed, yes," he added, remaining stoic.

The opposite happened to me, I began to lose myself to worry. He took hesitant steps my way, and I drew my hands over my chest, pinning my forearms crisscross to try and chase away the goose bumps pebbling my skin.

"Being with me won't change the past. It won't change whatever it is you're nervous to share." Trembling to the point he must've noticed, he knelt on the bed and hooked his arm behind my back, tugging me over to him.

I wound up on his lap, straddling him. Naked limbs tangling together. My cold skin warming against his hard, hot body. My breasts smashing to his wall of muscle while hugging him. His cock just beneath me now, with no barrier between us.

With my wrists linked behind his neck, I rocked against

him, finding a light rhythm that still provided exquisite pleasure, forgetting all about whatever he was too afraid to share.

"Angel," he rasped, drawing his lips close to mine without kissing me. "You're going to accidentally . . . I'm going to wind up inside you bare if you keep moving like that."

"I can't help it." I needed relief that only he could give me. So, I continued grinding against him. "I need you to help me feel better. To take away the pain." I rubbed against him, and he unleashed a deep groan that had every part of me tensing. "Let's pretend the world outside this room doesn't exist and be together, for just this little bit of time. Would that be so wrong?"

He leaned back to find my face, and I felt his tip press against my opening, so close to pushing inside me. "Are you sure?"

The gruff texture of his voice rolled over my skin, and I wet my lips. "Yes," I begged, on the verge of tears. Desperate to finally connect with him after what felt like a lifetime of waiting. "I have an IUD, and I've never had unprotected sex, but I get checked regularly. I haven't been with anyone since I last tested negative," I babbled, probably killing the moment, but these were details we couldn't really skip over even in the heat of the moment.

A growl-like sound rumbled from his chest, nostrils flaring. Was this reaction from how badly he wanted me but was trying to abstain? Or did I trigger the wolf to come out at the reminder I'd ever been with another man?

After a few calming breaths, he rested his forehead against mine. "I'm good to go in that, uh, department, too," he said in a strangled voice. "But are you really asking me to take you bare?"

Breathing hard myself, nothing calm on my side anymore with this moment so close to happening, I nearly panted out, "I am."

"Diana." He was begging again without actually doing it. Begging for me to resist him? To walk back my offer? No, I couldn't do that. Being with him was the only thing that made any sense to me.

"Do you know how many times I've thought about this very moment?" His voice cracked on that last word. "Now you're offering it to me, and how can I possibly say no?"

Pulling back to meet his eyes, I whispered, "You don't." I worked my hand between our bodies, never losing hold of his gaze.

Brows drawn, he hissed, "You're going to hate me for this."

"I won't," I promised, my body trembling.

Within seconds, he flipped me to my back and had me pinned beneath him. Hard ridges over soft skin. The most perfect contrast, and I wanted to run my fingers over every part of him.

"You will," he grunted before capturing my mouth, kissing me hard.

At the feel of his cock pressing against me, I clutched his biceps and rotated my hips as he destroyed every one of my senses. Our tongues dueled before I gave control over to him.

His mouth momentarily wandered along my jawline, then he nipped my earlobe before finding my lips.

"Just like this," he hissed. "This is how I've always wanted you. I don't need . . ." He let his words trail off, heavy in the charged air between us.

"You don't need to be that guy," I finished for him, and he gave me a nod, finally accepting and knowing it to be the truth.

He stared at me quietly, and I was worried he'd back down and leave me, but instead he started to shift down my body. I reached for his chin in an attempt to stop him. "Foreplay another time. I need you inside me right now."

He couldn't shield his concern and his guilt from me any more than he could hide his desire. They were mixing. Becoming one and the same. He finally relented, holding himself above me, our mouths once again aligned.

"I know it's going to hurt at first. It's okay. I trust you."

He nodded, then kissed me again. Gentle, soft flicks of his tongue and sweet, sensitive kisses all over my face.

Moving his weight to one arm, he traced my silhouette with his other hand before nudging the crown of his cock in place. "You can be as loud as you want. I'll catch your cries with my mouth, okay?"

"I'm not made of glass. I trust you to trust me. I need you to take me all at once."

He didn't argue, and instead, dropped his mouth over mine just before he thrust inside me.

A gasp that was a borderline scream escaped from deep within my chest. My entire body tingled as he stretched me out. He captured my sounds as promised, banishing the pain with his kiss.

He moaned right back, reveling in our connection as we existed together as one.

"Are you okay?" He went still, kissing a tear forming at the edge of my eye.

"More than okay." My voice was strained, but my heart was full.

He began moving. Slow and steady. Taking his time to warm me up, help me fully accept him. He brought the pad of his thumb to the top of my clit, rubbing in small circles as he began thrusting a bit harder, never fully pulling out.

"You're tight." His Adam's apple rolled in his tanned throat as he bit out, "You feel so fucking good."

And he felt like home to me.

My abdominal muscles tightened nearly to the point of pain as I tried to fight off my orgasm. I needed more time. More of him.

As if sensing exactly what I needed, he moved away from my clit to hold my hip, pinning me down as he increased his pace. His pelvic bone rubbed against me creating the most amazing friction.

"You're close, I can feel it."

"Are y-you?" I stuttered, on the edge of heaven.

"Fuck yes." His jaw was locked tight, and as I shimmied against him a smile cut across his lips. It was all I needed to truly let go, and I writhed harder beneath him knowing he was enjoying my movements. "That's my good girl. Come for me," he ordered, his dark tone sliding along my nerve endings and pooling between my legs.

I lost it then and there, letting the orgasm own me as I allowed this man to claim me. To take away the pains of the past and the hurts of tomorrow.

Screaming out to him, he swallowed the cries with his mouth as he shuddered on top of me, his orgasm cresting with mine, and we breathlessly rode the wave together.

My name fell from his lips between soft kisses as he came inside me.

I was still panting when he relaxed on top of me, not yet pulling out.

Lifting his head, he studied me. Were his eyes glossy, or was that my faulty eyesight playing tricks on me?

Spying a drop of liquid at the corner of his eye, I lifted a hand between us to find out if it was real. He squeezed his lids closed as I caught the tear with my thumb.

"I didn't know," he said, his hoarse voice catching on a shuttered sob. "I didn't know it could be like this."

58

CARTER

I'D CAVED. MY DEFENSES HAD BEEN SHATTERED. NOT THAT they were strong around Diana. She'd barely had to do anything other than exist to push me over the edge. I'd tried, though, hadn't I? I'd made as much effort as possible to refrain, but . . .

It'd been twelve hours since we'd first made love, and I still couldn't believe I'd taken her missionary. And bare. *Fuck.*

Who was that man who'd been with her last night? Not the guy who took what he wanted with zero fucks to give. Yeah, I had taken what I wanted, then two more times after that. But I *did* care, and I didn't want to hurt her. All I knew was the man staring back at me in the newest photos saved to my phone wasn't a man I recognized.

Selfies. I'm now a man who takes selfies. And grins in photos. On an op, no less.

I swiped through the four-hour-old photos. Diana had asked me to take them while we were still in bed. And I did. There was a first time for everything, and if I was going to take selfies, there was no one I'd rather take them with. At least now my phone was full of photos *legally* acquired and not from my stalker habits.

I paused on one outside that set of images of us. One of her laughing with Dallas in her lab. A good kind of pain filled my chest, and I leaned back in the desk chair, thinking about every hour spent with Diana since last night.

After we'd made love, she'd gone back to her lab to work, and I'd wound up lost in my thoughts, thinking about how I'd made love, not fucked. How I hadn't needed to dominate or control. Guided and led when needed, yes. My thoughts had run on a loop, and when I'd realized the time, I'd dragged Diana to bed to get rest at zero four hundred.

She'd requested to take a ride I couldn't refuse. On my cock. Sitting on top of me, hands planted to my chest, she'd asked me three more get-to-know-you questions while her pussy had stretched to accept me.

"Pretty sure you're getting to know me really damn well," I'd teased, dragging my hands up and down her back.

She'd asked them anyway. More like panted them out. I wouldn't be surprised if she asked them again tonight. I wasn't sure she registered any of my answers. I wasn't even sure what I'd said. Could've been responding in German for all I knew.

Her moans had also been loud enough to wake Dallas from where he'd been asleep down the hall with Oliver (per my orders). He'd come running to the door to ensure Diana wasn't crying from pain. The little devil. He'd known what was going on. She'd been in the middle of falling to pieces on top of me as he'd barked outside our door.

But this morning, fucking hell this morning, had destroyed me. Waking up to her scent, with her limbs tangled with mine, both of us naked . . .

That was how I wanted to wake up every day of my

life. Hell, maybe I'd even consider breaking my rules, letting Dallas sleep on the bed, because I knew it made her happy.

"What have you done to me?" I covered my mouth, finding a smile forming there as I stared at our photos.

After we'd taken those selfies, we'd showered together. Strictly for the sake of expediency to get back to work (her words, not mine).

As expected, we wound up making love there, too. She'd even let me play with her ass. Not with the limb I'd hoped for, but my thumb was my way of warming her up to the idea of my cock there one day.

While taking her hard up against the shower wall, she'd held on to my arms, and between kisses, rambled on about the laws of physics and how I'd never fit. It'd been cute. Endearing, even. I held back on reminding her that I knew a thing or two about defying laws.

I palmed my crotch at the memory, growing painfully hard again. Missing her already. So much so I almost texted her those very words when what I really needed to tell her was, *I'm sorry. I'm sorry I slept with you knowing there was a chance your friends were dead. And as of this morning, confirmed to be true.*

I steepled my fingers against my lips, trying to figure out how to tell her the news.

Earlier in the morning, the coroner's office positively identified Bahar's, Bonnie's, and William's bodies as the ones in the fire. And according to the CIA, it was, in fact, Pierce Quaid in that explosion. I wasn't going to shed any tears over Pierce or her ex-boyfriend, but I knew Diana would be in mourning.

I'd purposefully hid out in my office after Gray had told me, unable to look at Diana again and not feel guilty for withholding the information from her both now and last night.

I needed to be alone to work. To find a way to save Diana from this mess sooner than later.

So far, no one in the underground world had admitted to knowing anything aside from what we already knew— Serbian traffickers were outsourced to do the Amsterdam job. And radio silence on the domestic side of things as to who could've hit the lab in Montana. The fact I couldn't intimidate or bribe anyone to talk had me wondering if no one actually had anything to say.

Who were these shadowy pricks managing to outsmart the President's best along with my people, who were *also* the best.

I was being hit with the uncomfortable feeling of déjà vu. I hadn't felt this much like a failure since searching for Rebecca's killer, chasing my fucking tail for almost two years. I didn't have that kind of time now. Forget two years. We had two weeks until the election.

And at almost forty-eight hours since we'd arrived in Scotland, the little we did know didn't help us in any way. The blackmailer had never again reached out to Alyona, confirming that'd been a diversion. Given what happened to Diana's colleagues in Scotland, the odds any of the other hostages from either lab being alive was next to none.

Frustrated, I went for my phone, prepared to call the White House for my third time that morning and demand to speak to Craig Paulsen myself. I needed to be in a room alone with him to get him to open up.

Before I could get shot down again, my laptop buzzed with an incoming call from Gwen. I slid the laptop closer to the edge of the desk and accepted the video call. "Hey, what's up? I thought you were working with Diana and the others."

"I can write code in my sleep. We have the cyber stuff covered for the laser, don't worry." She gave me a smile that was most definitely forced. "My grandfather asked me to work on something else, which is why the call now."

I sat taller from my slumped position, unsettled by the news the Secretary of Defense had tasked her to do something and hadn't clued us in on it.

"Sharing my screen with you now." She replaced herself with the view of her laptop. "I was able to trace the source of a wire transfer to an account in the Caymans for Jared Felsely. The money was deposited at the same time he went MIA."

"Of course," I grumbled. "Someone's setting him up."

"Oh, it gets way more interesting." She pulled up photos of two people, then added a split screen of a clip from my personal footage from Amsterdam, pausing the camera right at the point when Diana and Bahar had been talking about time travel.

I had to squeeze the chair arms so I didn't lose my shit all over again, remembering the bastard who struck Diana, knocking her out. "I recognize the one photo. That's Diana's colleague from the fire, Bahar. Who's the guy, and why is my footage on screen?"

"That's Bahar's brother. He's in cybersecurity in Turkey. Like the best of the best in cyber. He wasn't on my suspect list of hackers who could've been connected to this, because he's not a hacker."

I pushed away from the desk and stood, not liking where this was going. "Not only is he capable of pulling off all the cyber stuff, he's also tied to the lab because of his sister. And you're about to tell me you traced the origins of that wire transfer to Turkey."

"Exactly. Two hours ago, Natasha let me know the CIA

intercepted 'chatter' about Deniz and his possible involvement to help take down a 'multi-government' project." Her air quotes suggested we were on the same page in not believing any of this garbage.

I set my hands on the desk, hanging my head in frustration. "Let me guess, since Bahar left the lab right before the attack, and we never see her on screen again after that, she was also an insider and working with her brother."

"And our bad guys in charge are tying up loose ends, which is why she's dead. And why the CIA believes her brother will be targeted next, if he hasn't been eliminated already."

"Please tell me you're calling to let me know your grandfather doesn't believe this bullshit. That he's aware someone's baiting us to Turkey, setting a bear trap for us to step in." Pushing away from the desk, I locked my arms over my chest. "Either that, or they set up this lead to direct us where they *want* us to look, get us off their backs and also off Craig Paulsen's."

"My grandfather ran all of this over with Bravo, and they're with you on this. They believe Bahar and her brother, Deniz, are innocent. They think they're being set up, and, as you mentioned, if we go there, we'll find the evidence these dickheads want us to find. Probably blame a terrorist group for all of this in hopes we wrap up the case and move on. This was just another one of their backup plans."

Thinking out loud, I shared, "Something tells me whoever's behind this isn't a head of state or one of America's main enemies." I shook my head. "I think our so-called puppet master may have military and war experience. They know our playbook. Not just because of their inside man at the White House."

Gwen switched the screen back so she was on camera again. "American military?"

I hated to believe that, but there were a lot of people from within our own country looking to destroy it. "Possibly even someone from JSOC or who worked with them." Having once reported to the Joint Special Operations Command with Delta, something in my gut told me this had JSOC's fingerprints all over it. Well, someone who'd either been a Tier One operator themselves, or had a hand in directing Tier One operations for DEVGRU, Delta, and the like. "We know they have D.C. connections, too, which is how they pulled in Jared or Craig for help. It's going to be someone with a lot of money and influence. Ties to the Intelligence community given how they'd had that intel to blackmail Alyona at their fingertips. Craig wouldn't have access to that, let alone Jared."

"There's no way they're coordinating with the Chinese government?"

"Doubtful. Whoever's behind this is fine with us believing that, though, just like they want us to blame Bahar and her brother." *My guess is blame Jared, too, and Craig's the guilty one.* Each thought was clicking together in a way it hadn't before, and I suddenly knew why I was hitting a roadblock when searching through the belly of hell in the underground world. "You said Deniz never made it to your hacker suspect list because he's a legitimate cyber expert not a criminal." At her nod, I continued, "What if that's our problem now, too? What if we're looking in the wrong place?"

She stood, eyes going wide. "Bloody hell," she began, her English accent slipping through, "you're right. We need to come up with a suspect list of 'good' people who'd have a reason to take us down."

My focus fell to my phone, to thoughts of Diana. "Whoever we're dealing with is tied to Diana in some way. This is beyond Craig, Jared, or her parents. This is someone who Diana must personally know, and they're confident she can not only stop their plan to attack us, but also identify them."

"Then why not kill her? Why risk it? Why didn't they drop a Hellfire on you in Poland instead?" She lifted her hand in apology. "I mean, glad they didn't, but . . ."

Sifting through my memories, I muttered, "Andrew Cutter went to great lengths to keep Jesse's sister alive even though she could've been the end of him. The psycho was in love with her. So much so he manipulated Rebecca and destroyed her life just to distract Rory from finding out he was The Italian."

"And as a byproduct, Rory wound up taking out Andrew's competition for him, which then led to Rebecca's death." She frowned as if regretting having to mention that detail, one which I knew all too well. "But are you saying whoever's behind this is keeping Diana alive because they care about her in their own sick and twisted way, like Andrew did for Rory?"

"Fuck, I don't know. Maybe?" I dropped back into my desk chair. *Is it Craig? Does he love Diana? Has he been stalking her?* How would I have missed the fact she had a stalker while I'd been doing the same? *No, that doesn't add up.* "I need to think." Gripping my temples, I asked, "Just tell me what the President's planning to do with this intel about Bahar's brother?"

"He's about to reroute Bravo from Scotland to Turkey. They're hoping they can intercept whoever will come after Deniz. Well, that's assuming he's still alive. At the moment,

Deniz is their only lead, whether it was planted for us to find or not."

"You said the hackers you've been tracking have a signature or something like that." I dropped my hand to my lap. "Was the wire transfer a match to the other hacks?"

"Yeah, and my guess is the hacker went to Turkey and completed the transfer there in order to set up Deniz and lead us to Istanbul."

"Then, throw in the bullshit chatter the CIA suddenly intercepted . . ."

"I'm going back to the drawing board of hackers who could actually pull this off. Based on our conversation, maybe he or she's also a legitimate cyber expert with no priors in hacking, which is why I'm struggling to pinpoint who's behind this."

"Because they're also not a known criminal." I turned at the subtle sound of shuffling behind me to see Gray and Griffin in the doorway, hanging back. "I have to go." I motioned for the guys to join me. "Thanks for the heads-up. Good work. Keep me posted."

"Oh, and, Carter?"

"Yeah?"

"I really like Diana," she said just before ending the call. I had to assume that was her way of letting me know she'd "read the room" at some point and figured out I had feelings for Diana. That was also probably Gwen's way of letting me know she was happy for me.

Now for me not to fuck everything up to actually be happy.

"I'm guessing you heard the same thing my dad just told us. Bravo's spinning up, heading to Turkey," Gray said.

I shut the laptop. "Yeah, to chase false leads."

"Maybe they'll turn something up," Griffin suggested,

perhaps trying to be the voice of optimism.

Gray shot him a puzzled look, as shocked as I was at his words. "You mean find intel suggesting a terrorist group was behind this?" he asked him. "Maybe drag us into a new war because of it?"

"If it's the Chinese government, they could be hoping to distract us in the Middle East from something—"

"Speaking of China," I cut Griffin off at the sight of Zoey's name popping up on my phone. "Hopefully Zoey has news." I stood, placing the call on speaker as Griffin and Gray rounded the desk to come closer. "Tell me you have something."

"Hey, Camila's here with me, and we managed to dig up some intel that I'd never have uncovered without her, um, abilities," Zoey began, her English accent muffled a bit from background noise. A subway station, maybe? "It's not the Chinese. Although they have a working EMP weapon, they're not the ones who plan to use it. In fact, their top-secret research center was sabotaged back in July. Their lead scientists were killed and all of their work around the EMP weapon was stolen. They'd been trying to keep it under wraps, not wanting anyone to know they had a breach."

I took a step back, bumping into the desk chair as I dragged a hand along my jawline. "So, shortly after America and eleven other countries agreed to work together on a project that was motivated by the fact China was on the verge of having an EMP weapon, China's secure lab was hit." Intel had been wrong. *Not* on the verge, because the Chinese already had a working weapon.

"Not exactly a coincidence." Griffin set his hands on the desk, his wedding band drawing my eye, a reminder of what I'd done with mine only last night.

I shook that thought free and focused. "Based on what

you know," I asked Zoey, "if someone had the weapon design plans since July, is that enough time to assemble the weapon and the reactor needed for it?"

"To build the weapon itself, yes. The reactor to charge it? No," Camila answered. "But if they had access to an existing nuclear reactor . . ." She let me connect the obvious dots. "And guess which country has the most nuclear reactors in the world."

My hands went to my hips as I cursed and answered, "Us."

"They're going to use our own reactor against us." Gray went for his phone, already on the move to call his father with the update.

"What do you want me to do now?" Camila asked. "Zoey's being ordered back to London. I'd come to you, but I don't want to run the risk of someone following me to your location."

"Stick with Zoey for now. Head to London with her. I'll be in touch when we know something." We exchanged a few more words before we ended the call and I chucked the phone on the desk. After letting the news sink in, I locked on to Griffin and went over the conversation I'd had with Gwen, hoping he'd have fresh insight on the matter.

Griffin folded his arms, quietly thinking, and I gave him the time to do it. "We should let whoever's really behind this think we've fallen for whatever bogus lead they give us in Turkey," he finally said. "Otherwise, these pricks may switch to the emergency part of PACE and move up their timeline on an attack before Diana and the others can finish their work."

He had a point, but we couldn't leave Scotland yet. Diana had work to finish, and I'd never let her step foot in D.C. until I knew it was safe. "Are you suggesting we let them think we're bringing Diana home?"

"Key word, *think.*"

I could get on board with a diversion plan. "Yeah, okay. In the meantime, we need to rethink our suspect list while we wait for word from Bravo."

"And are we still not letting Diana know her friends are dead?" he asked. His gaze abruptly shot behind me toward the door, and he winced.

Damnit. Had Diana just shown up at the worst possible time? I slowly turned to see her standing there, staring at me with narrowed eyes and lips parted.

"What do you mean they're dead? Who, exactly?" She removed her glasses, remaining in the doorway.

"I'll give you a minute," Griffin said, and Diana quietly stepped aside so he could leave the two of us alone.

As much as I wanted to go to her, I remained a block of unmalleable wood, fixed behind the oak desk, my heartbeat pulsing in my ears.

"Carter?" She chewed on her lip, keeping her distance while gripping her glasses to the point I was worried she'd break them.

"There was a fire. Three bodies were found. They were killed prior to the fire. Bonnie's, William's, and Bahar's remains were found here in Edinburgh. Pierce also died in a car explosion in Belgium," I spat out the details like bullet points, wishing that'd make the news less horrific somehow.

She let go of the glasses and dropped to her knees, her hands covering her face as she leaned forward, her body crumpling in grief.

I circled the desk to get to her, telling her the most inadequate words on the planet. "I'm so sorry." I crouched before her, urging her to sit upright, but she didn't move.

"Did you just find out today?" The fact she'd yet to look at me . . .

"Last night I learned there were three unidentified bodies pulled from a fire, with evidence pointing toward it more than likely being your colleagues," I admitted. The full weight of the world slammed down on me when she finally did push back to sit on her heels, eyes meeting mine.

"That's what you were afraid to tell me last night." The words came out so small, and how could I not read between the lines and assume she was upset with me for making love to her knowing there was a chance her friends were dead? Upset that I'd withheld that information instead of giving her time to prepare for the news.

I closed my eyes and surrendered the truth. My *yes* came out like a heavy breath. I was going to lose her. Because instead of being a thoughtful human and trusting her with the information, I was a selfish prick who took what I wanted because she'd offered it to me on a silver platter. I always fucked up, didn't I? It was inevitable. "Positive IDs were made this morning."

Tears streamed down her cheeks, and with a trembling hand, she picked up her glasses. "I just, um, need some time to be alone. To process this."

Assuming she didn't want me touching her, I let her stand on her own, and it took all my restraint not to draw her into my arms and console her.

Glasses back on, a hand to her abdomen, she went to the door.

Seeing her so broken and not being able to fix it was going to shred me. "I'm so sorry, Diana. For their loss." I swallowed. "For the fact I let last night . . ." She went still by the doorway as I left my thought unfinished, finding it too hard to say out loud. "How do I fix this?"

"You can't fix it," she cried, a quick and painful glance back at me. "They're dead."

59

CARTER

I'D BE LYING IF I SAID I HADN'T CONSIDERED CHECKING IN ON Diana over the security cameras at the property. But the last thing she needed from me was an invasion of her privacy, so I'd behaved.

I'd also kept my distance the last twelve hours like I figured she wanted me to do. I'd made sure Oliver had delivered her lunch and dinner. He said she'd refused to eat both meals, and he wasn't open to getting socked in the jaw for trying to force-feed her.

When Oliver had let me know he'd witnessed her blinking back tears while staring at a mess of equations on her whiteboard, I nearly ran to the lab to sweep her into my arms.

She had to be feeling remorseful that she'd lived while others had died. To make it worse, it'd be painfully clear to her their lives had less value than hers to the monsters behind this. And she'd hate herself for that, too. Maybe even blame their deaths on the fact we'd saved her.

This woman was too sensitive and caring, and I knew

545

how much of a struggle it must've been to compartmentalize today. To shut down her emotions and work. Did she panic clean and panic shower when upset? Yeah. But this was different. She couldn't panic think her way out of this situation.

She wasn't me. She wouldn't be consumed by the need for justice to push her on. Instead, she'd be consumed by *guilt*. Guilt was something I knew and lived every day, and I didn't want her feeling an ounce of it, especially not with everything she was dealing with.

Lost to my thoughts, I wasn't sure how long Oliver had been standing in the doorway of the office, holding his bum shoulder in the sling. I leaned back in the chair, wishing it was Diana there instead. "What's up?"

He tipped his head, a request to come in, and I motioned for him to sit.

While waiting for him to drop down in front of the desk, I checked the time on my watch. 23:00. It'd been nearly twenty-four hours since I'd first made love with Diana, and now it'd been almost twelve hours since she'd uttered a word to me.

"Hear something from Bravo?" I asked him. I figured Gray would've been the one to share that news, so I wasn't shocked to see him shake his head no.

Bahar's brother, Deniz, had gone missing before Bravo arrived in Istanbul, so they were now working to locate him. To follow the trail of breadcrumbs that'd been left for us to find.

"To be honest, I was just checking on you." He cleared his throat. "Per Diana's instructions."

I gripped the chair arms at his words—at the hope he'd just given me. "She did, did she?"

"Never thought my job would have me feeling like a kid stuck going back and forth between their parents." A smile cut across his lips. "No offense."

"A little taken." At the realization my death grip on the chair arms was dangerously close to snapping them off, I let go and clasped my hands on my lap. "Does she know everything now? Did Gray or Griffin fill her in? Does she know Bahar's brother may be dead, too?"

Oliver nodded. "She took it as you'd expect."

Horribly. More guilt.

"So, what am I telling her? That Dad is good? Not to worry?"

Dad, huh? Thank God that, despite all of Diana's father's faults, she didn't seem to have any underlying daddy issues. I wasn't sure if I could handle that given our age gap.

I'd had a great relationship with my dad, but when it came to . . .

Chills painted my skin in a thick coat as I put together issues I'd never realized I'd had with my mother. At forty-five, was it all just clicking now?

I brushed away the thoughts. There'd be time for me to psychoanalyze my past relationships later. Like when I didn't need to fully focus on the mission. I was having enough trouble with the present distractions in my life.

"I'm not good. All the worrying," I said under my breath, remembering Oliver's questions.

"Was that sarcasm?" Oliver grinned. "But you really aren't good, huh?" His smile vanished, replaced with a serious look I rarely saw him sport. "Shit, I'm sorry." He held up his palm. "How can I help?"

"Just make sure Diana gets to sleep within a few hours and that Dallas is with her. Tell her I won't be joining her."

An unpleasant image popped into my head, and I added, "No need to personally tuck her into bed."

"I'm not even going to respond to that," he muttered, his words barely cutting through my thoughts, which were all centered around Diana.

If she needed space, and I couldn't hold her in my arms tonight, I had every intention of locking myself in this office, trying to ignore the tick-tock sound from the wall clock while I worked on finding who was behind this, staying awake until my eyes bled if it took that long.

I glanced at that clock now. Tick. *Fucking.* Tock. I'd always loved time and clocks, and now I was on the verge of taking one from the wall and sending it to join my wedding band.

"You, uh, sure you don't want help with something?" Oliver stood, concern etched between his brows. The man knew what it was like to lose a loved one, he just hid his pain behind humor, and I hid mine in a much different way.

"I need to figure out who's behind this. It has to be someone connected to Diana in a way I've missed," I admitted. "Someone who truly knows her." I thought back to the months of "checking in" on Diana, cataloging in my head every interaction she'd had and with whom during that time frame. "Not just knew her from the outside." Like how I'd learned about her. "But someone who has an inside . . ." My words trailed off as a name came to mind. A name that'd fit. And they were tied to everyone, including Rebecca.

The truth had been staring me in the face the whole fucking time. We had most of the story right, we'd just been missing this one piece. But like hell would I bring this up to Diana, throw out these kinds of allegations, before I had more evidence.

"What is it?" Oliver asked as I reached for my phone, standing at the same time as I did.

My thoughts were racing. Memories triggered. Pulling and tugging at every corner of my mind. Peeling open to reveal the truth. "I have to talk to Diana's father," I rushed out. "Now."

60

DIANA

I'd TOSSED. TURNED. CRIED. THEN REPEATED THE PROCESS, losing track of time as I'd tried to, so far, unsuccessfully fall asleep.

Dallas had been cuddled up next to me for a bit, offering me comfort, but eventually, he'd grown too exhausted to stay awake, and he was now curled up by my feet. As much as I loved having him there, it was Carter I needed. I hadn't expected him to keep his distance for this long, but maybe he was waiting on me to let him know I was ready to talk? *Patient with me.*

Curious if the sun would be rising soon with how long I'd been up there, I rolled to my side and checked the time on my phone. Was it really almost five thirty in the morning? That left me less than two hours before I had to get back to work. I would consider giving up on sleep, but this was the only chance I had to grieve.

I hadn't given myself a chance to mourn anyone's loss while working earlier. Anytime I'd found myself drifting into the state of a breakdown, which would've been accompanied by an ugly cry, I'd pulled myself together. By some miracle,

I'd done it. I'd maxed out on my ability to remain strong, though, and the guilt and pain was finally hitting hard. Floodgates had opened, and they didn't seem to want to close.

Bahar, William, and Bonnie were gone. Pierce, too. But if he'd betrayed us, resulting in their deaths, then screw him. Screw him all the way to Hell where I hoped he was now.

Ignoring the tears falling again, I opened up my last text thread with Carter. We'd only exchanged pictures so far. My heart skipped into my throat as I took a chance he might also be awake, and texted him.

> Me: If you're still up like me, any chance I could ask you my three questions to help me fall asleep?

At the immediate sight of three dots bouncing that indicated he was typing, I nervously stared at the screen.

> Carter: You still want to know about me?

Cue more tears. They fell onto my screen at the anguished tone I could hear even through his writing. Why would he ever think I wouldn't?

> Me: Of course I do.

He started typing again, but then the bubbles stopped. He was as unsure as I was about how to navigate our way through this.

The last thing I expected was for him to text me a song from YouTube. It opened to one I'd never heard before. "Beautiful Things" by Benson Boone.

I listened to every lyric. To the message Carter was

expressing in the most amazing way—that he didn't want to lose me. Well, that made two of us. I never wanted to lose him either.

When the song came to an end, I sent him one simple message.

> Me: Come to me.

Teardrops splattered onto the screen, and my eyes were too blurry to see if he'd responded.

A minute later, the door slowly creaked open, and I was surprised Dallas didn't spring into action. It was still too dark to make out much, but I was pretty sure Dallas had lazily looked up, confirmed in the dark it was his dad, then went back to sleep.

The door closed, and I kept quiet as I waited for him with breathless anticipation.

The weight of the bed shifted, and I set aside my phone in time for his big, strong arms to envelop me.

"I got you," he whispered into my ear, shivers rolling over my skin as I broke down all over again and sobbed.

I turned to face him, hooking my leg with his to get as close to him as possible.

"Give it to me." His voice broke as he thumbed the tears away at my cheeks. "All of your pain," he begged, "please, let me take it from you. Let me hold on to it so you don't have to carry it."

Another harsh cry escaped from deep within my chest as I whispered, "Only if you let me take yours, too."

61

DIANA

I BLINKED, SLOWLY COMING TO, AND THE SIGHT BEFORE ME had me wondering if I was actually dreaming.

I did my best to scooch upright in the bed, setting my back to the headboard while drawing the comforter to my chest.

Carter was in the doorway, handsome as ever in his jeans and white tee, quietly studying me with a mug in hand.

Putting on my glasses, I checked the time and sputtered in horror that it was ten in the morning, "I slept in."

He shoved away from the door and strode in, his long legs carrying him my way. He set the mug on the nightstand like a peace offering and sat alongside me, resting his palm over my leg. I could feel the heat of his hand through the heavy layer of the comforter.

Why was he avoiding meeting my eyes? "You needed it."

Memories from yesterday, from crying into his arms hours ago, assaulted me hard and fast. I became a blubbering mess again, only feeling safe to be that way with him. I squeezed my eyes shut. "They're dead." An even deeper cry tore from my chest. "Why didn't Bahar become a vet instead, then she'd be alive?"

He pushed aside the comforter and pulled me against him, circling his arms around me to try and absorb my pain. He already had too much of his own, and yet here he was, shouldering mine, too.

"These things . . . when they happen to good people . . . they never make sense," he whispered, holding my head to his chest. "Anytime I lost someone while serving, I could never understand it. We were in a war, and even then, I denied the *whys* and the *hows*. It's human nature to feel that way."

The cycle of grief, and the loop would never close if I let it run on repeat. But I wasn't ready to close it yet, even if I had work to do.

For now, though, I had to make sure this incredible man, who'd only been trying to protect me, knew that my silence yesterday had nothing to do with him. I knew from his text he held a ton of guilt for not telling me, and I needed to fix that.

"I'm sorry I didn't tell you this earlier, but I—I'm not mad at you. And I—I don't regret making love. You better not be feeling bad about that either." A shiver shot up my spine, and he chased it away, rubbing soothing circles across my back.

I needed his eyes. To see him. For him to know he wouldn't lose me. So, I pulled myself together and leaned back.

"You made the right decision to not tell me right away. You didn't know for sure if they were really"—I fought back the surge of more tears—"gone."

He cupped my cheeks, wiping tears with his thumbs.

"You know me so well," I said around a hiccup.

"Maybe not enough, but I have plans to change that." He

kissed me so tenderly, gently calming the pain in my chest, walking me back from an anxiety attack.

"How?" I whispered, needing more of this, more of him, to help soothe my nerves. Find my way back to the mission to get justice for Bahar and the others.

"To start, after this is over, we have breakfast in bed every day," he murmured against my lips, "while I ask you every question I can think of. Then we'll spend the rest of the day together. Just us." He slanted his mouth over mine, kissing me. "Dallas can join us for some of that time, I suppose. Just not when I get to know your body more."

"Mmm. All that's missing from this dream world you're painting for us is dessert."

"I think I can arrange for that. Preferably while naked," he said in a deep voice that truly did have me feeling a moment of bliss in the midst of this chaos.

I set my hands over his. "Thank you for making me feel better. For being here for me."

"You sure you're not upset with me, though?" His nerves pushed through his words, and I hated how, accidentally or not, he thought my reaction yesterday had anything to do with him.

"I promise."

Lines cut across his forehead, guilt still heavy when there should have been none. "I should have been more focused on your needs than my own, and trusted you enough to share the entire truth. I highly doubt you'd have wanted to have sex knowing there was a chance Bahar and the others were dead."

I considered his words, then shook my head. "I've always known that was a possibility. I just chose not to believe it, or I'd snap. And you gave me exactly what I needed. To feel whole. To feel safe."

He locked eyes with me, a tear escaping his eye as he

finally came to terms with the fact I truly wasn't going anywhere, he wouldn't lose me.

"I will never wish any parts of my past away," I began, sniffling, "so as long as they involve you."

62

DIANA

FOUR DAYS HAD PASSED SINCE I'D LEARNED THE TRUTH about my friends' deaths, two since Bravo had confirmed Bahar's brother was also dead. As expected, a trail of evidence had led to a terrorist group, allegedly sponsored by Iran, being responsible for both the Amsterdam and Montana lab hits.

A lot had happened behind the scenes while I'd worked with my team.

Some good had come from the evidence planted for Bravo to find, including locating the rest of the hostages—those taken from both Amsterdam and Montana—alive. Their stories helped provide a convincing tale that it was the terrorist group who hit both labs. Exactly what the real bad guys wanted everyone to believe.

Bahar and the others died because they'd been unlucky enough to be grouped with me when they'd split everyone up before hauling us away from Amsterdam. It was my fault.

I reached for my coffee, noticing the tremble in my hand as I recalled my last moment with Bahar at the lab. She'd been on her way to get coffee, Elmo and Einstein mugs in hand. I was going to unravel all over again at the memory. It wasn't fair. *Life isn't fair.*

A teardrop fell into my coffee, which was more cream than anything else. Carter had obliged my sweet tooth the last few days. Despite being busy with a lead he was working, he always dropped by to check on me. And he always left me with a choice of two candy bars before walking back out the door. An Almond Joy or a Mounds bar. *Because sometimes you feel like a nut, and sometimes you don't.* My cry morphed into a small, sad laugh at that thought.

I swapped the coffee for one of the candy bars he'd placed next to me earlier. An Almond Joy was needed for sure.

Staring at my whiteboard, the numbers floating around like they had a tendency to do in 3D when I was both overtired and overthinking, I quietly ate the candy, thinking about Carter. About how he'd been my rock the last four days. All it took was a quick "I need you" text whenever I felt myself spiraling, and he dropped whatever he'd been doing to get to me.

He'd sit on the floor in the middle of the lab with me on his lap and hold me while I cried. No words needed to be exchanged.

Every night, he'd also let me ask him questions before I drifted off to sleep in his arms.

His mouth hadn't touched mine, though. Forehead kisses, which were highly underrated, yes. Hugs, of course. But we both knew if our mouths had touched at any point that week, we'd lose ourselves to desire. The world could be on fire and burning all around us, and we'd be too consumed by each other for the flames to consume us. Carter could so easily draw his cloak of immortality around me and shield me from everything. Everything except grief.

I missed his kiss, though. His skin against mine. The total state of calm and bliss we both had surrendered to when our bodies had been connected those few times earlier in the week.

Throwing away my wrapper, I was tempted to text him again. Even chance a kiss. Knowing he was close to solving the "who's behind it all" part of the equation, I decided to refrain and leave him be.

I rubbed my eyes beneath my glasses, trying to zip up my emotions. Mom had been doing it all week, even with her boyfriend still being blamed for treason and MIA, so I could do it, too.

"We're done!" I flinched at Mya's words, nearly dropping my glasses.

"You're good on the cyber end for the laser?"

"The calculations check out." Mya smiled, the first one I'd seen from her in days, and I managed a real one myself.

Her eager nod had my hand flying to my chest. Despite the news, the pressure was still there. It was solely on me to perform. "That's great."

"Hey, this is good news. We're close. Don't worry, you're almost there, too," she said, reading me well as she strode farther into my workspace.

I turned to the side, eyeing my work on the whiteboard. I'd yet to close the final gap needed to turn myth into reality, and I was a little terrified I'd oversold my abilities and wouldn't be able to deliver on my promise to stop the weapon.

"Listen," she began, arms folded and eyes on me, "we've been dealt a tough hand, and we're dealing with a formidable threat. We all know it's not really a terrorist group working for Iran. It was sure as hell also not the Iranians who sabotaged China's lab either. Whoever's behind this has gone through a lot of trouble to turn everyone in the world against each other so no one trusts one another, though."

"I thought we were focusing on the good news." A nervous laugh fell from my lips, and I cursed that coping mechanism.

She worked her lip between her teeth, appearing a bit stressed herself, despite trying to pull off optimistic.

"Election day is around the corner. Do you think we'll be able to stop who's behind this before we have to do a live test run to see if the laser truly works?"

"That's the plan." Mya stared at the whiteboard, combing her fingers through her hair.

From the looks of her dark roots, she was letting the blonde grow out. And what a thing for me to be thinking about, all things considered. My brain and the detours it took sometimes had me— "Detour," I sputtered, blinking quickly. "Holy shit, that's it."

I went back to the whiteboard, erased the last two numbers of my equation, murmuring my thoughts out loud as I worked through the problem. "The line won't be perfectly straight between two points like it is in a controlled setting." I closed my eyes, trying to visualize the curvature and math needed to bring theory to application. "With the earth's gravitational force . . . and when the electromagnetic pulse shoots out at that distance and speed . . ." I snapped my fingers. "That's it, I had the angle wrong. That's why the math wasn't mathing."

"Say what?" Mya said from over my shoulder.

"Just like when a sniper shoots from a long distance, you have to account for . . ." I kept going. Rambling away as if I were alone to my thoughts before enunciating the last few details with more clarity, "The number was off by three degrees. The laser will take the slightest detour." I did the math once more in my head, then checked it ten times over again on the whiteboard, then on the computer while Mya patiently waited for me. "I was off by three degrees." I spun around to face her, bringing my fists to my lips. "The laser will work."

"I have no idea what you just said other than the last part." She crushed me against her, my arms pinned between us as I caught sight of Carter and Dallas filling the doorway.

"Good news?" he asked, his tired eyes fixed on me. He may have been holding me while I slept at night, but I had a feeling he'd barely actually closed his eyes during that time.

"Your girl just figured out how to save the world," Mya said, pulling back to look directly at him. "Something about gravity and a detour, I don't know." She waved her hand in the air. "I'm going to tell the team. Would you like to do the honors and let POTUS know?" she asked me.

"No, I'm good, you can do it." I wanted to be alone with Carter so he could rip the Band-Aid of bad news off that I felt coming. Talk about counteracting the good with the bad, though. Story of our week.

Carter fixed his attention on Mya, giving her a go-ahead nod to alert the team, and she called out to Dallas to join her, giving us the room alone.

Carter closed the door and wasted no time getting to me. He pulled me into his arms, and I felt more than his gratitude in that hug. "I knew you could do it."

I allowed myself a few seconds to feel safe and at ease before asking him to share the news I knew would flip my world upside down again. "What do you know?"

"Who's behind this," he said in a low, gruff tone.

I eased back, hands to his chest to meet his eyes. "Who?"

His tense jaw strained as he revealed, "Your best friend's husband. Karl Novak."

63

DIANA

"KARL HATES YOU," I SAID IN PURE REFLEX AS THE ROOM started spinning.

Carter seized hold of my arms, recognizing I was about to fall. "I know he does, and I'm not sure how it took me so long to figure this out."

"He, um . . ." I worked my hand between us to rest it over my abdomen, the gnawing pain there definitely not from a lack of food. I was going to be sick.

"Sit down." He guided me over to my desk chair, kneeling in front of me as he guided me down to the seat. "I wanted to be certain before I shared my theory with you."

Karl Novak. Is it really possible? Based on what Sierra had revealed over the years, he definitely hated Carter. But did he hate the world and humanity, too? Why was he doing this? "I was with Sierra that night in June after I saw you at the office," I said, starting to piece things together. "Karl and Craig are friends. I'd assumed Pierce told Craig we'd spoken that day, then figured Karl told Craig where I was so he could talk to me."

"Assault you in the limo, you mean," he bit out, red-hot anger visibly flying up his throat into his face.

Was the truth in front of me all these years, and I just didn't see it?

He gave my hands a gentle squeeze, a way to ground both of us back to what we had to focus on. "It took me days to put everything together. I needed help on the cyber end of things, and help from a few people, like your dad and Sydney's father, to make sense of this."

You spoke to my dad? How in the world did that conversation go? My parents hated the man, and now they were working together behind the scenes?

"Tell me everything you know, and we'll work through this together. Okay?"

My eyes went wide at the first thought pinging to mind. "There's no way Sierra's part of this," I stated quickly, needing to set the record straight first.

"Gwen checked your personal emails. Voicemails, too. Sierra called and left you a message on Monday. An email on Tuesday. She thought it'd be best not to actually open the email or listen to the message, though. Sierra then called your mother yesterday, probably because you never got back to her."

"What'd Mom say?" *You talked to her one-on-one, too?*

"Given the lab hits are still classified, your mother lied and told her you were deep in a project and not allowed access to your phone. Sierra accepted that as the truth and ended the call."

"Sierra's on vacation." *Now I know why he took his family on such a long trip. He knew what was coming.* "Karl always takes her phone when they travel. He wants her to unplug, and he's also paranoid that people will track them when they're out of the country." I shook my head, trying to process what that meant. "Do you think he put her up to the emails? The calls? Is he going to hurt her because of me? I—I can't lose her, too. And she's a mom."

Carter held my hands even tighter, offering me as much comfort as he could to try and keep me from losing it.

"It's possible she's clueless. He may have given her the OK to talk to you, and so she reached out, but he did it with ulterior motives," he explained, and his words gave me some relief. "This could work to our advantage in drawing him out so we can find where he is. Gwen tracked Sierra's signal to the sky each time. They'd been flying, so that information is useless, and probably why he let Sierra call or email at those times."

"How are we using this to our advantage?"

"Gwen didn't listen to your voicemails, and she didn't open your emails, because we're assuming he's monitoring that. Karl knows you're with me, and he'll know I'd never let you check your personal messages."

"So, why'd he want her to call or email?"

He let go of a deep exhalation. "He's curious if POTUS took the bait about the terrorist group backed by Iran. He'd know I'd never let you check your messages if I thought you were still in danger."

"So if I do, he'll believe we really did fall for the bait."

He nodded. "Then once you open the messages, he'll pinpoint your location and come for you."

"And you'll be there waiting."

"Yes, but without you. I'll be the one opening those messages."

I still didn't understand why Karl was doing this, but we got a bit sidetracked by my focus on Sierra. Another detour. "Why the call to my mom, then?"

"Adds a layer of credibility and protection. If your best

friend couldn't get ahold of you and just went on her merry-fucking-way without following up with your loved ones, what kind of friend is that?"

"Right." I peeled one hand free from his grasp to remove my glasses, still unable to process all of this. "When are you going to D.C.?"

"Tomorrow. From there, we'll set the trap for Karl and his people."

I dropped my glasses on my lap at his words, at their intense and focused delivery. That was a moment Carter had been waiting for. The rip-Craig-apart one. "What about me?"

He let go of my other hand and returned my glasses to my face. "At this point, Karl must know we followed the lead to" —he cleared his throat—"your friends here. I can't keep you in Scotland while I'm gone, but I can't take you with me. You'll come to the airport with me tomorrow, and Gwen will manipulate the CCTV footage so it appears you're getting on the jet with me."

"Where will I actually be going?"

"We'll get to all that, I promise." He pushed up off the floor and stood, reminding me of the original plan before I'd been sidetracked by needing to clear my best friend's name of any wrongdoing. "Tell me what you know, and we'll go over everything from the beginning together."

"I don't know much." I sifted through my memories, squeezing my eyes closed, trying to concentrate and key in on anything important that might help. "Sierra's grandmother is friends with my mother, and my mother was close with the Barclays, and the Barclays were close with . . ." *Ohhh.* Opening my eyes, he offered a firm nod, clearly reading the direction of my thoughts. I'd dialed into the chain reaction of connections. "The Novaks." I stood, my right leg feeling a bit stiff, and I held my outer thigh, working at the knots rapidly developing everywhere.

"The Novaks were good friends with Rebecca's family. Had Karl not been in high school while Rebecca was in college, they probably would've arranged a union between their two powerful families by way of marriage." He kept his voice flat to get through this, and I reached for his arm, hoping to console him the way he'd been doing for me all week. "Gwen was able to curate a list of all the times the two families were ever publicly together. Like you said, they were close, and we have reason to believe the Novaks planned to meet with the Barclays that Christmas but—"

"Their plane went down." Chills skittered up my spine. I ignored them, working at the muscles in his arm instead of my leg, hoping to ease his tension as much as possible while he carried me through this conversation.

He'd been dealing with a walk down memory lane the last four days, confronting Rebecca's death all over again. I knew why he'd kept me out of it, but I wished he hadn't. So I could offer him hugs, candy, and comfort, too.

"Rebecca mentioned the Novaks a handful of times to me over the years, but nothing memorable from while she was alive. She also never said her parents' plans that Christmas involved anyone else. She would've brought that up had she known. And the Novaks didn't mention anything at the funeral either."

"A secret meeting, then?" So many secrets when it came to the Barclays, I couldn't keep up.

"Gwen found the flight details from the Novaks' personal jet. Same time frame and destination to the Alps that weekend of the crash. The Novaks had a property there in the mountains, and they sold it two weeks after the crash. It sounds like we're making a leap they'd planned to meet, but as the story unfolds, it seems much more likely to be true." He tipped his head toward the whiteboard. "Here's the part that gets a bit hard to follow. May be easier if I write it out?"

I followed his gaze to my messy board. Wild enough, it was still more organized than my chaotic thoughts. "If the news wasn't so horrible, watching you write on my whiteboard would probably be turning me on right now."

"I'll be sure to remember that for later." His smirk came and went so fast, I might have imagined it, the gravity of our situation tugging us both back to earth and reality.

I released his arm and went over and erased the half of the whiteboard that was only scribble. "All yours." I set aside the eraser and stepped back.

He pushed up his sleeves and got to work, creating a timeline with notes starting with Rebecca's parents dying.

Standing alongside him, I did my best to decipher his doctor-like handwriting, while also trying to ignore the vein popping in his forearm as he wrote. He started all the way back at his wedding, noting the attendance of the Novaks there, and hesitating for the briefest of moments as if not wanting to point out that detail to me. Not that I could be jealous or forget he'd been married. Rebecca was still very much at the center of both our lives, maybe more in mine than I'd ever realized before.

"Just noting that detail to show how far back the Novaks went with the Barclays." He'd spoken directly at the whiteboard, feeling the need to explain himself, but for some reason not wanting to look at me while he did. "I had Gwen check the guest list since I had no memory of them being there."

I set my hand on his back, letting him know as long as he was good, I was good.

He continued fleshing out details of any major

interactions the Barclays had with the Novaks over the years, stopping when he hit the year 2018.

He tapped the Expo at the date, and I read the words for him, sensing he needed an assist to get through this part of his past. "According to Susan Mackenzie, Rebecca received anonymous intel that her parents were murdered. Rebecca then shared the photos with Craig Paulsen for another opinion. Rebecca sold off all Barclay holdings except The Barclay Group. Susan said Rebecca wanted to focus on her father's dream of clean and sustainable energy and had concerns of an EMP weapon or solar storm threat." I took a breath and paused. "Evidence now points to Craig Paulsen first meeting with Karl Novak after Craig had spoken with Rebecca about the anonymous photos." *Wait, what?*

He set down the Expo and faced me. "Gwen confirmed that Karl Novak and Andrew Cutter were friends. Karl must've given Craig his name." Hanging his head, hands on his hips, he spelled it out for me. "Karl's why Rebecca is dead. He's why Craig set up the meeting between Rebecca and Andrew, which led to her death."

"Why would he do that?" I hooked my fingers through the empty belt loop of his jeans, urging him closer.

He lifted his head, letting go of a heavy breath. "To prevent Rebecca from finding out his family killed hers."

6 4

CARTER

"So, all that back-and-forth theorizing on the jet was right?"

All I could do was nod. Oliver had been right on the jet. I *had* missed these details back when searching for Rebecca's killer. "We should finish this with the others."

Only Falcon was still present on-site. Easton, Mason, and the others were prepping for the next steps. We'd be leaving tomorrow, but I needed my team's help to get through the rest of these details first. Sharing all of this with the woman I was falling for, having to dredge up memories tied to the woman I'd spent nearly half my life with . . . well, it was too fucking much, even for me.

"Yeah, um, of course. Let me take a photo of the equation to give to Sydney for the President's team."

That was an important detail I'd skipped over. Mya may have been letting POTUS know we'd been successful, but he needed the formula, too.

After Diana took a photo with her phone, she wordlessly threaded our fingers together, letting me lead the way.

Once in our makeshift command center, Sydney was the first to approach. "Congrats on coming up with the formula."

I let go of Diana so she could take the moment she deserved to celebrate something positive.

"Thank you, and thank you on the cyber side." Diana hugged Sydney and accepted a few more congratulatory words from the others. "We make a great team."

Diana gave Sydney her phone, showing her the screenshot of the equation from the whiteboard. "If you want to get that to POTUS's people, they should know what to do with it. I can walk them through everything when we're done here just to be sure."

My genius girl. Thank fuck for her in so many ways.

"On it." Sydney cut away from the group, leaving the room to make the call to the President.

"I'm still in the process of filling her in on the Novaks." I was addressing the entire team, but my eyes stayed on Griffin, a silent signal I needed help. I wasn't so great at verbalizing the need for it, but he knew me well enough to pick up the slack.

"How far'd you make it in the timeline?" Griffin asked, easily reading between the lines. He picked up the yellow legal pad with all of our notes and the timeline and began thumbing through the pages after I recapped what I'd already told Diana.

"So, you really think the Novaks had Rebecca's parents killed?" Diana asked, sounding a bit skeptical. "And then to hide that truth, they set Rebecca on a collision course with Andrew Cutter to sever any ties to her death?"

"We do," Griffin answered.

"But who sent Rebecca the tip?" Diana abruptly turned toward me, her mouth rounding as it all clicked for her. "Wait, that means your job isn't why she died."

I'm not the reason, no. It didn't change the fact she was gone, and I hadn't been able to save her, but she wasn't targeted because of me. All I could do was nod, the words caught somewhere between *Fuck this* and *I'm done.*

I was so tired and exhausted of years and years of this uncertainty and chaos since Rebecca had died. Now that I knew what it was like not to be consumed by so much hate and anger, to feel what it was like to be on the other side with Diana, I just wanted out. I wanted the peace she gave me. I wanted it so damn much it hurt. The tightness in my chest made it hard to breathe, hard to move, hard to speak.

That little tremble in Diana's lip as she did her best to resist hugging me in front of my colleagues, sent me over the edge. I reached for her wrist and gently pulled her to me, nearly crushing her against me as I wrapped her up in my arms.

Dallas beelined to us, his tail wagging against us as I rested my chin on top of Diana's head.

As the rest of the team resumed packing up around us, I caught Griffin's eyes across the room and nodded, the gratitude I felt for my friend only eclipsed by the love I felt for the woman in my arms.

After allowing myself a few minutes to hold her, and get my shit together, we finally pulled apart.

Blotting the tears beneath her glasses with the bottom of her shirt, still caught up in the same emotions as I was, she whisper-cried, "What were we saying?"

I tapped a fist against my mouth, scanning the room for a save from someone. Anyone.

Mya beat Griffin to it. Her days in investigative journalism had been helpful. As Gwen and Natasha had combed the web to pull out possibly pertinent details to fill in the puzzle, Mya had been pivotal in organizing the information we'd received to make sense of it all. "Two days after Craig met with Karl—presumably to share the news someone tipped off Rebecca—the Novaks' head of security mysteriously died in a boating accident while on vacation at his lakeside home. I don't know why Ivan chose to do it, but we believe he leaked the evidence to Rebecca that his employer may have had a hand in her parents' crash. Who knows why."

"The Novaks would've taken him out sooner if they knew he had something that could connect them to the crash. I'm assuming they considered him the guilty party after Craig gave Karl the heads-up about the anonymous photos," Oliver tacked on to Mya's explanation.

"After that, the Novaks distracted Rebecca by setting her in Andrew's path, which must have meant the Novaks were familiar with The Italian's true identity," Mya added. "They wanted to stop her from finding the truth, and possibly from also picking up where her father left off with his cold fusion dream."

Diana pivoted to Gray, as if drawing up a memory he'd shared previously. "Her father was the one making the most noise about clean energy back then, and he had the financial means to make cold fusion a priority. The Novaks wanted to stop her from being successful the way they'd stopped her dad."

"They stopped everything in its tracks for a long time, yet again," I said under my breath, and Diana turned her attention back on me. "Then the project was kicked off this summer because of the intel about the Chinese having a weapon, but shrouded under the premise of pulling off cold fusion as a viable energy source."

"When in reality, I was working on both an EMP weapon and its countermeasure, and they had inside knowledge to know I was on the verge of solving both. They knew I was the closest in the world to making cold fusion possible as an energy source." She covered her mouth as the responsibility settled in, and I refused to let her take that on.

I had her back in my arms again before she could say what I knew she was thinking. No other way around it, she wasn't confronting this alone. "This is not your fault."

"If I'd never accepted the job at Barclay, then maybe none of this would've happened," she cried into my chest. "Bahar would be alive. Bonnie. The world wouldn't be on the brink of chaos. And for what?"

"Jared pushed your mother into getting you to work with him so he could keep an eye on you. If not with him, then to work at Barclay where Pierce could watch over you," I explained the only thing that made sense. Jared was guilty, but so was Craig. Everyone was on my target list right now. "They've been pulling our strings for years. Both of ours." Diana's work in energy, and my marriage to Rebecca, placed us in the Novaks' crosshairs long ago.

"That's why Karl hates you? Tried to turn Sierra against you? So she'd try and turn me in that direction, too?" Diana sputtered, hands on my chest, peering up at me with glossy eyes. "She said he had footage of you killing people after Rebecca died. Warned her you were dangerous. He was trying to find you, wasn't he? Worried you could connect him to Andrew Cutter and the truth."

And I failed. Fucking hell, I couldn't let myself go there right now. Too much to deal with. "Yeah, and I'm confident that's why Karl smeared my name at parties, trying to convince people I was behind Rebecca's death, too." I'd heard he'd been tossing out rumors I murdered my wife, but so many others had as well. I never thought anything of it.

"When Karl learned you were in New York with me in

577

June, he wasn't just worried I'd told you about my work, he wanted a chance to get to you before you could upend their plans," Diana said as if putting more of the story together. All the pieces still didn't quite make a whole yet, though.

"The Novaks must've learned through Jared or Craig—maybe both—the President planned to join a project with eleven other countries. They had to try and control the narrative," Griffin said, joining in. "They made sure Barclay was chosen. They already had the pieces in place to manipulate it in a way that'd work for them. Insiders, including Karl marrying Sierra to keep a closer eye on Diana."

"Karl never served in the military," I added, "but he did have top-secret security clearance. Worked side by side with DEVGRU, outfitting them with the best of the best in weapons." Diana was nodding along, knowing all about DEVGRU given her dad had been a Teamguy. "I spoke with your father and confirmed he'd been meeting with the Novaks about defense contracts for the Pentagon at the time the first listening device was planted at his home. They'd even moved the meeting up by three weeks, which was odd, but given their relationship, he didn't think anything of it."

"They plotted and planned. Somehow sabotaged the lab in China after they completed their work, which means they have people on the ground there, too," Mya shared her thoughts.

"Their only fuckup in all this was never counting on the President to turn to Carter for help after the labs were hit," Oliver said.

Not to mention not knowing about my obsession with Diana.

"Wait." Diana abruptly took a step back. "What if this has nothing to do with the EMP weapon, just like those terrorists never really attacked the lab? It's another diversion to distract from their ulterior motives. They can't stop the inevitable—cold fusion as an energy source becoming reality—but they can control the narrative of how we view it."

I went to her. "What is it?"

She met my eyes and whispered, "What does an EMP weapon do? What would it do if used even on just one city?"

"Kill our power grid and make technology useless," Griffin answered somberly.

"And also," I began, understanding Diana's train of thought, "instill fear in people."

65

DIANA

CARTER DREW HIS HAND UP AND DOWN MY BACK WHILE continuing to stare at me as if we were the only two in the room.

"Why is a defense company so concerned with stopping cold fusion as an energy source? Isn't that what we should be asking ourselves?" Jesse spoke for the first time, and I peeked over at him as he continued to pack up weapons alongside Jack and Oliver.

"What if it wasn't just the Novaks meeting with the Barclays that Christmas of the crash?" Jack asked, gaze sweeping my way for a brief moment. "What if it was some bad-guy super club? A bunch of rich dicks—no offense, Carter—that work together in different sectors of society to influence their interests?"

I thought Carter might blow Jack off and tell him to stop watching so many movies. When he didn't, I started to worry he believed Jack was onto something. And what'd that mean for the future?

"The Barclays had energy covered. Novaks, defense," Mya said, picking up Jack's train of thought rather than shooting down his idea as ridiculous. "But then Rebecca's father deviated from some set plan they had in place, pushing for clean energy before they were ready for it to happen."

"Cue the oil and gas industry as part of the secret meeting," Jack offered.

I volleyed my attention around the room, listening to their speculations, putting it all together. Recognizing that a group of people may have been pulling everyone's strings. Not one puppet master, but a team of them.

"So, if this group had the Barclays killed in one massive coverup, who knows what else they've done over the years," Oliver added.

"I mean, is it really that shocking that a bunch of billionaires are orchestrating everything from wars to stock market crashes for their own motives?" Mya folded her arms, peering around the room, the investigative reporter in her taking over. "Probably working hand in hand with spy agencies when their interests aligned. You know, overthrowing regimes and installing dictators when it benefited them."

"That means even if we take down Karl and his family, we're only scratching at the surface," I said, finally breaking my silence. "Stopping the Novaks might not stop the use of the EMP weapon on election day either."

"Election day, right," Mya whispered. "They're probably trying to change the outcome of the election, too. President Bennett's not a man who can be bought or controlled."

"It may take us time to round up every asshole involved," Carter began, eyes steady on me, "but your laser will stop their weapon. They won't win. No chaos. No fear. No more fucking division in this country. Enough is enough." His voice kicked up at that.

"And how do we do that?" Mya asked him.

"We start with finding out who has the most to gain from an attack," Carter said, holding my arms.

"Whoever's making bank off building secret bunkers around the world is one possibility. Throw in pharmaceutical companies, for a number of reasons," Jack tossed out. "The fact this group has disrupted alliances could mean something, too. They might even want us at war with Iran or China. Or back in Syria, based on who they're trying to pin this on as well."

"Also, we can rule out industries who'd take a financial hit if an EMP weapon is deployed. Electric vehicle companies would be a victim," Oliver added to Jack's list of theories.

"It's also possible these assholes wanted Diana alive for when they deemed the world was ready for cold fusion as an energy source. They'd hold all the cards, be the ones to control its delivery to the market and world stage, come out on top as heroes. Assuming Rebecca's father had once been part of this group, they had him there for a reason," Mya suggested.

It was the first thing that made sense about why they hadn't just killed me. It was always about more than trying to keep me from stopping their attack.

"Right, they're not opposed to cold fusion as energy one day. They're just not ready for it yet. Gotta milk the oil and gas cow a bit longer." Oliver's words earned him an eye roll from Mya.

"I'll get both Craig and Karl to talk. If Jared's still alive, him, too," Carter gritted out. "I'll get answers." He kept hold of me, but turned his attention toward the others in the room. "If we can determine who the hell else was going to be at that meeting the Barclays never made it to in 2008, we'll have our target list. Then we pick them off one by fucking one."

"Starting with Karl, and saving Sierra and her daughter

from him, right?" *I can't lose anyone else.* At Carter's nod, I couldn't help but ask, "Why can't the President send the FBI or our military after them? Why is this up to you all? I mean, I get why he came to your team in the first place, but with this kind of national security threat from within our own borders now on the table, can't the President get approval for military intervention?"

A few uneasy glances passed between his teammates before Gray took point. "Homeland and the CIA could put together the most exhaustive and thorough case against the Novaks, but Congress would still shut it down. We're talking about a company that supplies a third of our nation's weapons. Let's just say a lot of politicians would have a vested interest in not seeing a company like that tank."

"Not to mention the Novaks more than likely have a network of people in D.C. aside from the few traitors we've uncovered who'd run their mouths about the plan the second it was walked up the chain," Jack pointed out.

My shoulders slumped, wishing it wasn't true. Then again, I didn't want to believe anything I'd learned tonight was true, not just this. "You said I'm not really going home, we're just letting the bad guys think we fell for the trap the terrorists set. So, where are you sending me?"

"Ireland," he answered. "The McGregors will take care of you, keep you safe. Mya and Oliver will be joining you. Dallas, too."

It was somewhat comforting to have people I now knew with me, but I still hated leaving Carter's side. "Ireland. You're sure?"

"Given we aren't dealing with criminals behind this, but the alleged good guys—who probably have their own spot reserved there—the Montana bunker is likely compromised," Mya said before Carter could answer. "So, we can't go there."

The lines aren't even gray at this point. They're just gone, aren't they?

"The McGregors are like the Irish version of Carter," Oliver said, drawing my eyes. "Especially Holly McGregor's husband, Sebastian." He stroked his jaw with his good hand, a hint of humor in his tone as he added, "Hell, they even kind of look similar, now that I'm thinking about it. I suppose everyone has a doppelgänger." Still eyeing me, he added, "You and Gwen could be twins, minus the almost decade age difference."

"Is triplegänger a thing?" Jack asked, eyes shooting back and forth between Griffin and Carter. "Because Griffin also kind of looks like Carter."

I inwardly smiled at their ability to make jokes under the circumstances. I couldn't fault them for it. I could use the humor, too.

It felt like the tide was finally turning, the momentum shifting. As scary as it still was, it felt good to be finally going in that direction.

"I mean, they're not wrong," Mya remarked with a small smile. "Shocking, I know. But I think everyone has a double, or even a triple, out there. Have yet to meet mine, though."

"God help us all if there's ever more than one of you." Oliver winked, and she flicked her wrist. "Of course, maybe we all have a bad twin out there in the world, a yin to our yang. Well, in Mya's case . . ."

"Smart-ass." Mya whacked his chest with the back of her hand, still careful to avoid his bad shoulder, and he was quick to catch her wrist before she pulled her hand away.

While they remained locked in some type of exchange, I pulled my attention to Carter, finding his brows drawn, silently staring at the floor.

"Change of plans," Carter said a beat later, eyes back on me. "I'm not going to D.C."

"Okayyy," Mya said, dragging out the word while pulling her hand away from Oliver. "Care to enlighten us on the rest of that thought?"

"Your ridiculous back-and-forth nonsense got me thinking," Carter started, never losing sight of me, "and it reminded me that most people only know one side of me."

"Your devil face?" Jack piped up, his tone more serious than joking, though. "Ohhh shit," he added. "You're right. You'd never willingly fly Diana back to the States without knowing it's safe for her. Not even if the President told you to. Karl would know that about you, so if you were to return to the U.S., he'd realize you're trying to set your own trap."

Carter reached for my hand, drawing me closer to him as I asked, "What are you saying? What am I missing?"

"He'd take you somewhere off-the-grid. Somewhere no one would think to look for him," Mya answered. "Somewhere a man with Carter's reputation would be safe from both criminals and authorities. A place like—"

"The Sapphire Hotel," Carter finished for Mya, offering a familiar-sounding name.

Had it been discussed on the jet? Along with something about a fork? "And you're actually taking me to this place? Or are we just letting the Novaks think you are?"

Carter cut his eyes to me. "I'll never even have to make it to the hotel. Once our jet lands, the Novaks' mercenaries will do a vehicle interdiction to stop us before we get there." Why'd he sound okay with that plan? "You won't be with me, no. But they'll think you are."

"And if they still want me alive, they won't risk an aerial attack." *What if they change their minds, though? What if you dangle yourself as bait and die?!* "How will you convince them I'm with you? Security footage being altered at the airport doesn't seem like it'll cut it with who we're dealing with and how good they are at all this stuff, too." My free arm banded across my stomach, nausea returning.

"Your doppelgänger," Oliver said as it all clicked for him. "Gwen will play the role of you."

66

DIANA

THE SUN HAD YET TO RISE, AND WE'D BE LEAVING FOR THE airport that afternoon, but Carter had woken me up twenty minutes before my alarm and requested I dress in something warm. He'd helped me into his jacket before leading me downstairs and outside.

An old-school Land Rover Defender had been parked out front, and he'd been a gentleman, opening the passenger-side door for me as if we had all the time in the world.

And there we were, quietly driving along a dirt road on the property, our hands locked over the console, the quiet sounds of nature stirring to life to keep us company.

"Where are we going?" I finally asked, curiosity getting the best of me.

"I want a few minutes alone with you before we leave."

"I'd love more than just a few minutes." *I don't want you to go.* I didn't let those words escape, though, knowing if I asked him to stay with me, he'd probably do that. I couldn't be selfish. The country needed him.

When he kept quiet and didn't say more, I turned my attention to the window and back to thoughts of last night.

After getting hit by one shocking revelation after another, I'd spent the remainder of the evening working with the President's team Stateside. President Bennett had chosen and vetted a select group of people he personally vouched for to work with me.

Although, even if someone did betray his trust and leak the fact we had a countermeasure in place, I supposed it wouldn't really matter. Worst case, the bad guys didn't attack knowing they'd fail.

With the formula and cyber aspect of the plan complete, all that'd been left to do was to talk the President's staff through how to reconfigure their existing defense systems to block the electromagnetic pulse and divert it to space.

While I'd been on that call, Carter and his teammates had created multiple contingency plans for when they arrived in Zurich, which was the closest airport to this "bad guy" hotel.

The President was rerouting all of his off-the-books operatives, including Bravo Team, to Switzerland to assist Carter. But as a key part of the plan in not letting the Novaks believe we were onto them, the President made sure to get word leaked that JSOC was putting together a target package for an aerial strike in Syria to take out "those responsible" for the Amsterdam and Montana lab hits. The hope was the Novaks and their group would lower their guard if they believed POTUS was taking real action toward the false lead they'd planted.

"We've got this. One problem at a time," Carter had said when he'd noticed me spiraling last night. I wasn't just worried about the *what-ifs* when it came to his dangerous mission. What if I was wrong about the formula?

What if it was four degrees not three? I'd gone back over the math a hundred times last night, and the President's brightest in D.C. who were given access to the mission had as well. Ninety-seven percent chance of success, and three percent chance I was full of shit. I wished I liked my odds, but I was more of a "sure thing" kind of girl.

Carter slowed the Defender and I looked out the front window at a helicopter in front of us. If only we were there because he was taking me up for a romantic joy ride, surprising me with his ability to fly among his many other skills. I mean, at this point, the fact he couldn't leap tall buildings in a single bound was almost shocking.

Carter quietly proceeded to get out and open my door. Taking my hand, he helped me step down, then he grabbed a pile of blankets he must've stashed in the backseat before waking me. Maybe this was going to be a romantic something after all?

Could I silence the noise of this last week, and the fears of what was to come, for a few minutes? God, I hoped so. I needed it. I needed every second with him before we parted ways. Before he made himself bait for some psycho group of billionaires.

Setting the blankets on the hood, he zipped up my jacket, bundling me up. "Warm enough?"

"I'll be okay," I promised, and he tucked the blankets under his arm and escorted me over to the helicopter.

Setting one blanket down, he urged me to sit, then draped the second thick brown blanket over my shoulders. I'd expected him to join me, but instead, he went over to the bird and smoothed a hand along its dark blue frame. "My father's dream was to get his license and fly one of these." He turned toward me, setting his back to the helicopter, resting a hand on his leg as he studied me.

The sun was starting to make its debut, and nature continued to unfurl around us, coming to life.

Tightening the hold of the blanket, I patiently waited for him to go on, realizing he had something he needed to share.

A gentle breeze caught some of the strands of his hair as he continued to peer at me. Unlike my jacket, his leather one was open with the collar popped, revealing a white shirt partially tucked into the front, and a glimpse of his belt.

It felt like forever ago since he'd used that belt to stop me from fighting him when I'd been unsure if he was my hero or my enemy. Was that only a week ago? That memory led to thoughts of Bahar. And maybe William was a shitty boyfriend, but he didn't deserve death. Neither did Bonnie.

Worried I was about to lose myself to tears, I pulled my attention back to his face, searching for comfort. For strength to keep it together in the few precious moments we still had.

"I realized something while we've been here this week," he began, lifting his eyes from the ground, his espresso-brown irises locking on me, "and I feel like it's important I say it out loud. Share it with you, so I can move forward."

This felt like a big-deal moment, and my panic intensified. Was he sharing this because he was worried he may not make it home alive? With my words lodged in my throat, I only managed a nod.

"This isn't easy for me to tell you." He peered off to the side as if he could find answers or strength in the woods. "The day I got the tattoo on my back was also the same day I confronted the man I'd become. I'd spun out of control, and needed to find answers where I could, including my encounters with women. Sex stopped being about connections. It became about power, dominance, and release."

His words coaxed more chills, and neither the blanket nor his jacket could keep me warm at his admission.

"I realized I had to be in control going forward. To feel in power because"—he closed his eyes—"I'd given over almost all of the control in my marriage to Rebecca. So much so I'd wound up losing most of myself. I resented her while we were married. Blamed her for pushing me to make decisions I didn't agree with and for becoming someone I couldn't look at in the mirror. Seconds before she died, I told her over the phone I hated her." He'd sped through the rest, and I let the blanket fall, prepared to go to him.

Sensing my reaction, he opened his eyes and held up his palm, a request to wait and hear him out before I came to him. "I didn't realize until this week, until being with you, what it was like to be someone's equal. And Christ, it feels so fucking good."

Holy shit. My heart. I couldn't *not* go to him now. I nearly tripped trying to get to him, too, but he caught me as I launched myself forward, hurling myself against him. I buried my face against his chest, and he held on to me.

After a few minutes of just coexisting, he continued, "I finally figured out this week why I married a woman like Rebecca, a woman who was all wrong for me. I had issues with my mother, ones I never recognized before." His heartbeat pounded into my ear, and I knew this was probably one of the hardest conversions he'd ever had. "Growing up, my mother dictated everything that ever happened in our family, right down to not letting us have a dog. Dad would've named him Dallas." He paused for a moment, emotion choking him up. "The man was so in love with her, though, he let her walk all over him. He took up smoking, most likely to cope with the side effects that came with loving a woman like her, and lung cancer eventually stole him from the both of us."

I lifted my chin to peer up at him, and his eyes were once

again squeezed closed. "I'm so sorry," I whispered, a few of his tears hitting my face.

"My father had always been obsessed with time, worried he wouldn't have enough to do everything he'd hoped to do in life," he continued, his voice still strained, and if I could possibly squeeze him any tighter, I would've.

That's why the clock and time tattoos. It all makes sense now.

"My dad never did fly a helo. He let his fears of failing or crashing get into his head. Well, my mom's fears, her lack of belief in him, stopped him." He met my eyes this time and added, "I don't want my own fears and fucked-up past to stop me from being the only thing I've never truly been. At least, not until you."

I blinked back tears. "And that is?"

He reached between us, forcing me to step away, so he could draw my chin into his palm. "Happy."

I let the dam break, and he caught my wobbly lip and my tears with his mouth. Giving me his love in that kiss even more intensely than ever before.

"Diana?"

"Yeah?" I asked, breathless, still coming down from the high his touch always gave me. My heart was still breaking at his painful memories.

"I don't want to wait until the mission is over to tell you I love you."

His words skipped through my mind so fast it took my heart a second to catch up with my head.

Eyes back on mine, he cradled my face in his hands. "I want a future with you, and a life of making memories together to form our past." More tears slipped down his cheeks, and from such a strong, tough guy, it was just . . . God, my heart ached for him. "I want our kids to wake us up, bouncing on the bed. I want to cook breakfast together, and do all those normal things I never could do. I want that. All of that. With you." He lowered his forehead to mine. "I don't want time to slip by."

Searching for my voice, strangled by emotions, I finally pushed out, "I don't need more time to know what I want. I've been waiting thirteen years for you. I've been waiting for our time, and it's now." I set my hands on top of his as we remained locked in that position. "I love you," I whispered on a breath.

"Good," he choked out, then he let go of me and dropped to his knees, like he was bowing to me.

I quickly sank to the hard ground, collapsing along with him, reminding him, "Equals, remember?"

A sexy smile cut across his lips as he reached for my hand. "Yes, but in this case, I was going to ask you to marry me." He cupped my face between his big palms. "Patience when it comes to waiting to be with you is not something I have." He swallowed, and so did I. "So, what do you say?"

I nodded, the tears flying nonstop now, splattering over his hands. "Spend the rest of my life with you and have your children? Save the world somewhere in there, too?" I leaned in so our lips were close enough to create fusion. "That's a yes."

67

CARTER

Standing inside our private hangar at the airport that afternoon while we waited for Gwen's arrival, as well as Diana's Irish escorts, I peered over at Diana as she spoke with Mya. I couldn't help but question whether I'd fucked up that morning. Should I have waited to ask her until after this mission like I'd originally intended? Picked out a ring for her first, even though I knew she didn't care for jewelry?

I'd planned my proposal while pulling together the evidence against the Novaks. Thoughts of Diana being my wife one day had kept me from falling apart myself. I had no doubts I wanted to spend my life with her, but I didn't want her to second-guess if my proposal had come from a place of fear. That I'd asked her to marry me because I was worried I wouldn't survive the op.

Had I planned to drop before her and ask her to be my wife that morning? No, I'd wanted to offer her the fairy tale she deserved. But instead, my head took a backseat to my heart. I was too eager to tell her how I really felt, and I'd been unable to stop myself.

She said yes, I had to remind myself. *She doesn't think I'm crazy.*

"You good?" I glanced up at Jack as he joined me between our two jets, his voice tight but steady.

"Are you? You sure you want to go to Zurich when your wife is pregnant?" I closed one eye, trying to remember if I was supposed to know that piece of intel.

"Ah, so my man told you? I should've known." Jack locked his arms across his chest, taking in the view with me, including both Falcon and my old crew loading the jets in preparation to fly to Switzerland.

"He did. Say the word, and you go with Diana, Oliver, and Mya to Ireland. Hang low. Stay safe there so you make sure you make it back to your family."

What am I saying? We're all going to be good no matter what. We have no choice. I may have been forty-five, but with Diana in my life, I felt like I was just starting out. I had no intention of missing out on this second chance at life.

Jack moved in front of me, blocking out everyone around us, forcing me to give him my undivided attention. That was always hard to do when Diana was within the same room. "You won't let us down. I'm not worried. I learned long ago to trust you know what you're doing. Who knew this better plan would be a result of heckling you about how much you look like . . ." His words trailed off as he smiled at someone or something over my shoulder. "Speak of the devil. Well, the other devil."

"Sebastian Renaud here?" I pivoted to the side to see the door to the connecting hangar open. I trusted the man enough to know he'd never let anyone know he was in Scotland, let alone taking Diana safely back with him to Ireland. Otherwise, she'd never be leaving my side.

Jack checked his watch. "Right on time with Gwen," he

added as she trailed in behind the man who reminded me a bit of myself, both in his looks and his overall demeanor. We had the vigilante thing in common as well.

Whatever alias Gwen had cooked up to fly abroad overnight made her unrecognizable as herself, or Diana, which was the point. Fake tattoos on her arms. Piercings on her face. A red wig. Black fishnet tights.

"Goth chick, huh?" Jack joked.

I wrapped a hand over his shoulder before he could leave. "You will make it back to your wife," I confirmed in a steady voice. "I promise."

He stole a look back at me, nodded, then continued toward the others.

Introductions were being made between Sebastian and Diana. Gwen removed her wig and flung it over her arm as she went in for a hug instead of a handshake with my fiancée.

Fiancée. *Fuck.* What a gorgeous fucking word, second only to wife.

"Nice to finally meet my partner in crime in person," Gwen was saying as I made my approach.

There was still one more question I had to mention to Diana about my plans for this mission, and I wanted to be honest with her. No secrets between us. I only hoped she'd understand my request. And if she didn't, I'd adjust course. For her, I'd do anything.

Hands sliding into the pockets of my dress slacks, I stopped alongside Sebastian. We were both in all black, the look I'd grown accustomed to during my dark years. If I were to slip back into this person one more time to finish the mission, it was only fitting I dressed the part.

"Dominick." Renaud tipped his head instead of offering his hand.

"Renaud." I nodded back. "You still doing the whole not-killing thing because your wife prefers you not to?"

The side of his lip lifted as if trying to fight off a smile. "And are you still killing people with silverware?"

"When the occasion calls for it," I mumbled, still shocked I was heading back to the very place where I'd killed an assassin with a fork. My teammates couldn't seem to let me live that down, and apparently neither would anyone else. Although, this time we'd never actually make it to the hotel. No, we'd be making a detour. If all worked out, that side trip would take us to the Novaks themselves. "So?" I prompted, waiting for him to answer my not-so-joking question. I had to know if he'd kill if it meant protecting my fiancée.

"When the occasion calls for it," he echoed back, not hiding a devilish grin.

"Are we sure this is going to work?" I wasn't sure who Diana's question was for, but there was only one acceptable answer. And I could read it in the faces of everyone around me.

I turned toward her, prepared to steal her away for a quick goodbye before she was snuck out through the back exit along with Mya and Oliver. I'd planned to send Dallas with her, but if he wasn't seen getting off the jet with me in Zurich where we assumed the Novaks' people would be watching us, that could tip them off. They'd know I wouldn't leave him behind.

"It'll work," Gwen said, catching my eyes next. "Once we're in Zurich, and the Novaks think I'm you, my overbearing father will be waiting with a plan to slip me away before all hell breaks loose. He doesn't want to run the risk I'm in one of the vehicles heading to the hotel if these assholes change their minds and decide they'd rather have you dead than alive. He's not a fan of me being bait."

Diana's skin blanched, and Gwen winced at the way her

words negated her previous "this will work" statement.

"Thank you for doing this," Diana whispered to her instead of melting down.

"Hey, us girls have to stick together against these evil goliaths of the world." Gwen pulled out a pair of glasses from her purse and slipped them on. "I also have a mission of my own when this one is done. I can't find the hacker who's working with them, and if you don't figure out who the Novaks hired when shit goes down later, I'll make it my personal mission to hunt down that SOB."

"Your dad will love that," Gray said, not hiding his sarcasm.

"As much as you do, Uncle Gray?" Gwen poked back, and Gray rolled his eyes and motioned for us to get a move on.

I tipped my head to the side of the hangar. "I need a word with Diana before we part ways. Give me a minute." *Or two.*

Diana stepped away from Dallas clinging to her side and cut through the crowd of operators standing there to get to me. I set my hand on her back and walked her away from everyone for some privacy. We hadn't mentioned the engagement news yet, and we'd decided to wait until the mission was over to share, but there was someone who did know, and I decided to go ahead and reveal that fact now.

"I asked your dad for your hand in marriage two days ago," I said, nearly blurting my words like she had a tendency to do. Maybe that side of her was rubbing off on me, too.

Her hands slipped to my chest, and I drew my arms around her waist, needing to feel her. "You knew two days ago? This morning wasn't an out-of-nowhere moment?"

"I did know, but I'd planned to wait and couldn't," I confessed.

Her smile faded when she asked, "What'd my father say?

Bet that went over real well."

"It went as expected. He said no. Hung up on me. Then he called me back, remembered how much money I have and changed his mind. Then I hung up on him."

"I'm so sorry." I leaned in and kissed her pout away, and she moaned against my lips. "I'm marrying you," she murmured.

"You are." I met her eyes. "I will make it back, and you will be my wife."

"I love when you're bossy about these kinds of things."

My hands at her waist slipped farther down, close to her ass. "We'll have all the time in the world for me to be bossy in other ways, too." I had to remain optimistic and forward-thinking, no choice. Fuck the alternatives and the possibilities of not making it home. "I do have to ask you a favor before I leave."

My heart was going to break through my rib cage. Talk about waiting until the last minute to bring this up, but it was no easier than revealing my post-Rebecca pre-Diana bedroom proclivities to her.

"I, um, have a favor to ask, too. But you go first." There wasn't any hint of concern in her voice. She really did trust me, and I loved that.

"How about you first?" I didn't mind stalling a bit longer.

She worked her lip between her teeth for a moment before asking, "Can you please make sure you save Sierra and her daughter? I've already lost so many people, and I can't lose them, too."

Ah, fuck. My chest ached all over again for her loss. Her pain. "I won't leave without them," I reassured her. "If they're not with Karl, I'll find them. I won't let you down." And I meant that. Whatever she wanted, I'd rearrange the solar system to make it happen.

"Thank you." Total faith in me. Just like that.

All her faith in me started to truly have me believing in myself, too. In the man she saw before her.

"Your turn." She gave me a small nod to go ahead.

I exhaled, hoping to get through this fast. "You already know Camila's meeting us in Zurich. It'll be helpful if she can foresee potential obstacles so we don't—"

"Do the dying thing I refuse to accept as a remote chance in happening," she sputtered. "So glad she's your friend and on our side."

Me, too. "We need all the allies we can get, though. The Novaks might have their own private army. Given the number of men who were sent to Poland, I wouldn't be surprised if we're up against a hundred tonight." Based on the frown now sitting on her lips, maybe I'd been a little too candid with mission details.

"I get why Oliver isn't helping because of his shoulder, but why aren't you asking Sebastian and his Irish friends for an assist?"

Easy. "If I can't protect you personally, I need the only other motherfucker as intimidating as I am to do it." At least that garnered a smile.

"I guess I'll agree to that. I know if you're worried about my safety, you could lose focus."

Also very much correct. "I do have other backups, though. Like Zoey." I lifted one hand to drag it through my hair. "And Alyona wants payback against the Novaks for their bullshit toward her, so she's agreed to help, too. In fact, having her act as though she's checking into The Sapphire as well helps sell the fact we're truly going there."

"I'm not sure what the favor is you're trying to ask me." She gave me a small shrug, seemingly unaffected by my words.

"I don't think it's appropriate to work with women I've, well . . ."

Her mouth rounded, and she dropped a long, "Ohhhh." Her hands slipped to the back of my neck, and she held on while pushing up on her toes to draw us closer. "You're asking if I can handle you working with Zoey and Alyona?"

"I am." I looped my arms back around her waist, relieved she'd yet to pull away.

"I trust you," she said without hesitation, then set a quick kiss to my lips. "But I love you for being honest with me that they're joining."

"No secrets between us." Well, technically there was one. A mission detail I'd refrained from sharing—that I planned to get captured by the Novaks' men in the "ambush." Assuming I'd be kept alive for an interrogation, drones and a tracker would monitor my movements from there, and once at a final destination, all teams would advance and move in. I just had to survive until they arrived.

At that thought, I dug into my pocket for my cross while pressing my mouth to hers, trying to push away any negativity. "Hold on to this until I get back, will you?" I closed her hand around the heavy chain and crucifix and promised, "This is not a just-in-case thing." My brows slanted at her trembling lip, and I kept my hand on top of hers, squeezing a bit tighter. "Hey, look at me, angel."

She pulled her eyes up, unable to mask her nerves. "Are you sure you don't need this?"

I smiled and reminded her, "I have an angel on my back to protect me. Been carrying you around with me for years, remember?" Kissing her deeply, pouring every ounce of intention and promise into it, I whispered, "If I have your support, why would I ever need anything else?"

68
CARTER

KARL NOVAK CROUCHED BEFORE ME WHERE I WAS LAID OUT on the concrete, soaking wet after being hosed down. He fisted my hair, jerking my head up to look at him. "I've been searching for you for a long, long time. All it took was a woman to bring you to your knees." He snickered. "Get him back in the chair, then leave us alone to talk."

The former soldier, based on his tattoos, kicked me in the side. He'd taken turns beating me up with the other two men in the large, empty floor-to-ceiling concrete space. "You sure you want to be alone with him?"

I forced myself to smile, showing my mouth full of blood, letting Novak know he wouldn't be able to break me. "Yeah, you sure about that?"

The other two soldiers, and I used that term motherfucking loosely, hooked their arms under my armpits, dragging me across the wet concrete, creating a trail of my blood.

Novak reached into his pocket for a remote and killed the

cameras in the room. The fact he seemed to be treating this as a legitimate operation and an on-the-books interrogation of a suspect made me wonder if these other men actually thought they were "mercenaries for a just cause."

I spit out blood and thankfully no teeth, while the two men hauled me to my knees. They needed a third to get my dead weight onto the chair. I'd been stripped down to only my dress pants. *No shoes. No shirt. No problem.* Had my dark humor stayed as a thought, or did I say it out loud? I wasn't even sure.

Two men held me down in the chair while the third reworked the ropes to secure me, binding my wrists and ankles. This would've been the perfect time for an escape, but now that I finally had Novak there, I *let* them overpower me, anxious for a one-on-one with him. I needed answers, and he was the only one in the room who could provide them.

"Unless you want to bolt the chair to the concrete," I taunted, pushing the balls of my feet against the ground, tipping back the chair, "you're making it way too easy to get loose and kill your boss." I spat out more blood, letting the front chair legs fall back into place.

Novak pointed to the only door in the empty space, a quiet order for the others to leave.

From what I could gather, between when my jet had arrived in Zurich and now, I'd more than likely been taken to an underground bunker. Though I'd been drugged after we'd let his people ambush our SUVs en route to the hotel in Switzerland, I doubted the plane ride had been longer than four or five hours.

Thanks to Sydney's father and his new-age technology he'd provided Gwen before she'd joined us in Scotland, there was an undetectable tracker injected under my skin. A conspiracy theorist's wet dream. One day, people could be easily monitored and tracked without anyone knowing about it, all under the guise of what looked like a shot. The government's version of tagging sharks, then throwing them back into the ocean.

Did I agree with that? Abso-fucking-lutely not. Did I need it to save my ass now, knowing the government's eyes in the sky would've more than likely lost me at some point after the ambush in Switzerland? *Also*, abso-fucking-lutely.

Because it was still a highly classified prototype, unlike the kind of tracker that'd been planted in Diana's glasses, the Novaks weren't yet aware it existed.

"You've been a thorn in my family's side for too damn long," Novak cut to it once we were finally alone. That was what I wanted, but it was a stupid idea on his part. He began rolling up the sleeves of his black dress shirt, his voice menacing as he added, "This ends now."

I echoed back his last words, injecting sarcasm in my tone to screw with him. "You see, the thing about feuds is that I'd have to know I was even in one. Do you think I give a damn about you or your family? I barely remembered your name until this week." Men like him were usually arrogant and narcissistic, and I'd use that to my advantage to get in his head. Reverse interrogate the prick without him realizing it.

Novak loosened the knot of his black tie and rolled his shoulders back, preparing for whatever beatdown he'd planned.

I sized up my opponent as he slipped on brass knuckles, striding my way with his ice-blue eyes laser-focused on me. He flicked his skinny black tie over his shoulder as he stood before me, scrutinizing me right back.

"Wondering if you could take me in a fair fight, aren't you?"

He kept quiet and smiled, showcasing his flawless white

teeth. He could be the poster boy for a dental commercial or a Calvin Klein ad.

I wasn't one to judge a book by its cover and assume he couldn't hold his own because of his polished appearance. No, this man hit the gym. Probably practiced martial arts. Clearly knew his way around firearms. By my estimates, he had something to prove to both himself and his father. He was itching to see if his skills in a controlled setting would translate in the real world. The fact he'd been hunting me for years, and he finally had his chance at a face-to-face with me . . .

I had to remind myself why I was there, though. I needed intel about who else he worked with to protect both Diana and the mission. Killing him would have to come later.

Finally breaking the staring contest we had going on, he asked, "How are we going to do this, Dominick?"

"Hell, I was hoping you'd tell me." I spat out more blood and grinned.

He set his fist against his palm, eyes on my bare feet, which were wet from the cold shower his men had so politely given me for thirty minutes straight.

Novak abruptly struck me across the face, sending my cheek to the side, blood flying with it.

Biting down on my back teeth, I slowly swiveled my head to find his eyes and shot him a menacing glare. "Best you got?" He really had no clue how much pain I could tolerate. "Come on now, take the knuckles off, be a real man and strike me with your fist. Risk breaking your hand on my jaw."

"I'm not worried about my hand, Dominick." He eyed the brass knuckles. "Only interested in breaking your jaw," he added before striking me across the face, then sending a second strike to my abdomen, his speed and force confirming this man boxed on the side.

"Where's Diana? She wasn't in the car, but my men clocked her at the airport with you. Tell me, and I take the knuckles off."

"Why do you want her? To corner the market on cold fusion as energy? Or are you afraid she can stop an EMP weapon? I bet the Chinese would love to know your family was responsible for breaking into their research center." I smirked. "I have a feeling they wouldn't use brass knuckles when they tie you up."

Without hesitation, he hit me again. That time hard enough to knock most men unconscious. Searing, hot pain beneath my eye, as if my flesh had been split open, had my muscles locking tight to resist showing him he'd hurt me.

More blows to the stomach sent my chair skidding backward a good foot.

Coughing up blood, I spat it off to the side. I'd save spitting blood on people for the savages. Although, he had me on the verge of breaking free earlier than I'd prefer to hit him back.

"Why'd you have security cameras in Amsterdam? Were you trying to steal their work out from under them because you were upset about the takeover?"

So you don't know how I really feel about Diana. You think I want her for what she can do. For her work. Of course you do, because you think with your wallet. "Did Jared or Craig tell you that? Or are both working for you?"

His smile was the only answer I needed to know the truth. Yes to both.

"Where. Is. Diana? I won't ask you again."

"Good, don't ask. You should know by now I won't tell you." Shit, I had to rethink this. The fire-with-fire approach wasn't working. Time for a change in tactics. I had to get into his narcissistic head and peel back his arrogant layers so he'd tell me what I needed to know.

He struck me, and the chair fell backward. I tucked my chin in to avoid slamming my skull against the concrete.

"Brody! Jackson!" he hollered, and the door opened a moment later. "Get him back upright."

The two men came over, and one slipped in my blood, falling to his knee, as he tried to help the other guy place the chair back on its legs.

I brought my face close to one and headbutted him, unleashing the devil inside me that time, and the prick startled back, falling onto his ass that time.

"Get up, Brody. Stop embarrassing yourself. Go find Sierra and Jake," Novak ordered, slipping the brass into his pockets as the two men left, shutting the door behind them. "Where were we?" Novak shook his hand out at his side.

Brass knuckles or not, you hit me and it'll hurt you more than it does me. "We were just discussing the fact you're the reason Rebecca Barclay is dead." It was time to change the conversation away from Diana.

Novak's lips parted, the shock registering there and in his eyes. "The Italian killed your wife. You killed The Italian."

So, you have a man inside the CIA with high-level security clearance. Interesting. Not even Craig Paulsen, and definitely not Jared, knew that information. "You can cut the bullshit. You know Andrew Cutter was The Italian, which is why you set Rebecca on his path to get her off chasing leads about who killed her parents and why. You knew it'd lead back to your family."

His gaze flicked to the camera in the corner of the room, the only other object in there besides the chair beneath my ass.

"Your father's not watching. You turned off the cameras.

Will he be pissed he's not able to see the interrogation?" I made the leap and guessed. "He must not be here, or he'd have come and asked why your cameras are glitching. Maybe you can blame it on your hackers." Time to get in his head. Find his weakness. With any luck, desperate for his father's approval would be his. Men like him . . . yeah, not a stretch to make that assessment.

I rocked back on the hind legs of the chair again, hiding the fact I was working the rope free at my wrists. That fall to the ground had helped loosen the knots at both my wrists and ankles. Brody and Jackson were sure as hell never sailors.

"Let's recap, shall we?" Since he wasn't hitting me right now, and I was running on adrenaline to push through the pain in both my face and body, I went ahead and shared, "Back in 2008, your family, along with others, had the Barclays killed because they deviated from the plan. Rebecca's father pursued cold fusion as an energy source and made too much noise at the government level about the need for it. So, he was silenced. The crash was made to look like an accident."

This had Novak's attention, and his arms went dead at his sides.

"All was good until Ivan, your head of security, grew a guilty conscience, or maybe always had one but finally stumbled upon evidence about the crash, and he anonymously sent it to Rebecca. The byproduct of this was not only her trying to determine if her parents were murdered, but she became hyper-focused on picking up where her father left off." I let the chair legs thwack back to the ground. "Rebecca was close to Craig. She told him about the photos, and you set her on a path with Cutter, knowing he'd take her out for you. Keep both your hands clean of her death."

Novak approached me and dropped to one knee, resting his forearm across his thigh. "Who told you this?"

Rebecca didn't tell Craig she told Susan about the photos, did she? At least I wasn't the only one she kept some secrets from. She saved Susan's life.

"Not as untouchable as you think, are you? Those skeletons in your family's closet are about to come out. Diana stopping your planned attack, or working on cold fusion as energy, will be the least of your problems."

His light complexion became paler. He closed his eyes, and I could so easily free my wrists and circle my hands around his throat and strangle the life from him right then.

"Rebecca was never supposed to die." The words squeezed out so slowly, I almost believed him. When his blue eyes flashed open, maybe I even did.

He pushed back up, careful not to slip in my blood, then went for a 9mm at his back. Resting it at his side he went on, "Paulsen loved your wife. But you know that, too, don't you?"

The truth and the weapon meant I was now on borrowed time. He was going to tie up loose ends and search for Diana another way.

"So, remove the guilt from your chest the way your head of security tried to do before you had him killed in that boating accident. Absolve your sins." I did my best to shift my wrists and ankles around as subtly as possible to loosen the knots even more for when it was time to make my move.

"I have no sins. Everything I've done is for the greater good."

"Hey, whatever helps you sleep at night." I rocked back on the hind legs again, preparing for the moment I'd launch his way and spring into action. Unfortunately, I wouldn't be able to pry the information about the other members of the group from him. I'd have to find another way to get to the truth. One problem at a time.

"Andrew Cutter was only supposed to be a distraction from her pursuit of the truth about the crash. I didn't know at the time he was The Italian. I only knew his reputation to fuck D.C. socialites and blackmail them with photos. I didn't even care if Rebecca focused on cold fusion; I could deal with that later. The Collective didn't want Rebecca to die. We just needed her to stop looking into the crash."

The Collective? What was he saying?

"We'd saved Rebecca's father's seat at the table for her ever since he died. In fact, we'd been on the verge of asking Rebecca to join, and explain how she could help make the world better. And, of course, get richer."

Chills rolled over my skin, and my tension had my arms stretching out the rope at my back to the point my hands were now free.

"Someone from The Collective, *not* my head of security, didn't want that happening and leaked the photos to Rebecca, knowing what would happen if they did," he went on, closing the space between us. "I found out a little too late, which is unfortunate, I liked Ivan."

I kept my hands hidden, waiting for the truth before I attacked. "This other person dead, too, then?"

He shook his head, smiling. "Sometimes I wish I could kill my wife, but sadly, no, she's very much still alive." Believing he'd delivered a final crushing blow, he leaned in and brought his eyes level with mine. "How does it make you feel to know Diana's best friend is why your wife is dead?"

69

CARTER

THE MOMENT NOVAK AIMED HIS GLOCK AT ME, PREPARED TO take me out after the bomb he'd dropped, I freed my wrists and lunged for him. Knocking the pistol from his hand, it went flying across the concrete as I wrapped both of my hands around his throat, throwing my weight against him.

With my ankles still attached to the chair, we both went down. I landed on top of him in an awkward position, but I used the element of surprise to my advantage.

Pulling my hands free of his neck, I fisted his tie, clutched his hair, then jerked his head up, looping the tail of the tie around his throat, tugging like it was a collar.

Novak latched on to my arm, his hold slipping in my blood as he tried to save himself.

Without losing my hold of the tie, I kept my weight on top of him to prevent him from getting free, then bent my knees, taking the chair up into the air to free my ankles.

The chair fell onto both of us as Novak continued to squirm under me. Now that I wasn't tethered to a piece of furniture, I freed the tie around his throat and socked him across the jaw, hearing a distinct crack of bone.

I struck him harder the next time, my rage feeding off the memory of everything he'd done to turn so many lives upside down.

I reeled my fist back, preparing to send a hammer strike to his skull, but hesitated at the sight of his head falling limp to the side. Most of the blood he was wearing was probably my own, dropping down on him like rain.

Realizing hitting an unarmed, beaten man made me no better than him, I refrained from striking him again.

Shoving him to the ground, I slowly made my way back to my feet while he rolled to his side, holding his jaw and groaning.

The comforting sound of gunfire outside the room confirmed my team was on-site, but that also meant his people would be coming in to alert him to the breach.

Grabbing his Glock from the floor while clutching my side, I returned to where he was trying to sit up. I knelt behind him, dragged him upright, drew my forearm across his throat and positioned the weapon at his temple, waiting for the door to open.

Novak grabbed my forearm, his last pathetic attempt to fight me.

"I guess now you know who'd win in a fight when your opponent isn't tied up and unarmed," I hissed in his ear as the door opened.

I looked up to see Sierra and another man standing there. No sight of the three who'd taken turns torturing me for hours.

Sierra's eyes flashed to her husband, then back to me, and she quickly shut the door behind her and the man armed with an M4.

"I told you this was a trap," she bit out, pointing toward the man at my mercy, at my human shield. "You didn't listen.

You never listen. Just like I told you not to bring Rebecca into the fold. But, no, you were going to do it anyway." Her hands balled at her sides as war echoed all around us. "I never thought you'd become this man, Dominick. I thought you were weak to put up with Rebecca for so long." She gestured to the armed guy at her side to come closer, and I applied more pressure to Novak's throat, signaling for him to stop. "We should have killed you at her funeral when we had the chance."

I kept quiet. Let her talk. Answering questions I'd yet to ask but needed to know.

"You couldn't just leave well enough alone." Was she talking to me or her husband that time? Hell if I knew.

She glared at Novak. "You listened to Craig over me, your own wife."

"Just like you always listen to Jake instead of me. He is our daughter's real father, is he not?" Novak shot out, eyes on the other guy in there, identifying him by name.

Sierra didn't acknowledge his accusation, which I assumed to be true based on her obviously contentious relationship with her husband. "Craig wanted Rebecca for himself. He actually believed she'd leave you for him. Then he could marry her and finally get his chance to sit at the table, to learn who all the players were." Pointing at Novak while keeping her eyes on me, she went on, "What my idiot husband and Craig failed to understand is Rebecca would've stayed in an unhappy marriage rather than wear the mark of divorce as if it were a scarlet letter."

"That's all your grandmother's BS in your ear," Novak muttered, his words strained by my arm at his windpipe.

"Nothing matters now, does it? We're blown, and The Collective will kill us for it. Our family is now a loose end." Sierra opened her arms wide, and I hated she'd been in

Diana's life and for so long. Diana was sweet and trusting, and she'd never have seen through this woman.

"You blame me for Rebecca, but this is all your mess, too," Novak gritted out, and I loosened my arm a bit to better hear what he had to say. "If you'd let me kill Diana and the others, we wouldn't be in this position."

"You don't kill the best minds in science, not when they can be advantageous later." Sierra folded her arms. "Rebecca was no Diana. Her life was inconsequential. She didn't deserve a seat with The Collective. She'd have handled it like her father, and my grandmother and I were the only ones with the foresight to know that. The rest of you men thought with your dicks."

I sucked in a sharp breath, my heart pounding as I worked hard to let these two fight and reveal details for me, suppressing the urge to kill everyone and end this right then and there. I'd never killed a woman before, but fuck . . .

"You do know your wife wasn't only screwing Craig Paulsen, but my husband as well, right?" Sierra came a few steps closer, meeting my eyes as my arm started to slip from Novak's neck. "They shared her at the same time. She had a thing for dominance, and I guess she wasn't getting her needs met at home. Wouldn't get a divorce, but she'd let two men fuck both her holes at—"

"She's lying," Novak hissed when I was seconds away from crushing his windpipe, killing him. "It was only Craig she was screwing. My crude wife is clearly trying to goad you into killing me so she doesn't have to do it herself. God forbid she gets her own hands dirty."

"He's right, I do want him dead." She whipped out a 9mm she must've had tucked behind her back.

Realizing what was about to go down, I flung my weight to the side in one fast movement, breaking away just as she shot her husband. While she unloaded on him, I neutralized the other threat. A head shot, and Jake went down.

I placed Sierra in my line of sights next. No obstacles or weapons in the way, but I couldn't bring myself to shoot her.

She slowly lowered her pistol, her gaze falling to Jake as if only now realizing through her haze of hatred and anger he was also dead. "I bet Rebecca would've loved the man you are now, though," she murmured before pointing her Glock at me. She didn't appear to be mourning the loss of Jake either.

Sociopath. I shifted to my knees, preparing myself for the last thing I wanted to do. Kill Diana's best friend.

"You won't pull the trigger, will you? I can see it in your eyes. Some devil you turned out to be."

Her lips stretched, and she readied her aim, but the door flew open a moment later, distracting her. Alyona stood in the doorway, and Sierra spun her way.

"We need her alive," I hollered out just as she shot her.

Sierra returned fire, striking Alyona in the chest. She stumbled back into the doorway in shock, sending another round at Sierra before they both fell to the ground.

"Damnit." I shifted to my feet, unsure who to go to first. "Alyona," I hissed, sidestepping Sierra as blood began to pool around her body.

"I—I'm okay," Alyona whispered, scrambling to sit up. "Chest plate caught it," she told me as Zoey and Griffin came up behind her. Dallas rushed between his legs to get to me. He dropped by my side, waiting for a command to move.

"We got held up out there," Griffin remarked, joining us. "But we have to exfil now."

"We need to drag Sierra out, she might have answers." I went over to her, finding her eyes closed, head lolled to the side. Checking her neck, my shoulders fell. "No pulse."

"I'm sorry, I didn't mean to kill her," Alyona said as Zoey helped her stand.

"It's not your fault," I mumbled, patting Dallas's helmet, signaling to him to start moving.

"We have less than three minutes to get out of here before this whole place blows," Griffin announced, grabbing hold of my arm to redirect me.

"Someone remotely hacked an explosive device that was down here. We can't turn off the countdown," Zoey rushed out, coming to my other side as if worried I couldn't walk alone.

Maybe I couldn't? Shit.

No, that wasn't why I wasn't budging.

"Sierra's daughter," I said at the memory. "Is she here?"

"Wyatt found her," Griffin shared, jerking my arm to get a move on. "She's already above ground."

Relief swelled in my chest, and although the pain was catching up with me, I finally managed to get myself to move. I had a reason to survive. Someone to come home to. "Where are we?"

"Greenland. A bunker." As Griffin and Dallas led the way, Griffin added, "We have more good news," he said as we stepped around dead bodies while traversing narrow tunnel-like hallways. "Bahar, William, and Bonnie," he added without slowing down, "they're not dead."

DIANA

DUBLIN, IRELAND

Wrapped up in Carter's jacket, his cross heavy around my neck tucked under it, I shoved my hands into the warm pockets, sitting on the steps out back alongside Mya and Oliver at the sprawling estate.

We weren't at Sebastian and his wife's home, but one of his wife's family properties. They'd been kind and gracious hosts, helping distract me the best they could so I didn't succumb to my nerves.

Up until this morning, when I'd learned how the mission unfolded, I hadn't previously been clued in on one key part of their operation: Carter being taken as a hostage.

Yesterday, in Zurich, he'd allowed himself to be a Trojan horse, and the Novaks hadn't figured out we'd been onto them until it was too late.

I wasn't sure if the team was ready to call this mission success yet, regardless of what went down seven hours earlier in Greenland. Not with an unknown number of enemies in The Collective still out there, and no leads on their identities.

Mya and Oliver had reported that Carter and everyone on the right side of the fight had escaped without any major wounds. Then Mya dropped the news about Sierra on me, sending me spiraling.

After breaking into a sweat and throwing up, I'd curled up by the fire with Carter's jacket over my shoulders, pretending it was him hugging me. Half listening to her and Oliver go over the details of the mission as they knew them, I'd simultaneously run every encounter with Sierra through my mind, wondering how I'd let her deceive me for half my life.

When the room had gone quiet, Mya sat next to me on the floor.

"We met at one of the Barclays' parties back when I was still in high school," I'd recalled. *"We became fast friends. Chose to go to the same college and be roommates. That was all orchestrated from the beginning, wasn't it? My mom was an ambassador back then and close to Rebecca. Dad was Speaker of the House at the time with connections in Intelligence. That's why I was chosen."*

Peering back, I located where Sebastian stood with his wife, all of us waiting for Carter's arrival via helicopter.

Sebastian caught my eyes and offered a reassuring nod before I returned my attention on Mya at my side. She patted my jeaned thigh twice, probably her way of reminding me she was there if I needed her.

I was pretty sure I did, so I asked for the tenth time that day, "How could I let someone fool me like that? Has any choice I've ever made been my own?"

"Carter," Mya whispered. "That choice has always been yours. Him being in your life."

I closed my eyes, thinking back to all the times and people who'd tried to change my mind about him. Mya was right, and that gave me some small comfort.

At the sounds of blades chopping the air, I opened my eyes, searching out the helicopter like an actual beacon of hope. It wasn't in view yet, but he had to be getting closer.

"Too bad Alyona couldn't have left Sierra alive so we could question her," Oliver said as the bird finally came into view.

"Carter couldn't pull the trigger," Mya said, her tone soft, as if almost surprised at that fact.

Not me, he'd never take a woman's life, let alone someone who'd supposedly been my best friend. I knew he was really a softy beneath those complex layers of toughness.

"Someone had to do it," she continued, "but yeah, we have no leads about who these other members are now. Or how many of them there are."

Not only were Karl and Sierra, and everyone at the bunker, now dead, so were Karl's parents. Black ice sent their vehicle off a bridge, plunging into a river that morning. The "accident" claimed their lives.

Loose end after loose end wrapped up.

Craig Paulsen was still in custody, but surely he'd mysteriously die, too, before we could ever get anything from him. Jared was definitely not missing but dead, probably at the bottom of the Atlantic.

Samantha Byrne, Sierra's grandmother—assuming she'd been a member of The Collective, given Sierra's comments— had already died of old age. Surely, she'd have gone down with Sierra as well if not.

But the question still hung over all of us: would The Collective go forward with their attack? And, if so, would our countermeasures stop it?

Would they wait for election day? Move up the timetable? Move it back? They still had their fall guys, the terrorists in Syria financially backed by Iran, to blame for everything.

Did this Collective want me dead now? Was I a loose end? My parents? Carter?

What if Sierra was the real reason I'd been spared? Mya had told me Sierra mentioned keeping me alive because my mind would be useful one day, but she'd had a feeling Sierra may have grown attached to me a bit, too, and couldn't go through with murdering me.

There were far too many questions without answers, and if I thought about it all right now, I'd lose myself to panic.

"So, you said the rest of Falcon is heading back to the U.S., but what about the other teams? And Camila?" I swallowed, pushing my hands even deeper into my pockets as nerves continued fighting to take control.

Two people I opted not to ask about were Zoey and Alyona. I was thankful they'd both had Carter's back, and Alyona hadn't stabbed him in it, but I wasn't eager to invite them to family dinners in the future anytime soon.

"We have to assume the worst, that The Collective will go forward with an attack, blaming terrorists. They're probably confident taking out the Novaks kept their identities safe," Mya began. "So, all of our people in the D.C. area are taking their families outside the city and staying with them until after the election."

"Surprised neither Camila nor Elaina saw any of this coming," Oliver said. *Elaina?* Catching my eyes, reading my confusion, he explained, "One of the guys on Bravo, well, his daughter has visions like Camila. What Elaina can do is far more shocking than even Camila."

"Camila and Elaina both live in D.C., and they have a unique connection," Mya continued. "Camila's sticking with Elaina for now. She knows we've got Carter's back here."

"What if that means our countermeasure will work?" I

asked, hopeful. "If they're not seeing chaos and destruction in the future, maybe it's because we stop it?"

"I like the way you think. That's a great point." Mya smiled, and I'd take that optimistic look, even if it'd been a bit forced. "I know we still have a ton of unanswered questions, but try not to let it pull you apart. We'll dismantle this group and keep you safe."

"Gwen's already heading back to the U.S. with her father and his team, busy working new cyber angles, too," Oliver noted. "She'll also make finding those hackers her own personal crusade."

"Yeah, sure her father loves that," Mya grumbled with a light shake of her head.

I stood at the sight of the helicopter finally about to land. It was far enough in the distance we didn't feel the wind whip us. Mya and Oliver were on their feet now, too, and Mya hooked her arm behind my back as if worried I'd run over too soon and have an unfortunate accident with a blade still whirling.

"You think Gwen can find out who else was supposed to be at that Christmas get-together, which was probably The Collective's secret meeting back in 2008 before they killed the Barclays?" I asked as I anxiously awaited the blades to stop so I could see my guy and run to him.

"That was a dead end. Only the Novaks could be tied to being anywhere near where the Barclays planned to vacation that Christmas," Oliver informed me. Poor guy seemed to hate being the bearer of bad news. "But don't worry, we'll draw up a list of assholes who'd profit off an attack who could pull this off, and go from there."

Mya let go of me, and I realized why. The blades had stopped and the side door was open. My heart was about to break free from my chest with anticipation.

"It's just Easton and Carter, right?" Apparently, Easton had been in the Air Force and could fly almost anything.

"Um," Mya said, shooting me a small smile.

I faced the helicopter again, catching a flash of fur. Oh, I had to assume she meant Dallas was there, too. Had he been part of the op? He had been when saving me from the human traffickers, and he'd held his own at the safe house in Poland.

Dallas hopped out, and at the sight of me, he eagerly began flying across the grassy field. I started in his direction, preparing to meet him halfway, then my legs buckled as Carter exited next.

Brown pants covered his long legs, a blue sweater jacket hid his broad shoulders, a beanie-type hat concealed his black locks, and a bag over his shoulder fell to the ground the moment our eyes locked.

At that, I turned my jog into a sprint. Dallas had already joined my side, and he switched directions to run alongside me back to his dad.

"Carter!" I cried, tears flying, hitting my face as the wind kicked back my hair.

He was moving too slowly, holding his leg while limping to get to me, so I picked up my pace even more.

And, oh God, the closer I got . . . I saw the damage to his face.

"Diana," he rasped, throwing his arms around me.

We fell to our knees on the grass together, Dallas hopping with excitement around us as we held each other, and I sobbed into his chest.

"You're okay." I knew he was because I'd basically had the same briefing as the President, but seeing him, feeling him, made it real.

"Sierra's daughter's safe in protective custody, too. She'll be given a new life. A fresh start," he said with a raspy, strained voice, offering me more hopeful news I could hold on to to help me get through this.

"You're hurt." I pulled back to take him in fully.

There was a Steri-Strip beneath a black eye, and more purple and black on his face than there was unharmed skin. Despite his lip being swollen and cut, he tried to set his mouth to mine, which sent me into another round of tears. He was risking pain to kiss me. I tried to kiss him back as gently as possible as he cupped my cheeks.

"I'm sorry about Sierra. That she betrayed you. That she's dead," he said between soft touches of our lips connecting.

"It's not your fault. I'm just so sorry you were pulled into all of this because of me." Well, I supposed Rebecca was somehow at the center of bringing us together in an odd way, when she'd also been the reason to keep us apart for so long.

"I know you lost your best friend, but I—"

"I did," I cut him off. "But I have you. Your team. Dallas. A new family." Tears cascaded down my face.

"You have someone else, too." He shifted to the side, putting eyes on the helicopter, so I followed his gaze.

Easton walked around to the side and offered a hand to—

"Bahar?" I gasped, unsure if my mind was playing tricks on me.

"The coroner in Scotland was paid off. The bodies in the fire weren't really your colleagues," Carter explained as Easton helped Bahar out. "I guess Sierra really did want to keep the best minds in science alive to capitalize on you all later."

Thank God for that.

"Diana," Bahar called out to me, and Dallas went running her way. Animals always loved her, and now . . .

"Thank you," I whispered through a mess of tears before

helping him slowly rise to his feet, knowing he wouldn't ask for the assist but needed it anyway.

He patted my ass and prompted, "Go hug her. I'll be okay here."

"Oh-okay," I said as Mya and Oliver joined us.

"Sorry, he asked us to keep this a surprise," Mya tossed out with a small smile.

The best possible surprise I could hope for in the face of all this hell. "Is, um, William okay?" I asked Carter, a bit hesitant, knowing he'd catch on to what I was really getting at.

Carter lifted a brow, then winced as if pained by the movement. "I may have taken a moment to have a word or two with him." He lifted a shoulder, then scowled as if that movement hurt, too. "But I left him in one piece if that's what you're asking," he said with a small, lopsided smile. "I promise."

"I'M SO SORRY ABOUT EVERYTHING." I GAVE BAHAR ONE more tight hug, then pulled back and removed my glasses to brush away my tears.

"No more apologies. Not your fault," Bahar said as Easton stood alongside her inside the lavish estate, a slightly smaller version of the one we'd spent a week at in Scotland.

I knew Bahar would try to brush it off, but knowing what she went through because of the people in my life would stick with me for a while.

"He'll take good care of you." Carter winced as he lightly rubbed a spot on his lower back. He'd never admit how much he was actually hurting, and I was anxious to get him upstairs, draw him a bath, and take care of him.

"I won't let her out of my sight," Easton commented, his tone steady, reassuring both me and Carter that he'd have my friend's six.

Carter had ordered Easton to escort her back to Turkey so she could mourn her brother with her family. He'd also given him the directive to protect Bahar until we knew more.

William and Bonnie were already in protective custody back in the U.S. Better to be paranoid and prepared until we knew more about The Collective.

Bahar fluffed the fur on Dallas's head before offering her thanks to Sebastian and his wife, Holly.

"I'll see you soon," I told her, sniffling, while returning my glasses in place.

"Thank you for taking them to the airport on your way home." Carter held out his hand to Sebastian next, and I turned to Holly, who pulled me in for a hug like we were old friends.

"If you need assistance down the road to go after these arseholes, let me know," Sebastian offered. "We know a thing or two about going up against these types of groups." He tipped his head, scrutinizing Carter for some reason as they unclasped palms. "You okay? I mean, uh, aside from the bloody obvious."

Carter stepped away from him, gesturing for them to head out. "Fine," he said a bit too gruffly for my liking. And why was he sweating?

Sebastian turned his attention to me, narrowing his eyes, implying Carter was anything but "fine." Yeah, I knew what that word meant, and I subtly nodded back, letting him know I'd address the issue once we were alone.

"Good luck." Holly squeezed my arm, and I hung back alongside Carter as we watched Bahar and the others leave.

As soon as we were alone, I shifted to problem-solving mode. Carter was standing, but his head kept nodding as if he might fall asleep. "You need to sit. You were tortured not even twelve hours ago." *Tortured.* Chills flew up my arms at that word, at the evidence of what happened to him written into every line of his face. No way to lie his way out of the fact he was anything but fine.

When he started to sway as if he might lose his balance, I wrapped my arm around his waist for support. I wasn't so sure if I could keep this six-two man of steel upright on my own, though.

With my other hand, I reached for his face and set the back of my hand to his forehead. "Oh my God, you're on fire."

"Am I?" he murmured, blinking, and stumbling back a step.

"Oliver! Mya!" I yelled, unsure where they were right now in the massive home.

Carter's knees buckled, and he turned his face my way, his lips parting. "Yeah, I don't feel so good," he rasped before dropping to his knees as if dragged down by an unseen force.

I went right with him, and Dallas rushed over, barking.

His face was more than just hot. He was truly burning up. How had he been standing that long without letting us know he was suffering?

As Oliver and Mya came flying into the room, Carter fell forward onto his hands.

Oliver quickly holstered his drawn weapon, realizing we were dealing with a different kind of problem.

"Oh, shit." Mya hurried over as Carter fell flat, then rolled to his back, groaning.

I took hold of his hand, interlocking our fingers as worry ripped through me. "He's got a bad fever," I told Oliver as he began checking him.

Carter's breathing was slow. Almost too slow. When he shut his eyes, his grip of my hand went lax. Dallas gently pawed Carter's chest as if trying to wake his dad, and that sight was heartbreaking.

"We need to get him to the doctor," Mya said, but Oliver quickly shot her a stern look.

"He's technically an international fugitive. We can't draw attention to the fact we're in Dublin. He wouldn't want us doing that." Oliver shifted Carter's shirt up, checking for wounds or some sign of an injury he hadn't noticed in his cursory check earlier.

"Screw that," I said, shaking. "Save him, or I'll drag this man to the hospital myself."

* * *

TWENTY-FOUR HOURS LATER

"You haven't left his side, have you?" Mya shielded her eyes from the light pouring into the room. I had all the curtains drawn and blinds open, hoping the sun might somehow help expedite the process and heal Carter. "You either, huh?" She peeked at Dallas on the bed, and he howled.

I removed the wet facecloth from his forehead and rested the back of my hand there. "I think his fever is finally starting to break. He's sweating it out."

Setting the cloth aside, I spied the crucifix on the nightstand and picked it up. I curled my fingers around it as I stared at my guy.

It wasn't fair. He'd been through so much. Tortured and narrowly escaped the explosion in Greenland. Now an infection was wreaking havoc with his system. Could we please catch a break?

"He'll be okay. Just give the medicine time. He'll beat this. I've seen much worse out in the field." At Oliver's words, I turned to see him hovering behind Mya in the doorway.

Though he'd been a medic in the Army, he could only do so

much. Thankfully, when Oliver called Sebastian to alert him to our problem, Sebastian had a better plan. He sent a doctor he trusted to the house, and he confirmed Oliver's assessment. A wound he'd sustained in Greenland had become infected, and with all of Carter's injuries on top of it, it'd taken him down fast.

Fortunately, the doctor gave him an IV of fluids, prescription antibiotics, and pain medicine we'd otherwise not have access to. Carter had come to here and there since yesterday, but he'd been groggy and confused. He'd never been alert enough to carry a conversation, but he no longer needed the IV, at least.

"Let me do another vitals check. Will that make you feel better?" Oliver offered, and I nodded my thanks.

Oliver sidestepped Mya to come farther into the room, reaching for his personal medic bag he'd left by the bed as I set the cross back on the nightstand and stood to give him room.

Dallas remained on the bed at his dad's feet, his tail flopping around while waiting for Oliver to provide news. Eager, like me.

"I know it doesn't look like it, but his oxygen levels are better. Heart rate, too. He's just gotta break this fever, then he'll be back to himself." Oliver closed up the bag, patted my shoulder, then stood.

"Want us to stay here with you?" Mya asked, but I was already busy pulling back the covers to crawl into bed next to him.

"You have leads to work, it's okay," I reminded her, drawing the comforter over us. "I'm going to stay and get some sleep with him."

Mya nodded, then wordlessly left with Oliver, shutting the door behind them.

I shut my eyes, resting my head near his, trying to find comfort in the steady beats of his heart.

Unsure how long I'd been out, when I slowly came to, I realized I was alone in the bed.

Seeing Carter in the armchair across the room, I sat upright in relief.

Only in his briefs, chest lifting with deep inhalations, he clutched the leather chair arms, head tipped back, eyes closed or on the ceiling.

"Searching for the writing up there?" I whispered, breaking the silence and doing my best not to cry with relief. If he could walk across the room and sit upright, he had to be doing better.

He slowly dropped his head, meeting my eyes. The side of his lip lifted, and that was all it took for me to jump off the bed and hurry to him. I fell to my knees in front of him, gently setting my hands on his strong thigh muscles as he dipped his hand between us, guiding my chin up.

"If I wasn't so sore and tired, and your world hadn't been flipped upside down . . . the position you're in right now, angel," he murmured, a dark edge to his voice.

"I see you're feeling much better." *Thank God.* I reached around his arm to check his forehead, confirming his fever broke.

"What day is it?" he asked, a bit of grogginess returning to his tone.

"Monday. Probably evening time now." *Depending on how long we slept.* "You passed out yesterday after Bahar and Easton left."

"I'm sorry I did that. Are you okay?"

"Did you just apologize to me for being sick?" *I swear, this man.* "Let's get you back to bed." I tried to stand, but he stopped me.

"Is there any news?" He frowned. "Did anything happen while I was out of it?"

I wished I could tell him something. *Anything.* But all I could give him was, "We're all safe, that's all I know." *And right now, that's all that matters.*

DIANA

FOUR NIGHTS LATER

"Craig still hasn't revealed anything new. Does that mean he doesn't know anything helpful? Is that why The Collective hasn't killed him, because they're not worried?" Mya paced the living room, and it took all my strength not to mirror her movements. "Jared must've known something, because he's already dead."

Oliver blocked her path with his body, preventing her from pacing again. "The President has him being held at the Pentagon. Kind of hard to kill him at one of the most secure sites on the planet. The second they relocate him, his ass is grass just like Jared's."

Mom was both grieving and furious to know her boyfriend had manipulated her the way Sierra had me. Turned out we had something in common after all. We'd trusted the wrong people.

Mom's apologies to Carter, right along with Dad's this week, wouldn't hack it, though. I needed some grade A groveling before I'd forgive them for how they'd treated him over the years. Carter had said he didn't care, but I had a feeling that was him being a typical tough guy. He didn't need to be accepted by my parents, but I knew secretly he'd like to be. They were about to become his in-laws after all.

"And when they relocate Craig, that's when we intercept the men sent to kill him," Carter said, breaking through my thoughts as he set aside his laptop.

While everyone continued talking, I went to the bar cart, deciding a glass of scotch might help take the edge off for Carter.

Although the rest of Falcon was part of our conversation right now, only Mya and Oliver were physically in the room with us. Sydney, Gray, and the others were split up all over the U.S., but we'd connected over a web call to see if we'd missed anything now that we knew Sierra and her late grandmother had been part of the group.

Our timeline had exploded with new details, going all the way back before Sierra was even born. Unfortunately, none of that information pointed anywhere new.

Maybe Mya and Oliver want something to drink, too? I decided on a bottle of Macallan single malt Scotch whisky and poured a few glasses.

Situating the bottle back in place, a bowl of M&M's caught my eye and I whispered my thoughts out loud, "If I gave you a hundred M&M's but told you six were poisoned, would you still eat them?" Armed with two glasses, I faced the room.

"This guy would," Mya said, nudging Oliver in the side. "He likes to live on the edge."

Carter's eyes shot to me as he accepted the scotch, nodding his thanks. "Why do you ask?"

Because the best minds in D.C. had downgraded the

probability of our laser being successful to ninety-four percent. "Six percent chance I will fail next week, and . . ."

Oliver declined a drink, but Mya accepted a glass while responding, "Not the same thing as playing Russian roulette with poisonous M&M's. Don't stress. Everything will be okay."

Ha. Allll the stress. But I kept that thought locked up that time and peered at the screens, curious if the others felt likewise.

"In two days, the laser will be good to go," Gray said with a confident nod, reading my worried look. "If The Collective goes through with their plans, we'll stop them." He whirled a finger in the air. "Let's take a breath. Regroup tomorrow and get back at it." Why'd it feel like he was worried about that six percent failure rate as much as I was?

"We'll be fine," Sydney added with a bit more confidence in her tone. "Camila would tell us if we wouldn't be. Elaina, too." She cut her attention to Carter, still quietly sitting on the couch nursing his scotch.

"Right," Carter finally spoke up, realizing everyone was peering at him.

"Talk tomorrow, then." Gray ended the meeting, and the three screens we had set up in the room went dark.

Mya set aside her drink and closed the laptops, gesturing to Oliver to head out. "We'll give you two some space. Come on, boy, want a snack?"

"Are you talking to me or the dog?" Oliver smirked, and Mya swatted his arm. "You're lucky that was my good arm," I overheard him say on their way out.

I fixed my attention back on Carter, who was quietly staring into his glass of scotch, wishing I could get a read on him.

I knew he was still worried about not only my safety, but

my overall mental state after what I'd learned about my *ex*-best friend. It was a lot to digest, but I'd opted to focus on the good. Bahar was alive. Also, Sierra, and presumably Jake's (not Karl's) daughter, was being placed with a couple in South Dakota who'd been trying to adopt for years without luck. That gave me some peace.

"You okay?" I toyed with the strings of the gray hoodie, which was actually Carter's, and my new favorite thing to wear.

He swirled the liquid around before sipping. "I don't want you to feel like you're in some type of prison until this is all over, but I have no idea how long this is going to go on." He gulped back the rest of his drink as I moved his laptop to the coffee table to join him.

I set aside his empty glass. "It won't be so bad if you're there with me."

"I can't take down these assholes and watch you at the same time." He rested his head back against the couch and closed his eyes.

His bruises were still prominent, but the cuts on his face were healing faster. I'd done my best not to hug him too tight, or kiss him too hard, worried about hurting him. Of course, whenever he'd realized I'd been holding back, that only seemed to encourage him to pull me in closer, kiss me with even more fervor.

"I had an idea, though, I wanted to run by you." He dropped his head and pivoted to face me. "What if we don't call it a prison, but a really cool and very safe lab where you can continue your work?"

"I suppose I was close to completing my mission before the lab was hit. I'd been on the verge of figuring out how to make cold fusion a viable energy source." I grimaced at the memory of that night. "Then wound up stumbling upon the equation to making an EMP weapon a reality instead."

"What if you can work alongside your friends again, too? Bahar and your colleagues need to be watched over, too." He was squinting as if worried how I'd handled this lab-prison idea.

"Lock me up with my ex, huh?"

"Trust me, I'm not excited about that, but if you don't want him to die, and he could be useful with your work . . ." He grimaced. "On second thought, fuck that guy. I'm not that much of a changed man. William can go into hiding somewhere else."

That's my guy. Right there. I leaned in and pressed a soft kiss to his cheek, doing my best to be careful with him. "I love you."

"Wait, so you don't hate the idea?"

I pulled back a touch to meet his eyes, and he palmed my cheek. "Will this lab-prison include candy, cake, music, and visits from my fiancé?"

"About that." His forehead tightened, and he lowered his hand, linking our palms. "I think we should make it official after you save D.C. from the attack." He casually shrugged as if he didn't just ask me to become his wife next week. "I'm impatient, what can I say? We could do it now here in Dublin, but I know you won't make love to me until I don't look like I was in the ring with Rocky and lost. And like hell am I not making love to my wife on my wedding night."

My stomach fluttered at his words, particularly one of them: *wife.* "Like you'd lose," I teased, then fisted his shirt and drew myself even closer to him, doing my best not to climb on his lap. "And yes, I'd love to marry you sooner rather than later. Also yes, we're waiting to make love until the doctor says it's safe."

He tipped his chin toward the door. "My doctor doesn't actually have a medical degree, and if I tell him to give me the OK, he will."

I smirked. "Which is why I gave him my own order, to not lie to me because my stubborn guy told him to."

"Wait, is that a yes, though? To marrying me next week and agreeing to let me tie you up?"

I laughed, and I swore it was the first time I'd done that since we'd been in Ireland. "Was that a Freudian slip, sir? Lock me up? Tie me—"

He caught my last word with a kiss before sharing, "Oh, if you give me the go-ahead, I'd tie your ass down right now and lower my face between your legs. I mean, it'd be the best medicine to heal me."

"Right, right." I grinned. "I think I read that in a medical book somewhere. Going down on each other cures any ache or pain."

"It'd make me feel a hell of a lot better." He lifted his brows suggestively a few times, and seeing him happy, even if we were only in a temporary bubble, made my heart soar.

"Hmm. Let me go talk to Oliver. I'll be right back." I stood, and he caught my wrist in one fast movement, pulling me back onto the couch.

"Ask that man if I'm allowed to eat your pussy, and I will spank that sexy ass of yours," he rasped.

"Mmm. Promise?" My thighs tightened, feeling desire unfold inside me for the first time since we'd made love in the shower what felt like forever ago back in Scotland.

Did that mean I was healing from the trauma of the betrayal? Sierra didn't deserve my pain, and Bahar was alive, so . . .

Yeah, screw Sierra and The Collective.

"Don't test me, angel." His warning was full of sugar and spice and everything nice, though.

"I just want to slip into something a bit more comfortable if we're going to, well, pleasure each other after not being together for so long."

He pulled on one of the hoodie strings. "You're perfect the way you are."

"Give me two minutes. Pour another scotch. I'll be right back." I winked, then tried to pull away to stand, but he stopped me.

"No talking to Oliver about your pussy or my cock, got it?" He arched a brow, his voice low and rumbly, and when my eyes shot to the crotch of his jeans, they were tented with his arousal.

I licked my lips, anxious for him. "Yes, sir."

At that, he released me, seemingly satisfied with my answer and how I'd said it. He propped his forearm up on the couch and palmed his crotch. He lifted his chin, urging me to get a move on.

Not wanting to waste time, I hurried from the room and down the hall.

Finding Dallas standing outside the laundry room, staring at it while cocking his head to the left, then the right, I quietly went over, curious what had his attention.

It sounded like a pair of tennis shoes were rolling around in the dryer. I set a hand to the knob, prepared to ease his nerves, then halted at what I heard next.

"Don't stop, don't stop . . ." A moan followed. "Fuck, yes, yessss. Right there. Ugggh, I hate you, but if you stop right now, I'll—"

"Sure you do, buttercup. You hate me all right. That's why you keep coming into my bedroom every night and . . ."

I backed up, nearly tripping over Dallas, forgetting where

I'd been going and why. No more eavesdropping for me. I was done with that.

A smile snuck up on me at the fact those two had finally given in to their desires.

Now, it's time to give in to mine.

73

CARTER

THE SNAPPING SOUNDS OF CAMERAS FILLED THE COLD afternoon air as reporters waited for President Bennett to approach the podium for the impromptu press conference he'd announced. I had to believe the location outside was very much intentional on his part.

Slipping on my sunglasses, I reached for Diana's hand as we hung back, waiting with her parents for him to speak.

We weren't exactly sure how much he planned to reveal about what *almost* happened on election day, but the President had requested we fly in from Dublin, promising I wouldn't be intercepted by the Feds at the airport.

"Thought you might want to see this." Susan Mackenzie stepped in front of where Diana and I stood, blocking sight of the podium.

"What is it?" Diana asked, accepting her mother's phone when she'd yet to accept any of her mother's apologies to me in the last week.

Diana had told her mother she'd have to do better. Be better. Beg on her hands and knees to me before she'd forgive her. Said as much to her dad as well, while I'd quietly listened to her grill them both, first virtually over a web camera and then in person today.

My sweet angel, wanting to fight my battles for me (and with me).

"It's a breaking news story," her father shared before her mother could.

Keeping hold of my hand, Diana pressed play with the other.

"The billionaire Novak family . . ." I barely registered the reporter's words, only catching a few select sound bites. "Responsible for the deaths of the Barclays . . . Carter Dominick's late wife, Rebecca, killed by Andrew Cutter because of . . ." More words. More explanations. Shocking details I'd had no clue would be aired. "Carter Dominick has been cleared of all charges related to his wife's death."

No mention of Craig Paulsen. *Good.* Per my request, he was still in the custody of Secret Service and had yet to be relocated. I had a feeling he knew something helpful, and I'd be the one to get it from him.

"You did this?" Diana pointed at the screen as her mom pulled the phone back. "You made sure the truth got out?"

"We had the President's permission, of course." Her mom returned her phone to her purse before Diana pulled her hand from mine and hugged her mother. Then father.

"Thank you." Diana faced me, and I wrapped my arms around her waist as she hugged me next. "Are you okay?"

Was I relieved my name was cleared? Sure. That the case surrounding Rebecca's death was finally closed? Definitely. I wanted to be fine and really mean it, but until Diana was safe, I was far from it. "I'll be good once we're back out of the country." I knew there wouldn't be an attack against us so out in the open, especially not on the White House lawn. But Diana was still vulnerable, and I'd never be "fine" until I could guarantee her safety.

Wild enough, it wasn't criminals or the underground world I was worried about. I'd already put word out Diana was off-limits, and Sebastian ensured that message made its way through his parts of the world, too. *Fuck with me and mine, fuck with him and the McGregors.* Message received in all languages.

It was The Collective, the faceless and nameless group of people hiding somewhere in plain sight (and behind their wealth), masking as "good," that had me terrified.

I hooked my arm behind Diana's back, catching sight of Griffin, Gray, Natasha, and Camila now arriving with Secretary Chandler. We were separated by the podium and the press, so we'd have to talk after the speech.

With the threat neutralized on election day, everyone on Falcon, as well as the President's SEAL Teams, had returned home.

My girl, my angel, my soon-to-be wife, had saved us. The ninety-four percent probability had turned into a hundred percent at precisely 14:05 on Tuesday, November the 5th. Crisis averted. The EMP weapon had been stopped. The pulse was diverted to space as Diana had planned, and by some miracle, missed hitting any satellites.

That'd been one of the longest days of my life, and for everyone on Falcon, as we spent the day video conferencing from our separate locations, waiting and wondering.

As a precaution, the President had grounded all incoming and outgoing flights in the area that day, not wanting to take any chances of a crash if the EMP weapon had been successful.

The President had opted to stay in the White House. *"If the ship goes down, I'll be going down with it,"* he'd said, and I respected him for that.

Diana had sobbed with relief. Tears of both joy and overall emotion had overwhelmed her after Secretary Chandler had joined our web call to let us know, *"Crisis averted. Mission success."*

Now to stop The Collective from ever striking again.

"Any clue what he's going to say?" I asked Susan, speaking to her directly for the first time since we'd arrived that day. It was as close to an olive branch as she'd be getting from me.

"Maybe," Susan said, shooting a nervous glance her ex-husband's way before shielding her eyes.

Real comforting.

"He's finally talking," Diana said, covering her mouth with her fist, eyes set on the President at the podium.

Aside from the cameras continuing to click, the outside grew quiet in anticipation of what he planned to say.

Maybe I was a little nervous, too.

"Tuesday, November the fifth, while Americans were voting in the election, the Calvert Cliffs Nuclear Power Plant, despite being on high alert, was overrun and used to launch an attack." The President had cut right to it, no fucks given for tempering the blow. Gasps fell from the reporters. The camera clicking intensified as he continued, "An electromagnetic pulse weapon was used to target D.C. and surrounding cities. From Baltimore all the way to Richmond."

I buried my fingers into Diana's side a bit tighter, drawing her closer to me, doing my best to shut out all other thoughts and focus.

President Bennett pointed to the sky. "This weapon was

designed to take down our power grid, Wi-Fi, stop all radio transmissions, and terrifying enough, cause planes to fall from the sky." As more sounds of shock, and a few of outrage, fell around us, Diana looped her arm across my chest, holding me back as we listened. "Yesterday afternoon, our newly refined missile defense systems successfully stopped the weapon in its tracks." He glanced our way for the briefest moment, a quiet thank-you to Diana in his eyes. "I'm making this public to the world because I want to be very transparent here. Not only will the United States not be vulnerable to such an attack, but in coordination with our allies, we're sharing the technology with them so they can protect themselves from anyone attempting to attack them as well." He set both hands on the podium, bowing his head for a moment. "I have also made the decision to share this technology with countries that aren't our so-called friends. The people of those nations shouldn't suffer because of the poor decisions of their officials. It's time we get back to remembering we're all just people trying to live. Doing our best to survive. Find some happiness or prosperity along the way, too." He slowly lifted his head, eyes on his audience. "It's time we remember our humanity. Our commonalities all around the globe, not just within our country." He paused, allowing his words to sink in.

I swallowed, hanging on to his every word the same as everyone in the country tuning in had to be.

"You see, it wasn't a foreign adversary behind this attack. It wasn't China. Iran. North Korea. It wasn't a terrorist group." His hand went over his heart. "The threat came from within our own country. From a group known as The Collective. Rich and powerful people attempting to manipulate and control. From starting wars to deciding how much you pay for gas."

Fuck. I squeezed Diana even tighter, and she squeezed right back.

"Well, I say, enough is enough. You will not divide us. No more choke hold on American lives or their wallets. Or the rest of the world, for that matter." He curled his hand into a fist. "You think your group is strong?" He smiled, shaking his head. "We're the *United* States of America. You're the few. The greedy. The corrupt. Well, I have news for you. Good will prevail. America will return to being a beacon of hope." He set his fist against his chest. "All your failed attacks did is make us stronger. Make us remember who we are." He shot his attention my way for a brief moment, then nodded toward the crowd. "Questions?"

"I have chills. My chills have chills," Diana sputtered, pulling away to tear her hands through her hair in shock.

"Did he just call out The Collective, and by name?" Diana's father peered at his ex-wife, clearly not clued into what the speech had been about.

"He's going to have them looking over their shoulders. Put them on defense." This wasn't the play I'd expected, but it might work. "It's bold," I said as I spied Camila making her way around the press hammering POTUS with questions. "You all might have targets on your heads now, though."

"It's not like people haven't tried to kill us before," Susan said, seemingly taking this all in stride. "You don't hold the positions we do without expecting shots fired."

Fuck, maybe I could even like Susan one day. *Maybe.*

"What does this all mean now?" Diana turned toward me, still shaking, so I drew my hands up and down her back over her wool coat.

"Plans stay the same," I said as Camila reached us. It was my first time seeing her in person since the party at Gray's house forever ago.

Camila barely had a chance to speak before Diana threw her arms around her. Camila smiled at me over her shoulder, and I smiled back.

My shoulders stiffened at the realization Camila might be seeing Diana's future right now.

The second Camila let go of Diana, she asked, "Can I steal Carter for a second before we head out?" Diana stepped back, her focus bouncing between us, then nodded. "We're still on for the next thing, right?"

"What thing?" Susan asked, removing her sunglasses.

Diana smirked. "Courthouse." She lifted her hand and wiggled her fingers. "If you'd like to join us, we're about to get married before we leave the country."

As Diana dropped the news on her parents about our plans to wed today, I followed Camila away from our group to talk out of earshot.

"Your bruises are getting better."

"Yeah, quick healer." *My bruises aren't what you want to talk about, though.* I swallowed, tensing up. My hands dove into my jacket pockets as I waited for her to tell me something horrible. To ruin my future and reveal I'd need to choose between happiness and saving the world.

"Easy there." She held her hand up. "I can see the panic in your eyes, and it's not what you're thinking. What I have to say isn't even about you."

The weight that lifted from my chest was short-lived, because was her premonition, or whatever they were called, about her? Was there something wrong with *her* future?

"After you get married today, I need to go away again. I can't help you take down The Collective, but I promise you don't need me. Everything will be okay." Well, that was comforting, and not bad news at all, so what was it?

"Everything will be fine for you two as well." Her gaze swept Diana's way. "More than fine, in fact."

Fine. The only time I'd liked hearing that word in months.

"There's just something I need to do. I can't tell you about it, but I need you to trust me." She reached for my arm and gave it a squeeze. "I'll be off-grid again, so that's why I'm telling you, so you don't worry. Okay?"

I frowned, not sure how I felt about this, but Camila was a grown woman and not technically my sister to boss around. "You promise you'll be okay?"

"Absolutely." She tipped her head toward Diana and the others. "You two are the definition of hope, you know that, right? About how even in the face of total darkness, the light can still find its way through."

Now she was choking me up. Turning toward the love of my life, I felt my body relax at the sight of her.

"Also," Camila said while playfully nudging me in the side, "I thought I told you to stop dressing like you're in the mafia."

Some things would never change, like the fact I'd forever be overprotective of those I loved. "Old habits." I grinned. "What can I say?"

74

CARTER

I'D MADE LOVE TO MY WIFE, SLOW AND SOFT, IN THE PERFECT storybook setting (her words). It really was bliss, though, with Diana wrapped up in my arms, and the white-sand beach, palm trees swaying, and the aquamarine sea (that we'd see better in the daytime tomorrow) right outside our open door.

Eight hours earlier, with Secret Service protection, we'd wed in D.C. It'd been perfect, even with Diana's parents there to "give her away" at the courthouse. Griffin, Camila, and Dallas had also attended. Dallas was currently staying with Oliver while Diana and I honeymooned.

In my paranoia, I'd called in a favor from a *former* bad guy who owned a hundred acres of property in Saint Lucia. It was highly secure, and we'd hopefully be untouchable from the likes of The Collective. After everything we'd both gone through, we deserved a week to ourselves as husband and wife.

I'd had another friend of a friend set us up with a jeweler

here, and we'd picked out two bands and had our initials interlocked and engraved inside them.

Then, I'd carried her over the threshold, and she'd immediately spotted our "wedding" cake. Devil's Food, of course. The woman had me taking selfies again, even with bruises still lingering on my face, as we made more memories. Smashing cake against each other's mouths had come next.

Now there I was, happily married and tangled in the sheets with my wife.

Diana lifted her hand, staring at the simple platinum band, a match to mine. Despite not being a jewelry person, she'd promised this would be the only ring she'd ever love wearing and cherish.

"Diana Dominick." She wiggled her fingers, studying her wedding ring. "Feels like that name's always been mine, like it was written in the stars."

I turned toward her, resting my hand on her hip. "Maybe that was the writing on the ceiling back then, we just couldn't see it."

"Mmmm, my hopeless romantic. Who would've known?"

"Don't dare tell anyone," I teased, smirking as I went in for another kiss.

That kiss turned into something more as it always did with us. Our tongues met, and my cock grew, ready to go again. But maybe this time, we'd . . .

"Angel?"

"Yes?" she whispered, hooking her leg with mine, arching into me.

"Any chance you're ready for me again?"

She chuckled. "I can feel you most certainly are." Shimmying against my cock as I snaked my hand around her side and gripped her ass cheek, she whispered, "I'm definitely ready, too."

"Good." I untangled our bodies, rolled off the bed, and bent down to retrieve my black slacks where I'd dropped them earlier that night, removing the belt from the loops.

She sat back on her heels, her tits in the air, and chin lifted. Eager and ready for something we'd never done.

I snapped the leather between my palms and winked. "Don't worry. Not on your ass."

"Was never worried."

I closed the space between us and turned my belt into makeshift cuffs, looping and tightening them around her wrists.

"We'll start slow," I rasped before sitting on the bed. "On my lap. Facedown. Pussy positioned against my cock so I have access to your ass." The commands came out rough. My eagerness obvious.

"I haven't been a bad girl, though. Still going to spank me?" She stood before me, her glorious body on display. Her blonde hair lay heavy over her breasts, and I stood and reached forward, shifting her hair to her back so I didn't miss an inch of perfection.

"I do recall you doing something I told you not to." I nudged my chin in the direction of my phone on the table in the room.

"Ohhh, about that." She wet her lips, drawing her tongue along the seam to tempt me.

"I told you what'd happen if you sent me a nude photo." She knew exactly what she'd been doing texting me that picture.

Sitting, I patted my thigh, reminding her of where she belonged.

Her linked wrists rested against her abdomen, and my

eyes dipped below to her pussy, swollen still from our lovemaking. Pink and soft. Ready for me again. "I suppose I also deserve your handprint on my ass for constantly wiggling it in your face for a week, taunting you about that backdoor access you hope to have one day. Still seems mission impossible, though."

At her words, I returned my eyes to her face. God, it was so good to see her smiling and happy. She'd been through hell, lost a best friend to betrayal, and we weren't out of the woods yet, but I'd do my best to shield her from everything and stay inside this bubble for as long as possible. It was the least I could do for her after she'd given me a second chance at life, not to mention helped me redeem my soul.

I cocked a brow. "You may be right. Your virgin ass would be a tight-tight fit for me."

"Ah, giving up, are we?" Such a little tease. "I didn't take you for a man so easy to surrender."

I scoffed. "At what point did I admit defeat? I was only suggesting we need to slowly ease you into taking all of me."

"You and your love for defying physics." She finally came over, and with her hands bound, I helped her across my lap facedown. My cock throbbed as I lifted my hand.

With her wrists still linked and her body stretched out across me, she peeked back just as I connected my hand to her ass, spanking her. She caught her lip between her teeth as I plunged my fingers deep into her pussy.

She began grinding against my cock, searching for relief, rubbing her arousal all over me. "You sure I'm not hurting you. Your bruises . . ."

"Trust me, this is helping." *In so many ways.*

I pulled my hand from her center to spank her once more, then growled like a damn caveman, needing to be inside her.

I fell back onto the bed, using the belt to draw her up, guiding her on top of me, her bound wrists behind my neck.

With my feet still on the floor, she straddled me, and I slipped my arm behind her back. "Now, be a good girl," I said in a low, deep voice, "and ride your husband's cock."

75
CARTER

"You've picked up a tail," Gray relayed the news we'd hoped for over comms. "Two black Escalades about two hundred meters back."

"Roger that. Hold positions until I give the order." I tapped my ear after Gray confirmed he'd heard me, muting my comm so Falcon wouldn't overhear the conversation I was about to have.

Gripping the steering wheel of the government-owned Suburban, I drove farther away from the Pentagon, heading for the bridge to cross the Potomac.

I fixed my focus on the rearview mirror, catching Griffin's eyes in the backseat. "It's time."

Griffin, his face covered with the exception of his eyes, nodded and repositioned his rifle so he could focus on the target—the gagged and cuffed mark sitting next to him.

The second he removed the black hood from Craig Paulsen's head, I adjusted the rearview mirror so Craig would see I was behind the wheel. That it was me escorting him away from the safety of Secret Service.

Staring at me in shock, blinking as Griffin removed both his headphones and gag, I calmly revealed, "The Collective is a minute or two out from ensuring this vehicle goes off the bridge and into the river, where you'll drown and be silenced."

Anger flared inside me all over again at the memories of everything this man had done to destroy lives just to have a seat at the table.

It'd been radio silence from The Collective since the President's speech. And no surprise, every mercenary who'd been apprehended at the nuclear plant on election day hadn't known who hired them. But Craig, damnit, he had to know more than he'd revealed to the Feds.

He may have beaten the polygraph tests, but with his background in Intelligence, I'd expected nothing less.

Unfortunately, like at the power plant, we doubted the men sent to kill Craig today would know who hired them. Not that we wouldn't attempt to get them to talk anyway.

"What do you want?" Craig finally breached the quiet, only the sounds of traffic around us filling the space.

"Oh, I think you know." I tightened my hold of the wheel. "We can either fake your death today, or you can actually die. What's it going to be?"

Craig stole a look out the window, then back at the mirror. "What if I don't know anything? Jared didn't. Not beyond what I already told the White House. We both worked directly with the Novaks, and Pierce worked for me. Pierce didn't know about the Novaks."

"But you know about The Collective, that they exist," Griffin hissed, drawing his masked face closer to Craig's.

My attention skirted back and forth between the heavy traffic and the mirror pointed on the backseat.

"From what I heard, thanks to POTUS, the whole world knows that name," Craig hissed, sweating. "Do you have any idea who you're really up against? This is much bigger than you think."

Clearly, you know something. "What. Do. You. Know?"

He shook his head, eyes on his lap. A beaten, broken man in an all-orange jumpsuit.

How the mighty have fallen.

"Get me out of this alive and somewhere safe, and I'll give you all I know. It's not a name, but it's a lead," he remarked, his tone wavering.

"Why should we trust you?" Griffin asked him.

"You don't have much of a choice now, do you?" Craig worked his gaze back to the mirror. "Same as me."

"Fine," I bit out. "Just one thing before we go off this bridge to fake your death. Novak didn't tell you this, but I want you to know." I let go of a deep breath. "Andrew Cutter killed Rebecca. He wasn't only a treasure hunter, he was The Italian."

I let the words sink in. Witnessed the shock in his eyes. Diana was right, wasn't she? Craig had loved Rebecca, and he'd believed I'd killed her. Based on his reaction now, it appeared Novak never told him the truth. Craig would have to live with the guilt of what he'd done forever.

"Do you know what that means?"

He lifted his cuffed hands, drawing his fists in front of his face. "It means I'm a dead man anyway. You're going to kill me regardless."

No, I'm not. Lucky for you, my wife wouldn't like that. Well, unless it's self-defense. Plus, death would be far too merciful.

"I did care about her. Loved her, and she loved me back, but she wouldn't get a divorce." He closed his eyes, accepting his fate, assuming I'd kill him before The Collective could.

I didn't care about their relationship. I didn't need to know the truth about Rebecca's indiscretions. Hell, maybe when Rebecca had thought she'd had a drunken night with Cutter, that was why she didn't tell Craig anything. She'd felt she'd cheated on *him,* not just me.

But screw the past. It was time for Rebecca to rest in peace, and for me to have peace, too.

"I'm a man of my word," I assured him. "You give us a lead, and I won't kill you."

Gray popped back into my ear, alerting me to the fact the Escalades were now advancing. It was about to be go-time.

"But," I couldn't help but add in a menacing voice, "if you mention Diana's name during the chat we'll be having . . . I will cut out your tongue."

DIANA

DUBAI – ONE WEEK LATER

I CHECKED MY PHONE FROM INSIDE THE BEDROOM FOR THE tenth time that hour, hoping to hear from Carter, but still no notification.

Going a bit stir-crazy, I set aside my book on quantum physics and went over to the window. We had a gorgeous view of the Burj Khalifa skyscraper. I could get used to a city like this. A gorgeous location, kind people, great food, amazing weather, and so much more.

I had no idea how long I'd be living there with Carter, but he'd already gone ahead with arranging for my lab to be constructed there. He had people working at hyper speed to get it ready. I'd once again be back to following my dream of making cold fusion as an energy source a viable option, and Bahar would be joining me as soon as the lab was set.

It'd be nice to have her there with my husband traveling so much lately. This time, he'd been gone for over eight days, and it was eight too long.

Mya had casually mentioned over a call a few days ago

that Oliver wouldn't be visiting us there. Apparently, he'd almost lost his head (quite literally) after being wrongly accused of a crime here. I'd yet to broach the subject about them having sex back in Dublin. I decided if Mya wanted to tell me about it, one day she would.

It was nice to have so many new friends. I'd done my best not to mourn Sierra. She didn't deserve it. Cold, evil, and heartless was how I needed to remember her.

Shivering from the thought of her, I turned from the window and went over to Dallas curled up asleep on the bed. Thank God for him being here, or it'd make Carter's absence that much worse.

Not only was Dallas with me, so were three of the President's Secret Service agents. That was in addition to the ten guards Carter had personally hired to protect me inside our highly secure skyrise in an extremely safe city. Everyone from kings to prime ministers had stayed here in the past, so it was already outfitted in a manner Carter had found "acceptable."

I was pretty sure that man would always be paranoid when it came to my safety, even when the threat of The Collective no longer loomed overhead.

Right now, Carter was chasing a lead he'd somehow pulled from Craig Paulsen last week. I didn't even want to know how he'd managed to get Craig to talk after Falcon faked his death.

Carter had smiled over FaceTime and casually promised, *"He's alive, and he can still walk."* Then he'd winked and added, *"Just not well."*

Honestly, I was just impressed Craig was still breathing. I knew Carter was trying hard, in his words, to be a better man, and I'd give the man an A for effort. I planned to thank him, too, in many, many ways and with a plethora of orgasms as soon as he returned home.

When my phone lit up from a notification, I hurried over and grinned at the sight of his name there.

> Hubby: Miss me?

> Me: More than a little.

> Me: Tell me your lead gave you a new lead.

Since the mercenaries who'd tried to kill Craig had been dead ends, we only had Craig's "tip" to go off, in addition to the name of one elite hacker Gwen had finally discovered. The problem was, we couldn't find the hacker, and Carter had concerns that was because he was already dead.

> Hubby: Yeah, we got a pretty big lead, but it's going to require some deep cover work.

I dropped onto the couch at his words, trying not to let the sting of disappointment that he'd be gone longer hit me. I understood why, but I just . . . well, loved and missed him so much.

> Hubby: Mya and Oliver volunteered to do it since they're the only ones on the team without families.

> Hubby: Go to the bedroom door, angel.

Before I'd even registered what Carter was trying to tell me with his last text, Dallas was on his feet. He ran to the door, scratching at it and trying to use his jaws on the handle.

I dropped the phone in my rush to get to the bedroom

door and unlock it, hauling it open with much more force than necessary.

Carter was standing there, hands bracing against the exterior frame, wearing a sexy smile and nothing else. There was a trail of his clothes behind him, and it was the best sight I'd seen in a long time.

"For the sake of expediency," he said with a smirk, then dragged me against him.

After coming down from the high of his arms around me and his mouth on mine, I murmured, "What a way to greet a girl. Guessing security's not allowed upstairs."

"Definitely not." Keeping my feet off the ground, holding me tight to his hard frame, he whispered, "Do you know what day it is?"

It took me a few seconds to work through the memories, and then it dawned on me. "Thirteen years since you rescued me. Since our first time meeting."

He brushed his lips against mine, still holding me up against him. "I'll never let you fall, angel. Not ever."

Pressing my mouth to his, I murmured, "Just fall in love. More and more."

PART IV

NEXT...

EPILOGUE

CARTER

BUSHKILL FALLS, PENNSYLVANIA – THREE MONTHS LATER

"Stalker tendencies, huh?"

I about dropped my phone at Mason's words. I closed the security app on my phone since he'd caught me *checking in* on my wife at her lab in Dubai. "Any news?" I asked, hoping to deflect from the fact I was most definitely obsessed with my wife, and I had no plans to ever change that. Thankfully, that was exactly how she liked me.

"Nothing from Oliver or Mya yet." Mason looked around Falcon's headquarters, his gaze shooting to Gwen working quietly behind her laptop. It was only the three of us there tonight.

Ironically, the two people who'd planned to part ways with Falcon were now the ones working the longest hours alongside my team. We'd take all the help we could get on our mission to continue crossing names off our list.

Unfortunately, anytime we'd managed to get a name (two at this point), they were killed before we could question them.

The Collective had eyes everywhere. The only bright side was that "they" took out the trash for us. Two more down. How many to go? We had no clue.

Until we cut the head off the snake and ensured it never grew back, we'd be chasing our tails. After months of working this case, we were all exhausted and frustrated, and the only place I wanted to be right now was with Diana.

I'd only flown back to Pennsylvania because the team was supposed to touch base with Mya and Oliver tonight. They were deep under and couldn't risk making contact more than every few weeks. This was our only shot at getting to The Collective before that lead was killed, too. If "they" didn't know we were onto them, we could silently move in that way. It was our best shot, and the team owed Mya and Oliver for embedding themselves so deep under.

"Hopefully Mya and Oliver have something when they make contact," Gwen spoke up, peering at us over her screen.

Mason checked his watch. "They should've reached out by now, though."

"They will." I stood. "Let me know when you have them on the line. Until then, I'm going to make a call." I nodded my thanks to him, then to Gwen for working so hard, then disappeared down the hall for some privacy.

I closed myself in one of the storage rooms and opened up the security app.

Sometimes I couldn't believe how much had changed since the night Secret Service had picked me up from my home in Pennsylvania to let me know the lab in Amsterdam was hit.

After the wedding, I'd sold off my home and the other office I'd kept in Pennsylvania. For now, my home was wherever Diana was. Once we took down The Collective, we'd plant some roots and maybe give Dallas a furry friend to play with, too.

Setting my back to the door, I turned on the volume so I could listen to Diana talking to Bahar inside her office at the lab I'd had constructed for them in Dubai. *Old habits and all.* At least this time she knew about it.

I drew up our last text thread to give her the heads-up I was watching.

> Me: You have a second?

Diana retrieved her phone, then peered straight at the camera while letting Bahar know she needed the room. "Watching me, are you?" she teased once alone.

> Me: Miss you. Can't help it.

> Me: Touch yourself. Let me see you.

She read my messages, chuckling. The sound was heaven, and just what I needed to help me get through the night. "Right now? In here? Is that an order?"

I palmed my dick over my jeans and let go of a gruff breath.

> Me: Absolutely. To all three.

She rested a hand over her abdomen, lightly shaking her head. "Your daddy is crazy. You'll love him, though, just like I do."

My shoulders fell at her words. My chest squeezed with emotion.

> Me: She's going to be just like her mother. My little angel. Or maybe there can only be one angel. You. She can be my little girl. How about that?

Talking to the camera, she told me, "We're only eight weeks. What if we're having a boy?

> Me: Energy doesn't lie ;)

"You're right about that. But the world could also use more men like you."

> Me: I mean, I have no plans to stop at just one child. We can have a boy next.

Finally obeying, she slipped her hand between her legs *but* over her jeans. No, those needed to be lowered so I could see her.

My muscles tightened with anticipation of what she'd do next. She usually made a show of slowly taunting me. Misbehaving here and there, more than eager for my reaction.

This woman, with my child in her belly, was all mine. It wasn't luck but fate. It was meant to be that we'd found our way to each other. A long, rough road to get there, but we made it.

> Me: I want to see my wife pleasure herself. Will you do that for me?

"Have you been a good boy?"

Before I could type a response, there was a knock at the door, followed by Gwen calling out, "Carter, we need you. Now."

Talk about timing. "Coming." *Well, I would've been.*

> Me: Hold that thought. I'm needed . . . I'll be back soon. I love you.

"I love you, too," she said to the camera, then blew me a kiss.

After pocketing my phone, I did my best to adjust my raging hard-on, then joined Gwen and Mason, assuming Mya and Oliver were on the line with urgent news.

"What's up?" I asked, not expecting to find Mason's fists on Gwen's desk, head bowed.

"Mya made contact, but she was cut off while talking," Gwen shared, eyes glossy. "I recorded the call, but I can't reach her. Their trackers are also offline."

I rounded the desk and sidestepped Gwen to press play on the video, anxious to find out why they both looked like someone had died.

Mya's tear-streaked face filled the laptop screen. "Our covers are blown." Crying, Mya went on as my pulse raced. "The Collective must've found us. Oliver just sacrificed himself so I could get away and—" The video ended there.

"Still nothing," Gwen cried, clutching her phone as Mason stood, his bloodshot eyes on me. "What if they're both . . ."

"Not an option," I hissed. "They're not dead." *Camila said everything would be okay, and I'm going to fucking make sure of it.* "Round the team up," I ordered, emotion starting to choke me up. "We're going after them."

I wrapped a hand over Mason's shoulder, and he hesitantly surrendered a nod.

"We'll find them. *Alive.*" Shooting my focus to Gwen next, grit and determination in my voice, I promised, "The Collective's going to learn their lesson once and for all. Fuck around. Find out."

AFTERWORD

The Falcon Falls Security mission continues in Mya and Oliver's book, *The Wrecked One.*

Some memorable moments from previous books:

- We first meet Carter when solving his wife's murder in *Chasing Fortune.*
- Falcon Falls Security is formed in the epilogue of *Chasing the Storm.*
- The "fork" incident at the hotel is in *The Taken One.*
- The undercover dating show game where Gwen develops a crush on Carter is in *The Wanted One.*

Where did we first meet Mya & Oliver?

Mya was first introduced in the book, *My Every Breath.* She joins the Falcon team in *The Guarded One.* This is the book where the chemistry (hate to love) starts with Oliver.

Oliver was first introduced in the book, *Chasing the Storm.*

CROSSOVERS

Previous Falcon Falls books

Griffin & Savanna - *The Hunted One*

Jesse & Ella - *The Broken One / The Lost Letters*

Sydney & Beckett - *The Guarded One*

Grayson & Tessa - *The Taken One*

Jack & Charlotte - *The Wanted One*

* * *

Aside from the Falcon Falls books - where else have you seen some of these characters?

Gray Chandler was first introduced in *Chasing the Knight*, and he's also in the epilogue of *Chasing the Storm* (Stealth Ops Series: Echo Team books)

Jack London was also in *Chasing the Knight*.

Gwen Montgomery - Wyatt's daughter - introduced in Wyatt's book, *Chasing the Knight*. She joins the Falcon cast in *The Taken One*.

Mya Vanzetti is a journalist in the contemporary romance, *My Every Breath*. And she is Julia Maddox's friend in *Chasing the Storm* (where she helps save Oliver's life). She joins Falcon Falls Security in Sydney's book - *The Guarded One*.

Carter Dominick was also in *Chasing Fortune* and *Chasing the Storm*. He guest appears in *Let Me Love You*.

Camila Hart was first introduced in *The Guarded One*.

Jesse & Ella - are first introduced in *Chasing Daylight*.

The McGregors- the Dublin Nights Series

Sebastian Renaud - *The Real Deal*

Constantine Costa is part of the The Costa Family Series

FALCON FALLS

Falcon Falls Team members:

Team leader: **Carter Dominick - Army Delta Force/CIA**

- A widower (lost his wife)
- Dog: Dallas
- Now married to Diana Mackenzie (pregnant)

Team leader: **Gray Chandler - Army SF (Green Beret)**

- Now married to Tessa (pregnant)
- Dog: Lucky

Other family members:

- Admiral Chandler & Mrs. Chandler
- Natasha (sister)
- Wyatt (brother-in-law)
- Nieces: Emory Pierson & Gwen Montgomery

Jesse - Army Ranger / CIA (hitman)

Family / Friends:

- Wife: Ella Mae (son: Remington "Remi" Tucker McAdams)
- Sister: Rory
- Parents: Donna and Sean
- Friends: AJ, Beckett, Caleb, and Shep Hawkins
- Beckett's daughter: McKenna (adopted son: Miles)
- AJ & Ana's son: Marcus (Mac)

Griffin Andrews - Delta Force

- Married to Savanna (baby: Tomas)

Jack London - Army SF (Green Beret) / CIA (Ground Branch Division)

- Divorced (Jill London)
- Married to Charlotte Lennox (pregnant)

Oliver Lucas - Army Airborne

- Tucker Lucas - brother (deceased)
- Tucker was engaged to Julia Maddox before he passed away.

Sydney Archer - Army

- Married to Beckett / Son: Levi
- McKenna and Miles Hawkins (stepchildren)

Guests on the team: Mason Matthews; Gwen Montgomery

STEALTH OPS

Stealth Ops Team Members *(Falcon is a spin-off from the Echo Team books)*

Team leaders: Luke & Jessica Scott / Intelligence team member: Harper Brooks; Bear (canine)

Bravo Team:

Bravo One - Luke (married to Eva)
Bravo Two - Owen (married to Samantha)
Bravo Three - Asher (married to Jessica)
Bravo Four - Liam (married to Emily)
Bravo Five - Knox (married to Adriana)

Echo Team:

Echo One - Wyatt (married to Gray's sister, Natasha)
Echo Two - A.J. (married to Ana)
Echo Three - Chris (married to Jesse's sister, Rory)
Echo Four - Roman (married to Harper)
Echo Five - Finn (married to Julia)

ALSO BY BRITTNEY SAHIN

Falcon Falls Security

The Hunted One

The Broken One

The Guarded One

The Taken One

The Lost Letters: A Novella

The Wanted One

The Fallen One

The Wrecked One

Dublin Nights

On the Edge

On the Line

The Real Deal

The Inside Man

The Final Hour

Hidden Truths

The Safe Bet

Beyond the Chase

The Hard Truth

Surviving the Fall

The Final Goodbye

WHERE ELSE CAN YOU FIND ME?

I love, love, love interacting with readers in my Facebook groups as well as on my Instagram page. Join me over there as we talk characters, books, and more! ;)

<u>FB Reader Groups:</u>
Brittney's Book Babes
Stealth Ops Spoiler Room

Facebook
Instagram
TikTok
Pinterest

www.brittneysahin.com
brittneysahin@emkomedia.net